In a mere few heartbeats, forty to thirty, and it didn't even a single scratch. Some wards into the forest, but a few were still game to try Vykers. Unfortunately, a few is not enough. They died before they even had time to regret the choice. Finally, as more and more of the band dissolved into the woods, Vykers stabbed his sword into a nearby corpse in frustration and yelled, "Well, I'm not going to go chasing after the sons-of-bitches!" He turned to the Five. "Go get 'em. Just bring me their heads." That was the first time he could ever remember seeing the Five smile. It was, he would later reflect, delightfully sinister.

Smiling at the sounds of horrified screaming in the woods, Vykers set about stripping and staking the leader to the ground. If he was a right bastard, he was still a man of his word. When the leader awoke, he'd find himself, as promised, buried in bloody heads, appetizers to the entrée he was to become for some predat

You don't call the Reaper a liar.

ISBN 978-1-949914-45-0

For information address Crossroad Press at 141 Brayden Dr., Hertford, NC 27944
A Mystique Press Production - Mystique Press is an imprint of Crossroad Press.
www.crossroadpress.com

First edition

STEEL, BLOOD & FIRE

IMMORTAL TREACHERY: BOOK 1

By Allan Batchelder

I would like to thank my first-round readers, whose support encouraged me to believe…

Gillian Avery
A. Bento
Benoit Deeg
Bobbi & Rusty Dreier
Rodney Sherwood

And also my wife & son, who endured my sustained absences from the living room when we might have been doing something together.

ONE

Vykers, In the Stocks

The beatings and abuse continued without pause, without end, due in no small part to the efforts of the two A'Shea on either side of him, who had surely foresworn their sacred trust in prolonging his misery. He had hoped for—even expected—death, by the end of his first day. But the Duke, the people of the Reaches and his healers would not be satisfied until the last victim had exacted his just measure of vengeance. An all-too familiar speech interrupted his reverie.

"You may strike him once," one of the guards told the next in line, "however you like. If your blow's the one kills him, though, you'll be whipped on this same post. Do you understand?"

"Aye."

Of course. They all understood; they were artists of understanding by now. And so he'd been punched, slapped, scratched, kicked, stabbed with needles in non-vital areas, spat upon, burned and had various things thrown on him, from rotten blood, to urine, feces, vomit and offal. He was a masterpiece of the people's understanding. And still, death would not come, nor the lines of peasants abate. He could endure the physical torture—what choice did he have?—but the constant insults and taunting were harder to ignore. He'd been a proud man. Once. Worse than the beatings and the verbal abuse, however, were the flies. There must, he concluded, have been one for each person he'd killed over the years. Perhaps these flies were even the shades of those unhappy dead, come back to join in the festivities. They made him itch something fierce. The only accidental mercy he enjoyed was that he'd been hung up facing west, and for the brief few minutes that sunset was in his eyes, he could see nothing.

But perhaps blindness had put him here in the first place.

One morning, he was awakened—shocking enough that he'd been asleep—with a crash of salt water, the cold of it practically stopping his heart, and the salt burning his countless wounds like hellfire. Miraculously, he found himself alone. Or nearly so.

"You look like shit, Vykers. Smell like it, too." It was Captain Brandt again, backed by a number of silent soldiers. "'Course, most of it probably *is* shit, but you get my meaning."

The best the Reaper could manage was to grunt in reply.

"I guess we all thought you'd be dead by now."

Vykers was silent this time. No need to respond to such an obvious truth.

"There's no good news, there, though. His Lordship says you're to live...after a fashion."

Brandt was setting him up. Vykers wouldn't give him the satisfaction.

"We're taking your feet and hands, Reaper, and then we're dumping you in the woods."

Vykers looked up, inquiringly.

Brandt shrugged. "His Lordship thinks there may come a day when someone will have need of your...talents. If you're still alive, that is."

Finally, Vykers spoke. "That's bad strategy."

"No shit. And I told him so. But he's convinced you'll be tractable." The captain reached over and unlocked the mechanism holding Vykers in place.

Slowly, the prisoner stood up.

"Enjoy it, Vykers. You won't be so tall in a few moments' time."

The odd sensation in his gut was fear, he realized. The first he'd felt in ages. He simply couldn't—or didn't want to—imagine life without hands or feet. His Lordship had finally accomplished what thousands of angry peasants could not: he had made Vykers feel something.

The actual taking of his hands and feet was more psychologically painful than physically so. The terror as the axe swooped down and parted his flesh was unlike anything he'd ever known. The pain was less significant, for a while. This time, the healers took no special care to sustain him, beyond cauterizing and wrapping his wounds. Watching them gather his hands and feet into a bucket and carry them off, Vykers felt unspeakable loss.

He spent the entire journey into the wilds in a semi-conscious fog, in the back of an old wagon that must once have been used to transport pickled herring. The smell and the rough jostling made him violently ill and, along with the weakness, fever and pain he was already feeling, he again found himself wishing, yearning, for death. This was immeasurably harder to endure than those days of beatings and insults in the public square. He almost laughed at the thought of it. Almost.

He must have lost consciousness, because the next thing he knew, he was crashing to the ground in a dark forest. The shadow of a fat man stood between him and the last of the day's light.

"See you in hell, Vykers."

"Oh, you'll be there, too?"

A moment of angry silence, and then Vykers felt a boot to his face. He might've lost a tooth. Another one. There was a bit of rustling, and then he felt hot liquid pouring onto his head.

Piss.

The fat man laughed.

Vykers shut him out and went back to sleep.

Aoife, On Her Mission

She had, she felt, spent most of her life second-guessing herself. Standing out of the rain under an old cedar by the side of the road, her mind circled back, inevitably, to the same conclusion: she should have killed him when she had the chance. And the same old retort tried to rescue her: how can a ten year old girl be expected to murder her little brother?

There was no way to answer these thoughts; she had tried for years. She was damned when he *became.*

She gasped. Sometimes, when she was wrapped up in these thoughts, she forgot to breathe. Or was that self-sabotage? Anyway, she sighed, shouldered her pack and set off again, hoping to make the next village by nightfall. A fire would be heavenly. And something to eat, something hot. She wouldn't be picky.

Of course, she felt guilt as she noticed the telltale scars of war on the landscape. But it had been a while. Maybe things were on the mend locally, and folks had begun to forget. Until he returned.

Gods, it was driving her mad. She needed to visit an herbalist. More than fire or food, she hoped the nearest settlement had an herbalist, even a hedge witch would do. She had to quell these nagging recriminations or she would lose her mind.

"Blessings, Sister. Walk with you?"

She turned. A withered old man in tattered clothing hobbled towards her.

"Best to have comp'ny along these roads, nowaday."

"Certainly, friend, certainly, and welcome."

Welcome, indeed. Anything, anyone to wrench her mind from its present self-abuse.

"Spreading the word, then, are you?" the old man asked.

"That's been done, I think." She responded. "I'm more for ministering to the sick."

He laughed. "Plenty of work for you in town, then. No shortage."

"And you? What brings you onto the road at this hour?"

"Was told there was a Mender approaching, and I came out searching, to be your escort-like."

"But wouldn't they send the—"

"I *am* the Captain of the Guard."

That stopped her in her tracks.

The old man shrugged, apologetically. "Times ain't what they ought to be."

Everything, everything made her feel guilty.

"What's the population of your town, sir? Captain?"

"Thousand, give or take."

"And how many men amongst you?"

"Of shaving and sword-bearing age? Maybe sixty."

She reeled. "But sixty?"

"Oh, there be a couple hundred boys, surely. But we're letting 'em *be* boys, for the nonce. All the rest—"

"Yes, I know, Captain," she said, a little more sharply than she'd intended, "the wars have been evil, inexcusably, unforgivably evil."

"That they have" was all he said before falling silent.

Up ahead, she saw the silhouettes of cottages in the gloom.

Vykers, In the Forest

Vykers woke up with dirt in his eyes. It took him a moment, but he dimly remembered crawling into an old log at some point. He was more thirsty than he'd ever been in his life, even more than in his various campaigns across numerous deserts, even more than during his recent days-long torture in the square of that nameless village. Thirst was a demon inside him. He felt that if he didn't get water in the next few minutes, he'd be dead within the hour.

He tried to move and was blindsided by an avalanche of pain. That's right: they'd destroyed him, taken his hands and feet. The stumps were itching and burning and throbbing all at once. It was by sheer force of will that he clung to consciousness and sanity. Water, first. Nothing else mattered.

Slowly, he inched his way out of the log and into the light of afternoon In the Forest. Questions were a swarm of bees in his head, but water first. Water first. What did he know about water? It flowed downhill. It was most likely to be found in the low places, in the gullies and ravines. He listened, but could hear only insects and birds. They knew where the water was, but wouldn't tell him, the little bastards. He raised his head and looked around. This was an old, old forest in a temperate climate. There were oaks and firs, alder and birch. The undergrowth was all but impassible. There would be water.

He had a powerful urge to sleep, but felt that if did, he would never wake up. Water first.

There was no obvious slope nearby, but he began crawling in the direction that most felt downhill. After an eternity of unrelenting effort and agony, he found himself looking down into the urine-filled tracks of a hoofed animal. He sniffed the liquid and almost threw up. But he bent his lips to the tracks and drank, anyway, and indeed had a very hard time keeping it down. His disgust and anger gave him a burst of energy, though. He considered a moment: was this beast coming from or heading towards water? Coming from, he decided and wriggled off in the direction from which it came. He almost burst into tears when, after a great deal of time, he came within sight of a bog.

With frantic energy, he shuffled into the water, almost completely submerging himself. It was not particularly cold and had a deep, woody flavor, but he didn't care. It was the most wonderful thing he had ever tasted. When he was satisfied, he crawled back onto dry land, exhausted. Again, he needed a safe place to sleep. He was ravenous, he was cold, but of all his basic needs, sleep was most demanding. Eventually, he found a dense thicket that backed up against a large boulder. He would be unreachable from behind and difficult to reach from the front. It was not perfect—nowhere near—but good enough.

He slept like a dead man.

Long Pete & Company, In Corners

Long Pete was a gigolo. He had been a lousy farmer, an inept fisherman, a hopeless blacksmith's apprentice and a middling soldier. In the dearth of men after the wars, he became very popular with the local womenfolk. Well, perhaps "very popular" was overdoing it. He became *necessary,* and that was good enough for him. That he could pleasure himself and a woman and make money at the same time was more than he had ever hoped for. Still, he couldn't escape the feeling that he ought to be doing something, when he wasn't doing some*one.* And the other men in town weren't exactly fond of him. What he wanted—what he needed—was a higher calling, some way to earn their respect and eternal gratitude. There had once been a statue in the town square, some honorable so-and-so, but the locals had been forced to smelt it down for swords, armor and arrowheads during the war. But they couldn't do that to the statue Long Pete hoped to have someday, if it were made of marble.

"Ho there, Pete!" Long Pete was shaken from his daydream by the voice of his too-constant companion, Janks. At his side was their friend, Short Pete, wheeling himself along in his specially made cart. Short Pete, whose real name was "Frayne," had lost both legs in battle, but not his sense of humor. If Long Pete was somewhat vain, the existence of a Short Pete would surely temper him.

"Shall we make merry this morning?" Janks bellowed.

"I'm a bit the worse for wear after last night's...celebrations, and I've work to do later."

"Work, is it? Work! I should be so lucky!" Short Pete replied. The fact was that, while Long Pete was tall and somewhat chicken-like, and Janks resembled nothing so much as a pig, Short Pete would have been a fine specimen, indeed, if not for the lack of legs.

"Lucky? I'd trade it all in a heartbeat for a title and a piece of land. Some of these women are impossibly demanding. The great Mahnus himself couldn't please them."

"Well, they do say he had two peckers." Janks offered.

"I'd rather have kept that image out of my head all day" said Short Pete. "But you couldn't work a bit of land to save yourself."

"I didn't say anything about working it. I just want a buffer to keep the riffraff out."

"But you *are* the riffraff!" Short Pete objected.

Long Pete choked. "With friends like you..."

"Got anything to drink about you?" Janks asked.

Long Pete sighed and pulled a flask from his vest. "Go easy on that, Janks. I won't be able to refill it 'til I see the widow Sorensen tomorrow night. Anyway, why don't you go over to the inn and drink your fill there?"

"I..." Janks began.

"He's got no credit left. Owes Arnet too much money." Short Pete said.

"It's true, it's true, and a terrible thing it is when honest men can't earn a decent wage." Janks lamented.

"Honest men?" Long Pete sneered. "Where? And why should the indecent earn a decent wage?"

"A man's gotta do something for money, hasn't he? Look at you!"

"I happen to perform a valuable service!"

"For yourself, maybe. I doubt all them widows'd miss you if you went off to war again."

Long Pete was indignant. "For your information, mate…"

"Ladies! Ladies!" Short Pete interjected, "This is boredom talking. What we need is some sort of cause, or purpose. We can't sit here drinking and whoring forever."

"They're not whores!"

"You know what I mean, Long. We don't have any goals. You want that title and piece of land, you'll have to earn it."

There was a long silence and then Janks said "I might have an idea…"

Vykers, In the Forest

When he had been whole, he had not been given to reflection; he took, he broke, he killed. Now, though, he had little to do but reflect. And he did not enjoy it. Memories of things he did—or even might have done—bedeviled him. Questions of why and what-for tormented him. Had he been given life only to take others' lives? What was his purpose now? Why was he even alive? *Countless Hells,* he hated these thoughts; they were the province of weak-spirited philosophers. If he had his way, he'd… but he did not have his way and likely never would again. He'd been reduced, he felt, to his primal state, that of a beast. He lived in squalor, ate whatever came within reach, slept, pissed. He'd long since lost his use for language—who was there to talk to? Ha! Was this so different from his former life, after all? Except for the thinking.

Without cause or warning, he remembered a particular battle a few years earlier. His army had swept into some backwater and pitched camp. Facing annihilation, the locals sent their beloved champion to challenge Vykers in single combat. The man was a legend among his people, with a near-mythical sword. He was tall, he was handsome, with the kind of charisma most only dream about. With a great, jubilant roar, they sent him forward. Vykers cut him down before he could even draw that sword from its sheath, and then broke it over his knee. The silence that followed was deafening. The hope and courage went out of the opposing army in a single breath, and they went to their deaths with little resistance. It was as if, in killing their hero, he had killed an entire people. The rest was just clean-up.

Vykers had never meant that much to anyone. He was universally feared, to be sure, but no one admired him. And no one missed him now, he was certain. But he would not wallow in self-pity. That, too, was for lesser men. He—Something... something was scrabbling in the back of his mind, like a rat in the walls. For a moment, he considered resisting. Then he realized the only way to catch this rat was to let it into the room.

"Warrior..."

Vykers was on all-fours, foraging in a gully. He paused.

"A moment of your time..."

He raised his head, held his breath, looked around. No one. This was something internal.

"Warrior."

He laughed. He was going mad. He'd figured it might happen, sooner or later.

"I am here."

Vykers looked around and noticed a pale root or stick under his left knee. Moving off it, he saw several more nearby. Not sticks. Bones. And there, between two stones, a skull. He scuttled towards it, laughed again. "Vykers, old man, you have well and truly gone 'round the bend!"

"Not so," the voice replied.

He dug the skull out with his wrists. The back was missing.

"I met my end here, yes."

Vykers sat back on his haunches, contemplating the skull.

"Will you not speak to me?"

"Why are *you* talking to *me*?"

"Because you're here. And I've been waiting too long for someone, anyone, to come by."

"And then...?"

"Take me away."

"You're out of luck," Vykers said. "I've got no hands and no use for your bones, if I did."

"But *I* may be of use to you."

This time, Vykers laughed himself faint. "Who are you?" he asked. "Who *were* you?"

"I was—am—Fourth Shaper to his Majesty, King Orstoth."

Vykers sat. "Was. He's dead, too."

The voice was silent.

"So, you're one of them Burners, huh?"

"We prefer 'Shapers'."

Vykers laughed. "And I'd *prefer* to have my hands again, but what we want's got nothing to do with what's coming to us. What's your name, Burner?"

"I was called 'Arune'."

"Huh. Never heard of you."

"And your name is Tarmun Vykers."

"Maybe you *were* a mage."

"Vykers-the-Vicious,' they call you, and 'the Reaper'."

"I doubt they call me anything, anymore. Far as anyone knows, I'm dead. How'd *you* die, anyway?"

"Long Teeth."

"Svarren?"

"That's an older name for them, aye." Arune said. They're also variously known as Svarrenii, Worrenu, and Varn. "I'm surprised you haven't encountered them hereabouts."

Vykers' head snapped up; he scanned the forest.

"I told you you weren't mad. A madman wouldn't care for his own safety."

"It's just that I hate those fucking things. And I'd hate to be set upon when I'm defenseless."

Now, it was the shade's turn to laugh. "The Reaper, defenseless? You underestimate yourself."

"I have no hands or feet, fool. I can't run from predators nor defend myself once they catch me."

"Take me with you, then. I can help."

Vykers glanced at the skull in irritation. "Assuming I haven't gone completely batshit, and you are more than you seem, how can you help?"

"Take me with you, and I'll show you."

"You're getting on my nerves, Boney. What the hell difference does it make if you lie here or in my cave for all eternity?"

"We won't be staying in your cave for all eternity, as you put it."

Vykers brooded.

"I offer you fire," the ghost said.

Vykers grinned, in spite of himself. "Fire? You can give me fire?"

"What sort of Shaper would I be if I couldn't conjure fire?"

"Yeah, but you're dead."

"For now."

"Okay," Vykers shrugged. "Let's go back to my cave..."

Aoife, On Her Mission

Aoife followed the old man to an inn, near the town's well.

"Here y'are, mistress: the town hall, the marketplace, the church and o' course the inn, all rolled into one."

"The church? Then your town has a spiritual leader?"

"It does now," said the old man, looking her up and down.

"But I can't stay" she protested. "Long."

Whereupon the old man laughed, "They all say that."

Turning, he led her inside, where a thick miasma of odors almost knocked her over. Here, she smelled sweat, mold, mildew, candle wax, stale beer, wood smoke, tobacco, animal fur, baking bread and...some sort of stew. Experience told her that her exact position in the room dictated the balance of these odors, and that moving around would produce both better and worse results. The trick was finding the good spots, which was often made more difficult by the other occupants of the room. This particular room was packed, as she suspected was usually the case, given its multifunctional purpose in this community.

Thus, her entrance was well and widely marked, and she felt a hundred eyes upon her instantly, some welcoming, some skeptical, a few apathetic and several, quite drunk. She turned to thank the Captain of the Guard, but he had slipped away, unnoticed. Steeling herself, Aiofe waded into the crowd and made for a pair of welcoming eyes, which belonged to an old red-headed woman with few teeth but countless wrinkles.

"Good e'en to you, Sister" the old woman chirped.

"Good e'en to you," Aoife replied. "How does one go about getting the innkeeper's attention in this…this…throng?"

Laughter. "He knows you're here, he knows you're here. He'll never miss a penny comin' through that door!"

A large bowl of stew and a tankard of ale clunked down on the table in front of Aoife, as a pair of meaty arms withdrew behind her. Aoife turned, only to see the innkeeper's broad back as he bustled through the crowd on his way to another table.

"That was fast," she observed.

More laughter. "Aye. There's none don't love Locksby. Best innkeeper in the Lake lands."

The aroma drifting up from her stew gave Aoife further evidence. "This smells impossibly good. It lacks only a small loaf of…"

Bread plopped down next to her bowl, but before Aoife could thank the man who brought it, he was gone again. "He must be spirit-touched" Aoife said, to yet more laughter. "I'm Aoife, by the way" she said to her table mate.

"Frieda," the old woman answered, "the town gossip," she finished, not without pride.

"I must say, Frieda, I've only met you and the Captain of the Guard, but you folks seem in surprisingly good spirits."

"Ah, there's plenty o' piss-and-vinegar in Shoulty—even some as use piss *as* vinegar, but all-in-all, we're a good-meaning folk."

"Then perhaps you're not in need of my services…?"

"Now, I din' say that. Kerbie's legs've gone foul—ya c'n smell him two homes away—Nell's not recovered from birthin'. There's many a widow needs comfortin', and then there's that odd Soolan boy…"

That odd Soolan boy. That odd boy.

Aoife looked into the fire and thought back to another, in the hearth of her parents' cottage. She remembered a winter storm had been raging outside. She and her parents were huddled close to the flames, while her brother Anders lolled on the floor, babbling to his fingers.

Anders was odd and more than odd. He had been born three weeks late, as if disinterested in joining the rest of humanity. Though his hair was black, his eyes were of blue so pale they seemed almost colorless. It was disconcerting, looking into those eyes. Fortunately, Anders never maintained contact for long. But he didn't speak well or often, so it was almost impossible to know what he was thinking. As the saying went, "there was no 'there' there." He just didn't seem to recognize—or even acknowledge—people or events around him. For Anders, Aoife believed, there was no difference between her family and the stones in the hearth; they were not human, they were simply more "things" he encountered. She found that heartbreaking for the first few years of Anders' life, but eventually came to accept it. No, that was wrong: she became *resigned* to it.

Aoife figured she must have been about nine years old that night, which meant Anders was six. She could still picture her mother, in the glow of the flames, plucking a bird for dinner, while her father sat nearby and smoked his pipe. He favored lowlands tobacco, and whenever she smelled it, it brought back a thousand memories. She loved her father and mother fiercely and wanted to love Anders, but…But.

It was a cozy little cottage—her parents had worked endlessly to make it so—but the wind nevertheless found its way through various cracks and crevices and whistled discordantly at her family like an angry guest, unhappy with his welcome. The rain battered against the roof and walls, as if trying to reduce them to rubble. Yet their little home remained defiant.

There came a banging on the door and not a polite banging, either. Everyone reacted, except Anders. Aoife's parents exchanged looks. Without a word, her father reached up, hefted a piece of firewood from a nearby pile and slowly approached the door.

Bang! Bang! Bang!

He looked back, and Aoife's mother stood, clutching her kitchen knife. Her father extended his club and used it to raise the latch. Suddenly, the door exploded inward and a tall, grey-black figure crashed through, stumbling a few steps before collapsing on the floor near the fire.

Aoife remembered the strange, crustacean-like appearance of the thing. He—it—was wearing armor, but it seemed more a part of its skin. No armor she'd ever seen fit so snugly or meshed so seamlessly with the material beneath and between its plates. And the color was so weird—not silvery, nor grey, nor even a proper black…more like an exhausted black, a super-murky grey, a shade heretofore unknown. There was, Aoife noticed, a sword in its belt, but by the look of its scabbard, the sword was as strange as the creature itself. As for the creature, a hairless, waxy yellow head emerged from the armor, with two shiny black orbs for eyes, but without ears or a nose. A sickly grey tongue darted out from its slit of a mouth. The creature shuddered and gasped.

"Kill it, husband!" Aoife's mother urged.

"Kill it? I'm not goin' near the damned thing. Look at it, will you?"

"What is it, father?" Aoife asked.

"Damned if I know," he answered. "But it don't look healthy, that's certain."

"We can't have it in our house!" Aoife's mother complained. "You've got to drag it back outside."

"In this weather? Are you mad, woman?"

"Are *you* mad, husband? We don't even know what it is!"

As her parents argued, Anders crawled over to the thing and moved almost face-to-face with it. Noticing this, Aoife shrieked in fear.

"Great One, preserve us!" her mother cried, while her father stood petrified.

The creature grasped Anders' collar and pulled him near. Aoife's father raised his club and took a tentative step closer. The thing appeared to be struggling to say something when, without warning, it vomited all over the boy and then went slack. Aoife's father finally rushed in and bashed it on the head, but it was clear it had already died. Her father stood over it, prodding it with his log. The girl and her mother stood nearby, in shock.

"I'm cold," Anders said, the first words he'd spoken in weeks.

Long & Company, Corners

Spirk Nessno was the village idiot or, more accurately, the prototype for a new generation of village idiots. There was nothing obviously wrong with him and, except for the port wine stain that covered the left half of his face, nothing remarkable, either. In fact, Spirk was so bland as to be almost invisible. There were occasions in which he would quite literally go unnoticed in a room of two. But he possessed transcendent gullibility. He was the Grand Master of Credulity and displayed a dizzying virtuosity in that regard. And, as a nothing who'd believe anything, he was paradoxically unique.

"He's our secret weapon!" Janks told his cohorts.

"Against what?" Long Pete asked, skeptically.

"Dunno. But I'm certain whatever-it-might-be's unequipped to deal with the likes of Spirk Nessno."

Long nodded. The legend of Spirk Nessno was not to be gainsaid...

When his parents were young, Spirk's mother ran afoul of a local witch, who cursed the poor peasant with infinite fertility, and by the time Spirk was born—twenty-third of thirty-seven children—the wretched Nessno clan had eaten itself out of hovel and home. So it came as no surprise—even to Spirk—when, at the tender age of fifteen, he was given his father's rusty sword and encouraged, rather forcibly, to go and find his fortune in the wide world. Or at least get a damned job. For a simpleton, however, he had a remarkable aversion to simplicity.

"I'm lookin' fer ad...adventure," he announced, as he burst into the infamous Hog's Tooth Tavern one stormy spring night. "Adventure and...uh...a job!" The patrons of the Hog's Tooth were a frightening lot and probably wouldn't have bothered to look up if Alheria herself had come cartwheeling through the door with seventeen demons in her wake, but most were so flabbergasted by the outrageous naïveté of Spirk's declaration that they felt themselves compelled to examine the boy for signs of madness. Spirk, uncomfortable with this sudden scrutiny, could only gasp and roll his eyes, like a fish thrown onto a dock. Shaken from his near catatonia by the waves of derisive laughter that thundered towards him from all corners of the tavern, Spirk turned on his heel and was just about to run weeping into the rain when a voice called "Boy!" Cautiously, he ducked back into the tavern and noticed a man waving at him, while his two companions regarded Spirk with expressions that approached religious wonderment. Occasionally, they whispered amongst themselves, squinted their eyes at the boy and dropped their jaws in even greater amazement. As he drew nearer, Spirk could make out snatches of their conversation, but try as he might, he could make no sense of it.

"I'm certain of it, Korith!" Spirk heard a rather large fat man tell the stranger who'd called to him, "He's the one. He's the one foretold!"

"Yes, by Frumda!" a second man told Korith with a tremulous voice, "He does bear the mark!"

"Dosin, Rundel," the man called Korith said calmly, "We must speak with the boy first, that our prayers may be answered."

Spirk was completely bewildered. Something in their conversation suggested these men thought him to be someone of great importance; he even believed they might be in awe of him. But that was ridiculous. Arriving at their table at last, he was able to get a closer look at his admirers and was quite shocked to find them ordinary—even non-descript. From the clothing they wore, they could as easily have been woodsmen as craftsmen or mercenaries. No more enlightened than he had been before, Spirk turned to the man called Korith and said "Yeah?"

"The simplicity of his words! The honesty! Surely, he is the boy of prophecy!" the thin man, Dosin, cried out enthusiastically.

"And look!" Rundel added, "He does bear the mark of the Rooster across his left eye..."

"That's 'Mark of the Griffin' weren't it, Rundel?" Korith corrected.

"Oh, aye...aye...so it is. And what a beautiful griffin it is, too." Rundel agreed, reaching out hesitantly to trace the angry birthmark on Spirk's face.

Still, Spirk found himself at a loss.

Finally, Korith spoke to him directly.

"I say, boy, my friends and I were wondering if...if er...we might have seen you somewhere before...?"

"Um, well...I sorta doubt it," Spirk began. "See, I'm not from 'round here. I'm from Bloodge, and I..."

"Bloodge?" Korith repeated in obvious amazement. "Did you say 'Bloodge'?"

"Well, yeah, and..."

Korith threw himself down onto the filthy floor. "He is the boy of prophecy!" the man exclaimed to his eager companions. "He bears the mark and comes to us from Bloodge! He is the one!"

"At long last!" Dosin cried joyfully.

"Truly, we are saved!" Rundel added.

"Whu...whu...'scuse me?" Spirk stammered.

"What is your name, honored one?" Korith inquired humbly, tears of elation streaming down his cheeks.

"Me?" Spirk looked around. "Spirk. Spirk Nessno." He answered.

"All hail Spirk!" Korith prompted his companions.

"All hail Spirk!" they obliged happily.

"Fuck Spirk!" someone in the crowed jeered in less than helpful fashion.

But Spirk was too caught up in the odd declarations of the trio before him to take any note of other goings on. "I...uh... don't get it." He announced unashamedly.

"Great Spurt..."

"Spirk. It's 'Spirk'!"

"Yes...yes, of course it is, noble Spirk!" Korith agreed. "Long have our people awaited your coming, and at last you have arrived."

"I didn't even know I was coming 'til my Da gave me the

boot last week..." Spirk protested.

"No, noble Sperm, your coming...er...your arrival was preordained, just as it is your destiny to lead our people out of oppression and into greatness."

"What are you talkin' about?" Spirk demanded, both disturbed and delirious as he began to feel the stirrings of greatness in his concave chest.

"Surely you know of the prophecy?" Rundel asked.

"Uh...'course. But...er...remind me a bit, okay?"

"Well..." Korith began, "the...the prophecy tells us that one of humble birth and bearing the mark of the rooster..."

"I thought it was a griffin," Spirk interrupted.

"Why yes. Yes it is. My mistake." Korith conceded. "Anyway, one of humble birth and bearing the mark of the griffin will one day...ah..."

"Arrive! Er...arrive and um..." Dosin added, excitedly.

"Arrive here! Yes, here at the Hog's Tooth..." Rundel declared.

"Don't be an idiot!" Korith growled under his breath as he elbowed his fat companion in the ribs. "Actually," he said, "the prophecy don't really mention the Hog's Tooth specifically, but, er, it does lead one to believe that the savior will be found in an establishment such as this here!"

"And one day become King of the West!" Rundel added quickly, as if attempting to gain the last word.

"We're in the East, fool." Korith glared at him.

"Did I say West? Ha! I meant East o' course. King o' the East!"

"Really?" Spirk asked, barely able to contain his growing euphoria. Gods, wouldn't his old man just die when he learned that 'Spirk the Jerk' had become King of the West! Or East.

"Oh yes, your magnificence!" Dosin fawned.

"Absolutely," Korith agreed, again lowering his face to the floor.

"You bet!" Rundel said.

"Then I'm gonna be your king, eh?"

"Yes!" the three men insisted.

"Then...I could give you orders, for instance?" Spirk asked, anxious to begin reaping the benefits of his newfound greatness.

"Why, uh, I suppose so, yes." Korith responded, with poorly masked surprise.

"Buy me a drink, then!" Spirk commanded.

After a brief moment of silence, during which Spirk's three subjects glowered at each other in irritation, Korith finally said, "Majesty, it is unseemly for so great a monarch to refresh himself in so base a tavern. Please, my king, permit my friends and me to escort you to a more worthy establishment."

"You mean, more expensive?"

"Aye."

"Well, escort away then!" Spirk assented gleefully.

"Let us leave by the back door then, my friends," Korith told his companions gravely, "that our king may not be mobbed by his adoring subjects."

"What sayeth you, my subjects?" Spirk demanded, trying his best to sound regal, "I art not a'feared of the adorishments of my people."

"Of course not, my king!" Korith quickly agreed. "I merely suggested we use the back door so that your loving subjects would not, in their excitement, tear your royal person limb from limb in search of souvenirs. But if you still wish..."

"Methinks thy first idea wert good, after all," Spirk admitted. "Let us leave by the backdoor then, for sooth."

And so, the odd processional marched toward the rear door: Korith, Rundel and Dosin in front, sporting the most solemn of expressions on their faces, and Spirk striding nobly behind them, his hand resting clumsily on the hilt of his father's sword. As they passed out the door and into the damp night, Spirk sneered disdainfully at a couple of toughs who were beating an old drunk.

"I care not for violence in my kingdom," Spirk proclaimed, stepping out of the tavern and into an oncoming fist. Instantly, he went blind with little white stars, but a follow-up kick to the stomach cleared his head.

"Whatsa matter, yer majesty?" He heard Rundel sneer. "Royal life too tough fer ya?"

"Lemme heap s'more 'adorishments' on 'im!" Dosin cackled,

smacking Spirk across the thighs with the flat of his old sword.

"Just take his valuables, if the cretin has any, and leave him to the scavengers!" Korith commanded, as he threw a knee into Spirk's ribs.

And the abuse got worse after that, so that, in a matter of minutes, Spirk lay semi-conscious and bleeding in a mud puddle, as the derisive laughter of his assailants receded into the distance. "I care not for violence,' Ha! Whatta rube!" he heard one of them say.

Short grunted, pensively. "If we do this by the book..."

"What book? Janks here can't read!"

"No," said Short, "but you and I can. Anyway, it's just a figure of speech."

"Whereas I'm a figure of *action*!" Janks proclaimed.

"You're a figure of moldering dunghill," Long countered, "but let's hear what

Short's got in mind."

"But I..."

Short cut in. "What I meant was we're still lacking a giant, a Shaper, and any number of worthy arms."

Long and Janks just stared at him.

He continued. "Look, a good crew's gotta have a little slight-of-hand, which I guess is Janks. It's gotta have a leader. It's gotta have a decent basher. And it's gotta have some magic. Now, we... we've got a whoremaster..."

"I'm not a whoremaster!" Long objected.

"A cripple..." Short pointed to himself, "a scoundrel and, counting Spirk, an imbecile. Y'see what I'm saying, lads? We're shy a bit of real flash and smash."

Long Pete considered. "Yes, yes, I see. Can't really call ourselves a decent merc squad without some magic and muscle. Any ideas, boys?"

"I hear there's a mighty big fella over to Farnsley." Janks said.

"None closer?" Long asked.

"War cleared 'em all out. They was all pressed into service on one side or t'other. Surprised there's anyone over five feet left alive, to be honest."

"You? Honest? There's a laugh." Short snorted.

"So, Farnsley." Long mused. "And what about the Shaper?"

"Well, there's always D'Kem." Janks answered.

"Dickum? Man's a wastrel, a drunk." Short said.

"Beggars can't be choosers," Janks replied. "And anyways, man's good company." He paused. "But he don't like to be called 'Dickum'."

Short sneered. "Until he's sober enough to stop me, it's 'Dickum.' So, to recap: we've got ourselves a whoremaster, a cripple, a scoundrel, an imbecile, a drunk and a could-be, might-be, possible giant living in a town a good three days' travel from here."

"Well," Long observed, "one has to start somewhere. Now, uh..." he continued awkwardly, "there's the matter of leadership..."

"This whole crew was my idea!" Janks reminded them.

"And we still don't know it's a *good* idea. So, that counts you out. Plus, you can't read." Long said.

"What's readin' got to do with it?" Janks demanded.

Short ignored him. "So, it's down to Long and Short. But here's the brilliant bit: we let everyone *think* it's Long, but it's actually me. That way, our enemies will waste all their time trying to kill him, when it's really me they're after!"

Long bristled. "Now, wait a minute..."

"I like it!" Janks bellowed.

"Done!" Short said.

"But I..." Long Pete stammered.

And so it was decided.

Vykers and Arune, In the Forest

Fire. So often, it had been his weapon of choice. There was a time when he'd burnt an entire city to the ground (and salted the farmlands around it), even after its people had surrendered to his host. He hadn't just wanted to incapacitate them; he'd wanted to burn their collective spirit.

And now it bolstered his. After placing Arune's skull on a stone ledge inside his cave, Vykers set about gathering wood into a pile, and the Shaper set it ablaze. He worried briefly about smoke, but his ghostly companion seemed to have that covered as well. All-in-all, things were almost…pleasant.

And he must have dozed off, because Vykers jolted awake, disoriented and famished. Strangely, the fire looked unchanged.

"Burner."

A pause.

"Tarmun?"

"Don't call me that. Why's the fire look like that, same as when it started?"

"We needed the wood to get it started, but it's not burning wood now."

"Huh. What's it burning?"

Another pause. "It's complicated."

"Fine, then. Look, I'm starving. I've gotta go out and find something to eat."

"And if I said I could bring something to you?"

Vykers sat back on his haunches, thinking. "Why are you being so helpful?"

"You'd rather I didn't help?"

"I just wanna know what you're after, what it's gonna cost me." He spat, "I can't see as I have anything you'd want. You an idiot, Burner?"

"Your meal has arrived" the shade said, and be-damned if Vykers didn't hear snuffling and grunting near the cave's entrance. In a moment, a wild pig wandered in.

"How'm I supposed to…"

And then it fell over dead, its legs kicking a final three or four times.

"That's a hell of a trick. That work with people, too?"

"Not that well. People are a little harder to penetrate. Anyway, I'm afraid you'll have to figure out how to butcher that beast on your own." Arune said. "There's not really a spell for that sort of thing, or, if there is, I've never heard of it."

Vykers would like to have been more cautious, but this was more meat than he'd seen in he-had-no-idea-how-long. He scrambled into a corner and retrieved the sharpened stone fragment he used for gutting rodents and frogs. He found he was drooling like a simpleton. Before he could eat, though, he'd have to figure a way to cut up that pig and put some on the fire. Hard to do in his condition, but he had every reason to try.

Young Aoife and Anders, At Home

With each day, Anders changed a bit more. He never became talkative in the fashion of regular folk, but neither was he as detached as he had been for the first several years of his life. Quiet as he was, his eyes were alive and utterly engaged, utterly present in whatever was going on. It was creepy, really. To Aoife, he was like cat watching a mouse, biding its time and waiting to pounce. "What?" she used to challenge him, only to be greeted by further silence or, worse still, the faintest hint of a smile.

She remembered the day her father was ill and asked Aiofe to take Anders and tend to the sheep on the North meadow. It was the warmest, most pleasant day of spring, and Aiofe could not resist running barefoot through the grass and wildflowers. When she looked up, her brother was already a good distance away, kneeling before one of the lambs. As she watched, he took its head in his hands and snapped its neck. Aoife ran to him in anger and horror.

"What in all hells have you done?" she yelled.

When he saw her approaching, he winked at her, stopping her dead in her tracks. Slowly, he laid the lamb down on the grass and placed his hands on its side. Again, he looked up at her, as if about to impart a mischievous secret. He squinted at the lamb and clenched his jaw. And then it opened its eyes and struggled to get up. Anders stepped back. It jumped up and ambled off after the other sheep. The boy looked over at Aoife with a smile that was more frightening than anything she'd ever seen. He had killed that lamb and brought it back.

Aoife turned and ran home to her parents, crying in fear and confusion. When she finally reached them, her hysteria had grown so intense she was absolutely unable to communicate, and her parents simply stared at her, worried and bewildered.

"Calm down now, Sweet. Calm down" her mother urged. "Are you hurt?"

Aoife shook her head.

"Your brother, then. Is Anders hurt?"

Aoife let out a wail of terror.

"Is it Svarren?" her father cut in.

Again, Aoife shook her head, gasping for breath.

"Is it the sheep, then?"

Finally, Aoife found the breath to speak, just as the door opened again and Anders walked in. She stared at him, her mouth open, words on her tongue. He looked right into her eyes and then casually nodded to his parents before heading over to the wash basin to clean his hands. Aoife's parents exchanged glances.

"Everything alright on the meadow, boy?" her father asked Anders.

He grunted in the affirmative. And then, "Everything is perfect," which amounted to a monologue for Anders.

Perfect? Far from it, Aoife thought. But how could she ever convince her parents of what she'd seen? And what could they do about it?

Months went by, years evaporated, and while Aoife witnessed many strange and disturbing things from her brother—things that made her fear him like nothing else in her life—he never revealed himself to his parents. They seemed to have no idea of what he'd become...or perhaps he had them under some sort of spell. Eventually, Aoife knew, she'd be expected to marry and make a home of her own somewhere else, leaving her parents alone with Anders until it was time for him, too, to make his own way. But the thought of leaving her parents alone with him, sleeping in the same house without her nearby to keep the boy in check was terrifying.

Vykers and Arune, In the Forest

Vykers lay back, firelight reflecting off the grease on his distended gut. He couldn't remember ever feeling so full.

"Burner?"

"Vykers."

"It's time you told me what you want from me."

"I felt I had to earn your trust first."

"Not gonna happen. But, as you can see, I'm not really in a position of strength right now. So?"

"So...you've seen a small sampling of my abilities..."

"Mmmm."

"And you must realize we're in a similar predicament... me being completely without a body and you, dealing with a greatly damaged one."

Vykers rolled over and looked at the skull, suddenly alert. "And...?"

"What if I said I could restore your hands and feet?"

"I'd say you're full of shit."

"I didn't say it would be easy or enjoyable. But I can do it."

"Huh. And you're gonna ask some terrible price..."

"Terrible? I don't think you'll find it terrible."

"You wanna eat my soul, or some such shit?"

"Eat your soul?" Arune laughed, "No. I'm not even sure that's possible."

"Well, spit it out, damn you! What's the cost?"

"You'd have to allow me in, to share your body until such time as I found a more-suitable host."

"Alheria's poisonous tits! That's some fuckin' cost, alright."

"It wouldn't be permanent."

"So says the spook." Vykers scoffed. "You might be like the plague, not to be shook off for love or money."

"I understand your skepticism. But I'm offering to restore your hands and feet in return."

Vykers fell silent and turned away.

Arune waited.

"You wouldn't think you'd miss being able to wipe your own ass." Vykers finally said. "Destroyer of legions, brought low by his own stench." He paused. "Fine, then. How do we do this?"

"Take my skull," Arune answered, "and throw it into the fire."

Vykers laughed. "Well, there's one wish granted."

He ambled over to the ledge, pinned the skull between his wrists and swung it towards the fire, letting it fall into the flames.

"You're one o' the Burning now, in truth." Almost immediately, he was overcome with a lassitude, a strange fuzziness of thought. The more he fought it, the worse it became, until he simply collapsed on his side in the dirt, writhing helplessly like a turtle on its back. Eventually, fatigue overcame him and he drifted into a fitful sleep.

Later, he bolted upright in a panic. His head hurt. His vision was blurry. And his joints creaked. He felt hung over, was the problem. Terribly hung over. And he still had no hands or feet.

"Burner! Where the fuck are you?"

Without warning, he doubled over and vomited in the dirt.

"I know how you feel." Arune muttered in his mind. "Actually, I *feel* how you feel."

"Can't you make this experience a little less...shitty?"

"I'm trying. Believe me. Whatever fairytales you may've heard, this kind of thing isn't easy."

Vykers grunted.

"I'm trying to work with your body, and it's trying to throw me out."

"Can't say as I blame it."

"And I thought you were immune to a little misery."

He'd had a sort of mentor when he was starting out, an old veteran by the name of Tewkes—but everyone called him "Hobnail," on account of he was always threatening to plant his hobnails in someone's ass. "Tarmun," he'd say "kill their spirits, and their bodies'll follow hard after."

Vykers killed 'em, alright. By the hundreds of thousands. He spread corpses like fertilizer across the North, until the land was more lush and green than any time since Creation, itself.

Despite his injuries, his own spirit was very much alive and, even in a magic-induced fever dream, Vykers yearned to get back onto the battlefield.

Long & Company, On the Road

In the absence of a consistent work force to maintain it, the road to Farnsley had become overgrown in places. In others, holes that ought to have been filled had simply gotten worse. It would have been slow-going under the best of conditions, but with the motley assortment of mounts the gang had been able to assemble, the mere three days' journey was likely impossible.

"A goat, Nessno?" Long sniped. "Mahnus save me. Who rides a goat?"

"Well...it's a big goat." Spirk answered.

"And that makes two of ya."

"Take it easy on the boy," Short said. "If nothing else, we can eat the damned thing if food gets scarce."

"And you!" Long shouted.

"Now don't start in on my ram!"

"It's a sheep. A bleedin' sheep!"

"Ram! It's a ram. Classic war mount of the Southern Dranavians."

"Damned scrawny for a ram, ain't it? And where's his horns?"

"Yeah, and why don't we eat him instead 'o my goat? I like me some good mutton."

"I am surrounded by idiots!" Long muttered.

"Look, Long, this here ram's only got to carry but half of me, and it's all I could afford. Anyway, it's a lot further fall from the back of a horse."

"And you wouldn't be riding one, neither, if it weren't for me!" Janks cut in.

"Yeah, thanks. You stole me a horse. Or at least she was a horse once upon a time. If you've got to risk the stocks, couldn't you have found something a little less ready for the knackers? Or did you choose this old nag to humiliate me?"

"I am hurt, Long."

"Morally hurt." Spirk added.

"Mortally hurt." Long corrected.

"That, too" said Spirk.

Long sat back in his saddle and surveyed the crew: Short Pete, the half-man, strapped to the back of a boney sheep; Spirk Nessno, standing—actually standing—astride a wall-eyed goat; Janks, sitting smugly on the back of a filthy draft horse and, of course, the old Burner, half asleep on the back of his donkey. It was as ridiculous and inauspicious a beginning as Long could imagine, but he figured perhaps—perhaps—they could purchase or steal better mounts later. He looked glumly at the road ahead and back at his friends. What in all hells was he doing?

"Whenever you're ready, '*boss*,' we'll move out" he called over to Short Pete.

It had been a long and tedious day without much progress. Farnsley seemed as far away as ever, but the campfire warmed the group's spirits and loosened their tongues. All except D'Kem, and Long found that especially irritating. The Burner slumped against a log and stared sleepily into the fire.

"Look here, Dickum. Are you a member of this expedition or ain't ya?"

The Burner rubbed his stubbled chin and lifted his bloodshot eyes to Long Pete. "I am here." He said, as if that explained everything.

"Oh," Long replied with melodramatic surprise, "are ya, indeed? And how would we know that?"

Janks cut in, as expected. "There's naught for him to do, yet, Long, except follow the road with the rest of us."

"Why doesn't he *talk* with the rest of us?

"Maybe he's got nothing to say."

"Or too much." Spirk added blithely, causing D'Kem to glance over at him with an appraising eye.

"Too much? That's rich. I bet he doesn't know shit!" Long spat in the dust. "And you, Nessno! Ya spent more time walking *beside* that mangy goat than riding it. You're slowing us all down."

"Feffles don't like to work so hard!" Spirk answered, defensively.

"Feffles?"

"That's his name." Spirk said.

"Feffles. Boil me in tallow. Fuckin' Feffles."

"Why are you so ornery tonight, Long?" Janks asked. "We made us some miles today, got a nice fire going, the stars are out and we got food."

"Well said, Janks, well said!" Short cheered.

"Ooh, high praise, coming from the sheep rider!" Long retorted.

"It's a *ram*! Gods, Long, why don't you go take a piss or something? You're souring the whole ambiance!"

"Amb...what?" Spirk said.

"It means 'stew'," Janks whispered to him.

"Oh!" Spirk responded, "I think the amby yawns is delicious!"

Long looked over at him with a jaundiced eye. "Yeah, I think I will go for a walk" he said, as he wrapped his cloak tighter about himself and wandered off into a nearby thicket.

This was a right balls-up, and no two ways about it, far as Long could see. Back in the day, a team like this would've had ten-to-twelve strong-armed and savvy veterans. They'd each have had specialized equipment—the best that money could buy or cunning could steal. They'd have had horses. Real ones. They'd have had a goal and a plan to carry it out. None of this bullshit charging off with your prick still hanging out. And it rankled him mightily that Short had seized command and done virtually nothing with it. Command weren't no popularity contest. It was all about—

Long heard a dull grunt followed by a high shriek, back towards camp. He wheeled about and saw dark figures struggling in silhouette before the fire. Drawing his short sword, Long ran in their direction. As he got near, he could see Short down in the dirt, while Janks and Spirk each struggled with separate arms of a single attacker. A second man held a knife at D'kem's throat and was shaking him violently. Long bellowed in what he hoped was a terrifying manner and threw himself at the back of the already besieged attacker, leaving D'Kem to his own devices. With three men climbing all over him, pulling him to and fro, the first assailant toppled sideways into the fire, where he landed with a scream of alarm. Fire was working its mischief elsewhere, as well, as the second assailant's beard burst into flames that quickly enveloped his head. Soon, both attackers were screaming in earnest. In a moment, they managed to right themselves and scramble off into the dark, fanning the flames as they went.

Long took a deep breath and resheathed his sword. He did a quick survey of his companions. Janks and Nessno seemed okay, if rattled. D'Kem had slumped back down against the log, and Short was still lying on his side.

"Planning to sleep through all our scrapes, are ya?" Long asked him, sardonically.

Short didn't respond.

"Hey, Short, they put a scare into you?" But as Long approached, he could see that his friend was dead. There was a bloody, jagged hole at the base of his neck on the left side, between the clavicle and shoulder blade, as if one of the attackers had come up behind him and...

Long sank to his knees, lowered his forehead 'til it touched Short's cheek.

"Long Pete?" Spirk ventured.

"Fuck off." Long replied.

"Now hold on, Long." Janks objected, "He was our mate, too."

Long wasn't interested. "He died for nothing, you stupid shit! For nothing! All this farting about in the woods at night, that's child's play! That's wooden swords and unicorns and mountains of gold. It's all crap!"

"It ain't crap. Short believed in it, too."

Long rolled onto his back and watched the smoke rise into the night sky. "He was my oldest and dearest friend, was Short. And he died for nothing."

"He died how he wanted to die, Long. On the road, doing. Being. Not stuck back in town, a burden to his community. Short wanted this journey as bad as anyone."

"There's few can choose the manner of their deaths" D'Kem croaked from across the fire.

Long sat up. "Who the fuck asked you, old man? Where was all your wizarding when my friend was sent packing?"

D'Kem fell silent again.

"We go back." Long said, after a lengthy pause.

"That's not what Short woulda wanted." Janks answered.

"Yeah, well, he's dead. We ain't...yet."

"We can't go back, anyway, Long." Janks breathed.

"We can't? Who says?"

"I do. We can't go back, because I stole from the town hall's coffers to pay for this trip. We go back, they'll put us all in the stocks, sure."

Long couldn't remember ever having felt so old, so worthless.

Vykers and Arune, In the Forest

Vykers was furious. But his voice was cold, steady. "You're a woman."

"I was," Arune answered dryly. "Now, I'm a man."

"You knew if you'd told me, I'd have never agreed to this."

Arune laughed. "Oh, you would have, you would have. The offer was too sweet."

He felt a moment of panic, something like claustrophobia. "Where's my hands and feet?"

"I can't repair them overnight. It'll take a while."

Vykers brooded.

"Don't worry, though. It's in my best interest to make you whole again, unless we want to spend eternity in this cave."

Another silence.

"Ah. You're worried I'll make you weak, then, is that it? You think that because I was a woman, you'll start collecting flowers?" Arune asked. "You don't know women."

"I know..."

"No, you don't."

"You can read my thoughts, can you?"

"Not yet," Arune admitted. "You've let me into the castle, so to speak, but kept me out of the throne room."

"And how do I know I can trust you?"

"Does it matter, at this point?"

Again, Vykers was silent.

"Look, I'll share this with you: you don't have to speak aloud to me. If you wish me to hear your thoughts, I will. That could work in our favor in any number of situations."

"For instance, it'll save me looking like a babbling idiot wherever I go."

"Wherever *we* go." Arune corrected.

Vykers scowled and looked into the fire.

Young Aoife and Anders, At Home

And then came the day Aoife woke up to find her parents butchered and her brother casually eating a crust of bread near the fire. Emotions assailed her so heavily, the girl could not speak. Anders glanced at her as he might a fly that had landed on his arm.

"I was going to do this eventually," he explained in a flat voice. "I thought I might as well get it over with."

Aoife felt her heartbeat in every part of her body, in her fingertips, in her toes, in her eyes, and in her tongue. "And me?" she managed.

"You?" Anders laughed. "You, I'm going to leave alive."

Every word was an effort. "But why?" Aoife asked.

"Why what? Why did I kill our parents or why am I letting you live?" He shrugged. "The answer's the same, I suppose: because I can. Because I'm going to keep doing this—killing—until you stop me." His smile made her flesh crawl. "Do you think you can, sister? You think you're up the challenge?" He tossed the remains of his meal into the fire, got to his feet. "Because I'm going to kill everyone and everything I meet until this world's naught but a smoking ruin." He paused. "What do you think about that, eh, sister?"

She watched in silence as he threw a cloak over his shoulders, hefted a large sack he had hidden behind him and strode over to her. He bent towards her until their noses were nearly touching. His eyes were afire with dark, seductive energy and intent. Slowly, slowly he drew closer until his cold lips brushed lightly against hers. She felt his tongue snake into her mouth, and then she felt nothing at all.

She had terrible dreams, nightmares beyond imagining or explanation, and when she awoke, she found herself in a pool of sweat in the middle of the floor. There was a dampness between her legs that she dared not investigate or even consider, for it suggested things too abhorrent to be borne.

The bodies of her parents were as she'd seen them earlier—broken and blood-drenched, draped over their bed like filthy, discarded clothing. Aoife felt a hollowness in her gut that made her ill. She staggered outside for some air and was steeled by a cold rain on her face.

Kill him? Kill *him*? Gladly…but how?

Vykers and Arune, In the Forest

"I would have thought self-pity was beneath you."

Vykers wouldn't rise to the bait. *Where's the hands and feet you promised?* He thought back at her. He felt her pause, sigh.

You're not going to like this, but what else is new? she responded.

Let me guess, you lied about this, too, he sent, disgusted.

No. Not entirely. And then she was silent.

Another game. Okay, 'not entirely.' What, then? I'm to get rat's feet? Hooves? What?

They'll be incorporeal.

They'll be what? What's that mean?

You'll be able to use your hands and feet soon, just like always. But they'll be invisible.

Invisible? What the hell kind of bullshit is this? How the hell am I supposed to use a sword?

You'll figure it out. Or wear gloves. It's the best I can do. I'm a Shaper, not a Mender. And you'd need one of the best to restore your hands and feet completely.

"Is there no fucking end to this nightmare?" Vykers roared aloud.

Take what I've offered, and you can walk out of this cave by dawn tomorrow. Arune suggested. *What is it with you men, anyway? When you're down to one choice, you always love to pretend you* have *a choice.*

Fine! Vykers replied petulantly. *Gimme the ghosty parts.*

There's one more thing…

Vykers yelped in pain. It was nothing he couldn't handle; he'd known pain of every kind. But the sudden shock of it caught him off guard.

Gods, I'm burning all over. What is that?

That, my friend, is the cost of channeling and shaping magic. It's what we feel every time we make the effort. It is, in fact, the reason we're called 'Burners.'

Vykers was shivering, pulsing and shaking by turns. *Thought it was because you loved fire.*

Arune snickered. *Hardly. Pain is the price for using magic. The more we use it, the bigger the effort, the more it burns throughout our bodies. More than a few of my brethren have been driven mad by it, others try to deaden themselves with smoke or drink.*

I'm not surprised. Vykers thought in reply, wiping sweat from his brow.

But some, some become addicted to the sensation. They're the ones you want to avoid. They're the ones…

Vykers couldn't understand the rest, wracked as he was with uncontrollable spasms. Eventually, all he could do was moan.

He could stand. It was hard to believe, since there was no obvious means of support beneath his ankles, but it was hard to deny as well.

Vykers grinned. "That's more like it!" He made a fist.

Can you feel that?

Yes. He laughed. *It's the damnedest thing. Feels just like it should.*

Do you trust me now?

Again, he laughed. *Not a chance!*

What's next?

I need a weapon.

Have you forgotten my other talents?

Let's just say I'm not anxious to feel that burning again.

You're smarter than you let on.

Part of my training. Now, I think I'll make me a good, heavy staff and a couple of spears. Vykers said, looking out into the morning through the mouth of the cave. *And then…then, the long slog back to civilization.*

TWO

Long & Company, On the Road

What he'd done back in Corners, he could do just as well in Farnsley, Long figured. The women might even be better looking or more grateful. He damned sure wasn't going to continue on this schoolboy's fantasy, not with what happened to Short.

"Who's up for a little warm brekkie?" Janks asked.

"Fuck that!" Long spat. "Let's just get to Farnsley."

Long saw Janks and Spirk exchange sullen looks, but he couldn't have cared less. He glanced over at D'Kem; the cryptic bastard was as unreadable as ever. Once they got to town, they'd have a reckoning, Long thought. He'd never liked Burners, especially ones who didn't pull their own weight. Finished saddling up his nag, Long didn't wait for his companions' consent, but started off down the road.

Janks watched him with a mixture of frustration and disgust.

"Everyone mourns after his own fashion," D'Kem said softly. "Does him credit, in a way."

Janks snorted. "He'd spit in yer eye for saying so."

"Mmmm," the old Burner nodded. "Nonetheless."

By the time his fellows had mounted up, Long was a good quarter mile down the road. "Just get to Farnsley," he told himself, "just get to Farnsley."

Two days later, they did get there. At first glance, Long was not impressed. Spirk, on the other hand, seemed impressed by everything.

"Wouldja look at this place? They got a wall and a gate and everything! I mean, look at this place!"

"So long's they've got beer, I'm happy." Janks said. "I could really use a beer."

"You could really use a bath," Long retorted, in the closest thing he'd shown to good humor in some time.

"If I remember rightly, there's an inn just off the Guards' Walk, to the left over there." D'Kem pointed.

Long glared at him and headed off to the right.

"'Course, we'll probably find something that way, too." Janks added, helpfully.

"No." Long said firmly. "I need some time alone. You go off with the idiot and the Burner and I'll catch up with you later."

Janks was about to yell at him, but finally shrugged and headed off to the Guards' Walk. "Suit yourself, Long. You always do in the end."

Spirk and D'Kem stood between the two men and watched for a moment in silence as they continued off in opposite directions.

D'Kem turned to Spirk. "Well, boy?"

"Janks is better company just now." Spirk said.

"Just now?" the old man asked. After a pause he said, "You don't get irony and sarcasm, do you, boy?"

"It's 'cause I try to bathe at least once a fortnight."

Aoife, Remembering

In the intervening years, Aoife hadn't come close to catching up with Anders, much less killing him. And even if she had, she still had no idea how to best him. From all she'd seen and heard, he had grown more influential and powerful by the day. Though she travelled more or less in his wake, she never ceased to be amazed and appalled by the magnitude of his dark talent or his hunger for destruction. Every new town, battlefield or corpse seemed even more uniquely defiled than its predecessor.

But what in Alheria's name was he after? What did he want?

After leaving her parents' home, Aoife had seen no choice but to enter the Sisterhood. Her brother—her own brother!—- had taken her maidenhead and spilled his seed inside her. She needed every tool at the Church's disposal to insure that seed did not quicken. She would rather have died.

But the Church and Alheria smiled on her. The Sisters bought the sad tale she told them of having been waylaid by bandits on the way to market, bandits who killed the rest of her party—including her parents—and then took turns raping her. The Sisters ministered to Aoife's physical and spiritual wounds for months, and then one day the Mother Superior came to her cell.

"Aoife," she said, gently, waking her from a day dream.

"Mother Superior!" the girl gasped, shocked and surprised to see the head of the order in her room.

"I hope I am not intruding..." the Mother trailed off.

"No, no. Not at all. I am honored." Aoife answered.

"Thank you, child. The Sisters tell me you're as mended as you're like to be. And so the time has come for you to make a choice."

Aoife said nothing, afraid she was about to be turned out.

"Though it may not be the choice you're expecting. I am told you have some talent, but you may be unaware of it."

"What?" Aoife asked, feeling stupid. "Talent?"

"Don't be alarmed. It's not a major talent, but it's more than sufficient for our work, here." The bemused look on Aoife's face was so comical, the Mother Superior couldn't suppress a grin. "You exhibit some beneficial energies that can be trained to aid in healing. Elsewise, you probably wouldn't have recovered as quickly as you have. The Sisters have recommended I offer you the rank of initiate."

Aoife remained dumbfounded.

"Which carries with it a life of service and marriage only to the Faith."

And still Aoife was silent.

The older woman finally bowed her head. "That," she said, "is too long a pause. In such cases—and we do get them—I recommend the girl in question return to the village until such time as her thoughts on the matter are more clear."

"Yes, Mother Superior," Aoife replied, deflated.

"Our door is always open to you, child. Remember that. We have many sisters who did not join the order until much later in life. You can come back, if you wish. When you're ready."

And ready she was, for better or worse, with the passage of six long, heartbreaking years. Aoife had accepted the hand of a tinker's apprentice in marriage. He was not a wealthy man or ever like to be one, but he loved her—or said he did—and, being a young woman without family, name or dowry, Aoife believed she could do no better. She tried to love him in return, how she tried! But when year-after-year brought no children, her husband lost interest, grew distant, apathetic and then downright hostile. Divorce was not common in their village, but when a wife proved barren, a husband was invariably forgiven his vows and allowed to move on.

With a profound sense of regret and not a little bitterness, Aoife realized that motherhood and romance were not to be part of her destiny. For a few days, perhaps even weeks, she was lost, unsure what to do with herself. And then she remembered the A'Shea and the Mother Superior's offer. Yet there remained a shadow over her future, in the form of her brother. Aoife felt such anger towards him, such need for vengeance. It frightened her how much she hated him. At the same time, perhaps healing was her only option to counter Ander's destructive nature. And, in her previous sojourn with the Sisterhood, she'd come to like and respect more than a few of the A'Shea. Also, she felt...safe.

Finally, nervous and with great humility (as if she needed more), Aoife returned to the Mother Superior.

The older woman raised an eyebrow upon seeing her and sported a wry smile. "This is a good day, an excellent day. Welcome to the Sisterhood." And that was it.

And the Mother Superior was right: it had been an excellent day, but those that followed in its wake were long and hard. It seemed to Aoife that she spent every waking moment learning the names of useful plants, minerals and other natural substances, in addition to various bodily organs and their functions, along with more menial tasks like mopping floors, carrying firewood and cleaning the jakes. And, of course, there was always plenty of praying to be done.

The first of her teachers—and by far her favorite—was the Tarn A'Shea, Henta.

"My job," Henta told her one day, "is to teach you as much as you can absorb..." Then she trailed off laughing. "Absorb! As much as you can *absorb* about water!"

"Is there truly so much to know?"

Henta giggled again. "Of course. It's water than humbles the mightiest mountains, carves the widest riverbeds, quenches the fiercest fires. It's water that cleans a wound, satisfies the thirsty, nurses the seedling."

"I see."

Henta's eyes twinkled mischievously. "Do you?" She strode to a nearby table and snatched an apple from a wooden bowl in its center. Opening her hand, she let the apple rest in the flat of her palm. Slowly, the apple shriveled until it was less than a quarter its size. Juice oozed out its top and coalesced into a small, sparking sphere just above the stem. Henta let the apple fall away, keeping her focus on the free-floating pool of liquid above her hand. Suddenly, it froze and plopped into her palm. "Open up!" Henta commanded, pointing at Aoife's mouth. Nervously, the girl did as ordered, and Henta popped the grape-sized sphere between her lips.

"Mmmm!" Aoife smiled, her eyes wide as saucers. "That's delicious. And chilly, too!"

"Bah!" Henta laughed. "A cheap parlor trick! Still, it illustrates my point: those who know how to command water and its cousins are never without resources."

Aoife was less fond of Zaff, the Gale A'Shea, who seemed in a permanent state of irritation and impatience. Perhaps both her magic and her personality came from the winds.

"Pay attention, girl!" Zaff yelled, batting Aoife about the ears. You will either master the winds or they will master you."

"M-m-master?" Aoife managed. "The Mother says I've only a small talent."

"Well, if that isn't the pot calling the kettle black..." Zaff muttered, sourly.

Aoife was shocked at such disrespect.

"Oh, don't look so stunned, you idiot child! Myeen's a

wonder at administrative tasks, but she's far from the most gifted among us."

"But...but..."

"'T'ain't me, neither, if that's what you're thinking."

Then who? Aoife wondered. *The Green A'Shea? The Blood A'Shea? Or the ever-imposing Ember A'Shea? Surely not the ethereal Moon A'Shea.* Perhaps there were others she hadn't yet—

"Oh, stop that. You're transparent as one of Henta's ice crystals. It's Shestie you're after."

Aoife could not have been more surprised if the Baker's man had stripped himself naked, painted himself purple and danced around the courtyard singing "All Ye Wenches, Dance A the Daye."

Shestie was, from all appearances, touched in the head... and not much else in the head. She was short, round and rather homely. She was missing several teeth and her stub nose veered decidedly to the left, which might have explained her painful shyness. Shestie spent most of her days waving at dandelion fluff (when the season was right) and chasing dust bunnies (when it was not). Aoife was embarrassed to think she'd mostly regarded the older woman with pity, but now...Zaff claimed she was the order's most gifted A'Shea? Such a thing could hardly be credited, had it not come from the largely humorless and never generous Gale A'Shea.

"W-w-what is her...I mean, what does she...?" Aoife began.

"That's just it: she seems to be able to do just about any damned thing she wants. None of us has the first idea how she does it, or why she chooses to spend her time as she does." Zaff scratched her somewhat hairy chin and turned away. "Begone, urchin! You've ruined my mood. There'll be no more lessons today!"

As Aoife turned to go, she marveled at these mysterious Sisters she'd chosen to dedicate her life to serving.

Unlike Shapers, for whom channeling mystic energies was painful at best and excruciating at worst, the A'Shea felt euphoria as long as their casting endured. In its aftermath, however, they felt emptiness, despair, even occasionally suicidal. For some, this caused a desire to begin casting again immediately. Others decided the boundless pleasure of casting was not worth the bottomless depths of depression they felt afterwards, better to keep an even keel.

Vykers and Arune, In the Forest

"So, you think you can get us back to some peopled lands?" Vykers asked Arune as he strode out of the cave and into the morning sunlight. "I've got folks who owe me favors just about anywhere we might go."

Yes, along with just as many or more who'd want your head on a spit.

"They want it, they're welcome to try and take it. It's been a long time, but I'm in a killing mood, now. A little bloodshed to wash the dirt from my skin would suit me fine."

Don't get yourself killed, Tarmun…

"Vykers, to you. Vykers."

Vykers. Remember: it's my body, too, for the time being.

"Heh."

It was good to feel tall again, the big man reflected, good to be able to see a ways into the forest, good to be up where an honest breeze brought him more information than was otherwise available to one slithering across the ground. He clenched his jaw and grinned; the urge to do violence was upon him in an almost sexual way.

You're not right in the head.

"Oh, and your being up there has nothing to do with it, I suppose?"

When Arune lapsed into a sullen silence, he could feel it. But…she must know that, so perhaps she was trying to manipulate him. Laughter.

You learn fast.

"You're the first to say that, believe me."

Somehow I doubt that.

The forest ahead of him sloped slightly down to his left, and Vykers followed. "Listen, might be as there's things in my head I don't want you spying on."

And you've done a good job of keeping me out.

"Or so you'd have me think."

Can you read my *thoughts and memories?*

"Not so much, no."

That's how it is, then, with us. For the moment, we can talk and... that's about the extent of it.

The warrior forded a large stream, its icy waters sending an invigorating shock up his legs and lower torso.

I felt that!

"Did you, now?" Vykers felt Arune urging him to the right. "This way?"

Yes.

"Huh. I'd have gone the other."

Interesting. There are people that way, too. Eventually. If you call Sholdorn Heretics "people."

Vykers stopped short. "I've got a score to settle with the Sholdorn."

Which is why I suggested the other direction.

"Ah, maybe you're right. This once. I need about a week's worth of good meals, a decent bed and a good sword before I get to settling scores."

Just a week? You're a man of iron.

The big man laughed. "Not iron, steel. Steel, blood and fire."

By sunset, Vykers had traveled several leagues and felt utterly exhausted.

"Fuck me, but I am out of fighting trim" he spat as he threw himself down on a fallen log.

If it's any comfort, I understand most fighters don't outlive their twenties.

"No, that's certain."

And even most peasants don't reach the half-century.

"So, I'm getting old. That your point, Burn?"

<Sigh>

"Speaking of which, how 'bout a fire?"

Gather your kindling and we'll set it ablaze.

But as he bent to retrieve a broken branch, Vykers froze. He thought at Arune: *You smell that?*

I smell what you smell.

Svarren.

It would seem they smell you, as well.

If the Mahnus-cursed Savages can smell me, I must stink something awful.

Well…

Vykers shoved the two spears he'd made into the dirt at his feet and took hold of his staff. "Rather have a nice cross-hilt long sword, but this'll kill 'em just as dead. What can you tell me?"

They're getting closer.

No shit.

There may be more than you can handle.

The warrior broke into his biggest, most chilling smile. *There's no such thing, little spook. No. Such. Thing.*

In the waning light, Vykers could hear the pounding of countless feet on the forest floor as the swarm of Svarren raced towards his position. Near cities and towns, Svarren preferred to gibber and ululate, perhaps in attempt to terrify their prey. In the deep woods, however, it appeared they favored silence. And if it was silence they wanted, they'd come to the right man.

Moments before the creatures burst into view, a wall of fire exploded into existence around Vykers. It was not terribly high, reaching only two or three feet into the air, but it did give the Svarren pause. They stumbled to a stop just at the flames' edge, and Vykers sneered at them. "Gods, but you're ugly fuckers."

"Ug-lee fuckerzzzz," one of them echoed, flecks of spittle flying from his lips.

While Arune could easily have enumerated the several intelligent and semi-intelligent races apart from men, Svarren were not of that number. Because Svarren were not completely separate from men. They had, in fact, once been of mankind, but centuries of inbreeding, cannibalism and other equally unpleasant practices had reduced them, as individuals and as a people, to malevolent and misshapen perversions of their former race. Some were fully eight feet tall, covered with warts and bristles, while others were diminutive and sported extra digits or tusks. Some had only one eye, while others boasted several. A rare few even had extra heads, though not all of them functioned. The universal attributes were nakedness, a putrid stench, long, filthy nails and jagged teeth.

In their hunger, several jumped through the fire and came at Vykers with their jaws hanging open and arms outstretched, but the big man was a fire in his own right. He swung his staff faster than his enemies could track, in a series of blows that seemed to have been choreographed days if not weeks before. Eventually, the Svarren made a bridge of their fallen brethren and poured into the circle, only to be smashed and broken by Vykers' impossibly prescient blows. Even creatures as primal as Svarren could sense they were witness to something preternatural, for the longer the fight went on, the stronger the warrior became. It was as if he was somehow feeding on their rage, their fear, their very life-energies.

Arune remained quiescent after the fight was joined. She had meant to help her host, but even she had never seen his like in combat. Few men live up to their reputations, and while slaughtering a score of Svarren in a remote stretch of woodland was hardly the same as leading an army into battle, Vykers was clearly up to his legend and then some. She, too, felt there was more to the man than made sense, something either divine or infernal, but in any case somehow beyond simply human. Even inside him, as she was, she was awed. Despite being a Shaper, she was mystified. In mere moments, it was over.

"Douse these flames, Burn. Might be there's worse than savages in these woods, and I don't want their attention right now."

That was...fast.

"Heh. Best way with Svarren. Get into it, get it over with. Don't want 'em calling out for kin."

I meant, your skill is impressive.

"Put a sword in my hand, Burn. Then, you'll see 'impressive.' Although most of the Svarren had been largely naked, Vykers was able to salvage a very shoddy pair of boots and an equally shoddy—and mismatched—pair of gloves.

Good thinking.

"If folks want to assume I've got real hands and feet, I see no reason to make 'em think otherwise."

Clever. There may be some advantage in that.

"'S what I figured. Anyway, let's camp somewhere else. I got my wind back, feel like I could go all night."

Some time later, Vykers managed to pounce on an orris—a large, nocturnal rodent—and, with a fire of Arune's creation, was enjoying a hot meal.

"So, Burn, how'd you end up in the dirt, anyway?"

Why do you refuse to call me by name?

Vykers rolled his eyes.

I just felt that, you know.

Vykers sighed, exasperated. "Look, in war, we don't use given names. You got a title, you got a nickname...that sorta thing. I ain't courtin' you, anyhow."

Arune had noticed that whenever he felt belligerent, his language got more rustic. *Courting me?* She laughed. *You don't have to worry about that.*

Vykers grimaced. "You're not one o' *them*, are ya? One of those girls who only goes for other girls?"

And what if I was? Besides, you're too old for me.

"Too old for a ghost?" It was Vykers' turn to laugh.

How old do you think I am—or would be if I were still alive, anyway?

"I don't know. I've seen some damned old Burners."

I was seventeen when I found 'the dirt,' as you so eloquently put it. I would be over eighteen now. Far too young for a relic like you.

"Seventeen's young for a Burner, ain't it?"

I was good. And I'm even better now.

"Huh."

I've learned a great deal since my body died.

"And, again, how'd that happen?"

Savages. Perhaps even the ones you killed tonight. I came into the forest with a few companions, looking for Theulia resin—

"Toolia what, now?"

Theulia resin. It's what we call a 'Channeling Enhancer.' It makes magic easier. But the Svarren overwhelmed us.

"Yeah? I thought you said you were good."

Yes, but overconfident, too. I've learned my lesson. And I'll be back.

"I hope so. I don't like you poking around in my dung bucket."

Your…what?

"My skull, my skull! Ain't you ever been around soldiers?"

I've tried not to let them get too close.

"Well, this is about as close as you can get, now, ain't it?" Vykers chuckled sardonically. "Anyway, I got another question…"

You're in a mood, aren't you?

"You got anything better to do right now?"

What's your question? Arune asked.

"Menders and A'Shea are the same thing…"

Yes?

"How come A'Shea have an old name, but Shapers are just Shapers?"

Who says we don't have an old name?

"Well, what is it?"

There's a reason Menders are only Menders. They share their knowledge; we keep ours close.

"Must be some special fuckin' name," Vykers remarked, irritably.

And what about you? Arune asked, deftly changing the subject. *How was the mighty Vykers brought so low?*

He was silent for a moment, as he thought about it. "I was… overconfident, too." Then, he said nothing more for several minutes. Arune didn't press, because she sensed more was coming.

Vykers chewed an orris haunch, watched sparks from the fire float up amongst the tree branches. For the briefest of moments, he wondered if stars were, in fact, sparks that had escaped the forest canopy. "I was replenishing my host. Told the people of the Tenbrae region I'd wipe out their rivals over to Bysvaldia, if they lent me their husbands and sons. Then, I told the Bysvaldians the same. I really only wanted an army big enough to take out the Virgin Queen."

Arune gasped.

"Hey," Vykers shrugged, "if you're going to go big, you might as well go the whole hog. Anyway, she's sharper than you'd think, and she slapped me down pretty good. Then she sold me back to the Bysvaldians. Love to know what she got for me."

I imagine you'd be disappointed.

"I expect so. But that's life, ain't it?"

So, what's next?

"After you get out of my body, you mean?"

Yes, well, that's going to take a considerable amount of gold.

Vykers stretched. "I've got gold. I just need to dig it out."

You buried it?

"In a manner of speaking. I've got various...business ventures, I guess you'd call 'em. My money'll keep building up ten years after I'm dirt."

And you don't think anyone's stolen it?

Vykers stared into the fire. "Terrible things happen to folks who steal from the Reaper."

I'll bet.

Long & Company, Farnsley

Long Pete looked up from his plum wine. Shit. The gang just wouldn't leave him alone. Janks and Nessno muscled towards him through the crowd, while D'Kem stayed back near the door with another man, dressed somewhat pretentiously, and a monstrous, hulking figure. So, they'd found the giant.

"Good news!" Janks smiled. "We picked up another sword arm and landed our giant, as well."

"I'm happy for you," Long answered sourly, and turned back to his wine.

"Means we can get back on the road, soon!" Janks prompted.

"Have fun." Long said.

Janks and Spirk exchanged glances, looking both hurt and

confused. "Um, well, we sorta need you to…what I mean is, we can't…"

"I'm not going, Janks. I don't want to die leaking my guts out in the underbrush, just off the Queen's Road."

Janks grabbed him by his shirt collar and pulled him nose-to-nose. "And how *are* you wanting to die, then? In a big feather bed, surrounded by all of your rosy-cheeked grandchildren? That ain't gonna happen, for fuck's sake! You're well past marryin' age, Long. You got no one but us. If you're lucky—lucky!" Janks yelled, spittle flying in Long's face, "you'll go out like Short did, with all of your mates nearby, keepin' you company and holding your hand as you go over!" Suddenly, all the air seemed to rush out of Janks and he slumped, got smaller. "Ah, forget it. Goodbye, Long."

Janks took Spirk by the arm and Long watched as both men worked their way back to the front door. "Lads!" he called out. They turned. "Wait up! Wait up a second!" Slowly, cautiously, Janks broke into a smile.

Long was disappointed, but, after Janks' outburst, he was loathe to show it. Still, their new giant was *female*. He didn't see how a woman, no matter how big, could possibly serve as the basher their squad needed. And the new man was an actor. An actor!

"Long Pete," Janks said, indicating the giantess, "this towering beauty is Mardine. And this," he added, pointing to the actor, "is the famous Remuel Wratch."

"Friends call me 'Rem'," the man said, bowing deeply.

The giant said nothing, but watched Long with eyes like two tiny currents peeping out from an enormous shortbread scone.

And Long watched her. She was big, he'd give her that. Maybe ten feet tall. How'd she'd gotten through the door—in or out again—he'd no idea. Her enormous, pasty face was surrounded by a cloud of wiry red hair. Her arms were covered in red down as well, and even the backs of her massive fingers sprouted red hairs. She was massive and unlovely, and the look in her eyes seemed to be challenging Long to say so aloud.

As for the actor, although Long had worked as a gigolo, Rem actually dressed like one. His attire seemed more aimed at women's tastes than men's respect. He was decked out in opulent black fabrics embroidered with red and gold thread from his collar to the top of his thigh-high boots. His blue-black hair was wrapped in a gem-studded bandana, while the plunging neckline of his shirt offered full view of his quite hairy chest. He sported an enormous belt with a custom-made buckle that spelled out the mysterious initials "W.C," along with a scabbard that held some sort of dueling sword. Finally, he wore the best pair of gloves Long had ever seen. He couldn't believe this man had ever been in a fight. Not with another man, anyway.

"So…uh…Rem," he began, "you ever been in the army?"

"The army? Absolutely!" Rem replied.

"Really?" Long asked, unable to keep the surprise from his voice. "And where was this?"

"Well, let's see. I played General Zardrakkis in *The Tyrant's Demise,* and I was Commander Voobs in *Die King, Die!* That was an especially popular play. Of course, I started my career playing no end of 'third-spearholder-on-the-left' roles. And I…"

"No," Long interrupted. "I mean *actual* service. Actual *combat.*"

"Whatever do you mean, 'actual combat?' I've fought in dozens of plays. Dozens!"

Long took a deep breath, willing himself to calm down. "Right. Look, I don't mean to sound, uh, judgmental, but actual fighting's a bit more difficult and dangerous than play-acting with prop swords. For one thing, it draws real blood."

"Oh! Real blood, is it?" Rem countered, indignantly, "do you see this?" he asked, pulling the neck of his shirt open even further and revealing a small scar above his left nipple. "I got this when my scene partner scratched me with an unbated foil! Bled like a bitch, too!"

"Of that, I'm certain," Long muttered.

"Look, Long," Janks broke in, "what are you after? We needed a giant, and Mardine's here to help us. We needed another sword, and Rem's here, too. Now, I say we gear up and see if we can find some work!"

"Work! Work! Work!" Spirk cheered. The others didn't join in.

After three hours of searching, the best they could find was a merchant offering them twelve pennies apiece to escort him and his wagons to Milford. After agreeing to the merchant's terms, they retired to a tavern to sulk—at least that was Long's plan.

"Well," he sighed, "if we don't eat, we might just break even."

"Ah, but Milford's a much bigger town!" Rem offered. "We're bound to do better there."

"Bigger, aye. And more dangerous." D'Kem replied.

It was what Long would have said, too, but the grudge he was nursing against the Shaper wouldn't allow him so much as a nod in agreement.

Mardine pounded the table top with a fist the size of an anvil. "I can't live on twelve pennies a day. I need to eat!"

Long sighed. "The rest of us'll have to pitch in, say, five pennies each then, to make sure you don't go hungry." Seven pennies a day? That probably seemed like a fortune to that idiot, Nessno. It sounded like fuckin' poverty to Long. He looked over at Janks, caught the other man's eye, and they both frowned in response. Seven pennies. Seven Peasants. Seven Shims, so-called because they were so low in value, they were often used to level wobbly table legs. They weren't good for much else.

Janks rose. "I can put us up for one night's lodging, and then we've gone through the money we brought with us. That is, unless anyone wants to dip into his private funds?"

Everyone looked at the table top.

"Right, then. Let's all get one good night of sleep and see what the road brings us on the morrow."

When morning came, the group climbed back on their various mounts, except for Mardine who was forced to walk and made it plain she was none too happy about it.

"I understand, I understand Em," said Long.

"Em?" Spirk asked.

"Em's the first letter in 'Mardine'," Long explained.

"Truly?" Spirk said. "What's the second letter."

"Vee," Mardine answered, the trace of a smile on her lips.

"Really?" Spirk said again.

Everyone but Spirk exploded with laughter.

The merchant's name was Fiebers, and he sold soap, which, not being considered a necessity amongst the region's poor, did not sell particularly well. Hence, the low wages he offered his escort.

As he surveyed the cargo, Spirk whistled. Or tried to. "All hells but that's a lot of soap!"

The merchant eyed him askance. "It is."

"I bet you'll make a fortune selling all that." Spirk gushed enthusiastically.

Suddenly, the merchant got that look in his eye, that particular look that meant he thought he had the advantage. "Yes, well, I expect to. It's worth a mountain of gold, you see."

Long was about to intervene on Spirk's behalf, but Janks put an arm across his chest and winked.

"A mountain of gold?" Spirk murmured. "What are you gonna do with all that money?"

"Well," the merchant sighed. "The sad truth is, that's more money than I can spend. I'll probably have to dump some of this soap in the woods somewhere..."

"Wait!" Spirk said. "Don't do that! I'll...I'll buy some off ya and then I'll get rich, too!"

The merchant pretended to be thinking it over. From Rem's perspective, he was overplaying his part. "I suppose I can part with a crate. But it'll cost you twelve pennies a bar."

"I'll do it! I want it!" Spirk proclaimed.

"Er, Spirk," Long intruded. "You're only making twelve Shims a day on this job, and five of that goes to Mardine."

"Oh," Spirk said, clearly deflated. Just then, an idea came to him. Or near him. "I'll work in trade for soap, then!" he declared.

"Done!" the merchant said, too quickly for Long, Janks or any of the others to intervene.

Long turned to his old companion, a look of disgust on his face. "You idiot! Now, the rest of us have to make up the difference in Em's food money!"

Unable to retort, Janks rode his nag to the front of the wagon and started slowly towards the town gates. The merchant climbed onto the wagon-driver's bench and flicked the reins on his horse, setting into motion after Janks. D'Kem and Mardine followed along on the wagon's far side, while Long and Rem took the near. Spirk trailed behind, gazing lovingly at all of the soap that might someday be his.

The End, At War

The End-of-All-Things sat astride his charger, atop a cliff overlooking the city he had just destroyed. Though the flames rising from the ruins were incredibly hot, Anders remained cold inside, impossibly, transcendently cold. Without taking his eyes off the fire, he raised a hand and summoned his generals to his side. The largest of them, Shere, spoke first.

"Lord?" he asked.

"The numbers." Anders whispered, flatly.

"Numbers. Well, they're all dead. As you commanded. The whole city. But, er, specifically..." he opened a scroll, "specifically, seventeen thousand, six hundred twenty three men, fifteen thousand, four hundred eleven woman, forty-two hundred and eighty-one female children, thirty-nine hundred and fifty male children."

"And the infants?" Anders hissed.

"Four hundred and sixty six," Shere replied. "All spitted, as you commanded."

Anders turned and looked directly at Shere. "I believe I like you" he said.

Which was amongst the most disconcerting things Shere had ever heard in his life.

"I can taste your fear. Did you know that, General Shere?"

"As you say," he answered.

"The scent of your sweat is many things to me. I know not only when you bathed last, but when you ate last. I know *what* you ate last. I taste the health of your internal organs. I know when you bedded a woman last. And I know whether she's ever been with child." Anders paused, watching his general for any response. "She has. Find that child, Shere, and bring it to me."

Woodenly, Shere bowed at the waist, turned and made his way down the cliffside trail.

"General Kine," Anders said.

"Here, Lord."

"Tell me, how many cities above, say, twenty-five thousand remain on the continent?"

Kine's eyes went wide. "A...a moment, Lord." As he turned to consult his fellow generals, he collapsed in writhing fury. Looking up, the other generals saw Anders scowling at Kine, just before his body exploded in a shower of gore.

"General Omeyo!" Anders yelled.

"Twenty-seven, Lord. Twenty-seven of that population or higher."

"And how long will it take to obliterate them all?"

"F-f-four-to-five years," Omeyo stammered, nervously.

"Can you guess what I'm going to say to that, General?"

"I agree that it's too long a time, Lord. We will find a way to reduce it."

"Yes," Anders smiled. "Or I will reduce you."

The End-of-All-Things turned back towards the fire. Funny how it didn't warm him, how it never warmed him. He would leave his remaining generals waiting at his back for the dismissal he would not grant them for hours. They were his dogs, and they would heel.

THREE

Vykers and Arune, In the Forest

Vykers felt the butt of a spear or some such in his shoulder and he bolted awake, his gloved hand already bringing his staff into attack position. As he got to his feet, he found himself surrounded by armed men on horseback.

Dammit, Burn! He thought at Arune. She had no physical responsibilities. Why had she let him be caught unawares like this? Unless...

Hear them out.

"I knew it," Vykers grumbled. "I fucking knew it."

One of the mounted men pushed forward until he was directly in front of Vykers. He was a big man, bigger than Vykers. Of middle age, balding and sporting an iron-gray beard, he was decked out in full armor, over which he wore a tabard with a crest the Reaper not seen before.

"Tarmun Vykers?" the man asked, in a rumbling bass.

Vykers was sure the Shaper had betrayed him. What he couldn't fathom was why. Why rescue him from almost certain death, only to deliver him to...Vykers studied the odds, found them prohibitive.

"Yeah, I'm Vykers." He paused. "Who in the infinite hells are you?"

"I am Den Marrish, Earl of Bransiel. These men and I have come to escort you to the Capital."

"Which Capital?"

"You're in the realm of the Virgin Queen."

"Since when?"

"Her Majesty acquired these lands a fortnight past, through compact with Bysvaldia."

"Well, that's just great." Vykers said, his voice dripping with sarcasm. "What are you planning for me in the Capital? A big parade? A holiday?"

"You're to be turned over to her Most Excellent Majesty."

Vykers started laughing, and the more he thought about his situation, the harder he laughed. When he looked up into a circle of bemused faces, he laughed even harder. At last, he fell to the ground, roaring uncontrollably as tears streamed down his face.

Vykers! Vykers! Arune called to him.

And again, he laughed harder.

Finally, impatience getting the best of him, Marrish drew his sword, prompting his fellows to do likewise. Vykers stopped laughing and got to his feet, angry now.

"Do you stupid fuckers want to die? 'Cause I'll kill the lot of you right now!" he bellowed. "I'll shove those Mahnus-Be-Damned swords right up your asses!"

Marrish was not used to being spoken to in that manner, even by the likes of Tarmun Vykers, and he abruptly swung his sword at Vykers' head, intending to brain him with the flat of it. In the blink of an eye, Vykers ducked the blow and pulled Marrish from his saddle and into the dirt. Before he could land any sort of blow, however, Marrish had dropped his sword and was gripping Vykers' neck with both hands. *So!* Vykers thought, *a challenge at last!* He kneed the bigger man in the crotch and felt his grip weaken. Vykers was just about to deliver an elbow smash to his opponent's jaw when the other men encircled him and began kicking and clubbing him.

"You boys are starting to piss me off!" Vykers yelled.

And then he blacked out.

When he woke up again, he was tied up and draped across the back of a horse. *Burner*! he yelled in his mind.

Vykers?

What did you do to me?

I can't afford to have you get killed, Arune explained.

Vykers seethed. He felt absolutely at the Shaper's mercy, and he hated every second of it. He wanted her gone, but how could he achieve that without her stopping him?

You betrayed me, he said.

No, Arune countered. *I'm trying to help you.*

Oh, yeah, this is a big help! Tied to the back of a horse, taken somewhere against my will—much better than walking somewhere of my choosing under my own power.

Think, you big oaf! You're being taken to see the most powerful woman in the world. If she'd wanted you dead, you'd be dead right now. But you're still alive. Why do you suppose that is?

Rather than concede her point, Vykers simply brooded until he fell back asleep.

Lunessfor was an ancient city. Nobody knew exactly how old, but she predated the Awakening by centuries, at least. Solving the mystery of her age was the sole occupation of some of her most celebrated scholars. Vykers didn't give two pennies for that. She was an amazing city, that was all he knew, and he wanted every brick of her.

It had taken the Earl's men eight days to get there, during which time Vykers knew not a moment of comfort. Halfway through the journey, though, the Earl had at least allowed Vykers to ride upright, if still tightly bound. The warrior was grateful for that much, anyway, as it afforded him a much better view of his surroundings and, since he had never been to Lunessfor before, he felt like the proverbial child near the honeypot.

"Nice little burg you got here!" Vykers called to the Earl.

Marrish slowed up, until Vykers drew even with him. "You'll never see its like anywhere else," he smiled proudly.

"How many people you got living here?"

"Why? Are you planning to sack the city?"

Vykers smiled back. "Might be."

Marrish laughed.

Vykers joined him. "So..." he said, finally, "what's this Queen of yours want with me?"

"If it were up to me, you'd be swinging from the gibbet by noon."

"They tried to hang me once," Vykers said, calmly. "Early in my career."

"Ah, yes. I've heard that little fairy tale," the Earl chuckled condescendingly.

"Fairy tale, is it? Hurt like you wouldn't believe. My neck wouldn't snap and my windpipe wouldn't collapse. In the end, my captors decided to take me down and behead me, which, of course, was their final mistake."

"I haven't seen anything that convinces me you can defeat fifty men by yourself."

"You took me half-asleep and half-starved. But we'll have our reckoning one day, you and me." Vykers assured him. "And it won't be the stuff of fairytales, but nightmares."

The Earl regarded him in silence a moment, and then said, "As you say," before spurring his horse forward again towards the front of the column.

The trip through Lunessfor's streets took the better part of the morning. Vykers was shocked by the diversity and variety of its people, its businesses and its architecture.

It is inspiring, isn't it? Arune asked.

Vykers hadn't answered any of the Shaper's attempts at conversation in days. But he was feeling generous. *Magnificent,* he thought.

I can answer that question you had about the city's size earlier. The last census showed this to be the largest city in the lawful realms, more than twice the size of my home city, Nespharia.

Nespharia, huh? Vykers thought, intrigued.

Yes. Arune answered, cautiously.

I knew a girl there, once.

A…girl.

A woman, then. A woman. But she had a girlish air about her.

The great Vykers, waxing nostalgic? Arune asked, at once skeptical and amused.

Never mind, then. I hate having you in my head like this. The sooner you're gone, the better.

Vykers, I—

But he had closed down again.

The Queen's castle was many times the size of most villages Vykers had visited; it was, in fact, a city unto itself, with its own guards, its own currency, even a slightly different take on the common language. It felt a little odd in the ears, but Vykers wasn't troubled. Inside the gates, the Earl dismissed his men and joined a retinue of the Queen's Swords, who led him and Vykers through labyrinthine hallways and corridors the opulence of which defied imagination. Surely, there was not so much wealth in all the world, much less under one roof. Finally, the Queen's Swords halted outside an enormous pair of double doors, watched over by still more guards. The Captain of the Queen's Swords exchanged a few quiet words with one of the door guards, who promptly turned to his partner, nodded and began to open the door. Moments later, the processional moved into the Royal Presence.

To call this new chamber a throne room would be making a molehill out of a mountain. It was simply vast—at least a hundred paces across, with ceilings equally high. Around its circumference stood a series of statues of Lunessfor's previous rulers. Toward the back of the room was an enormous dais, reached by a long series of steps, atop which sat a monstrous throne. Vykers' eyes were drawn, however, to a small chair at the foot of the dais, in which sat a smallish figure in black. Vykers noticed no less than fifty guards stationed at regular intervals around the chamber, with four more near the base of the dais. In the shadows at its side, Vykers spied another figure in long, colorless robes, perhaps attempting to remain inconspicuous. At last, Vykers and his escorts drew within fifteen paces of the figure in the chair, and everyone stopped moving. The Captain of the Queen's Swords dropped to one knee and spoke.

"Majesty, as you commanded, we deliver Tarmun Vykers, the Reaper, into your hands."

This was the Virgin Queen? She looked like an ancient gnome! Granted, her gown looked expensive and of intricate and complex design. Still...

Be very careful, Vykers, Arune thought at him.

The Queen walked, brazenly, right up to Vykers. After a moment, she snorted. "Hmph! I thought you'd be bigger."

"Oh, I'm bigger," Vykers smirked, "where it counts."

The Captain of the Queen's Swords made to draw his weapon, but Her Majesty stopped him with a gesture.

"Are you, indeed?" The Queen asked, raising an eyebrow. Turning to address her captain, she said, "You have done well, Captain. And you, as well, your Lordship. You and these others may retire now."

The captain, his guards and the Earl, of course, immediately protested. "Your Majesty," the Earl began, "is this...is this prudent?"

"We will see, soon enough. I have said you may go. Do not make me repeat myself."

The captain and Earl exchanged looks of profound confusion and concern, but bowed to Her Majesty, turned and left, with the rest of Vykers' escort. The Queen turned back to the warrior.

"Drop your hose and let us see this colossus."

Vykers winced and looked about, taking in the distant guards and the figure in the shadows.

I don't like this, Arune thought

"Was I unclear?" the Queen asked. "Drop your hose."

Vykers shrugged, unlaced his britches and dropped them.

The Queen breathed a whimsical sigh. "Days gone by," she mooned. "Days gone by." Seconds passed, and then she emerged from her reverie, hard and sharp as obsidian. "Any man can wield a massive sword. The question is whether you know how to use it."

"But...they call you the Virgin Queen."

"Propaganda," she scoffed, dismissively.

"Surely you didn't haul me in here to discuss my wedding tackle..."

"Well, you certainly fucked the North, but good."

Vykers was silent. Mercifully, so was Arune.

"Nothing to say?" the Queen asked.

"The way I figure it, you could have me killed in a heartbeat, if you liked. On the other hand, I'm pretty sure I could snap your neck before your friends' swords found my back. So, what

I'm wondering is, what in the hells is this all about?"

The Queen ignored him. "I was told your previous hosts had taken your hands and feet."

"You're well-informed"

"Apparently not."

"Why do I get the feeling you're disappointed?"

"Because I'm the one who ordered it done."

Vykers paused, taken aback. "You…?"

"Yes, you brainless Svarra: me." After another pause, the Queen continued. "I am old. Unspeakably old. I have no heirs, but enemies on all sides, including my allegedly noble cousins. You have potential, but were also a possible threat to my kingdom, so I needed to remove you from the field of play until I could figure out what to do with you. And here you are, with hands and feet intact. Tell me, Colossus, how did you manage that?"

Say nothing.

Really, Burner? Say nothing? How would I ever have reached that conclusion without your help? Vykers thought back with as much sarcasm as he could muster. To the Queen, he said "A magic pixie restored 'em in exchange for a kiss."

"Oh," the Queen responded suggestively, "I'll wager it was more than a mere kiss." Again, unexpectedly, her demeanor changed. "Here's what you need to know: as you did to the North, another is doing to the East."

"Huh." Vykers scratched at his scruffy beard. "And you want—what?—me to stop him somehow?"

"I don't believe you *can* stop him. But you might slow him down, weaken him."

"You don't think I can stop him? Is that supposed to goad me into accepting this challenge?"

The Queen's tightlipped smile was more a grimace than a grin. "Not at all. You see, you don't have a choice. And not only because I'll have you killed otherwise, but because you know you can't resist. What? The idea that someone out there is mightier, more ruthless than you? Heresy!"

"Hard to win much at cards when the dealer holds all the best. Are you going to tell me of this enemy, or am I to be surprised?"

"Well, man-of-a-thousand-names, you'll love this: they call him 'The End-of-All-Things'."

"Sounds like my kind of guy."

"Except that we're not sure he's even human."

"What, then? Svarren?"

"No."

"Not human, not Svarren. What else?"

"In addition to the fact he leads a massive, relentless host?"

"Well, I sort of assumed that, yes."

"Two things, then: he's some kind of sorcerer and carries a magic sword."

"Magic sword? Ha! Stupidest thing I've ever..."

The Queen turned and strode towards the shadowy figure near the dais, then returned with a sword in hand. "Let me see..." She pondered, and approached a nearby statue. With one swing, she cut it clean in half, the sound of its upper portion crashing to the floor startling many of the men-at-arms around the chamber... "I never liked that fellow, anyway." She said, turning back to Vykers. "What do you say now?"

"Every magic sword I've ever encountered turned out to be crap."

"So, if you've never seen it, it doesn't exist? You're an idiot."

"Fine. I'm an idiot. And this End-of-All-Things is a sorcerer with a magic sword and an enormous army. What is it you think I can do against *that*?"

"I think I can come up with an army for you. As for the magic sword, well, you can't have this one," the Queen purred, coquettishly, "it's mine, and it's worth more than this castle. But I might know where you can get one of your own..."

Aoife, On the Road

Years had gone by since her time with the Sisters, and still she had found no peace, drawn no closer to the vengeance she sought. Although pleasant, she considered reflecting upon her time with the Tarn A'Shea and the others a distraction. If she had been truly called to heal, there could be no better way than to prevent the destruction her brother had wrought and seemed bent on continuing to wreak upon everyone and everything in his path. There was indeed no shortage of work in this latest village, but Aoife knew she could not stay. She did as much good as she was able, purchased a few small supplies and headed off, in the opposite direction from which she had come.

The townsfolk were naturally very sorry to see her go, but they were also used to disappointment, so they let her depart without much drama. Privately, Aoife wouldn't have minded just a little drama. To feel that someone wanted her, really wanted her, would be wonderful. Sentiment! It bedeviled her.

She decided to travel to Lunessfor. Perhaps there, she thought, she might encounter that person or thing that would crystallize her thinking, galvanize her efforts. It was a long trip and time seemed short, but Aoife could think of no other choice.

Long & Company, On the Road

On the third night of their trek towards Milford, the merchant and his mercenaries were set upon by bandits. More of the same desperate filth that had killed Short, in Long's estimation, and he was glad for a chance to pay back that debt.

The squad had just settled into dinner when eight or ten dark shapes came boiling out of the underbrush around them, swords, axes and clubs in hand. *Amateurs,* Long thought. *Better to lead with arrows, maybe take out the giant.* "To arms!" Long shouted and was pleasantly surprised to see his people—including the merchant—rise into cautious crouches with weapons at the ready. The only exception, predictably, was Spirk, who stood fully erect, swinging a club back and forth with full force.

"Easy there, lad, easy. Don't wear yourself out in the first few seconds." Long said.

He studied the situation. In the firelight, he counted ten bandits—as bedraggled a crew as he'd seen in a while. They looked hungry, nervous and ill-at-ease with the presence of a giantess. "There any point in trying to talk this out, or are you bent on killing yourselves this night?" Long called out, loudly.

Though he wanted to avenge Short's death, he wasn't stupid. Anything could happen in brawl like this. Any one of them could become worms' meat.

One of the larger bandits stepped forward a bit and said, "Talk? Sure, here's some talk: throw down your weapons and walk away."

"You can't be that stupid!" Long replied.

"Yeah, stupid!" Spirk chimed in.

"Shut it, Spirk." Janks warned.

"Stupid, is it?" the bandit leader said. "You're outnumbered and surrounded!"

"You willing to die for a wagonload o' soap?" Long called out into the darkness.

"Soap?" he heard someone's incredulous cry from somewhere behind him.

"Don't listen to 'im!" the bandit leader yelled off to his left. He turned back to Long. "You, big nose! You say it's soap? Show me."

Slowly, carefully, Long crab-walked over to the wagon, tore open a package in one of its crates and grabbed a slab of soap, which he then tossed towards the bandit leader. It thumped in the dust at his feet.

"Nice toss," he told Long.

"Yeah, well, I used to play stones for drinking money."

"So, it is soap. Fuckin' soap."

Long could hear grunts and groans of disappointment from the bandits. "Hardly worth dying over, is it?"

"No, you're right there. Still, might be you mercs have got a few things that'll improve our lot."

"Fine sense o' humor, you've got. I can see why you're the leader o' the gang. Know what we're gettin' paid for this little adventure? Wanna guess?"

The bandit was silent.

"Twelve fucking pennies a day, and almost half o' that goes to buy extra food for my large friend over there!" he gestured towards Mardine.

"Twelve pennies?" the bandit asked. "Twelve pennies!" Suddenly, he began laughing. "Twelve pennies!" he cackled.

Soon, all of his mates joined him in boisterous laughter. They laughed long and hard. Every once in a while, one of them yelled something like "Ooh! Look at me! I'm a wealthy merc! I make twelve pennies!" and the laugher redoubled

Finally, the bandit leader called out "Come on, lads. His Lordship's got the right of it. Twelve pennies and soap ain't worth dying for." With that, the bandits receded into the night, marked only by the occasional giggle as they disappeared.

Long exhaled, lowered his sword. As he stared into the darkness, he felt one of his companions approaching from his right. D'Kem.

"That was well done."

Great. A compliment from the Mahnus-cursed Burner. "Huh," Long replied.

"A less-experienced man would have led us to catastrophe."

Long didn't respond. Truth be told, he was a little embarrassed. He didn't care for the Burner. He'd made that pretty clear, but the man didn't let that stop him from speaking his mind and behaving in a...*professional* manner. Long didn't want to give the man credit for anything, but...he was beginning to hate him less.

"Darn!" Spirk yelled. "I was gonna bash some heads in!"

Two days later, more bandits appeared, and this time they attacked.

It was late morning, and Mardine had taken the van. She was an immense woman, but there wasn't much she could do against arrows, so when two of them hit her in the shoulder and hip out of the blue, she immediately bellowed and dove under the wagon. "Bandits!" she roared. Every one of her companions looked her way, every one noticed the arrows.

"Defensive positions!" Long yelled, and his team drew tightly about the wagon, while the merchant dove in amongst the cargo.

Five men in ragged clothing and gear rushed forward from the trees on the left side of the road, while another four came from the right. And there was still the unseen archer in the trees. An arrow thunked into a wagon plank not two inches from Long's head. *That's what I get for yelling,* he thought. And then the first man was upon him.

He had little time to study the man's face but he could tell his adversary was ill and mad with hunger. The man's gauntness accentuated his sickly pallor—or perhaps it was the other way 'round. Whatever the case, he came right at Long's head with a rustic axe in his right hand and a rusted knife in his left. Long held his sword straight out, curious to see how his assailant would parry. All around him, he could hear the clash of steel on steel, grunting, and cursing.

Long's attacker backhanded the sword out of his way with his knife and came in with his axe in attempt to gut his opponent, but Long had anticipated something along those lines and continued to spin with his sword until he had come full circle with enough momentum to chop deeply into the man's shoulder. The fellow screamed and dropped his axe, and Long bashed his teeth in with the butt of his pommel. The man wasn't a complete pushover, though, as he surprised Long by lashing out with his knife and tearing a rent in his tunic, narrowly missing his chest. Sometimes, Long knew, the grievously wounded made the most dangerous of enemies, as they had little left to lose. Long swiped at the bandit's head with his sword, just to back him off a bit and followed up with a swing at his right knee. His opponent surprised him again, however, by spitting blood and bits of teeth into his eyes. In disgust more than injury, Long stumbled backwards, but was saved from falling by the wagon behind him. He saw a large shadow as his frantic assailant launched himself at him. Stabbing blindly, Long thrust his sword up and out again, this time scoring a solid hit in the bandit's belly. The man tumbled sideways in slow motion, sliding off the end of Long's blade.

Long dared a peek over the top of the wagon and saw Mardine swinging the corpse of a bandit back and forth like a monstrous two-handed sword. Elsewhere, Rem was putting on a fencing exhibition, all the while spouting what sounded like poetry. Janks was sitting on another bandit's chest, pulverizing his head and face with a mace of some sort. Spirk stood in the center of the conflict, howling incoherently and completely unnoticed. As advertised. Finally, D'Kem stood just off to Long's left, staring intently at an arrow he held in his hand. Without warning there was a tremendous fireball off in the woods and an agonizing scream. Scratch one sniper. D'Kem looked up from the arrow, caught Long's eye and gave him a most disconcerting smile. So, the crazy old son-of-a-whore could magic, after all. Long stood up and circled the wagon. There were three bodies on the ground. Two more figures could be seen running off in different directions. After a moment's silence, a voice asked "all clear?" and the merchant sat up from inside his wagon.

"Twelve pennies is hardly worth that kind of trouble," Long told him.

"Maybe. Maybe not. But it's all I can spare," the merchant replied.

"Well," Janks called over, finally done cleaning his mace, "let's see if they've got anything on 'em." He immediately began rifling through the corpses' clothing and gear.

Long staggered over to Mardine. It looked like she'd pulled the arrows herself, and her bleeding had stopped to boot.

"I saw you get peppered with those arrows; I thought you were a goner for sure." Long commented.

"Nah." Mardine laughed dismissively. "We heal fast."

Long nodded. "I've heard that, but I never knew how fast. How many o' these cutthroats you take down?"

"Me?" Mardine asked, coyly. "Four, five. Not as many as I wanted. You?"

"Uh...just the one. Got a little complicated there for a bit."

Janks strolled over with various knives, clubs and short swords under his arms. "Got a couple o' coppers and some kinda brass-colored coin I never seen before. And this pile o' beat up weapons."

Spirk came over, too. "I must have scared the piss out of them! Did you see me? I must've scared 'em bad. Not one of 'em wanted a piece of me!"

Long had to cover his mouth and Janks turned away to avoid laughing out loud. D'Kem was standing off by himself, so Long took a deep breath and approached him.

"That was something, whatever you did to that sniper," he told the Shaper.

"Do you recall the flaming beard I gave that one bandit a while back?"

Long nodded, reluctant to revisit the topic.

"This was a hundred times as much." Silence. "It felt like redemption and revenge."

"Well, uh, I s'pose we'd better get back on the road. Don't want to waste daylight." Long offered, feeling old and awkward.

Later, he found his chance to ask Rem about his odd behavior during the fight. "Heard you shouting some kinda poetry at your man, back there."

Rem coughed, embarrassed. "Iambic pentameter, actually," he said. "I, uh, find I can't fight without it."

If Long had possessed the energy, he'd have blown his top at this tardy revelation. Now, he was just too damned weary. "Verse, huh?"

"Yes."

Well, Long had been bored almost to death the last time he'd seen a play. Maybe this was Rem's version of two-weapon fighting.

The End, the Forest of Nar

When the host reached the borders of the great Forest of Nar, its generals asked The End-of-All-Things how he wished to proceed. "Burn it," he said, flatly.

"Burn it, my Lord?" they might have responded, or "Are you serious?" But of course they did not, for that would have meant death. Even to think such things was dangerous around a man—a being—as skilled in the mystic arts as Anders. Still, burn the Forest of Nar? Madness. Though they were to a man remorseless, treacherous scum, the generals inwardly balked at his order, for the Forest was legendary, home to the ancient gods, if the stories were to be believed. One thing was certain, though: it held more life and a greater diversity of it than all the cities of man combined. The destruction, the desecration of this forest would be by far their most heinous act to date, the one crime above all others that absolutely insured their damnation. And yet, Anders' generals were too terrified of him even to save their own souls, much less pause for a moment's reflection before action.

Except for one. General Wims Deda was as ruthless, unfeeling and cruel as his brethren, but he didn't much care whether he lived or died, whether his death was a satisfying fading or lingering agony; it was all the same to him. As he watched his peers break up and head back to their respective legions, Wims thought about The End-of-All-Things and how his response to every obstacle was predictably the same: destroy it. But to what end? Who wants to be the King of a wasteland? And who wants to be Prince to the King of Nothing? Part of Wims admired his master for his singular focus and determination, but part of him struggled with the conundrum at Anders' core: if one's sole purpose is truly the end of all things, what does one do *after* the end? Did Anders intend to finish himself when everything else was gone? If so, was this whole effort nothing more than suicide on an impossibly large scale? And why should Wims—or anyone—die because Anders wished to do so? Again, Wims reflected he didn't care either way for his own life. But he didn't feel the need to take everything else in creation with him. Why, then, did Anders? What secret was he privy to that Wims and his fellows were not? Wims kicked a rock from his path and sighed. The only way to find out was to play along. He headed towards his own legion.

The burning took much longer than anticipated, and many of Anders' officers at every level of command were punished as a result, with death being the least of their penalties. But the forest resisted, fought back, even went on the offensive at times. One might have assumed the End-of-All-Things felt frustrated, but in fact he gloried in the struggle. This was the closest he'd come to any kind of challenge, and it stimulated his imagination. Where he sent tens of thousands of soldiers with fire and axes, the forest responded with strange magics, living undergrowth and fey folk. While the chess match amused him and he cared literally nothing for his own forces, Anders recognized they might be hard to replace quickly and in such numbers, so he pulled them back and resorted to flaming arrows, catapults, ballistae and sorcery. Inevitably, he knew, the fire would grow too big to be stifled.

The forest howled in fear and torment, a cacophony that could be heard for leagues and would never be forgotten by those who did. Animals, creatures and even plants fled in all directions from the conflagration. Game burst from the undergrowth with their fur and flanks aflame, only to be cut down by opportunistic troops on the front lines.

Wims watched, his thoughts and feelings in turmoil.

Anders watched, exulting.

The old gods watched, and they were wroth.

Long & Company, On the Road

On such journeys, the real talk happened around the campfire—the wishing, the dreaming, the reminiscing, the self-recriminations, and the self-aggrandizement. Fireside conversations became contests of one-upmanship in who had suffered, achieved or just plain lived the most. Occasionally, Rem would recite extended passages from various plays he'd performed in, sometimes even using multiple voices to fill out the other roles. Janks was the biggest braggart, Spirk the most nonsensical. Mardine told the most traditional tales, Long the most self-critical (the more he ruminated on his recent work as a gigolo, the more embarrassed he became). Even the merchant pitched in once in a while. Of them all, however, none commanded the group's rapt attention like D'Kem. He rarely spoke, but when he did, his advice, his opinions, his tales had a gravitas to them the others could not ignore. One night, after Janks had finished telling the group how he'd once killed four men with a single arrow, and the giggles and guffaws of disbelief had subsided, a silence fell over the companions. The dark sky drizzled lightly upon them, and as they stared into the fire, each felt the need to fill that silence with...something, anything to keep the quiet at bay.

"I don't like this quiet." Spirk complained.

"Gives me the creeping Johnnies, for sure." Rem added.

"No, no." D'Kem said. "This silence is most meet." Everyone looked at him, sensing that more was imminent. "Do you know what tomorrow is?" D'Kem asked.

"Lons?" Spirk guessed.

"Aye. 'Tis that. But it's also First Day." D'Kem responded.

First Day. Of all the annual festivals, celebrations, and holy days, Long cared least for First Day. It was an observance too fraught with unanswerable questions, too haunted by the unknown.

"First Day!" Spirk said, cheerfully. "My mum used to make an egg pudding with rum that was the pride of our village. I always hated having to wait a whole year to have more."

The silence descended again, the old Shaper inhaled, and Long wasn't sure he wanted to hear what was coming on the exhalation.

"Mayhap you've heard the details of the original First Day, but it doesn't get the reflection it deserves. Its mysteries are central to our existence as a species, perhaps even our survival. And yet, we dress the day up in frippery and egg puddings." Spirk was about to protest when D'Kem continued. "Nigh onto three thousand years ago, our forebears woke up one afternoon, right after the third bell, it's said. They woke up, not knowing why they'd been asleep at that time of day. Not recognizing their surroundings or each other. Not remembering their own names or even their language. Imagine the chaos. Husbands and wives fought one another in fear. Children fled from their parents."

"This sounds like the tale of Ahklat." Rem interrupted.

D'Kem silenced him with a doleful eye. "You're not the first to make that observation, but you would be the first to explain the connection, if ever you figured it out. At any rate," D'Kem continued, staring back into the fire, "it must have been days if not weeks before anyone had calmed down enough to join hands with another in effort to settle the rest of our ancestors. They must have been like frightened pups in a thunderstorm, dashing this way and that, hiding from the least disturbance. But calm they did, eventually. Scholars write that leaders arose—warlords, holy men, even mountebanks, though what they had been before the Awakening, nobody knows."

"That just proves a man can remake himself," Long offered.

"Might be you're right. Or it might be they were warlords, holy men and mountebanks *before* the Awakening. You can cast a spell on a pig turns him into a wolf, but he's still a pig inside."

Long wasn't sure if he'd just been insulted or not, so he let it slide.

"Some of these new leaders," D'Kem went on, "were afraid of losing their power, so they banned all forms of writing and ordered anything with writing upon it destroyed. The present and future were all that mattered, they argued; no point in fretting about a past now lost to them. There were even a few cults that made it their personal missions to eradicate any evidence of our collective past. Such stupidity! Such evil! And it has only been in the last few hundred years that scholars and politicians have begun to appreciate what may have been lost, and what still remains to be found."

"Like what, for instance?" Spirk asked.

"Surely, three thousand years ago, we had great magicians, alchemists and scientists working on wondrous discoveries and inventions. Surely, there were poets and playwrights," D'Kem said, looking at Rem, "whose work would have amazed and delighted us. It may be we were all closer to Mahnus. Or it might be we worshipped someone else, entirely."

"That's ridiculous!" Janks cried.

"Is it? We have no idea how old our civilization is, no idea how long we've been here. There's some think Mahnus killed our proper gods."

"Not likely," Janks muttered, dismissively.

"Not likely, is it? Impossible to prove otherwise. And other harrowing questions remain: why were we stricken thus? What's to keep it from happening again? How can we preserve what we've learned if it does?"

"If we can't positively identify our forebears, what's to keep us from bedding down our cousins?" Rem jumped in.

"Ah, the light dawns at last!" D'Kem observed, looking at Rem appreciatively. "Some say that's how the Svarren began. And might we not, over time, not knowing our origins, grow into something even more monstrous?"

Long felt himself shiver, despite the fire's proximity.

"And there's another thing bothers me: there are other sentient races in the world. Did they, also, experience First Day, or have they continued to grow and progress unabated, gaining an advantage over us that we can never hope to overcome?"

"Ah, now you're raving, old man!" Janks said. "I've never seen hide nor hair o' these other races folk talk about." Mardine snorted. Janks looked up at her and bit his tongue.

"You haven't looked very hard, then, my skeptical friend. Some final questions occur to me: was this done to us by some external force? Did another god, another race, another people somehow hex our entire species, and, if so, what's to say they won't do it again? How can we stop them?"

Long pulled his cloak a little tighter around his neck and shoulders. "Happy First Day," he said, humorlessly.

Vykers, In Lunessfor

"Ahklat? She's out of her fucking mind!" Vykers complained. "The fucking Mahnus-cursed 'City Outside Prophecy.' What next? A tour of the countless hells?"

You are a legendary warrior, Arune responded, *in service to a legendary monarch, on a voyage to a legendary city. There is a certain symmetry to it.*

"I don't even know what you just said, Burn, but I don't like the sound of it," Vykers answered, as he sat on the bed in a room the Queen's Steward had provided for him.

What would you be doing otherwise?

"Me? Amassing an army."

But the Queen is amassing an army for you.

"I don't care; it don't feel right."

So what are you going to do?

Right now? I'm gonna take a bath. First one I've had in I don't know how long. Might take hours. Then, I'm gonna find me a barber. I'm a soldier, not a barbarian. Next, I'm gonna do some serious drinking. Lastly, I'm gonna find a brothel and…

Agggh! Arune cried out. *You can't!*

Why the hell not?

Because I see what you see. I feel what you feel.

What's that to me?

Okay, then. If you won't cooperate, I'll have to stop you.

Stop me? Did you forget whose body you're living in, Burn?

If only I could. But if you try anything, if you so much as touch one of those women, I'll make sure you never get stiff again in this lifetime.

Vykers was quiet for a moment, seething. Did I ever tell you how much I hate you, Burn?

Somehow, Vykers got back to his room in the castle and managed to tumble onto the bed before passing out. When he finally cracked his eyes open, he realized how much he hadn't missed hangovers.

"Nnnnnnnrrrggghhh," he groaned.

It lives.

"I was hoping I'd drowned you with rum." Vykers breathed.

You tried, you tried.

Can you do anything about this headache? Vykers thought, as talking was only making him more uncomfortable.

And why would I do that?

Stop being such a bitch! Ya spoiled half my evening's fun, the least you can do is clear my head a bit.

Vykers heard a low musical tone inside his skull, and as it faded, so did his pain. Carefully, he sat up, rubbed his new-shaven chin. "Better."

You're welcome.

Someone knocked on the door.

Three men, I think. Two are guards.

Vykers pulled his gloves and boots on, cast about for a weapon, not that he needed one to kill just three men. He found nothing. Ah, well, always the hard way.

"Enter," he said.

A short, bald man stepped just into the room and stopped. He was dressed in leather and light mail, with a series of belts, buckles and straps around his waist and across his chest that held more daggers than Vykers had ever seen on one person.

Over all that, he wore a black woolen cloak that fell almost to his ankles. He said nothing, as if daring Vykers to speak first.

But when it came to being stubborn, he had nothing on the bigger man. Vykers flexed his arms, crossed them and stared back.

Does it really matter which of you can piss the farthest? Arune asked.

Yes. Yes, it does, was all Vykers thought in return.

Finally, the little man spoke. "I heard you were broken, damaged goods, dead even. But they do say one man's trash is another man's treasure..."

Vykers inclined his head to one side, considering. "And which o' those are you calling me?"

"That remains to be seen, doesn't it, Vykers-the-Vicious?"

"Aye, that's my name. Or one o' them. What's yours?"

"Kendell."

"And your business with me?"

"Ahklat is my business with you, or, rather, seeing you get there and back alive."

Vykers laughed. Kendell bristled.

"Let's pretend," he said, "even half the stories they tell of you are true. You're about to go blundering into one of the world's deepest, darkest mysteries. Are you really going to turn up your nose at a little extra manpower?"

Vykers sat on the edge of his bed, pursed his lips. "What's the offer?" he asked.

"Five mercs." Kendell replied.

"And what's the Queen providing?"

Kendell repeated himself. "Five mercs."

You think it's a trap? Arune wondered.

No, that doesn't make sense. She coulda killed me a hundred times over by now.

Then what?

Dunno, yet.

They must be some special mercs, Arune thought.

They'd better be, by Alheria's tits.

"When can I see 'em?" Vykers asked at last.

"How's now work for you?"

"Good a time as any," the warrior replied, getting to his feet again.

The two men walked into the corridor, where they were soon flanked by guards—not the Queen's Swords this time, but household guards nonetheless.

"Isn't this where we make small talk?" Vykers said.

"That a crack at my height?" Kendell answered.

"Your height? You don't look that tall to me."

"And you don't look that smart to me."

Vykers thought he heard one of the guards suppressing a snicker. "So...you're a knife man."

"And my suspicions are confirmed."

"Knives ain't much good against a sword."

"They are if you can't get close enough to swing it."

"Oh," Vykers said, "I get close enough. There's countless dead'd say I get too close."

"This is gonna be a bit of a hike. Are you planning to talk the whole way?"

Vykers stopped. The guards and Kendell were forced to follow suit. "I was just being social. But if you forget who I am for one minute—a single minute—it'll be the last mistake you make."

Kendell was good. He didn't look frightened in the least, but it was clear he understood Vykers' message.

After close to an hour's walk in and out of buildings, across courtyards, down side streets and up back alleys, the four men rounded a corner and came to the enormous gate of what was clearly a private compound of some kind. A large crest above the gate confirmed it.

Vykers looked up and spied something unusual at its center. "What kind o' weapon's that?"

"It's not a weapon; it's a trowel. We came up as stone masons, when time was."

"Stone masons, eh? It's an honest trade."

"It can be," Kendell agreed.

"Still," Vykers said, "I imagine you know a thing or two about Her Majesty's castle that you don't share with just anyone."

The cryptic smile Kendell offered in response was confirmation enough. *I'll have to remember that,* Vykers thought to himself.

"You go through this gate with me," said Kendell, "you've stepped in the shit."

<???>

"What's that supposed to mean?" Vykers asked. "Thought you wanted me to follow you."

"And I do. I'm just saying, coming through this gate is taking a side. Taking a side is making enemies."

Vykers queried Arune, looked around as if checking for signs of an ambush. *What's he on about?*

I'm not certain. They say the noble houses of Lunessfor engage in some fairly nasty in-fighting. You might ask...

"You wanna explain?" Vykers asked, aloud.

"Inside."

Well? Vykers asked Arune.

There are men on the other side. But I don't feel any immediate threat.

"Inside it is," the warrior told his guide.

Kendell approached the gate, opened a small hatch and spoke something into it, or to someone behind it, and the gates began to rumble open. Without waiting or turning back to see if Vykers was following, Kendell walked through. Vykers looked at both guards, but neither was giving anything away. "Alheria's tits!" he muttered.

The estate on the other side was beautiful, if smaller than he'd expected and in some disrepair. Surprisingly, the guards had not followed their charge and his escort through the gates, momentarily leaving the two men alone together.

"Here's your chance, Reaper. Kill me before my men get here." Kendell said.

It's a test of some sort.

I figured.

What are you going to—

Kendell moved with alarming speed, grasping and tossing a knife in Vykers' direction almost faster than the bigger man had time to note it. Vykers, however, was alarming speed incarnate; he ducked backwards and slapped the blade from the air as if he were swatting at flies. The knife clattered onto the cobblestones and skittered another ten feet into a corner.

"Of course, it's better to take some people in the back," Kendell said, calmly.

"But then you miss out on the look in their eyes when they realize they're done for."

Kendell walked over to retrieve his knife. "Well," he admitted, "there is that."

Vykers was beginning to like the guy.

"Hungry?" his host asked.

"Always."

"Good. Let's go through the breezeway, here, into the inner garden. Wonderful place for lunch...and secrets."

Once more Kendell took the lead, and Vykers followed him through a sort of alley into an exquisite little garden with a waterfall, a pool, and numerous benches scattered throughout. Just off-center from the middle was a tiny gazebo, barely large enough for two. Vykers hadn't seen Kendell signaling anyone, yet lunch was nevertheless prepared and arrayed on the small table inside the gazebo.

Kendell picked up a decanter and began pouring a pale, yellow wine into two crystal glasses. "There are, as you may have heard, eight noble houses vying to succeed the Queen upon her eventual death. This," he gestured to the grounds and buildings around them, "is House Blackbyrne. At any given time, all eight houses are at war with the other seven on a number of different fronts and levels."

"What do you mean?" Vykers asked.

"We're constantly trying to embarrass or damage the other houses, so they lose favor with the Queen, and the other houses are constantly returning the favor. In fact, not so long ago, we were considered the favorites to inherit her throne, but some of our less-careful members fell for a rather nasty political trap that cost us a tremendous amount of credibility. We've been scrambling ever since."

"You look to be pretty well off to me."

"We do a nice job of maintaining that illusion. We've

fallen fast, far and hard. Time was, we had the best credit in the kingdom. Now, the dung merchant won't sell us fertilizer without cash up front. We're barely maintaining position above the Amberlys."

"I take it they're now the furthest from the throne?"

"And always will be. Right bunch of fuck-ups, they are. But, you know, being in the seventh spot isn't all bad. When you're in the top two or three, everyone's always trying to poison you, stab you in the back, throw you in the dungeon. In the seven-spot, nobody takes you seriously."

"*Eight* houses, you said?" Vykers clarified. Kendell nodded. "Then one of 'em's her own, right?"

Kendell offered a thin-lipped smile. "You count well."

"Yeah, well, I got ten fingers. Ask me to go any higher than that an' I'm lost. So, I'm guessing the Queen's a Blackbyrne."

"Actually, no. She's a Gault. But she hates those bastards."

Vykers shook his head. "Then, why did the old crone hand me over to you?"

Kendell grinned. "She's got a soft spot for Blackbyrne. Oh, public opinion and the banks may think they run this town, but the Queen's always several steps ahead of 'em."

There's a lot he isn't telling us, Arune said.

No shit, Vykers told her. *But if he told me something that sounded like the full story, I'd be even more suspicious.*

Good point.

"So..." Vykers trailed off, hoping Kendell would spill the rest and be done with it.

"So. As I said, I've got some mercs for you. Just prepare to be...surprised, I guess I'd say."

"Surprised, huh?

Kendell reached over behind the decanter and picked up a small bell. It made no sound when he shook it.

"That's cute," Vykers said. "Does a little fairy come flittering in and grant you three wishes?"

Kendell didn't reply. Instead, he turned towards a nearby archway and stepped back somewhat. Vykers followed his lead and stepped backwards as well. A few moments later, Vykers heard the sound of several feet walking their way.

You ready to act if we have to? Arune inquired.

I'm always ready.

You're not ready for this, she thought back.

What—

And then they arrived, and Kendell was right: Vykers was surprised.

'Reaper, may I present the Unborn?' Kendell said, without a hint of drama in his voice.

There were five of them, roughly humanoid in shape and appearance, except that Vykers could clearly see they weren't human. At least, not entirely. Instead, they were a mish-mash of features from several different races and species, some of which the warrior had never seen before. One was tall, lanky and very hairy, with claw-like nails and pronounced canines. Another was as broad as he was tall and looked like nothing so much as a living boulder, if boulders wore four foot long beards. A third was covered in quills and had solid black eyes. The next was almost as tall as the first, but was utterly hairless and the eyes in his over-sized head seemed to have no lids. The last was the ugliest of all, with scales, tusks, the ears of a bat—and cloven feet.

"I've been in the wild a while now. Might be I've lost track of time. It's not Mummer's Week, is it?" Vykers asked Kendell.

The mercs didn't appear offended or amused by the jest.

Kendell looked at the five, appraisingly. "As best we can tell, they're all chimeras of one sort or another."

"Chimeras?"

"Just what they look like: a little of this, a little of that."

"What's their story?"

"Why don't you ask them?"

"Vykers pivoted to face them better. "Right, uh…who's your leader?"

The ugly one answered, in a voice that was amazingly beautiful. "You are. Or so we understand."

Good start, Vykers thought to himself.

I wouldn't trust them, Arune answered without invitation.

"And who am I?" he asked.

"You are the Scourge of Empires, the Reaper, the Merciless

One, Vykers-the-Vicious, He Who..."

"Yes, yes, you can skip all that," Vykers snapped, impatiently. "Where did you come from?"

The one without eyelids chuffed and chortled and wheezed like an asthmatic serpent. Vykers figured he was laughing. The ugly one regarded his laughing companion with a stern eye.

"We're not entirely sure."

"One of our agents found them about a year ago, wandering the Rehlorn. They broke out of some manner of subterranean laboratory in the mountains north of there. Place was a ruin, they told us, as if the whole thing collapsed on them unexpectedly. Our man brought them here. We've done all kinds of tests on them, magical and otherwise—believe me, we've been thorough. But their story seems to hold up, so we put 'em to work for us, and they've served us well."

Vykers was skeptical. "Uh-huh," was all he said. *Got anything more for me?* he asked Arune.

Not much, she admitted. *They don't seem to have much in the way of memories beyond the last few months. But—*

But?

Well, they've obviously had training—in magic, in arms, in languages. It's odd they'd remember all that but not how they came by it.

You mentioned magic—

Yes. They all register to some degree, though a couple of them fairly reek of it.

Is that good or bad?

I can handle it.

That last seemed a little cocky. Good, maybe he was rubbing off on the Burner. Vykers looked over at Kendell, who was clearly waiting for him to say something. "Right. Good," was all he offered.

Kendell cleared his throat and continued. "Now, the Queen's sending you to Ahklat, and these fellows have been there recently on another errand, they know the territory, so it seems prudent to send them along with you, too."

Vykers didn't like it. Of course he didn't. But as murdering him didn't seem to be in anyone's immediate plans, he nodded his assent. "Can we eat some o' this food now, or is it only for show?"

Long & Company, On the Road

Long, his crew, and their charge came across any number of small farmsteads willing to sell them a bit of cheese, some bread, even a chicken or two, and most of it went, as expected, to keeping Mardine happy. There was nothing of the glutton about her, she just needed twice or thrice as much nourishment as the men in the party. Much to his chagrin, Long found himself wondering, in his idle moments, what a giantess looked like naked. At such times, he'd look up and find Mardine looking at him, too. Then, they'd both quickly look away, embarrassed.

"Have you lost your mind?" he muttered to himself. "A giant?"

Spirk overheard him and mistook that as his cue to chat, which he was capable of doing for seemingly limitless periods of time. "I like giants!" he began.

But Long had learned in his short time in Spirk's company to simply walk away. Half the time, the young dolt didn't even notice he was talking to no one. Instead, Long sidled up to Janks. "What do you reckon?" he asked his old companion.

"'Nother day, maybe two." Janks replied, spitting into the mud by the side of the road. "And maybe we'll have more luck with our next job, eh, Long?"

"Hope so. It doesn't need saying, but say it I will: I don't fancy spending my waning years making twelve pennies a day..."

"Seven."

"It *is* seven. You're right! Seven pennies a day." Long looked at his feet and chuckled ruefully.

"Well, there's one sure way t' make more money..." Janks began.

"Stealing or service?"

"That's two!" Janks laughed. "But I meant enlisting again."

"Shit, Janks. I'm a thousand years old. Leastways I feel like it. But I do hate this hired hand crap." Long paused. "What side were you figuring?"

"Whichever side's the stronger, I guess. Or the richer. Often, it's both."

"I overheard that old farmer a while back saying the Virgin Bitch was pressing men into service."

"Yeah, but we've been officers. Low-ranking ones, but officers. Could be, we sign on before we're pressed, we'll get a choice spot."

"And with six of us—assuming the others agree—we'd just about have a squad by ourselves. Might be able to set things up that way, anyhow."

"I like it."

"So much for our dream of riches and glory, huh?"

"Who knows how this next war's gonna turn out? They might make you king, old man!" Janks laughed again. "They might just!"

One shitty march of several days and being beset by bandits at every turn had fairly killed the whole team's zest for adventure. What the death of Short Pete could not accomplish, drudgery had. In the end, it had been damned easy convincing Rem, Spirk, Mardine and D'Kem to stick with them in joining the army, although each had his own reasons. Rem seemed to think that exposure to war would make him an even greater actor. Spirk, well, Spirk had a puppy's enthusiasm. He didn't care, except to be included. As for Mardine's motivations? Long got nervous just thinking about them. And D'Kem…no matter how Long looked at it, D'Kem's continued involvement made no sense. The old Burner was washed up, filthy, haggard and just plain spent. Except for whatever he'd done to that sniper In the Forest, Long hadn't seen much out of him. But he had signed right up with the rest of the crew. It seemed the title "Shaper" could get you through doors that most would have slammed in their faces.

"What's this, then?" the recruitment officer asked as Long and his fellows approached.

"Sergeant Major Peter…" Long fumbled for a moment. It had

been so long since he'd used his surname, he'd almost forgotten it. "Fendesst, sir. Formerly of His Majesty, King Kronnr the Third's Royal Forces, Red Company, having also served time in Badgers Elite and Stormite Regulars. This here's Corporal Esmun Janks, of the same. And the rest are our crew."

The officer looked him over. "Bullshit."

Apparently, Mardine didn't take kindly to the man's attitude or language, because she pushed her way forward and towered menacingly over him. "Truth," she insisted.

The officer took the tiniest step backwards. He looked up at Mardine and back down to Long. "This your giant?"

"And his Burner," D'Kem added.

The officer seemed surprised.

"And his actor!" Rem offered, cheerfully.

"And his...me!" Spirk finished.

"Some kind o' merc squad tired of working for bread and carrots?"

Long grinned, sheepishly. "That's about it, yeah."

"Six of you."

"Yes."

The officer made his decision and nodded. "Have it your way. You know the drill, then: one Merchant a week for regulars, a Noble for officers below captain, two meals a day at the company mess, march at sunrise, camp at sunset, all o' that shit. Report to Major Bailis at the muster standard outside town."

"Much obliged," Long said, before leading his crew out of the man's hearing. "This is it, friends. We meet this Major Bailis and we're in, we're committed. You can't back out o' the army if you're bored or ailing or feeling afraid. You serve your time or else. Anybody got anything to say?" Long looked at each of his companions in turn. None of them budged an inch. "Well," he sighed at last, doffing his cap and scratching his head, "I don't understand your reasons, but I'm glad to have you. We're brothers now, in truth."

Major Bailis was shorter than Long had expected, maybe five and a half feet tall. But he was nearly as wide and, dressed out in full battle gear of chainmail and steel breastplate, helmet, greaves and pauldrons, looked like nothing so much as a human battering ram. His hair was a sandy blonde, slowly going white. He had five days' growth of beard and large, bushy eyebrows that threatened to take over his face in the near future and obscure his blue eyes forever. His nose appeared to have been broken at least once and twisted ever so slightly to the right. Finally, when he spoke, it was plain he'd lost a couple of teeth on the lower right side of his jaw. Out of the corner of his eye, he caught the companions' approach and turned to watch, waiting patiently.

"I know you," he said to Long when the group came within ten feet or so. "We were in the same trench at Bull's Blood."

Long searched his memory. He remembered a slight fellow—"You've filled out, sir," he said at last.

The major patted his breastplate with a mailed glove, clank, clank. "Yes, well, decent grub and lots of exercise makes a difference. You make captain, you start eating better and sleeping worse. Funny thing, that."

"Yes, sir. What's the story, sir?" Long asked.

Bailis tilted his head, inquiringly. "Recruitment Officer should've told you: Queen's mustering."

"Yes, sir. I was wondering what the objective was, sir."

"I haven't been briefed, yet, but scuttlebutt says she's tapped the Reaper to serve as Lord General."

Long about pissed himself. "Sir? The Reaper? I mean, er, ain't that...?" Long had fought against the Reaper a time or two. That's what had convinced him to retire from the military.

"Don't finish that sentence, friend. As I said: scuttlebutt. But if it comes to pass, you and I have to toe the line same as if he were one of our lads." Bailis was silent a moment, regarding Long and his friends. "So...let's hear your particulars."

"Sergeant Major Peter Fendesst, sir. Formerly of His Majesty, King Kronnr the Third's Royal Forces, Red Company, having also served time in Badgers Elite and Stormite Regulars at your service. With me are Corporal Esmun Janks, same companies. Then we have, uh, Mardine..." Long was surprised to discover he didn't know that much about the giant. "Mardine of Farnsley, Remuel Wratch of...various and sundry, Spirk Nesso of Bloodge, and our, uh, Burner, D'Kem, of..."

"I thought I recognized you, old man!" Bailis interjected. "Thought you were dead, though."

"Everyone says that," D'Kem smiled, grimly. "Sir."

If Long had gained any status or respect for having been recognized by the major, he had to allow the same for D'Kem. So, the old Burner had served. And Bailis didn't seem unhappy to see him. Maybe this would actually work. Bailis addressed Long, "What are you thinking, then?"

"Well, sir, I thought we'd make the bones of a decent squad. Add three or four more and we're ready to take it to 'em."

Bailis' eyes took on a faraway look for a few moments and then he snapped back to the present. "Yes. I've got a couple of good bowmen for you. Twins, actually. I don't bother with their names, 'cause I can't tell 'em apart. And there's a real mean bastard, just loves to scrap. Finally, I've got a kid does some healing. Not much, but better than nothing, I'm sure."

Long wasn't wild about the idea of a real mean bastard, but he wasn't about to second-guess his new superior. "Thank you, sir."

Bailis surprised him by taking him into a bear hug and thumping him powerfully on the back. "Looking forward to this fracas, I can tell you. Should be fun. Historic, even."

Well, some of his crew had been itching for glory. If the major's rumors were true, they were about to get buried in it.

FOUR

Aoife, On the Road

In general, the A'Shea could walk unmolested along any road in civilized regions, such were their reputations. Hunters' paths through forests, smugglers trails, goat tracks and other, less-travelled byways were infinitely more dangerous. The world seemed increasingly out of balance of late, however, and people and creatures alike behaved in unpredictable, irrational ways. Thus, as Aoife walked East Hitchens Road one afternoon, she was beset by highwaymen. There were five of them, and they came at her dead-on, as if seeking her help. When they got near, though, they began to encircle her.

How to describe these ruffians? They didn't much differ from the universal image of their kind: worn-down, ill-equipped, with unkempt hair, ragged beards, countless missing teeth, scars—the whole Traveler's Kit, as the saying went. One of them stepped right up into Aoife's face and leered.

"And how may I help you gentlemen?" Aoife asked, nervously.

The bold one turned to his fellows and sniggered. "Ya can start by doffing them robes, missy," he drawled.

Men! Aoife thought. How come she'd never heard of a female rapist? She feigned difficulty with the clasp on her cloak, and as the presumed leader stepped forward to speed her efforts, Aoife laid hands on his face. At first, the man grinned, as if he thought Aoife welcomed his advances. Then he began screaming, as his eyeballs dried up in their sockets and twin wisps of steam floated out of his face.

"I'm blind! I'm blind! The bitch fuckin' blinded me!" he screamed in panic. These were not your top-drawer highwaymen, but neither were they imbeciles. Seeing their leader's plight, they turned and ran for the trees. The blind man drew his rusty sword and took a series of gigantic swipes through the air, in vain attempt to catch Aoife with one. The A'Shea were primarily disciples of mercy, however, and Aoife stepped in to touch the man again. This time, he keeled over in sleep. When he wakened, he would still be blind—Aoife lacked the power to reverse that—but he would be more at peace with his new state. In fact—

Aoife felt a sudden, severe pain in her right buttock. She twisted to look and saw she'd been hit by an arrow. She'd been a fool to assume she'd scared the rest of the band off. She—

Passed out from the pain.

When she awoke, it was night. She was lying, tied up, at the base of a tree, while four figures sat around a small fire nearby.

"It's a crime in the Four Kingdoms to assault an A'Shea," she breathed.

One of the figures mumbled something to the man on his right, got up and walked over to Aoife. "Shut up, bitch!" he yelled, and kicked her in the stomach. Aoife could barely breathe through the pain.

"Gag her, Lempz, before she does any more casting," one of the others said.

Lempz kneeled down and, despite Aoife's attempts to prevent him, succeeded in binding her mouth with a soiled kerchief. This gag was like to *make* her gag, she thought bitterly.

Lempz giggled stupidly and said, "We hear there's an underground slave trade in Tarith-Tae. You'll make some fat lord very happy, we think." With that, the man got up and sauntered back to the fire. Aoife heard him say something unintelligible to his mates and the whole group burst into laughter. After a while, she grew bored of listening to them and her focus turned inward, so she could examine her condition more carefully. The arrow had not been poisoned, but it had been filthy, which could lead to disease in a normal victim. Aoife, however, was schooled in dealing with such things and felt she could heal herself over a few days without much effort. As long as they didn't abuse her further, and, if they truly intended to try to sell her into slavery, that didn't seem likely.

In her mind, Aoife recited a prayer and put herself into a deep, refreshing sleep. This battle was far from over.

The End, On the March

General Shere looked down at the infant in his arms. He had briefly considered bringing a different child, a substitute, but of course the End-of-All-Things would have known. Still, he could hardly bear to contemplate what he suspected was to come.

As he entered his master's tent, Anders stood fully erect, facing the entrance, as if he'd been expecting Shere's arrival at any moment. This prescience of his was one of the many things that kept Shere awake at night.

"And here he is at last," Anders said, warmly. "Your son."

Shere balked, inwardly. "Yes, my lord."

Anders held out his arms, waiting to receive the child. It was the single-most agonizing moment of Shere's life. Yet, somehow he managed to hand the child over. Tenderly, almost lovingly, Anders embraced the child so that his head rested on Anders' shoulder.

Anders smiled darkly. "Oh, yes. I'm fully capable of doing everything you've feared and more. Far more. But it amuses me to keep the child. Train him, perhaps, in my arts, but also to hold him against any thoughts you might have of treachery or flight."

"I…I would never, my lord."

"So you say. So you all say. But I mean to destroy the world. Will you be content to help me, or even to stand by and watch?"

Shere said nothing.

"We shall see." Anders concluded, then turned his attentions to the babe. "Shall we not, little one? Shall we not?"

Shere realized without having to be told that he'd been dismissed.

The next man through the tent's entrance was General

Deda. Wims was a little taken aback to find Anders holding a baby, but did his best not to seem surprised. "You wanted to see me, Lord?"

Anders looked over at him, his weird, pale eyes revealing nothing. "Come closer," he said, and "here," as he put the child into Deda's arms. "You do not fear me," Anders said. It was a statement, not a question.

"I do, my Lord."

"No, not as the others do. I would know why."

"Life is pain, Lord; pain is life. I expect to die in pain someday. What have I to fear, knowing that?" Wims answered, as honestly as he could.

"You would not rule at my side in what's to come?" Anders asked, perplexed.

"Your pardon, Lord. As I understand, what's to come is annihilation, oblivion. Would I help you rule over nothing?"

Anders' eyes glittered in the light of a nearby brazier. "You are a dangerous man, General. I think, despite that, I will allow you to continue to live and serve me. You will keep me from becoming...over-confident, complacent."

Wims searched his master. "As you will, Lord," he responded.

"Indeed," the End-of-All-Things said. "And how long until we've finished the razing of this forest?"

"It has been an interesting challenge, but all signs point to a successful finish by the end of the week."

"That is far longer than I had hoped."

"We are being thorough, my Lord, very, very thorough."

Anders reached out and reclaimed the infant. "Very well," he said. "The end of the week, but no more. Make sure that is widely understood."

"Yes, Lord." Wims bowed from the waist, briefly presenting the top of his head to the End-of-All-Things and then turned and left the tent. Wims observed that he ought to have felt uneasy; instead, he was merely baffled. Anders could see through him—or so it seemed—why had he left him alive, yet again?

Vykers, In Lunessfor

Vykers was sitting on a bench in one of the estate's many kitchens, his feet up on a nearby table, a large flagon of ale in his hands. "Let me go over this again," he told Kendell, who sat across from him, drinking from a flagon of his own. "And you tell me where I'm wrong. The old hag—I'm sorry, Her Majesty—is afraid this sorcerer-warrior with a magic sword is coming to destroy her Kingdom. So she had me captured, maimed and dropped smack in the middle of her newly acquired territories. After letting me cool off a bit, she sends the Earl of East Bumblefuck to come get me and bring me back to her court. How am I doing, so far?"

Kendell put down his flagon and began to clean his nails with one of his ubiquitous daggers. "Sounds about right."

"I meet the wretched crone—I'm sorry, Her Majesty—and she tells me she wants me to meet this boogeyman in battle. But since I don't have a magic sword of my own, she passes me off to you, with instructions to get me up to the infamous City Outside Prophecy, where someone is supposed to reveal the location of another sword. Your solution is to equip me with a freak-show of an escort."

"Right."

"Have you all been eatin' wild mushrooms? And what's the point in all the tip-toeing around? Why not just raise the largest army ever assembled and go crush this bastard?"

"Has it occurred to you that Her Majesty might be concerned this End-of-All-Things is actually that? That it takes a legend—or a fiend—to defeat one? A better question is, do you think you can beat him?"

"How do you know I wouldn't join with him?"

Kendell chuckled. "Her Majesty guessed you might say something along those lines, so part of your journey up north will include a little side trip to witness this monster at work. Maybe once you've seen what he's capable of, you won't be so cavalier."

Vykers put his flagon down and, out of nowhere, a servant

girl came and refilled it. Vykers eyed her.

Careful, Arune warned.

Mind your own business, Vykers thought back at her. "Okay. I can't think of anything better at the moment. Now, tell me a bit more about this Ahklat."

"What do you know right now?"

"Uh...the city's supposed to be cursed. The people are cannibals or some damned thing. I was never really interested in the place before."

Kendell resheathed his dagger, took a massive swig of ale, swallowed and began, "Long ago, the city of Ahklat was a thriving metropolis that rivaled Lunessfor in size and influence. One summer evening seven hundred years past, however, the people of Ahklat were stricken with a strange madness that caused them to hunt and consume all of the city's children. When the madness disappeared as quickly as it came, the people of Ahklat were so filled with revulsion, guilt and rage that untold numbers killed themselves, while others sought vengeance through killing any and everyone else they came across. In the end, nigh onto two hundred and sixty thousand lives were lost during the slaughter. The survivors—less than thirty thousand—were cursed by more than the memory of their misdeeds, for they soon discovered they no longer aged or suffered illness of any kind. Indeed, it seemed they'd been granted immortality, so they might live with their shame for all eternity. Of course, once it was discovered what had taken place in Ahklat, many argued the King should take his army north and eradicate the city and its citizens. The King, however, feared that his army might contract whatever illness it was that had befallen the people of Ahklat and therefore simply ordered a quarantine, which stood, incredibly, for more than two hundred years, until it was broken by a rich merchant who cared more for money than his own health. When nothing untoward befell that merchant, others followed, until Ahklat eventually rejoined the realm. Still, the city remains a cursed and haunted place, nothing like the majestic center of industry and commerce it once was. No children play in the streets, no music or laughter is ever heard."

Vykers stared at the other man, slack jawed.

Kendell shrugged. "The Queen told me you'd ask, so I memorized that out of Phinestre's Chronicles."

"And how much o' that is bullshit?" Vykers asked.

"None. Phinestre's is the authority on the subject. Plus, I've been there a time or two."

He's right about Phinestre's Chronicles, anyway, Arune offered.

Huh. "So, it's a city full of immortal former cannibals?"

"Yes," Kendell answered. "But it's the immortal part we're interested in."

"Because...?"

"Because they've had a long time—hundreds of years—to try and divert themselves from thinking of their deeds. And in looking for diversion, they became some the world's greatest scholars, historians, artists. In fact, there's a weaver in Ahklat who spent two hundred years on one tapestry. It's impossibly long and uses every color known to man. They say it depicts human history from the time of the Awakening."

"And somewhere in this city is someone who knows where I can find a sword..."

"Yes."

"Anything else?" Vykers said.

"Yes, don't eat outside the merchants' quarter, or you'll be sorry. The local cuisine is notoriously bad."

The next morning, while it was still dark, Vykers and his escort left the estate through what was essentially a secret passage. They emerged in the backroom of a tobacco shop.

"Oh, I've missed that smell!" Vykers said.

"We do not have time to waste, begging your pardon," one of his companions said.

"Did you forget who you're talking to, ugly?" Vykers retorted.

"I am called Number Three."

"You look more like Number Two, to me," Vykers replied.

That is so juvenile! Arune intruded.

Why are you always busting my balls? Leave me in peace or I'll piss you right outta my body. "You lead the way, I give the orders. Understand?"

The beast looked at him, utterly mortified. "Yes, yes, you are right. I am deeply, deeply sorry."

"If we don't have time for some smoke, we really don't have time for your apologies. Let's just get moving."

They hustled through the front room, out the front door and onto the street, where they found a large wagon full of barrels waiting for them, as planned.

"If you boys weren't so ugly, we could be riding in style," Vykers noted.

"As you say," Number Three said.

Quietly, the five chimera climbed into the wagon and then into their separate barrels. Vykers put lids on each, and then climbed onto the bench beside the driver, to whom he only nodded. Wordlessly, the driver snapped the reins and his two draft horses began pulling the wagon down the street.

Vykers thought about the sword at his hip, as he watched the city roll by. It was beyond comforting to be wearing a sword again. It was almost sexually pleasing. He put his hand on the sword's hilt and imagined how easy it would be to kill his companions and the driver, whatever their abilities.

Arune intruded, again. *Whatever you're thinking, it's disturbing.*

To you, perhaps.

I would just ask that you don't do anything rash. Things are going well right now.

Oh? Vykers was intrigued. *How so?*

You jest, I assume? If you make the Queen happy, you'll have conquered half the continent.

And what's that to you? What's a Burner want with half the continent?

You may amass the money and influence needed to get me my own body, to separate us once and for all.

And here I thought you liked running around inside me.

No, Vykers. I do not and have not. This is what they call a "marriage of necessity."

Whatever that means, the warrior thought, derisively. Arune went silent. He'd hurt her feelings. Big fuckin' deal.

Vykers looked down at the wagon driver. The man was

a touch on the heavy side, but otherwise nondescript and, in that regard, well chosen for his task. No one would remember much about him if questioned later. Just another laborer in rustic homespun and a ten-penny cloak.

Lunessfor was beginning to awaken in earnest by the time Vykers and his team reached Traders' Gate, the one reserved strictly for commerce. After an interminable wait in line behind dozens of other wagons, Vyker's driver presented the guards with various documents, all impressed with the crest of a house that was definitely not Blackbyrne. It seemed that lying was standard operating procedure in the Capital. Good to know, if Vykers ever came back. The guards looked suspiciously in the big man's direction, but the driver quickly assured them the warrior was his personal bodyguard. That was rather far-fetched, as far as Vykers was concerned, but as long as the guards bought it, he didn't care. At last, the wagon pulled through the gates and moved out onto the massive bridge connecting Lunessfor to the mainland. From its center, the northern branch of the Aumbre was impressive, indeed. Biggest damned river Vykers had ever seen—and this was just half of it, as the southern branch forked around the far end of the Capital. A quarter of an hour later, they had moved well into the farmlands that surrounded the Queen's city and wouldn't escape them until noon or so the next day. If Vykers feared anything, it was boredom.

"You ever kill a man, driver?" he asked his taciturn companion.

The driver looked up at him, as if Vykers were something of dubious origin that had washed up on the shore. "No," he said, curtly.

"Wanna learn how?" Vykers asked, jovially.

"No," the driver said again.

"Alheria's tits, man! You're an irrepressible bundle of giggles, ain't ya?"

"No."

Vykers fell silent. Then he had an idea. *Hey, Burn. Burn!*

Yes? Arune answered.

You ever kill a man?

Silence. *Yes.*

This was more like it!

Aoife, On the Road

Aoife had been assaulted before, beginning with Anders, but continuing through any number of bandits, pimps and mercenaries. With the exception of her brother, Aoife inevitably bested them all. She would defeat these villains, as well.

In the morning, Lempz came over near Aoife to relieve himself. Presumably, he thought the sight of his pecker would intimidate her or awaken her desires. It was ridiculous, really. And when his piss trickled down the slight incline upon which he stood to soak into Aoife's clothing, she had the link she needed. In a heartbeat, she temporarily paralyzed him. Without thinking, she kicked out and toppled his rigid form, so that he tumbled down the slope and bumped into her. Cautiously, Aoife hazarded a look over his body to his comrades. None had noticed. With perhaps less than a minute remaining before Lempz recovered, she fumbled with her bound hands to find and retrieve his dagger. Once she had it in hand, she sawed furiously at her bonds. Just as Lempz began to stir, Aoife's hands came free and she renewed his paralysis. That done, she pulled off her gag and crawled on her belly towards the fire. She lacked a Shaper's gift for true pyrotechnics, but she was able to enrage the thugs' campfire, such that it tripled in size in one mighty explosion, dousing the last two bandits with sparks and flames. As they jumped up in panic, their clothing caught fire and they danced like madmen trying to put it out. Aoife seized the opportunity and destroyed the taller one's balance with a word and a wave of her hand, and he promptly fell into the fire. As the second man bent down to help his partner, Aoife made the fire explode again, engulfing both men. Immediately, she suffocated the fire, extinguishing it completely. The two men crawled from the fire pit and collapsed in the dirt. Behind her, Aoife heard Lempz calling, "Hey! Hey!" She hit him again with temporary paralysis and then gathered herself and the few things the bandits had taken, and walked away. She hadn't killed those men, but at least two of them would wish she had for a couple of weeks.

By evening, she was within sight of a very small village—just a few cottages, really—but A'Shea were welcome virtually everywhere, and she knew she would find succor.

She spent the night in a small farmhouse that made her somewhat nostalgic for her own childhood home. The sad old couple who lived there had lost all of their sons in one war or another and their daughter to the Fevered Death. They had a room that was spare in both senses of the word and no one to keep them company, so they were glad of Aoife's presence.

She asked them for news of this part of the world, and they asked her for stories of her travels. The old man had pain in his knees, which Aoife alleviated as best she could. The old woman had a terrible toothache, and Aoife was able to put the nerve to sleep forever and kill any rot that might be troubling her jaw. They fed her mutton stew with carrots, onions, potatoes and parsnips. She fed their souls and lightened the pain of their memories.

In the morning, they gifted her with cheese and bread, dried fruits and a newer, warmer cloak. She kissed each of them on the forehead and bid them goodbye. She felt it unlikely they would see another spring. She stopped by each of the other cottages to see whether she might be of aid, and then resumed her journey.

Late morning, she heard a wagon approaching from behind. She stepped off the road to allow it to pass, and its driver pulled to a stop just past her position. The young man offered her a ride for as long as their paths coincided, and Aoife accepted. The wagon was full of more onions than Aoife had ever seen, their fragrance strong, but thankfully not overpowering. The young man's name was Mix. Or perhaps that was his nickname. In any event, it suited him. He was skinny and tall, with hands that looked two sizes too large for his body. Though he was shy, he warmed to Aoife quickly—and she to him—and they were soon exchanging stories like old friends.

During such encounters, Aoife often found herself wishing she could settle down. Not in the standard domestic fashion, but at least as a member of a community, a small town in which everyone knew and looked after one another, some place she could have a deep and lasting impact. A home. Invariably, though, when she began to yearn for such things, she remembered her brother and how his sole purpose in life appeared to be the destruction of those same things—not just for her, but for everyone. It seemed laughable on its surface, but if anyone existed who could destroy Love, it was Anders.

Long & Company, In the Army

Short Tempered, the new squad called themselves. In honor of Short Pete, though four of their number had never met nor heard of him. Looking them over, Long was almost convinced. With their company-issued leathers, mail and weapons, all ten of them looked much deadlier than they had any right to. Even Spirk looked capable of hurting someone other than himself.

"Corporal," Long called over to Janks, "take these men through the basic attack and defense drills."

"What are you going to do?" Janks asked.

"What are you going to do, *sir*?" Long corrected him. "We're in the army again, Corporal. Best set a good example and remember that."

Janks scowled. "Question still stands, *Sir*."

"I'm going to pitch my new tent and take a nap." Long replied, smugly.

"How come you get to nap while I get drill duty?"

"Because," Long began with deep satisfaction, "I'm the sergeant and you're the corporal. You remember how that works, don't you?"

"I do, sir," Janks admitted in disgust.

Long winked at him and headed off towards his future tent.

Later that evening, the squad was sitting around a cook fire when Long approached.

Rem leapt to his feet a little too eagerly. "Orders, sir?" he asked, while saluting.

"At ease, soldier," Long said.

If this was all a grand charade of some kind, they were pulling it off remarkably well. Everyone looked and acted his part, and even D'Kem seemed to have a little more life in his eyes. Long looked at the four newest members of the squad. The two archers were in fact twin brothers, long and lean; no question they looked like bowmen. The new basher, the mean son-of-a-bitch that Bailis had mentioned, was more interesting. He was some sort of half breed, though Long had a nagging suspicion that neither half was human. The basher was big—not Mardine big, but big enough. He had massive shoulders and no neck. His hands were like mallets. And he had tattoos over both eyes that made them look monstrously large from a distance. He didn't say much, but he laughed often, in a deep, rumbling bass. Finally, there was the healer, the youngest, most unassuming A'Shea Long had ever seen, a slight, wisp of a thing with mousy-blonde hair. He'd be amazed if she could handle the hiccups.

"What do you hear, boys?" Long asked the group.

Janks was a little less pissy than he'd been earlier. "They're still sayin' it's to be the Reaper. Can you imagine? The Reaper and the Virgin Queen on the same side?"

Truth was, Long could not imagine it. It made no sense. "And who or what is the target?" he asked.

It was Spirk who spoke up this time. "Everyone's saying it's some end-o'the-world fellow."

"End-of-All-Things," Mardine corrected him, not ungently.

Long squinted. "End-of-All-Things? What's this?"

Janks answered. "There's a fella calls himself the End-of-All-Things. They say that's his name and his deepest desire."

"The End-of-All-Things?" Long repeated, stupidly.

"That's what they say. All kind o' stories going around about him burning crops, razing entire villages, poisoning lakes—all for sport. They say he's even laid waste to some of the East's largest cities."

To Long, this made less sense than an alliance of the Reaper and the Virgin Queen...which gave the whole thing the disturbing ring of truth. Long pulled up a good-sized chunk of firewood and sat on it, right between Rem and one of the twins. "So, what do we think?" he asked the group.

"I think we're going to whip the End-o'-the-World fellow's ass!" Spirk shouted.

"Well," Janks began, sinking into a familiar but long

unpracticed role, "if the Queen's worried enough to forge an alliance with the Reaper, this fella in the East has gotta be one nasty fucker." Suddenly, he became aware of the two women present and self-consciously added, "if you'll pardon my language."

"Sort of like fighting fire with fire," Long observed. "But do we have anything more than rumor to suggest the Reaper's our new general?"

"I've heard it ten ways from Shars day, all over the camp." Rem said.

"Might be it's just an attempt to raise morale." Janks replied.

"This early? Before any fighting?" Long asked.

The A'Shea's small voice cut through the conversation. "What do we know about this Reaper person?"

Everyone turned to stare at her in unison.

"You kidding?" Janks said. "The Reaper's flat famous. He's a legend. You tellin' me you don't know about him?"

"Not…much," the A'Shea finally allowed.

"Well," Janks said, loosening the top button on his britches and propping his feet up on a log. "Lemme tell you about the Reaper," he began. The rest of the squad seemed to lean just a bit in his direction. "The Reaper started out in the army, just like you all," he said, waving his arm at the rest of the group. "Now, every good warrior usually has some kinda edge, some kinda way he's just a little bit better than his enemies. Might be he's big and stronger than most," he pointed to the basher. "Might be he's faster, or more creative when it comes to attack and defense, might be he don't feel pain like you and me, or maybe he anticipates just a mite better'n most. Well, the Reaper's a freak o' nature. He's got all o' them gifts. All o' them. You name it. First battle he was in, they found him at the end, surrounded by a wall o' bodies. I mean to say he'd killed thirty-forty-fifty foes in that one fight. He got promoted pretty quickly after that."

"We had a favorite story about the Reaper in my players' troupe. It was one we always wanted to work into a play, but none of us could figure out how to do it." Rem paused. "There's a story up North that the Reaper was owed some money, once upon a time. He had loaned one of his sergeants a fortune in gold, in order to help the man build his own keep. When the debt was due, Vykers sent couriers to collect it, but his sergeant killed the men and fled. When the Reaper found out, he chased them into a large city—Qarms, it was—and the culprits tried to hide there. In his rage, the Reaper went through the city like a bladed whirlwind, killing everything in his path, not caring one whit whether his victims had participated in his men's murder or not. Qarms released the city militia on him, but he just went right through them like a forge-heated blade through a snowdrift. They say that's where he got the name 'Reaper'."

"No, no, that wasn't it," Long objected. "It was back in Agondria. The Reaper had laid siege to the walled city and was ever-so-slowly starting to prevail when the Agondrians challenged him to face their champion, instead of prolonging the conflict. When Vykers showed up at the appointed field for the challenge, the Agondrians had a group of two hundred knights ready for battle. When the Reaper demanded to face their champion, the Agondrians insisted their two hundred knights were their champion, that they fought as one and must therefore be considered as one, single champion. Vykers didn't even reply, but flew into their ranks with his sword flashing. When it was over, he'd left a lone knight standing, uninjured. The Agondrian witnesses and the knight were both terrified and bewildered. Then, the Reaper told the knight, 'you assured me two hundred of you were one; now one of you is two hundred. Go back and comfort the dead men's parents, wives and children, for they are now your own.' It's said the Agondrian killed himself within a fortnight."

"Two hundred men?" the basher scoffed. "Ridiculous. Ain't no one alive can defeat two hundred knights."

Long glared at the man with a look that bordered on contempt. "That a fact? You ever see action against the Reaper and his forces? You ever seen the man fight?"

The basher just shook his head and spat into the fire.

"You might want to check that, soldier. Attitude like that can get you killed but fast," Long cautioned.

"Yes, sir," the man said, somewhat mockingly.

"Yes, sir," Long repeated. "Once you've seen Vykers fighting, you'll know the truth of it."

"The truth of it," D'Kem uttered into the silence. "The truth of it," he repeated, as if he was testing the weight of those words. "The truth of it is, Tarmun Vykers once fell in love—against his instincts, against his principles, and against his nature. And he paid dearly for his mistake. Her name was Hesh-Tu, a slave girl from halfway 'round the world. Vykers had liberated her from a vanquished foe and took her, at first, as a curiosity. He had never seen her like, and she intrigued him. They grew closer, however, and over time, he could not do without her. Hesh-Tu became great with child, and Vykers knew contentment. But a challenger arose in a nearby land, as challengers will, and Vykers rose to meet him. This adversary was King of the Daemites and, with the help of one of Vykers' inner circle, he conceived a plan to blunt the Reaper's sword by kidnapping Hesh-Tu and holding her hostage. For a brief time, the plan worked. Vykers was truly unable to think or to act without Hesh-Tu at his side. The thought of endangering her unmanned him. Uncharacteristically, Vykers sued for peace. The Daemite King, however, like Vykers before him, had fallen for Hesh-Tu's exotic beauty and would not part with her. In fury, Hesh-Tu attacked the King with tooth and nail, and he killed her. They say the Reaper heard her death wail half a league away, and when he learned for certain of her death—and of his unborn son—he fell upon the Daemites with singular ferocity. He swore to kill them to the last member of their race. And once his army breached the Daemite Capital's outer wall, he was as good—and as bad—as his word. Vykers and his army killed every man, woman and child they encountered. They killed livestock, dogs, cats and birds. They desecrated temples and ruined art wherever they found it. Within a moon's time, Vykers erased the Daemites from the face of the world." D'Kem paused, breathed. "Look for them now. You will find them only in books."

Again, a silence descended on the squad, as each member reflected upon the Shaper's story. Long and Janks exchanged thoughtful glances. Rem looked pensive. Spirk looked lost. The others looked equally troubled by the story. An entire people erased for the treachery of a few? What kind of man would do such a thing? What kind of man was their new leader-to-be?

Vykers, On the Trail

The Five, as Vykers had come to think of them, could not pass for normal in daylight and so could not be allowed to accompany him into villages and towns for supplies and information along their journey. Bad enough being the Reaper, but having the freak show in tow was asking for trouble—not that Vykers wouldn't welcome a little trouble, but he wanted to get this Ahklat business out of the way as soon as possible. He did not relish the thought of sleeping amongst apparently immortal former cannibals, or whatever in Mahnus' name they were.

Whenever he and his driver returned to the wagon, though, Vykers was invariably treated to fresh game the Five had killed, usually without need of weapons. He was of two minds about this: on the one hand, he loved fresh meat and appreciated the skill of the hunters; on the other hand, he was somewhat disconcerted by the notion of a "man" who could bring down an elk using only his teeth. He had no doubt he could kill the Five if it came to that, but it would, without question, be one of his more memorable and challenging contests.

At a certain point in the journey, the group passed out of what might reasonably be deemed the civilized lands and into the wilderness. At this point, the wagon driver bid Vykers and the Five farewell in his typically loquacious style. "So long," he said and rode away. A normal man might have had a moment's unease about leaving the only other full human within several days' travel. *Ah,* Vykers thought, *fuck normal.*

Excuse me?

Oh, that's right: he still had Arune. *Well, if it ain't my favorite infection,* Vykers thought at her. *Whatcha been up to these last few days?*

Studying your friends, here.

And?

There's something...fey...about them, and some sort of taint, as well.

There's taint in all of us.

Arune actually laughed. *There certainly is in you,* she observed.

Yeah, well, I earned it. Vykers paused. *So, what's this fey business?*

You can smell them, right?

'Course.

What you may not smell is magic. They give off a faint whiff of magic not of human ken.

Why the fuck do you talk like that?

Because I've read a book or two. Why the fuck do you *talk like you do?*

'Cause I was too busy killing to read much.

Silence.

So, some sort of weird magic was used to create our friends. We knew that.

Ah, but they may also be capable of Shaping.

This was a surprise. *What does "may be" mean, exactly?*

In this instance, it means "definitely." I just don't know what it will look like when it happens.

I need to see what these boys can do. Any way you can scare up some bandits or wolves or some kind of threat for us?

Pause.

You want me to scare up an attack?

Yes. Please, Vykers added, as a special touch.

You're crazier than a rabid dog.

No sense goin' all sweet on me, Vykers replied.

Okay, then. This may take a while. I need to send out a signal, for lack of a better term.

Good. Thank you. Think I'll start a fire. The old-fashioned way.

They were eating wild boar. Vykers preferred his cooked, but his companions did not share his dainty sensibilities. Instead, they tore into bloody slabs of boar as if they hadn't eaten in days. Then, Vykers heard the barely audible sound of a twig snapping In the Forest. Immediately, the Five raised their heads, too, sniffing the breeze, listening, scanning the shadows cast on the surrounding trees by the fire.

We've got company, he told Arune.

As requested.

Wanna tell me what you know about them?

Oursine. Maybe...fourteen?

Huh. Better'n nothing, I suppose.

You're impossible.

So they say. Vykers turned to the Five. "Well, boys. What can you tell me?"

"Boys?" Number 17 said.

"He means us," Number 3 pointed out. To Vykers he replied, "We seem to be surrounded by several large carnivores."

"How many is 'several'?"

"Fifteen," Number 17 answered.

You missed one, Vykers told Arune.

It happens.

Vykers took a moment to recall what he knew about oursine. They were big creatures, about the size of a cow, and they looked like a lunatic's imagining of a cross between a bear and a wolf. Typically, where you found oursine, you found neither bears nor wolves. Unlike either, oursine possessed a primitive grasp of the Queen's tongue. At least in this part of the world. Vykers assumed they spoke other languages elsewhere. He stood, drew his sword and walked to the edge of the campsite.

"We know you're out there, ya big, shaggy bastards! If your race aren't all cowards, why don't you come into the light and show us what you're made of?"

That was subtle, Arune said.

A massive black and grey form moved into the firelight. "There just six of you. Small dinner for great Mehrohr."

"On the other hand, I wouldn't bother to eat *your* mangy flesh. Probably riddled with maggots!" Vykers taunted. He looked over at his companions. Clearly, they thought him more than a little unbalanced. Good.

Without another word, the oursine burst from the darkness on all sides. The black-and-grey reared up just as the Reaper knew he would and his sword intercepted its right forepaw, just as he knew it would. Out of the corner of his eye, Vykers discovered the oursine had surprised him in one respect: the black-and-grey was not the leader, but the runt of the litter. The other beasts assailing his Five and closing on his back were huge! Enraged, the black-and-grey fought to overwhelm Vykers with its size, weight and momentum. It might as well have charged an avalanche. The warrior danced one way and the other, whipping his sword through the air as if it were a hickory switch and not a three and a half foot length of Imperial steel. The beast died, bleeding profusely, having failed to land a single blow.

Instead of aiding his companions, now that he was free of his adversary, Vykers simply stepped to one side and threw his sword over his shoulder, in an attitude of complete nonchalance. In reality, he was watching the Five with rapt attention. Five-on-fourteen didn't seem like favorable odds, but Kendell's chimera fought with unearthly skill, with steel, fang and claw, and, yes, with magic. All five occasionally blasted their foes with bursts of arcane power between sword swings or bites, but the tall, lidless one, especially, unleashed a spectacular array of magical assaults.

That's pretty damned impressive, Vykers told Arune.

Mmmm, she responded. *I'd like to learn some of those attacks.*

So, the beanpole's better'n you?

Different, yes. Better? You don't want to find out.

For a moment, the skirmish looked like it might go the wrong way, so Vykers stepped in and put a sword through one creature's ear and drove it all the way out the other. He turned and found another looming over him. He gutted it from groin to mouth, jumping just wide of a cascade of steaming entrails. At some point, the oursine tried to retreat, but the bloodlust was high in the Reaper and his fellows, and they cut down every beast. As Vyker's head cleared, he noticed one of the Five literally bathing in the blood of the fallen. Another was urinating on some of them. He'd seen worse. He'd worked with men who took souvenirs—teeth, ears, privates. He'd seen men who shit on their kill. These creatures, his companions, actually seemed civilized by comparison.

Number 3 approached him. "Master, you watched?" he inquired.

"Yeah," Vykers said, "I did. Wanted to see what you can do."

"Did we meet your approval?" Number 3 asked.

"You'll do," Vykers replied, not willing to give too much away.

The group had little trouble the rest of the way to Ahklat. Creatures and men who spied them from a distance somehow realized the little band was not to be trifled with. Even the large group of hungry mercenaries who crossed their path deemed an attack unwise and potentially fatal. Mostly, the mercs just stared in unease as they marched past. And it wasn't Vykers they were staring at. The warrior was big, but not uncommonly so. He had no truly distinctive features that marked him as Tarmun Vykers. If you didn't know him, you wouldn't know him. He was just a big merc. The Five, however, were another story altogether. They gave off a funny odor, moved in an alien manner and made no effort to hide their decidedly strange faces. Vykers was really enjoying their company.

Aoife, the Forest of Nar

Aoife came to a point in the road from which she could see the horizon for miles in every direction. In front of her, the land was black and smoking as far as she could see. This had been the Forest of Nar. There had been a trading road that skirted its edge, but now, to save time, a person could conceivably walk straight across. Aoife considered that this strategy might literally save her days of travel and decided to risk it. It would not be her first mistake.

The closer the A'Shea came to the blasted area, the more she noticed signs of a great host: churned up soil, bits of refuse, horse droppings, and more. This forest had been purposefully, willfully burnt down. What kind of person would…? But Aoife knew, of course: her brother, who disdained all life. Now, she felt a responsibility to traverse the blighted region, to understand and perhaps somehow answer for this latest of her brother's crimes, as if to say, "For this, too, he shall pay." Aoife looked around herself again, before venturing into the black. On this side, the sky was a light blue, with wisps of clouds, on the other, a smoky and steaming grey. She steeled her nerves and strode resolutely into the damaged zone. The air was noticeably hotter here. Despite its warmth, Aoife felt goose bumps rise on her arms. She felt, too, the grievous wound her brother had inflicted on this place, as if the ghosts of all that had lived here still suffered, still endured their private cataclysm. And yet the A'Shea knew this was a loss for all the world, as well. She felt she should cry for the tragedy of it all, but found she could not, as if other emotions battled with grief for her attention. She quickened her pace, hoping speed and exertion would quell the rising storm within.

After several miles of this, Aoife was ready to scream herself into unconsciousness. Desperate to escape, she decided to retreat the way she'd come. She looked back and could not even make out the trail of her own footsteps. She spun in circles, but everywhere she looked she saw the same vistas of smoking ash. The hems of her robes and cloak, she saw, were now stained black, and her boots were caked with tar and ash up past her ankles. What had possessed her to act so rashly, so stupidly? Aoife would die here, she felt certain. She began running. Running and running and running. Eventually, she paused to drink from her water skin. She had an ample supply and skills to divine more, if necessary, but what she really wanted was a river, stream or even a pool. She wanted to bathe more than she ever had. She wanted to wash the ashes from her clothing and hair, wash the filth of her brother's evil from her soul. But she'd felt that way before, and look where it brought her. She resumed running.

The sun went down before Aoife came anywhere near the former forest's edge, as she might have guessed it would, had she taken the time to investigate her options properly. The sun went down, but she was not in total darkness, as little pockets of embers continued to glow throughout the blackness. Invisible during the day, they popped up like smoky stars in the blackness all around her. Well, she would not freeze tonight, anyway. She had thought, naively perhaps, that she might find the cooked remains of game, but the conflagration's intense heat had turned everything to dust. Exhausted, Aoife attempted to clear away enough ash to lie down, but it simply could not be done. Damn it, then. She would walk 'til she dropped.

The next thing she knew, Aoife was asleep and dreaming fitfully. She understood she was asleep, but could not force herself to waken. Strange, susurrant voices faded in and out of her dreams, whispering in languages she did not speak, but nevertheless understood, to some degree. *Want him to suffer,* they said. *Want him in agony forever. Find the man, find the man.* And then, a surprise: *her brother? This one's brother? Find your brother, girl. Make him suffer! Pain without end to your brother, your brother, your brother!* Aoife spasmed awake. She was shivering and sweating profusely simultaneously. She was about to rub her eyes when she noticed her hands were covered in soot, as were all her clothes, her arms and legs and, presumably, her face. Alheria's mercy upon her! What had possessed her to make such a foolish choice? She stumbled to her feet and staggered into motion.

Around midday, or what she guessed to be midday, Aoife came upon a stream so choked with ash it looked like nothing so much as a river of black mud. Here and there, she spotted fish floating belly up. There were even a few dead birds that must have succumbed to the smoke and fumes of the fire. The effort involved in retrieving one of them, along with cleaning and preparing it for consumption seemed too great. Aoife had enough provisions in her travel sack to last her another two or three days, and she could stretch that with her art, if needed. Still, the thought of some relatively fresh fish or fowl made her mouth water. Which then made her thirsty. She doubted she could filter the stream's water enough to make it drinkable. Checking her water skin again, Aoife was comforted by its heft. If she were judicious in her drinking, she might just get through this without too much additional trouble.

Evening came again, and still the A'Shea trudged through barren fields of ash. Mahnus grant her a brain in her next life! Aoife was fortunate to be able to augment her stamina, her food and her water with the skills she'd learned among the Sisters. Anyone without a gift in magic would surely die attempting such a crossing. Cresting a small rise, Aoife came upon a circle of raised stone about man-height. There was also a slab the size of a farmer's wagon lying off to one side. At least she'd be able to sleep in a bit less ash this evening, Aoife thought, as she climbed atop it. She was just about to lie down, when she remembered the voices that had intruded upon her sleep the previous night. As a precaution, she enspelled herself for a more-restful, unbroken sleep. It did her little good.

Again, the voices came, chanting this time, penetrating her defenses without difficulty. But rather than hearing about the voices' anger, she felt it. Rather than being commanded to seek revenge, her own desires exploded in their potency. In her mind's eye, she was naked in the center of the circle of stones. Green vapors, saps and pollens invaded her body from every direction, in every direction. It was a dream, had to be. And she had endured worse at Anders' hands. At the thought of her brother, an ecstasy of fury filled her. There would be no end to her vengeance, or his torment. Gradually, gradually her rage subsided, and she began to see visions of the greenwood before its demise, then farther back, before the Awakening, and farther back still. Great behemoths stalked its verdant alleys, and tiny atomies lived in its blossoms. Creatures unseen and unknown outside its boundaries roamed freely within its borders. But there were also the old races, the Chook-Na-Cha, the Arbint, the Sperleen, and the Drey. One-by-one, they turned to regard her, as if she were in their presence and they in hers. *Avenge us!* Their looks told her. *Avenge this crime!* She wept in truth, at last.

She rose with the sun this time, feeling strangely energized. She was not naked. No fresh footprints gave evidence of her ever having moved from the stone slab. And yet...and yet she was not the same woman who had fallen asleep in this spot the previous night. She did not know, could not say how she had changed, only that she had. As she got to her feet, her path out of the once-forest was as clear to her as if it had been freshly paved. A day, a day at most and she would be back upon the road. And that much closer to finding her brother.

Long & Company, In the Army

"Sergeant?" Major Bailis called, "You awake, yet?"

Long rolled over and glanced through his tent flap towards the sky. Not dawn yet. "I can be, sir," he said, working his way to his feet and stumbling outside.

Bailis was standing beside him, holding a flagon of hot broth in his direction. "Got a little brandy in it," he said.

"We marching, sir?" Long asked.

"We are. We have orders to move north and await our new general's arrival."

"So, it's true, then?"

"So it seems. It'll be a little odd fighting on the same side, though." Bailis admitted.

"I've been thinking the same thing."

"But I imagine it goes to the seriousness of our predicament."

"Sir?"

Bailis exhaled. "What do you know about this End-of-All-Things?"

"Not even gossip," Long said.

The major eyed him, surprised. "Really? Well, there's plenty to gossip about, that's for sure. But I don't want to, er, undermine the troops' morale. When Vykers gets here, we can fill everyone in fully; his presence ought to counteract the effect that learning of our enemy will have."

"Can you tell me anything now, sir?" Long asked.

Again, Bailis eyed him. "This is shaping up to be the battle of our times. This End-of-All-Things is very nearly a god, if reports be true, and a wicked god at that. Scouts and refugees tell us he's got a hundred thousand men, women and children in thrall. Story is, they carry out his orders mindlessly, like rabid dogs."

"Right," Long said. "Right. Guess I shouldn't have asked, after all."

"But," the Major reminded him, "on the other side o' the scale, we've got the Reaper and the Virgin Queen."

Long felt better. A little.

"Anyway, you've got a while to rouse your squad. Second trumpet'll be the sign to move out."

"Aye, sir."

"See you tonight, in the officers' mess," Bailis said.

Long didn't usually dine with the other officers, preferring instead to eat with his squad. If you were going to ask a man to die for you, you had to be willing to eat with him. Janks wanted to come along, felt he deserved it, but Long needed someone to stay behind with the squad and keep them in line. Also, the fact was, Janks hadn't been invited, which pissed him off something fierce. The corporal had actually outranked Long in younger days, when he'd made captain. Then, he'd been busted down for insubordination and that was that. But he'd never quite gotten used to taking orders from Long.

Entering the Officers' Mess, Long was instantly greeted with aromas he hadn't experienced in a long time: maple-glazed duck, sautéed onions, rosemary…and expensive cologne. He had blessedly forgotten how vain some officers were. Looking around, he spotted the major waving at him from the far corner. He made his way through the crowded benches and joined his commanding officer.

"I was afraid all the mead would be gone before you got here," Bailis joked.

"Mead?" Long raised an eyebrow. "Been ages, sir. Is there any left?"

Bailis laughed. "There's plenty, Sergeant," he said magnanimously, as he passed a pitcher of the stuff.

Long poured a generous goblet-full. "I guess there are some benefits to being in the army," he said.

Bailis was in high spirits. "Indeed, indeed. For an officer, at least."

Long heard that. His squad was likely drinking goat-piss ale right now, if they'd gotten their hands on anything over the course of the day's march. "Sir?" he ventured.

"Yes, Sergeant?" Bailis responded, around a mouthful of rabbit.

"Any more news on our basic strategy?"

The major nodded as he swallowed, giving himself time to clear his throat. "The idea seems to be to amass as big a force as possible and park us up north, so that, if forced to choose between the threat our army presents or the jewel of Lunessfor, the End-of-All-Things will choose the threat."

It sounded like good reasoning to Long. If their enemy decided to move on the capital, he'd have Vykers at his back and the Queen in front. Not even a wicked godling would be that impetuous. Unless he was insane. "Sounds good to me," Long offered.

"Unless our foe is insane," Bailis grinned.

Hearing his fears fed back to him did not seem grin-worthy to Long.

One of the other officers, a tall, thin red-head, asked "Are we going to be able to match this End-of-All-Things' numbers, though? I mean, the countryside's pretty much been picked over from the last few campaigns against our new general."

"That's the irony," another man chuckled, "isn't it? The Reaper empties the cupboard, and now he's the one needs to find dinner there!"

"Doesn't seem that amusing to me," the red-head replied.

"Amusing or not," Bailis interjected, "that's our lot for the foreseeable future. Unless Vykers can conjure men out of the ground like he put them into it."

There was probably not enough mead in the world to bolster Long's sagging mood, but he figured he'd never know unless he tested the idea.

Vykers, In Ahklat

The city of Ahklat was quite different from Lunessfor. Whereas the latter was noisy and bright with soaring structures of numerous architectural styles, the former was subdued, dark, quiet and all of a style. Its ancient walls were covered with ivy and other vines, and no guards stood atop its walls. In fact, the four gates (one for each season) stood wide open and unattended.

Vykers had recently learned plenty about the place, but seeing it sitting almost forlornly beneath the Sthalshouf

Mountains evoked an emotion within him that he could not readily identify: pity? Sorrow? Dread? At the very least, it confused him. "You coming in?" he asked Number 3.

"They are acquainted with us. I see no reason we can't join you."

As he understood it, the chimeras' job was to escort him safely here, but he wouldn't mind their continued company. It wasn't that he feared Ahklat or anything therein, but the chimeras made Vykers feel more...normal...by comparison. And it didn't hurt that they were serious bashers. "Come along, then," he said.

Passing through the Autumn Gate, Vykers marveled again at the lack of guards or other, obvious surveillance. His companions didn't seem concerned, so the Reaper walked on. Unlike any city or large town he had ever visited, Ahklat had no crowds, no citizens with diverse business thronging the streets. But for the presence of a few figures in various locations in the distance, Vykers might have thought the city abandoned.

They're here, Arune assured him.

Yes, I can feel them. But...

It's the lack of children. The population never grows or shrinks. Over the centuries, the locals must have learned one another's rhythms.

The Shaper seemed unusually chatty to Vykers. Strange, that a ghost could have nerves. The Reaper turned to Number 3. "Any idea where we're supposed to go?"

It was Number 17 who answered. "The one time we came here, the Ahklatians anticipated our arrival and our mission. Perhaps they will do so again."

Vykers didn't wait for an answer, but pressed on until he came to a vast square, the city marketplace by all appearances, but more like a library in tone, such was the atmosphere. The merchants in attendance looked normal enough, but spoke to one another and their customers in whispers.

Okay, this is creepy, Arune said.

I like it, Vykers countered. *Bein' yelled at doesn't make me more likely to buy something.*

Just ahead, a merchant was huddled with a taller figure who

suddenly seemed to notice Vykers' approach and politely broke away from his companion. Gracefully, the figure approached, and Vykers could see he was not quite human.

"Greetings, Tarmun Vykers," he said, drawing closer. "I am Nnsht-ttnntr," he added—or at least that's what it sounded like to Vykers. At the warrior's frown of concentration, he clarified, "but you may call me 'Nestor,' if that helps."

Nestor was slightly taller than the Reaper, but wire-thin and as pale as snow. Even his hair seemed bleached of color. The only exception was his eyes, which looked like gleaming orbs of obsidian, devoid of whites, iris or perhaps even pupils.

Now, that's what I call creepy, Vykers nudged Arune.

Nestor was dressed in a plain grey robe of linen, with a simple belt of corded rope. He wore no jewelry or ornamentation of any kind, and his feet were bare, as well.

"We were advised of your coming," Nestor continued in a barely audible monotone, looking dispassionately at the Five. "If you will accompany me, I will take you to the home of our historian. We feel he may be most able to advise you."

I'm takin' too much on faith, he told Arune.

<???>

I keep telling myself they don't want me dead, or I'd be dead. But I don't quite believe it.

Undoubtedly, that's wise.

You want to share any o' your precious insights, here?

This Nestor is old. I imagine you figured that out already. I get nothing else from him. He is like a closed door.

Great, Vykers griped.

I wasn't finished. This place reeks of sadness and regret. And more than a little shame. It's really quite oppressive. One can almost—

Any threats? Vykers interrupted.

I don't sense any, Arune answered curtly.

Vykers turned to the Five, in attempt to gauge their mood. Two or three of them looked back, inquiringly. Nothing useful, there. "Okay," Vykers told Nestor, "lead the way."

They passed through the market and down quiet street after quiet street. Sometimes, Vykers saw other Ahklatians—a man sitting in a garden, a woman painting a still life, another woman pruning a small plant on her balcony. The most common activity Vykers witnessed, however, was reading. Nine times out of ten, when he caught a glimpse of someone, that person was reading—a book, scroll, a sheaf of documents. At last, Nestor came to a stop in front of the smallest abode Vykers had seen.

"You may enter alone," the man told him. "Your friends will not be required and, as you can see, there is hardly room for all of you."

"We will wait for you here, then," Number 3 said.

You're not going in completely alone, Arune reminded him.

Every man dies alone, whether he's surrounded by friends or not. It's a journey he takes without company, Vykers responded. *If something happens, it happens.*

As you say.

Vykers ducked through the door into a single room with a low ceiling. There were more doors off to either side, but the man he'd come to see sat behind a table directly ahead of him, eating something out of a bowl with a spoon. He didn't even look up when the warrior entered. Vykers felt awkward standing in the tiny chamber, so he sat in a chair, opposite his host.

"Please, sit down," the man said, belatedly.

If that was a joke, Vykers didn't take the bait.

The man laid his spoon down, exhaled and sat up. Whatever he was eating smelled absolutely loathsome. Vykers had a strong stomach, but he was having a hard time keeping his last meal down. His host must have noticed his discomfort, for he said, "For seven hundred years, we have vowed to make eating an unpleasant chore in remembrance of the Great Crime."

Again, Vykers must have looked confused.

"Come, come now. You know the stories. We ate our own in a short span of madness. And yet, we live...and live...and live. We determined it unfair that we should enjoy life's pleasures when our beloved could not. Thus, we make for ourselves trials out of the things most people enjoy. It is our custom, it is our penance."

The Reaper studied the man. He might have been Nestor's twin, except that his hair was black and he seemed a bit shorter in stature. "I see a lot of reading," Vykers said, for lack of anything better.

"What else is there to do? We do not make war. We do not make love. We do not truly make art. Oh, we try, but…well, I'm sure you seen examples of our efforts. What else is there, but the endless quest to find the 'why' of our past?"

"Huh," Vykers intoned, feeling a need to say something, any damned thing.

"You cannot pronounce my name, Tarmun Vykers, but I am also called 'the Historian'."

Say as little as possible. This one frightens me, Arune cautioned.

"You know my name. I'm guessing you know my mission."

"You've come for a sword."

"But…you don't make war," Vykers reminded the man.

"We do not," the Historian agreed. "That does not mean, however, that we cannot choose sides."

The Reaper leaned back, taking the chair's front two legs off the floor. "You say you don't take pleasure in anything? I know the feeling," Vykers said. "Ever since I was captured in Bysvaldia, I've been living, eating and shitting at other people's mercy. And that ain't me. The Queen wants me to have a magic sword; you people might be willing to choose sides…what's in all this for me? What if I decide to just drop out o' this little game?"

So much for not talking too much, Arune sighed in evident frustration.

Sod off! Vykers thought back.

The Historian placed his hands on the table, on either side of his unfinished bowl of…whatever. Vykers could see he had impeccably maintained finger nails. Countless hells! What kind of man had perfect nails? Finished gathering his thoughts, the Historian spoke.

"I am not a seer, Vykers-the-Vicious," the man began. "But I've learned enough about the world to make an educated guess, and it is this: if you refuse to participate, this so-called End-of-All-Things will have his way."

Not a very compelling answer, as far as Vykers was concerned.

"Which will mean," The Historian went on, "that several important questions will go unanswered, amongst which are: what caused the Great Crime? What caused the Awakening..."

Vykers couldn't have cared less.

"And, of course, how great a warrior is Tarmun Vykers? The best that ever was or will be? Or something else, something... less."

Oh, please, Reaper. Don't fall for that line of—

"I could use a really good sword, though," Vykers grinned.

Shit.

The Historian steepled his fingers in front of his bowl. "I assume Her Majesty is unaware of your...guest?" he asked, nodding at Vykers' chest.

Shit! Shit!

Vykers let the chair's front end slam back onto the floor. He thought he saw the trace of a smile on the Historian's lips.

"Well," the man confessed, "you don't get to be seven hundred and forty-two years old without learning a thing or two."

The warrior crossed his arms over his chest and stared into the other man's eyes.

"Very well," the Historian said, "tell a secret to save a secret."

"Which means what, exactly?"

"Tell me who is riding along inside you, or I'll tell Her Majesty."

"Unless I kill you," Vykers answered. It was always one of his favorite trump cards.

"As much as I might enjoy the escape that entails, it wouldn't be helpful to the success of your quest."

Still at someone else's mercy. "Fine," Vykers said.

Vykers, don't!

"Her name's Arune. She was Fourth Shaper to his Majesty, King Orstoth."

"Fourth Shaper?" the Historian repeated. "I'd say she's a good deal stronger than Fourth."

Vykers was silent.

"Forgive me my greedy curiosity. Knowledge is the only pleasure we allow ourselves. Arune, you say?"

"Yeah."

The Historian took a small book out of his robes, retrieved an equally small piece of charcoal from a nearby shelf and proceeded to write something down.

"You didn't say anything about writing this down," Vykers growled.

"Ah, but I may be able to be of some help to you and this 'Arune' of yours," the Historian replied.

"And why would you do that?"

"As I said, we do choose sides, from time-to-time. I am simply choosing yours."

Why?

"Again, why?" Vykers demanded.

"For the questions unanswered, and for one other reason..."

"Which is?"

"This End-of-All-Things may be one of our own."

The End, On the March

The End-of-All-Things arrived at an idyllic mountain lake. "Take what you need for the host and poison the rest," he instructed his generals.

"As you wish, Lord," they replied in unison.

Privately, this sort of thing simply bolstered Wims' concerns. He had no use for people or, indeed, most living things. But he could see this place as an excellent spot to retire, if he happened to live long enough. It was remote, quiet and clean. Why destroy it just for destruction's sake?

"Wims," Anders called, disrupting the man's reverie. "To my side."

Wims walked over. Had the End-of-All-Things been reading his mind? Was this it, then? "Yes, my Lord?" he asked, bowing.

"That midlands Queen is up to something. I can sense it, but it isn't fully clear to me yet."

"What would you have me do, my Lord?"

"I need you to travel to her Capital—what is it called, again?"

"Lunessfor, my Lord. Although in the North they call it Moon's Crossing and in the South, simply Lunsford."

"Yes, yes," Anders said, irritably. "Go to this Lunessfor and infiltrate the Queen's inner circle."

"As you wish."

"Make whatever preparations, commandeer whatever supplies you think needful. I will equip you with the means to report what you've discovered."

Secretly, Wims was relieved. True, he had no particular fear of death; however, his master was as unstable as certain alchemical compounds, unpredictable and likely to blow at the least provocation. The chance to move out of Anders' immediate sphere of influence was highly attractive to Wims. "Yes, my Lord. Immediately."

After seeing his general off, Anders climbed a small hillock and surveyed his host. What they lacked in training and skill, they more than made up for in numbers and ferocity. Either his magic had worked especially well upon his unwilling draftees, or humans were all more savage than they cared to admit. Looking out upon them, he saw them huddled in large, teeming masses around myriad bonfires. They were always ravenous for food, of course, but also for sex and violence. The End-of-All-Things would be happy to destroy them all, once they had served their purpose.

Pivoting to his left, he held out his arms and a slave laid the infant into them. It was a funny looking thing, this child. And would get funnier still, by the time Anders was through with it. He had decided, after some thought, that it was time he created something for a change. He would be the *end of all things* presently in existence, but this child would be the first of his new race, beings made especially to serve and obey him. Worship would not be required, as he felt he would probably kill large numbers of them whenever he got bored. Perhaps he should also create a competing race and pit them against one another!

Long & Company, the Army

Long had been deliciously, decidedly, stinkin' drunk. Officer's prerogative, he told himself, and it was true, too. That probably accounted for Janks' obvious envy: he couldn't get anywhere near as plastered on the gaseous swamp-waterlike ale the regulars drank. But now, Long was terribly, annoyingly, painfully hung-over. And in the wrong tent, to boot. This one was huge! Forcing his eyes all the way open, Long took a good look around and just about pissed himself. There, on the ground next to him, lay a semi-naked giantess of familiar features!

Long bolted to his feet and instantly stumbled over his britches, subsequently tumbling over Mardine's sleeping form. She giggled in her sleep. He gasped in horror. What had he done? Well, it was bloody obvious what he'd done. The real question was how he could be so stupid. But even that was obvious when the odor of mead wafted up from his shirt front.

"Alheria's tits! You've done it now, old boy!" he chastised himself, as he rooted around for his stockings. If the rest of the gang found out…and then he heard laughter.

"How's it going Long Peter?" Janks' voice cackled at him through the tent, placing special emphasis on the word "Long."

"Were you long enough last night?" Rem's voice snickered. "Or was it rather a long night?"

Gales of laughter washed over the tent, threatening to wake Mardine. Long hissed through the canvas in an urgent, angry whisper, "Will you shut it, lads? I'm in a tight spot here, and…"

More laugher, bordering on the hysterical.

"Ah, for Mahnus' love, can you please, please, please just go away?" Long pleaded.

Of all people, it was D'Kem whose voice shooed the merry-makers away. "Come on, lads. You don't want the sergeant assigning extra drills, do you?"

The laughter subsided into the distance, and Long was about to peek out the entrance, when a powerful hand yanked him back down onto the ground. "Once more before brekkie?" Mardine asked playfully.

Long was never so scared in his life.

Breakfast was more like the mid-day meal by the time Long was composed enough to approach the squad's campfire. He walked with as much dignity as he could muster and kept his head down, so he wouldn't have to see the self-satisfied smirks of his men.

"Any of that sausage left?" Janks called across the fire.

"Just a couple," said one of the twins.

"Well, gimme the long one," he smiled.

At once, the whole squad—minus Mardine, who was still dressing—struggled to contain the giggles.

"Seems to me," Long mused, "that someone I know was once busted down from captain to corporal for insubordination."

Janks stopped giggling. Which made everyone else giggle all the harder. "Oh, so that's how it is, huh?" Janks snapped resentfully.

"Sounds like one of you two's taken a giant step forward, so to speak, and the other, a giant step back!" Rem offered, quite proud of himself.

Even D'Kem was laughing. Finally, Long started laughing, too, and it wasn't but a few moments later when Janks joined in. Soon, the whole squad was howling. Until, that is, Mardine showed up. Everyone grew deathly silent. But the baffled look on the giant's face was too much, and the campsite exploded with unabashed hilarity. There are worse ways to bring a squad of disparate parts together.

Unfortunately, Spirk never knew when a joke had died and kept rambling on and on in a beyond-feeble attempt to land a good punch line of his own. Long rolled his eyes and clenched his jaw in exasperation and salvation came from an unlikely source. Out of the corner of his eye, he saw Bash lean over and pick a small stone off the ground. Casually, the big bruiser sauntered over to Spirk and interrupted his sadly uncomic monologue.

"Know what this here is?" he whispered to Spirk, holding the stone up in front of the lad's face.

"A rock?" Spirk guessed, hopefully.

"Oh, aye, but not just any rock," Bash said.

Spirk scrunched up his face in a parody of concentration. "A *special* rock?"

Bash winked at him, held a finger up to his lips. "A magic

rock," he said, his voice heavy with portent.

"Magic?" Spirk's face lit up like...something really, really bright. "Where'd you get it?"

"Been in the family for generations. Trouble is, I can't figure out how to work it," Bash replied wistfully.

Watching all this, Long was impressed with the man's artistry. The fellow was good enough to give Rem a run for his money.

"Maybe I could figure it out!" Spirk said.

Now, it was Bash who looked excited. "Could you?"

"I could give it a try."

"Thanks, lad," Bash said and passed the stone into Spirk's waiting hands.

Without another word, the young man wandered off, struggling to decipher the mystery of the magic stone.

Aoife, In the Forest

As an A'Shea, she knew the signs, but did not want to believe them. Her brother's attack had left her barren, or so she'd thought. And her failed attempts to bear children for her long-ago husband only served to emphasize that brutal truth. Now, impossibly, inexplicably, the sickness was undoubtedly upon her and her belly swelled and rounded with new life. But whose life? Of what nature? Instinctively, she knew the answer to that, too. Foolishly, she had chosen to try and cross the incinerated Forest of Nar, and its ghosts or gods, or the ghosts *of* its gods, had chosen her to bring them back. Because they enjoyed the irony of it? Or because she had simply presented the opportunity? It mattered little. Soon, uncannily soon, she would serve as the instrument of their return.

Aoife sat on a mossy stone next to a creek and ruminated on her plight. There was no such thing as a pregnant A'Shea. Oh, some had found the order after raising families, that was true. But Aoife had never seen or even heard of an A'Shea with child. She was fairly certain that was enough to get her drummed out of the Sisterhood, unless she could prove she had not had sexual congress with a man. Well, she thought wryly, whatever she gave birth to should be proof enough of that. Unfortunately, that would lead to a whole other series of questions she could not and perhaps would not answer, beginning with her relationship to the infamous End-of-All-Things and her subsequent quest for vengeance—about as unbecoming an objective as an A'Shea could imagine.

Aoife looked down and, for the hundredth time that morning, placed her hand on her belly. This was happening too quickly. Where a human child would gestate for about nine months, the life inside her was fairly charging into the world. She might not carry him—it—for a month. And so, the A'Shea began to rethink her plans. Rather than pressing on to the Capital, it might make more sense to go to ground for a few weeks and wait this...experience...out. What Aoife needed was an abandoned hovel, a cave or an old ruin, someplace with a bit of cover over her head and room for a fire. Fresh water nearby would be nice, too, but again, this was something she could divine if necessary.

She sighed and stood up. Time to begin looking for a suitable nest.

Not two miles downstream, Aoife found an empty and rundown farmhouse just across the water. After exploring a while, she discovered a tree that had fallen across the stream ages past. It made the perfect bridge. The farmhouse was, as expected, missing a good deal of roof, but there was one corner in particular that looked more than serviceable, being situated out of the wind and potential rain. Nearby, Aoife found everything she needed for a small fire. In fact, she could easily have built an enormous fire, but smaller was better if she hoped to remain inconspicuous. Casting about with her mind, the A'Shea discovered an old root cellar, concealed beneath some half-rotten planks, a large sheet of oilcloth and a mountain of straw. Within the root cellar, she found some tiny, withered things that might once have been apples. But she also found six earthenware jars sealed with wax. Breaking the seal on the first, she discovered it filled with a delightful jam made of spiced apples, raisins, nuts and brandy. Another jar held the same, but the third held a hard, yellow cheese, the fourth was empty and a fifth contained some sort of smoked and dried meat. The seal on the final jar was broken, and the odors emanating from it did not smell inviting, so she put that one aside. Still, this was a wealth of food, and Aoife would not gainsay her good fortune. She knew things would get worse some day and possibly soon.

The next morning, she woke up and saw that, yes, indeed her belly was growing at an accelerated rate. She worried, briefly, that childbirth might kill her, but as the resultant adrenalin surged through her body, it was countered and overwhelmed by something else that left her with profound feelings of comfort, safety and peace. Was she being used? Perhaps, she mused, but at the moment she was too relaxed to care. The important thing, to Aoife's mind, was that this child was coming, and she needed to be prepared. Given its growth rate (and, frankly, its mystical origins), she had no idea how much time she had, so she assumed the farmhouse would be her home for the foreseeable future.

It wasn't until moonrise that evening that Aoife understood the timing of her baby's gestation. He or she (Aoife was already thinking of it in those terms) would be born on the night of the next full moon. Again, she felt a surge of fear, followed by an opposing surge of serenity. Of course a child of the old gods would be born when the moon was full! And that was just a few nights away.

Returning to the bedroom she'd fashioned for herself inside the farmhouse, Aoife was surprised to see a will-o'-the-wisp floating and bobbing in the air around her bed. The A'Shea had never seen one before, but somehow recognized it just the same. Stepping closer, Aoife noticed the wisp made a soft fluttering sound, and the intensity of its light wavered ever-so-slightly.

"Hello," she said, shyly.

The wisp suddenly glowed a warm, amber color and bobbed a little faster.

"Can I help you in some way?"

The wisp changed hues to a soft pink and sank slowly.

"Or are you here to help me?" Aoife tried.

The wisp bounced back up, glowing the warm amber again.

The A'Shea took a wild guess. "Are you here to help with the baby?" she asked.

The wisp bobbed rapidly up and down and made a noise that sounded like a whispered giggle. Aoife was not yet convinced they were communicating.

"If you can understand me," she said, pointing, "can you land on that old barrel?"

The wisp chirruped and did so.

Company, then. Aoife would have company through the childbirth.

Two nights later, she was joined by another will-o'-the-wisp. This one, however, favored blues and greens. The next day, she encountered an unusually large frog that faded in and out of existence. At least, that's how it looked to Aoife. The frog took up a station at the foot of her bed and would not budge. That afternoon, a talking hedgehog surprised her by introducing himself as she bathed in the stream.

"I am Mik Mik," he announced, right out of the blue.

Aoife didn't know which to feel more, embarrassed at her nakedness or astounded at meeting a talking hedgehog. "I am Aoife," she replied.

"Ah, yes, I know, Miss. And I am here to help you, Miss," Mik Mik answered.

"Well," Aoife said, "I suppose you can join the others inside the farmhouse."

"The farmhouse, is it? I shall be delighted, Miss, most delighted." And, with that, Mik Mik scampered off into the farmhouse.

The last to appear was a tiny brown dragon, no bigger than the end of the A'Shea's little finger. At first, she thought it a grasshopper or some other sort of insect. But as she looked more closely at it and witnessed it breathing miniature gouts of flame, she knew it for what it was.

"And how are you all to help me?" Aoife asked the assembled menagerie.

"We're here to keep off the darklings," Mik Mik said.

"The darklings?" she inquired.

"Them as feeds on nature's young," the frog said. Aoife

hadn't known he could talk.

"And we're to be here for the birth. An honor it is," Mik Mik added.

Aoife glanced down again at her amazingly distended belly, passed a hand over her swollen breasts. The moon would be full tonight, she thought. Yes, tonight. She didn't know about protection from darklings, she just hoped her strange guardians would not be underfoot when the time came.

At moonrise, she felt her first contraction, which was completely unlike anything she had expected. Instead of pain, she felt gentle, satisfying flexing throughout her abdomen. She had assisted in enough birthings to know this was not the way of things; then again, her child was most likely not human. Every time she started to panic, though, the familiar wave of calm descended upon her, and her fear evaporated.

With her contractions increasing in frequency and intensity Aoife began to make her final preparations for the birth. She cast a series of small, helpful spells that all A'Shea used in such circumstances. Her guardians continued to hover around her, doing mysterious things of their own and keeping themselves quite busy. Carefully, Aoife lay down on her back in the straw. The wisps floated near her face; the hedgehog and frog settled in near her shoulders; the little dragon flew around the entire area, as if greatly agitated. At last, the birth began. As with everything else in this otherworldly experience, the results were not what the A'Shea had expected.

FIVE

Vykers, In Ahklat

The Reaper was not surprised. Nothing that had happened since his capture surprised him any more. "One of your own," he repeated.

The Ahklatian nodded, almost imperceptibly. "In the old tongue, we call him N' Athka-T'ren, the Renegade. In the days following the Great Crime, N' Athka-T'ren continued the killing so many others had indulged in—not out of vengeance or disgust, but because he had come to enjoy it. As sanity and calm returned to the rest of us N' Athka-N'Amesto—'survivors'—we quickly expelled him from our community. We were done with killing, forever, but could not, dare not tolerate that mad dog in our midst." The Historian sighed. "It has been seven hundred years, and while rumors and anecdotes appear throughout the land from time-to-time, we have not been able to locate him."

Ask him about the magic, Arune prompted.

"Assuming your renegade and this End-of-All-Things are one and the same, what can you tell me about his magic or his sword?" Vykers asked his host.

"His magic," the Historian said, almost to himself. "We Ahklatians have an...*affinity*...for basic magics of all kinds. We assume the renegade made use of that to access those with greater knowledge and ability."

"Access? Kidnapped, tortured and killed, you mean."

"Likely," the Historian admitted.

"So, how powerful is he?"

"If what we hear is true, that he holds entire populations in thrall, he may be the most powerful sorcerer alive."

"And his sword?"

"Yes," the Historian paused to collect himself. "Mythology is rife with tales of magical swords, but few turn out to be genuine when found."

"You're tellin' me," Vykers agreed.

"There is, however, a handful of weapons scattered around the world that are known to be, er, *legitimate*. Your Queen possesses one."

"So I've learned."

"Another such is said to exist within Morden's Cairn, the great tomb of the Northern Clans."

Vykers shook his head in amused disbelief. "Morden's Cairn, huh? Sounds like a cheerful place."

"The sword's remoteness and inaccessibility are what have kept it safe all these centuries."

"Right. And, uh, what's this particular sword supposed to do?"

"Whatever it wants," the Historian said.

"Whatever it wants…"

"Yes. It's alive, after a fashion. Possessed of its own thoughts, desires and abilities."

"No shit?" Vykers said, rather impolitely.

"No shit," the Historian repeated, dryly.

There was only one inn in all of Ahklat that catered to "outsiders" tastes—Landy's Palace, and Vykers was finally directed there after visiting almost all the native-style inns in the city, places with names like Repose, Silence, Remembrance, Lassitude and Memory's Corner. In deference to the locals, Landy's Palace still observed the unspoken anti-noise ordinance and featured the same, intentionally spartan foyer as all the other inns, but its rooms were a bit more traditionally furnished and comfortable, and, more importantly (from Vykers' point of view), its meals were considerably more pleasant. Too bad his companions didn't know how to enjoy such fare. While the Reaper was enjoying pork with roasted apples, the Five were dining—if dining was the proper word—on raw legs of lamb and venison. Vykers had eaten raw meat many a time out of necessity; it would do in a pinch. But he preferred it well done and slightly charred on the outside.

A sword that can Shape? Arune asked. *That will make my job easier.*

Your job? Vykers countered. *Your job is to find a way out of my body and into one of your own.*

Arune offered a mental shrug. *That's as may be, warrior. In the meantime, I need to handle those defenses that fall outside your... expertise.*

I did okay before you came along.

May I remind you that when I came along, as you put it, you were crawling on all fours like a mindless beast, missing your hands and feet and shitting yourself at every turn.

And you were dead. Still are, truth be told. And I'm still missing my hands and feet. Don't think for a moment these ghostie parts are better n' my own flesh and blood.

I could remove them again, Arune thought to herself. *But no point in further irritating the big oaf.*

Vykers speared a roasted apple with his knife and took a bite. "What do you know about this Morden's Cairn?" he asked Number 3.

"Nothing," the creature confessed, regretfully.

"Wonderful," Vykers said, sourly.

"Are you worried, Master?" Number 17 asked.

Vykers looked over at him. "Worried? No. But I like to be prepared. If I'm to beard the dragon in his den, I like to know how big he is, how he likes to attack, that sort of thing."

"We're going to fight a dragon?" Number 12 gasped.

"No. No dragon," Vykers corrected. "It was just a what-do-you-call-it..."

Metaphor, Arune offered.

"A, uh,...dammit, what's the word?" Vykers continued to fumble.

Figure of speech.

"A figure of speech," Vykers finally said.

You're welcome.

I didn't use your suggestion. I thought of it, just as you were yapping at me.

I'm sure.

Vykers shut her out. Sometimes, the Shaper was worse than living without hands and feet.

"We need to find a map," Vykers told Number 3. "Everybody wants me to save the world, but nobody's makin' it easy."

"Off the market square, there's a collector of old books, papers and maps."

"And you know this from your previous visit?" Vykers asked.

Number 17 cut in, "We may look savage, Master, but we're not savages."

Vykers stood up. "I'm off to find this collector. Come along or stay here, as you wish. But be ready to leave by sunrise."

The Five looked at one another, briefly. "I'll join you, Master," Number 12 said. Vykers had never heard him speak before; he had the odd, cracking voice of a teen-aged boy, which didn't sit well with his bizarre, many-fissured appearance.

"Suit yourself," Vykers said, indifferently.

When the two had gotten a couple of blocks from Landy's, Number 12 spoke again. "Excuse me, Master…" he began.

"Yes?"

"Why do you kill?" the creature inquired.

In unusual circumstances, Vykers had learned to expect equally unusual events, so he was not completely surprised by the non sequitur. "I like it," he answered flatly.

"So do I," Number 12 said. After a while he added, "But why?"

The Reaper had been asked this very question by a thousand whores and ten times as many widows, many of whom would be forced into the same profession themselves as a result of Vyker's actions. "It's a simple enough question, my friend, but the answer's anything but: I'm good at it, it's easy. I like the feeling of power and control it gives me. I like the struggle, the contest of wills and skills as we used to say in the army. But mostly, killing's who I am."

Number 12 made a strange chittering noise that might have been laughter. "Yes," he said, "I see. Like a spider."

"Yes," Vykers agreed. "But a damned big one."

They walked on a while longer, turned a few corners, and then Vykers said, "You ask, because you want to understand yourself, your own urges."

"I do," his companion admitted.

"Then you'll get to know yourself right well in my service," the Reaper said, as the two came to the edge of the market square.

"The shop we want is over there," Number 12 pointed.

Vykers noted a narrow building, wedged in between two much larger structures. "Huh," he said, making straight for it. When he made his way through the door, the shopkeeper looked up from behind the counter and nodded.

"Ah, an honor to have such a renowned warrior in my establishment," he said softly.

"How in the infinite hells does everyone here seem to know of my coming before I get where I'm going?" Vykers complained.

"It's quite simple, really. We..."

"Never mind. It doesn't change anything."

"No," the shop keeper replied with mild disappointment.

"I'm guessing you know why I've come to your shop, then?" Vykers asked.

The shopkeeper brightened. "You're looking for a map of the Morden's Cairn region, or, perhaps, for a map leading from here *to* Morden's Cairn."

Vykers eyed Number 12, who said nothing. "Yes," the warrior told the shopkeeper.

This was the shortest Ahklatian Vykers had seen, a least a head shorter than the big man, with the same pale skin and washed out hair as all the others he'd seen. And the same black, almost soulless eyes.

"What do you know about Morden's Cairn?" the man asked.

"Nothing. Ghost stories and such."

"Then you know the truth of it: the place is well and truly haunted, rife with the undead and the spirits of the dead," the shopkeeper finished, with a morbid smile.

"O' course," Vykers said, his voice dripping with sarcasm. "Naturally. I'm sure the place is Evil's summer home."

The shopkeeper must've taken umbrage, because he frowned at the bigger man. "Do you take evil lightly, warrior?" he asked in his darkest tone.

Vykers almost laughed at the melodrama. "I get it, my friend. I'm well aware that you're acquainted with evil. As am I." He paused, "As will I ever be."

The other man dropped his gaze and let out a long, slow sigh. "It grieves me nonetheless," he said, almost to himself. Wordlessly, he extended a small roll of leather and placed it into Vyker's waiting hand. "If I believed in prayer," the smaller man said, "I would pray your own evil outweighs that you face."

The Reaper didn't know what to say to that, so he regarded the shopkeeper quizzically, turned on his heel, and left.

The next morning, Vykers and the Five set out through the Winter Gate for the wild northwestern part of the continent. It was a damp, drizzly morning, but Vykers was excited. It was territory he had always wanted to explore and now he had the freedom, no, the mandate to do so. He was further pleased by his little team of chimeras; they fought like demons but talked little and obeyed him without question or hesitation. He could see why House Blackbyrne had taken to them, but remained confused as to what they received in return. At the same time, the idea that he might have to face and kill one or all of them was never far from his mind. He didn't relish the idea, but neither was he afraid of it.

The trees up here smelled different to the warrior, and the wind had a different flavor to it, too.

Those are pine trees you're smelling, Arune informed him.

Was I talking to you? Vykers asked.

Must you always be so disagreeable?

No, I'm in earnest: I didn't know I was talking to you.

Well, Arune hedged, *you weren't, not really...*

Oh! Now you're reading my mind?

I'm learning to, Arune admitted.

You don't have my leave.

Your leave? I may save your mangy hide a thousand times before we part ways.

Are you bored, spook? Is that it? Vykers taunted.

It's an absolute wasteland in here. You should see all the cobwebs…

You're so smart, tell me something useful.

You need a bath.

Another? I had one yesterday.

It didn't work.

Maybe Arune liked this kind of banter, but it was wearing on Vykers. *Tell me something that ain't about me.*

Your five bodyguards are a mix of races—you know that. But some of those races aren't of this world.

Vykers wasn't sure what to make of that. *Uh-huh…*

And they honestly aren't aware of that. They're telling the truth when claim they know little of their origins.

But they were made for killing. That much is clear.

No one would know that better than you, I guess, Arune allowed.

There's something going on here, a bigger game being played than I can see or figure out.

I feel the same.

Huh, Vykers said. *A ghost moving in with me, this End-of-All-Things, the Virgin Queen making me her general, a noble family in the Capital offering me a bodyguard of creatures not of this world, and now I'm off to a haunted ruin right out o' the fairy stories to find me a bleedin' magic sword. And those are just the pieces I can see on the board. Mahnus knows whatever else is in play.*

That's a pretty fair assessment.

Vykers spat into the dirt beside the trail. "Thanks," he said aloud, forgetting the whole conversation thus far had been internal. Number 3 looked over at him, but Vykers just shook his head and looked away. He didn't feel like explaining.

Several hours later, Arune intruded again. *Large raiding party on both sides of the road, with a third group moving into place behind us.*

Vykers was about to ask how many men, when he remembered how the Five had gauged the oursine more accurately. "How many in hiding around us?" he asked Number 17.

"Thirty...eight," the chimera answered.

Forty, Arune corrected.

"Forty," Number 17 echoed, unknowingly.

Well, I'll be damned, Vykers thought at Arune.

Probably, she smirked back.

A big, wide man in a fang-studded helmet and breastplate stepped out of the underbrush just ahead and to the left of the party. He had an enormous brown beard, a wide mouth, and large, bulbous nose separating his green eyes. In his right hand, he held a mean-looking double-bladed axe.

"What in the endless hells have we got here? Some kind o' circus?" the man joked loudly, as he looked over Vykers and the Five. Since Vykers and his crew said nothing, the man continued. "Or is this more of a travelling zoo?"

"Ah," Vykers said, "there, you've hit it. We're a travelling zoo, and it's feeding time."

"Only I'm the one doin' the eating," the man said. "Hoick!" he yelled.

Out of the bushes and woods all around them, the other 39 members of the stranger's band appeared, weapons in hand.

"What the hell kinda signal is 'hoick'?" Vykers asked. "That some special code only idiots can understand?"

Some of the larger group laughed, others growled in disapproval. Their leader was of the first group, laughing heartily, but in an aggressive manner. "Well," he said at last, "I've got to give you credit for havin' some spleen about you. But you're outnumbered four-to-one. You know how this works, old son, bigger group plants the smaller under the leaves and pine needles. Your corpse'll be sprouting mushrooms inside a week."

The fellow's cronies laughed hysterically and repeated a few of his choicest words.

"Last time someone talked like that to the Reaper, I poured molten iron into his asshole."

The big man stopped smiling, and every member of his

band did, too. Most took one or two steps back. "You're lyin'," the leader said. "The Reaper's dead. 'Sides, he was a giant of a man. You ain't."

Vykers drew his sword and walked calmly towards the other man, who, not yet ready to lose face, stood his ground with a most concerned look upon his face. "Tell ya what I'm gonna do," Vykers whispered. "I'm gonna take the heads off every man in your little band, stake you to the ground, and pile all 'o them on top of you. They should make for great company 'til the nighttime predators arrive." The man's eyebrow began to twitch. Vykers ducked just as his foe was about to deliver a sideways blow with his axe, sending him flying over the Reaper's back. Instantly, Vykers wheeled and kicked him in the jaw, knocking him unconscious or close to it.

The rest of the bandits came to life and made to close with Vykers, but the Five stepped into position and their frightful, alien aspects momentarily stunned their assailants. "Let me!" Vykers told his companions. "You boys can sit this one out, get some rest." *And that means you, too!* He told Arune.

You're going to fight forty men by yourself? She asked, incredulous.

Shut up! Don't distract me! He countered.

"Flank 'im!" one of the bandits yelled. "Flank the fucker!"

Vykers swung his sword in series of mighty figure-eights, more to clear some fighting room around himself than to do any actual damage. Still, he caught a couple of his opponents on the arms and shoulders and they stumbled backwards, gasping or groaning in pain. "Shit, lads, I ain't even gotten started!" he roared. Two more men tried to rush Vykers on his right, while a third came in from his left. Vykers tumbled left, swinging as he went, and took out the man's knee. As the man went down, the Reaper was able to turn and bring his sword across the midsections of both attackers. One parried, the other died. Three more men came at Vykers' back. With his left glove, he reached out and grabbed the solo attacker's sword. While the man struggled to wrench it free, Vykers put his own sword through the man's right eye. Still in control of the dead man's body, Vykers wheeled it around and threw it onto the incoming threesome. Two of them wrestled with the corpse, and the third came in, swinging north to south. Vykers parried and kicked the man in the balls. As his sword rebounded from the other man's, he smashed him in the face with his quillons, catching the fellow by the inside of his right cheek and dragging his head down, where the Reaper could bash it with his rising knee. There was a great snapping sound, and the bandit collapsed. By now, the two wrestling to get through or past the body of their comrade had worked their way free, only to witness this latest casualty fall at their feet. They looked at one another and decided, without discussion, upon a more cautious approach. Meanwhile, more of the group continued to move into flanking positions, in hopes of catching Vykers off guard. Vykers feinted for the man's right knee and when he parried, swept over the top and cut his head clean off. Following the momentum of that blow, Vykers spun completely around and caught the second man on the shoulder, while he was busy looking at his now-headless friend. The Reaper ran right into him and knocked him ass-over-teakettle in the dirt. He then jumped on the man's torso, snapping numerous ribs for good measure.

In a mere few heartbeats, the bandit gang had gone from forty to thirty, and it didn't appear their target had sustained even a single scratch. Some of the band began fading backwards into the forest, but a few were still game to try Vykers. Unfortunately, a few is not enough. They died before they even had time to regret the choice. Finally, as more and more of the band dissolved into the woods, Vykers stabbed his sword into a nearby corpse in frustration and yelled, "Well, I'm not going to go chasing after the sons-of-bitches!" He turned to the Five. "Go get 'em. Just bring me their heads." That was the first time he could ever remember seeing the Five smile. It was, he would later reflect, delightfully sinister.

Smiling at the sounds of horrified screaming in the woods, Vykers set about stripping and staking the leader to the ground. If he was a right bastard, he was still a man of his word. When the leader awoke, he'd find himself, as promised, buried in bloody heads, appetizers to the entrée he was to become for some predator.

You don't call the Reaper a liar.

Deda, On the Road

Wims Deda had disguised himself as a caravan guard, quite common throughout the Kingdoms and unlikely to attract much attention. The three men he took with him were similarly disguised, though each wore different armor and carried his own weapons. Best not to look too organized or well-funded. Wims figured to take the trade road from Wareth to Lunessfor, but he was still over two weeks' travel east of it. It was distances like this that kept great armies apart long enough to become great armies.

Personally, Wims never cared for the East. Too grassy. Too wide open. If Anders wanted to incinerate the whole thing, it was just fine by him. No, Wims much preferred the Queen's realm, or the far West. The South was tolerable, if a bit warmer than Wims liked. Sweating in armor all day, every day was something he could never come to appreciate, though others he'd known didn't seem to mind it. If Wims lived or was meant to, he wanted perhaps a small island in the middle of a big freshwater lake. To his mind, freshwater fish tasted much better than the saltwater variety. And storms weren't anywhere as bad on a lake. Plus, there were things in the ocean—or so he'd heard—that you simply did not fuck with. So, a lake it would be. If he survived. A lake and a score of women. Why not? He didn't enjoy their insipid conversations, but they had other uses, and the prospect of an eventual son or three was not altogether unpleasant.

His horse kicked a piece of loose shale, disturbing his daydreams. He looked around. The men who rode with him seemed equally lost in thought. Just so they stayed on their own damned islands.

Wims thought for a moment about the massive and far-flung Deda Clan, of which he was not even the most famous, successful, powerful or wealthy. To be Deda had never meant much to him, not like it did to the rest of the Clan. But that might change if he outlived his master's plans. For the thousandth time, he wondered what those plans really were. What kind of being intentionally destroys everything he encounters? Where are you supposed to live when you're finished? How can you occupy your time? What pleasures will be left to indulge? His horse dropped dung behind him. Dung was more than Anders would leave behind, that was certain.

Wims was ambivalent about his master, ambivalent about his mission, even ambivalent about his own life or death. But the great puzzle it represented fascinated him.

Long & Company, the Army

The worst part was, Long didn't even remember screwing the giantess. What was the point in unusual sex if you couldn't remember or talk about it? How had it gone? How had it even worked? Clearly, she hadn't been on top, or he'd probably be dead. Did she enjoy his efforts? Did he enjoy *hers*? He was afraid there might be a repeat performance in the works, and Long didn't know how to feel about it, other than to dread the inevitable ribbing he would again receive from his men.

And he did have other, more serious, concerns, like getting Spirk Nessno ready for eventual combat. Those who could not dance at festival time were said to have two left feet. Those clumsy with their hands were said to be "all thumbs." Spirk was all left feet, all thumbs and very little brain. After much consideration, Long decided to train the kid in mace. A sword was beyond his abilities, but a mace required less subtlety. The only remaining question was whether Spirk could handle a shield or should simply be armed with another mace. Sure, he'd look foolish, but at least he'd hit something—himself, most likely, but perhaps the occasional enemy, too. While Long was still grappling with this conundrum, Janks sidled up to him.

"Hey-ho, giant killer!" he joked.

Long sighed. He could either do what he'd always done—attempt to defeat this kind of nonsense with bluster—or he could play along and hope his lack of annoyance took the fun out of teasing him. "What can I do for you, Corporal?"

"The basher ever tell you his name?" Janks asked.

"I never asked."

"Good thing, too," Janks said, "'cause it's the longest damned name I ever heard. For a while, I thought he was singing."

"Well, I'm not gonna sing every time I need to address him. What do we call him for short?"

"Fuck if I know. Let's just call him 'Bash'."

"There's one in every squad!"

"That's perfect, then, ain't it?" Janks retorted.

Long shivered. The days were getting shorter and colder. "We get any messages from the command tent today? Has Bailis come by?"

"Nah," Janks frowned. "Nothing. I hate waiting around, doin' nothing."

"Would you rather be marching?" Long asked, raising an eyebrow at his old friend.

"Did I ever tell you how much I love waiting?" Janks responded, with haste.

"Need I remind you, Corporal? You're the one wanted to get up and out of that little town. Now, you're a verb."

Janks screwed up his face. "A what? A verb?"

"Sure, a verb. You march, you wait, you sleep, you eat, you sleep, you fight, you drink, you screw..."

"Speakin' of which..." Janks cut in, "what's it like?"

"Oh, for Mahnus' sake!" Long pulled his cap off and pushed his thinning hair back. He paused, then, sheepishly, said "I don't remember."

Janks howled at that. "How in the world can ya forget something like *that*?" he cried.

"I was drunk."

"Sorry excuse for a gigolo, you are!" Janks remarked.

"Those days are past, Corporal, and I'll thank you to remember that."

"You want me to remember your days as a gigolo?"

"No, forget those."

"So," Janks scratched his nose, "you want me to remember to forget those?"

Long groaned in exasperation. "Look, don't you have anything better to do? Supervise the latrines? Swindle some rube at dice? Have a wank in your tent?"

"Be a lot easier if you'd just tell me what she looks like nekkid."

"Go and train the kid to the mace!" Long shouted and kicked his old chum in the seat of his pants to get him moving.

The sergeant was just getting comfortable on his cot when Mardine tried to sneak in behind and snuggle with him. Long's eyes shot open. This was a nightmare, despite his open eyes.

"Er, Mardine..." he began.

"Yes, sweetums?" she asked, in as close to a seductive voice as a middle-aged giantess can come.

"Folks are beginning to talk around camp. Perhaps we'd better..."

"No one will know," Mardine interrupted. "No one will believe it."

"What's that supposed to mean?" Long asked. Granted, he wanted this whole thing over with, but he also had his pride.

"A big girl like me? A little fella like you..."

"And where do you think I came by the nickname Long, eh?" Long snorted, indignantly.

"Ooh! I thought it was on account of that long face you always have."

"Oh, ha ha, private, ha and ha!" He wanted to be furious. He wanted her out. Who would have thought she'd have such nimble fingers?

"Long!" a voice shouted in his ear. He sat up. He was on the floor. Next to Mardine. Janks was yelling at him. Perfect.

"What? What is it, Corporal?"

"You're wanted in the command tent, soon as you can get there." Janks rolled his eyes towards Mardine and back to the sergeant. He smirked.

"You wanna get busted down to private, Corporal? I understand there's nothing they won't make a private do!" Long threatened.

Janks saluted silently and withdrew.

What a mess, what a mess, what a mess. *Well,* Long thought, *only way out is forward.* He got to his feet, scrounged around for the elements of a decent uniform, struggled into his clothing and stumbled off towards the command tent.

What could it be? He wondered as he walked. *We're too far away to have sighted the enemy, and the Reaper's not due for some time, yet.* Had the news of the tryst with Mardine undone him already?

Too soon, Long appeared before the command tent and was ushered in. Bailis was in the far corner, deep in conversation with a couple of higher-ups. When he saw Long come in, he saluted his comrades and made his way in the sergeant's direction. Such was Long's unease that Bailis' march across the tent seemed to take an eternity and no time at all. Arriving, the man pulled his jacket taut beneath his belt and straightened his collar.

"It's funny. When you're in armor, you can't wait to get out of it, and when you're in uniform, you can't wait to get back into your armor."

"Yes, sir," Long agreed, for want of anything else to say.

"So, Sergeant. Short and sweet: we've reports…"

Here it comes, here it comes, Long fretted.

"Of small scouting parties from the enemy's host making a few forays into our territory, to the northeast. We don't mind them coming by, we just don't want to them to leave."

Long felt like a man who'd just been spared the block, only to be put in line for the gallows.

"Something wrong, Sergeant?"

"Uh…no…I was just…I thought…"

"Worried about your little assignation?"

For a moment, Long couldn't breathe.

"Relax, Sergeant. Things don't work that way any more. And besides, any man who can bed a giant, well…" Bailis started chuckling.

"It was that bloody mead, sir!" Long whined.

Bailis grinned like a madman. "I'm sure, I'm sure," he chortled. "Usually has the opposite effect on me, but everyone's different, I imagine."

Long stared miserably at his feet. "Yes, sir," he said again.

The major got right back to business. "Now, about these scouting parties," he said. "We'd like you and your crew to intercept one. Seems likely you'll have to do some fighting, if you run across anyone at all. *Fighting*, I say, but no killing. We want these scouts captured and questioned, here at camp."

"Captured and questioned," Long repeated.

"Correct."

"And, uh, how many men are in these scouting parties?" Long asked, beginning to get the feel of it.

"Three-to-four, we hear. Not how I'd do it, but that's another reason to C and Q them: get a little insight into their leaders' thinking."

C and Q. Long liked that. He was going to have to use that when he got back to his squad. That kind of jargon made a man sound more experienced, more authoritative than he actually was. Right now, the illusion of command was about all he had going for him, especially after Mardine. Suddenly, Long realized he hadn't been listening.

"...Like you to set out by dinner. Head north, northeast. Don't wander any further than ten miles beyond the pickets. If you see anything bigger than a scouting party, send your fastest rider back with news and the rest of you follow. Do not engage. Am I understood?" Bailis finished.

"Do not engage a bigger party, yes, sir!" Long said.

"Excellent. Good luck, then and dismissed."

Long saluted and fairly ran out the entrance and back to camp. He wasn't surprised to see Janks waiting for his return, like a dog awaiting its master's return from the hunt.

"Well?" Janks prompted.

"Just a little C and Q," Long answered, smugly. "Nothing to worry about."

As Long had hoped, Janks was baffled. "C and Q?"

"Yeah, you know," Long said as nonchalantly as possible, "just a little C and Q."

Janks was in a bind, now. He had no idea what C and Q meant, but he couldn't let on that he didn't, or he'd lose face to his longtime friend and closest rival. He threw out his chin, stretched his arms and tried to appear bored by it all. "Yep, yep, the old C and Q. Q and C. First, comes the C and then the Q." He looked at Long out of the corner of his eye, trying to gauge how well his bluff was going. "Of course, some try to Q first and then C, but that's just nonsense, ain't it? Any thinkin' man knows it's Q first."

Long squinted at him.

"I mean C! C comes first, o' course. Any fool knows that. Hells, even Spirk knows that!"

"I reckon so," Long agreed, giving away as little as possible. If he could stretch this out just right, he might get a little payback for all the jokes he'd endured about Mardine.

Janks was as wary as a kid about to smack a hornet's nest. "So, er, how do they want it done—this particular time?" he asked.

"Oh," Long said, blithely, "the usual." He smiled inwardly as he saw Janks' expression cloud over. "Why don't you take the lead on this one, Corporal?"

"The lead?" Janks croaked, in a voice that suddenly climbed an octave.

"Sure, you know, get the boys ready to perform their duty!"

"Their duty..." Janks repeated, in slow motion.

"Come on, man, don't just stand there!" Long urged, "Let's get to it!"

Janks sleepwalked over to the rest of the unit and began rousting them. "Up and at 'em, lads! Up and at 'em!"

"What's going on?" Spirk asked in pitiful excitement.

"It's time to do your duty, o' course!" Janks bellowed. "Up and at 'em. Everybody into line!"

And line up, they did: Rem, Spirk, D'Kem, the twins, Bash, Mardine and the A'Shea. Janks strutted up and down in front of them like a rooster.

"Time to do our duty, yes, sir! And a mighty important duty it is, too—the kind of duty that can only be done by duty-doers doing their own, but also others. Duties, that is. A man who does his duty is a man worthy of respect, and this duty here, the one we're about to embark on..." Janks boiled over. "Oh, Alheria's tits, Long, I have no idea what in all hells I'm talking about!"

Long stood by, smiling so hard it hurt. But he loved it. "You have no idea how many years I've waited to hear you say that!" he laughed.

All the air rushed out of Janks. "You wanna tell us all what C and Q is?" he asked, sourly.

"Well, squad," Long said, "it seems we've been tasked with intercepting some of the enemy's scouting parties—if we can. We run into anything bigger 'n us, we're to run back here as fast as our mounts will take us. The C stands for 'Capture,' and the Q stands for 'Question.' We do the first part and the higher-ups do the second. We're to leave before dinner." He looked at his squad. "We take only what we need for a night or two at a time and we don't travel more than ten miles out. That's it; that's all."

Immediately, everyone began packing, saddling horses, checking and rechecking weapons. If everything went well, Long mused, they'd be right back in this very spot within a few days. If not, they might be attending a funeral. The important thing there was going as guests and not the departed.

Aoife, In the Forest

The light was the first thing that alarmed her, though again, as always, she no sooner experienced the feeling than it was replaced by calmer, more soothing sensations. She'd been prepared for her water to break, for the rush of fluids. She had not been expecting an eerie glow to emanate from between her legs, nor the coils and clouds of low-lying fog that issued from her, either. Stranger still, the fog did not dissipate, but simply got thicker and thicker. She felt herself trembling down there, convulsing, stretching. She did not, however, feel pain. She became sleepy and began fading in and out of consciousness. She heard, or thought she heard, odd twitterings, ululations, giggling, even snatches of song here and there. It made absolutely no sense to her whatsoever. And yet, she had never been happier. Somehow, incredibly, she was pulsing with joy, with sheer and unadulterated euphoria. There was no better place she could ever be, nothing better she could ever do.

She fell into a deep sleep.

And awoke on a natural dais of sorts, composed of the softest fungi and mosses, around which a large moat of brownish-green water swirled. Sitting up, Aoife was greeted by a chorus of odd voices, gently, reverently chanting a word she knew was alien to her, but which she nevertheless understood to mean "mother." Mother. Aoife was now a mother, had given birth, in fact. But to what?

Rising out of the mist peeped tiny heads of various shapes, none bigger than an apple. Here was a little fellow who looked like a juvenile satyr, there, a winged sprite, a female, perhaps. Nearby, a small mound of leaves and roots rocked back and forth on two gnarly legs. Further away, a sticklike figure that resembled a troll hopped up and down in apparent delight. Aoife attempted to count them all, but some were in movement continuously, and the sight of the collection overall so dazzled her that she gave up and sat back on her haunches, silently, waiting for some sort of sign or signal to enlighten her. Slowly, cautiously, they crept towards her, one by one, so that she might know them.

The satyr was the first to approach, as she suspected he might be. The horns on his forehead were little more than bumps, and the mottled, downy hair on his head matched that on his goatish legs exactly. He was precisely what Aoife had imagined an infant satyr might look like. The little satyr purred the word for mother again and climbed into Aoife's lap, which, she was relieved to discover, had been reclothed with her robes. The next creature was a miniature sword fern... except that it hummed, murmured and was inexplicably able to walk. The A'Shea had known plants were living things, of course. Who didn't? But to see one so clearly sentient was an epiphany that practically overwhelmed her. The next creature in line was a flying hybrid of insect and faerie. And there was another creature in line behind him, and another behind her, and another...

It was insanity to think that Aoife had birthed all of these things, but what else could she conclude? And how could she pursue the vengeance that had been her life's goal for so many years in her current situation? Surrounded, cloaked in her children, the A'Shea sat for hours, pondering her suddenly short list of options.

It was morning. Some of Aoife's children had grown tremendously since the previous night; others remained small. As she stood among them, one of them moved forward and spoke.

"You are troubled, mother-sister?"

"Not troubled, little one," she said, in her most loving, motherly tone. "Confused, slightly, but not troubled."

"What is it confuses you, mother-sister?"

"First, why do you call me 'mother-sister'?"

"We are born of the same father, though you are also our mother."

Aoife shook her head, no less confused. "There is another, more troubling issue."

"Tell."

"I have had some unfinished business I've needed to resolve for years. Now that you're here…"

"But mother-sister," the little satyr said, "you goal is also our goal."

"Indeed?" Aoife laughed, in the way that all mothers do when their clever babes have said something amusing.

"You seek revenge against your brother…"

Aoife gasped.

"And so do we."

At last, the A'Shea understood. It was her brother who had leveled the fabled forest, her brother who had desecrated the oldest temple of the old gods. Of course the people of that forest would want revenge. Of course they would use her, if they could, to exact that revenge.

"And how is that to be accomplished, little one?" she asked.

"Whenever we find a suitable place, you will birth the children of Nar. We, in turn, will spread forests wherever you birth us. In time, we will be able to attack your brother from every direction. There will be nowhere he can turn that he will not see one of our faces snarling back at him. He would burn the greenwood? The greenwood is a fire all its own, and we shall burn your brother in return."

Aoife nodded. What else could she do? She had never been able to find the means to punish her brother. Now, that means had found her. It felt wonderful. And terrifying.

Vykers, On the Trail

They were all tearing into their venison as if they hadn't eaten in weeks. Vykers suspected they might have eaten just hours ago, and their meal had been human. He didn't much care how those bandits died, and he didn't much care for cannibalism, either. On the other hand, he wasn't sure the Five were even remotely human, so perhaps it wasn't cannibalism, after all. Still, would it kill them to try roasting their meat once in a while?

"So," he said, leaning into the firelight to make eye contact with Number 3. "Tell me where you came from, where you started."

"We don't recall much."

"Well," Vykers growled, "whatever you do recall."

Number 3 looked to his peers to his left and right. None of them so much as stopped eating. "Very well," he said. "I was sleeping….somewhere. An earthquake or perhaps an explosion awakened me. I found myself on the floor of a prison cell. All around me, I could see others asleep in cells of their own. The noise awakened one or two of them. The bars of my cell had been damaged by great stones that fell from the ceiling, and I was able to squeeze through a gap near one corner. From there, it was simple, really. I wandered the place until I found a dead guard with keys. I opened each cell that wasn't damaged beyond repair and what you see before you are all that remained."

"We spent some time trying to make sense of our predicament and our surroundings. We all had—and still have—dim memories of excursions outside the complex at night, memories of marching, memories of killing on command. We were familiar to each other, but concrete recollections eluded us, one and all. And we had these…"

Number 3 pulled up the cuff of his sleeve, revealing an unfamiliar sigil branded into the back of his left hand, in the meat between his index finger and thumb. As if on signal, the remaining chimeras revealed their sigils, as well. Each was slightly different.

"These," Number 3 continued, "are numbers. How we know this or in what language, I cannot tell you. But this," he pointed again to his own sigil "is 'Number 3,' and 'Number 3' I have been ever since."

"In scouting the rest of our prison, we discovered a laboratory of some sort, in which one of our brothers was rapidly dying from countless wounds apparently sustained during torture. We returned to examine the other cells and found many times our number had died in their sleep, some through poison, some through starvation, some through injuries they incurred in desperate attempts at escape. At one time, it seems, there were close to fifty of us. Imagine..." Number 3 trailed off.

Imagine what? Vykers wondered. *Imagine the damage fifty of you could do to a small village or keep? Imagine the cost, labor and arcane power required to make you? More likely, imagine friends you'd lost...*

"At any rate," the chimera continued, "we discovered one hallway that had collapsed during the catastrophe—whatever it was—and determined it to have been the only exit from the compound. Elsewhere, we found a second collapse that left a pile of rubble and a hole in the ceiling. It was a simple matter to climb the pile and boost one another out the hole."

"In summary, we believe we were created and trained by someone with less than benevolent intentions. We call him 'Number 1,' although that is surely not his name. Whether he still lives, or knows that some of us still live, we do not know. Yet, we hope for a reckoning some day."

"Right," Vykers said. "And who doesn't?" He paused. "And your language? I don't get that bit. Seems like scary monsters should be a lot less...less..."

"Eloquent?" Number 17 asked, with just the tiniest hint of irony in his voice.

A hint, but Vykers got it. "Yeah, wise ass, eloquent."

The chimeras laughed in the variety of peculiar ways unique to them, and Vykers sensed they had all just enjoyed a moment of what passed for fellowship in a freak show. And again, he was struck by the frequency of uncanny coincidences—dominos, puzzle pieces—that, impossibly, seemed somehow connected.

He was also itching to meet this "End-of-All-Things." What was it the Historian had suggested—if you want to be the best, you have to beat the best? He looked over at his comrades again. What if they had somehow been steered into his hands, only to turn on him when the time was right? He began planning, in earnest, how he might kill each of them, if it came to that. No sense in being caught unprepared.

He could feel Arune tip-toeing around his thoughts. But he had no time for her at the moment; he needed to think without distraction.

The trail climbed steadily, so that the end of each day was a little bit colder, the air, a little bit thinner. The massive firs that had been the group's constant companions for days gave way to smaller, often stunted pines. Big game became far less plentiful, although large predators were still common. Clearly, there were enough rabbits, wild pigs, and big, flightless Doona to keep their population well fed.

Vykers wasn't concerned about predators—especially not in his current company. But he did enjoy a nice, big meal at the end of the day and meat, in particular, was essential. In that respect, he reflected, he wasn't so different from the Five. So, as long as the wolves, mountain lions and other, less savory predators didn't impinge upon his diet, Vykers wouldn't impinge upon their continued existence. He could eat wolf if he had to.

At midday, the group stopped at a mountain spring Arune had discovered a short distance from the trail. Vykers watched as each of the Five got on all fours and drank from the spring like animals. *All hells,* he thought, *why not?* He bent to do the same. About ten feet to his right, he heard one of the chimeras grunt, pensively.

"What is it?" Vykers asked.

Number 4 gestured to the water. "Flecks of gold."

The Reaper examined the spring bed beneath him. It was true. Countless gold particles ranging in size from almost imperceptible to pebble-sized spread throughout the stream. Vykers drank.

Aren't you going to collect any? Arune asked.

What for? I've got enough gold already in various banks and hidey-holes to buy my own kingdom.

You can never have too much gold. And this is ready-access. We may not see one of your banks for a long time.

Vykers hated it when she was right. He sighed. *Oh, very well,* he told her and bent down again to begin collecting the larger pieces.

"Shall we gather some, as well?" Number 3 asked.

"Sure," Vykers answer. "Couldn't hurt."

In an hour, the group had collected enough to fill a small pouch, about the size of a fist.

"Rich again." Vykers grinned, hefting the gold. He studied his surroundings, in case he ever wanted to return and investigate the gold's source further. Who could say? There might be a major vein nearby, enough to buy and sell the Virgin Queen herself.

"Is this unusual?" Number 17 asked.

Vykers laughed. "I've heard about this sort of thing before, but I've always been more of a warrior than a prospector, so I thought it was just bullshit. First time I've ever seen it like this."

Number 17 nodded, thoughtfully.

"The damned stuff comes in handy," Vykers continued. "I'll say that for it." The chimera wandered off to join his brothers, and the Reaper was left alone his thoughts. Just then, something occurred to him.

Burner? He asked.

Arune, she corrected.

Right, fine: Arune.

Yes?

You knew this gold was here all along.

Of course, Arune answered, matter-of-factly.

Don't play me, girl. You got something to say, say it.

We need every advantage we can get, no matter how small. A little detour for some water and *gold doesn't hurt anyone, does it?*

Vykers brooded a full half minute. *Maybe not. Still, you get any more ideas, run 'em by me next time.*

Consider me chastened, Arune replied.

Again, Vykers paused. *What do you do all day while I'm hiking and hunting and what not?*

Suddenly, Arune was coy. *What do you mean?*

It's pretty obvious what I do all day and night. Any fool can see what I'm up to. But you're hidden away up there. You're in my own skull, and I don't even know what you're doing most of the time. For Vykers, this amounted to a lengthy diatribe.

I watch, Arune replied. *I listen. I search our surroundings for any sort of threat.*

Threat? Vykers mocked. *We ain't come close to trouble. It's all I can do most days just to stay awake on the trail.*

You wouldn't feel that way if you knew the things I've saved you from.

You're playing me again, the Reaper growled, inwardly.

Really? Arune challenged, clearly annoyed. *There's a large raiding party about a day's travel west of here. There's a good chance we'll cross paths unless I divert them somehow or you change course.*

Vykers sat on a rock, pulled off his left boot and shook gravel out of it. *How big is this raiding party?*

More than two hundred.

Two hundred what?

Men. They're men.

Vykers pulled his boot back on over his invisible foot, then pulled the other off and shook it for good measure. *Might like to see that.*

I remember how you tested the Five. Are you planning the same for me? Are you going to do some damn-fool thing and see whether I'm able to save you or not?

Vykers nodded appreciatively. *So you can read my mind.*

And a pretty dull read it is, too, Arune complained.

So, how about it, Burn? You want to show me what you can really do? Vykers asked.

It'll be painful.

Isn't everything?

Have it your way, Arune responded. *Just don't forget I warned you.*

Vykers turned to the Five. "We're goin' hunting," he said.

All day and into the evening, Vykers felt an irritating prickling across and throughout his body—the Burner at work, he supposed.

The Five had brought down an enormous elk, but it was barely enough to feed them all and Vykers. The lucky part, from Vykers' perspective, was that his companions preferred the elk's innards, so he was always able to carve off a healthy-sized piece of flank before they moved on to the parts he enjoyed. Still, he was amazed at how much and how rapidly the chimeras ate. And given the volume of meat they took in, he shuddered to think how much they put out, while doing their private business off in the underbrush.

News? He asked Arune.

They're coming, she answered. *Two-hundred and forty-eight of them. They've got two Shapers and three A'Shea amongst their number.*

That worry you?

No.

No? That's it? No explanation? Vykers asked.

What's to say? I'm not worried about their magic. I do think we should talk with them before we start killing, though. Where I come from, information's more valuable than gold.

And we've got a shitload of gold now, anyway. Fine, we'll talk, Vykers replied. *When'll they reach us?*

Sometime after dawn. You can sleep in your usual shifts.

Dawn came and went, and the advance scouts of the approaching band had yet to find them. Vykers grew impatient.

I don't like this waiting shit, he told Arune.

And I thought you'd learned patience back in that cave we shared.

Now that I can walk and fight, I like to do it. This here's for old women and invalids.

They come, Arune replied.

Twelve men stepped out of the trees on the far side of the trail. In the quiet of this wilderness, it was enough to get Vykers' attention without any kind of hailing. He rose from his crouch slowly, and gestured "hold" to his comrades. Vykers knew a bit of Mountain Tongue, so he said, "Something we can help you boys with?"

A broad-chested fellow with an axe slung over his shoulder stepped forward. He was about Vykers' height and years, though his shoulder length hair was a good deal redder. His nose had been broken too many times to count and half his left cheek was caved in. When he spoke, his bearded jaw moved awkwardly to the left every once-in-a-while.

"We're not lookin' to fight," the man said. "Less we have to, in which case..." he trailed off.

"Not lookin' to fight," Vykers repeated. "What is it you want, then?"

The other warrior looked to his mates and then back at Vykers. "That's a broad question, ain't it? For starters, what in Tors Mima are those things you're travelling with?" he gestured to the Five.

"These are my brothers," Vykers said. "You sayin' they're not handsome lads?" He paused, "Cause I don't take kindly to folks mocking my brothers' looks."

The other man laughed.

"I'm still waiting to hear what you're aiming for." Vykers reminded him.

"If we don't have any trouble here, we're heading south to the Virgin Queen's realm."

Vykers raised an eyebrow. "Really? You planning to attack her, you twelve?"

The man raised his arm and more figures emerged from the trees. "Oh, we're a good deal more than twelve. More 'n twelve-times-twelve. A good number, no?"

Vykers shrugged.

"But no, we're not for fighting Her Majesty. We hear the Great War's a-coming, and we plan to take her side."

Arune was curiously silent. Vykers looked to the chimeras, who were likewise quiet. "What in the infinite hells for?" he demanded. "Way up here, you're likely out of the fracas."

"No, sir. We got cousins to the East who say otherwise. There's some sort of mad demon, wipes out every living thing in his path. They say a million or more have gone to it, already."

Vykers adjusted his gloves. "Sounds like the strong one, you ask me. Why not join up with him, instead?"

The other man bristled at this. "Are you mad? We got wives and children back home." He took a moment to compose himself, reassess. "Sides, they say the Reaper's joined up with the Queen, too."

"The Reaper? What's so great about him?"

The raider was astonished. "You been living in a cave, man?" he asked.

Why, yes, in fact, Arune thought.

It was all Vykers could do to keep from laughing. "I know of the Reaper," he said, "but he's just one man."

Several of the raiders guffawed at this. Their leader spoke. "One man? He's a force o' nature, is what he is. And a right bastard, too. A ruthless, brutal son-of-a-bitch who cares not one whit for this demon nor anyone else, I'll wager."

"Oh, he's all that, is he?" Vykers asked. "And I s'pose you'd say that to his face, would you?"

The man laughed heartily. "I ain't stupid, stranger."

"Then maybe you'll say it again to me, if ever we meet again?"

The sound of one hundred and forty eight men laughing echoed through the woods.

Well played, Arune said. *Shall I kill them all now?*

The Reaper—the Mahnus-cursed Reaper—stayed his hand.

Let's just get back on the trail, he grumbled.

"On your way, then, brave warrior!" the man across the trail yelled.

Vykers smirked at him and led his companions away.

You're not well, you know that? Arune asked.

The Reaper looked back one last time, to watch as the unnamed raiding party proceeded across the trail behind him and into the woods on the far side of the trail. They looked healthy and well-equipped. Good.

So? He responded.

You were actually planning to kill all those men!

So? He repeated.

They're men! They're people. They have lives, families...

Blah, blah, fucking blah. Yeah, I was planning to kill them. I was planning for us *to kill them. Why does that surprise you?*

I guess the joke's on you, then, huh? It'd be kind of foolish to kill your own troops.

And I didn't, which means I'm no fool. Now, how much farther to this Morden's Cairn?

You read the map.

I did. But I want you to do something other than annoy me.

A week, maybe.

A week? Dammit. I feel like everything's moving into position for the big dance with this End-of-All-Things, and I'm off in East Bumblefuck pickin' daisies.

Northwestern Bumblefuck, more like. But we're hardly picking daisies, and the Queen knows how to draw things out if she needs to buy us some time. The important thing is that we find this sword the Historian spoke of.

Vykers wasn't mollified. He felt drawn to this coming war like a lodestone to an iron shovel. He wondered if the End-of-All-Things even knew he was coming.

Deda, In Gabesh

Wims Deda came into Gabesh at the reins of a cheese monger's cart, the original owner of said cart having perished at Wims' hands earlier in the day. It wasn't that Wims disliked the man or had any particular objection to cheese, but his clothing and cart provided a plausible disguise for the warrior, and Wims always took what he needed. He thought, for a moment, of the men Anders had sent with him on this journey, all dead or gone now, butchered or chased away by the general. He didn't want allies, couldn't work with them. Better to have them out of his way and be done with it. The only thing that mattered to Anders, he was sure, was information. Wims would get it.

He studied the port town with a jaundiced eye. There was absolutely nothing—nothing!—remarkable about it, nothing of the slightest interest to anyone who had options elsewhere. This was the kind of backwater Wims was only too happy to see Anders eradicate, and he looked forward to seeing this one die, as well. When he finally made his way to what laughably passed as a market in Gabesh, he stationed his cart next to a chandler's and set about arranging his cheeses for sale, as he imagined the cheese maker might have done. Between customers—and they were few and far between—the idiot chandler attempted to befriend Wims and make conversation. This was, Wims reflected, the closest he'd come to torture since his long-ago incarceration in the Yellow Lands. Still, he had a role to play and information he needed to acquire, so Wims kept up the charade. Customers came and customers went; Wims sold seven cheeses, most of which he had to invent names for on the spot, since he'd never known them in the first place. "Ah, the DeBleck!" he heard himself proclaim, "Finest in the land! Favored by the Virgin Queen herself!" Or, "Hurry and buy the last of my special edition Blue Gnarsooge!" "This Rippling Dog's Pizzle has never been more flavorful." It didn't seem to matter what he called it, anyone inclined to buy cheese was going to buy it, any how. *Huh,* Wims thought, *this is almost like theft. Maybe I'll go into cheese making when I retire from mass murder.*

Over the course of the day, Wims heard enough gossip to piece together a reasonably accurate picture of events in the Queen's Realm. The big news, of course, was that she was mustering a host of her own, to counter or perhaps engage the End-of-All-Things. But there were also rumors of her having enlisted the services of someone called "The Reaper." Wims sat on the bench of his cheese cart and brooded. Years ago, he'd heard campfire stories about this so-called Reaper; they were more like fables and fantastic legends than anecdotes derived from personal experience. Wims had heard, for instance, that the man had once defeated an entire army by himself. Even six months ago, he might've laughed off such tales as absurd and impossible. But he'd seen the End-of-All-Things do that and more. Was it possible there were two such beings? And what would happen if they were to clash in battle? Would anything survive the meeting of the End-of-All-Things and the Reaper? Wims realized he'd been holding his breath for some time—perhaps even over a minute. He exhaled slowly and grinned a terrible frightened and frightening grin: he was going to have a front row seat. More than that, he might just find himself in a position to tilt the scales one way or the other.

Wims realized quite suddenly that his unsettling smile was scaring away potential customers, which only made his smile bigger and broader. Fucking peasants. Without even packing up his stores, Wims stalked off through the market and down a side alley. He'd played his role in Gabesh. It was time to move on and corroborate the rumors he'd heard in some other town, farther down the coast.

The End, In Camp

The child was developing a disturbing aspect, which was all to the good as far as the End-of-All-Things was concerned. Anders prodded him with a long, boney finger. The little boy didn't move a muscle, but watched his master with dark, dead eyes. *Dead eyes in an infant! Wonderful, wonderful!* Anders thought. *Truly, he will be my squire one day, my apprentice, or perhaps my next vessel.* He dipped his index finger into a nearby goblet of blood and then inserted the tip into the boy's mouth. The boy tasted it, curious, and then sucked it all off. The End-of-All-Things had no taste for blood, himself, but he knew the fearful power that blood-drinkers had over the weak-minded, so it was useful to have a few in his retinue at all times. Fear was a power greater than magic, fire or gold. Fear could raise great pyramids, and it could raze great pyramids, too. It was all at the discretion of the wielder.

In another part of his consciousness, Anders noted the approach of the boy's father, General Sherc.

"Yes?" he intoned, without looking up from the child.

"A local Baron and his leal knights approach our pickets, to challenge us," Shere reported, keeping his emotions at bay.

Anders turned and placed the boy in Shere's arms. "Is that so?" he asked, like a child responding to news that the circus had come to town. "Well, then, I think it is time to justify my legend. Must keep the host amused, after all, mustn't we?"

Shere always felt it best not to answer such questions; you never knew what Anders was after. He stared down at his son and saw nothing he recognized.

The End-of-All-Things lifted his sword from a nearby stand and left the tent. With a gesture, he summoned a boy who rushed off and returned with Anders' mount. The End-of-All-Things climbed into the saddle, put spurs to horse and rode out toward the pickets surrounding his host. Shere hadn't provided a direction, but it was laughably simple for Anders to sense it.

In ten minutes' time, he arrived within sight of the approaching knights. Well over two thousand of them. Fearlessly, almost carelessly, Anders continued to ride until he was within fifty or so strides of them. Each one had his weapons drawn; a number had crossbows trained on him. Anders didn't care. He jumped from his horse.

"And who leads this party of lemmings?" he sang out.

"Tis I," said a knight with particularly ornate armor. "Baron of Eemonfeld. We would know your intentions in our lands, End-of-All-Things."

Anders smiled. "My reputation precedes me," he beamed.

"It does," the knight replied, "And so I ask again, what would you?"

"Why," Anders chuckled, "I'm planning to kill you all! What else?"

"A lone wizard against the pride of Eemonfeld? That won't come cheap," the Baron answered.

Anders howled. "They all say that, little man! They all say that." He continued walking towards his opponents.

"Be warned, we've got Shapers of our own, tyrant!"

The End-of-All-Things waved an arm and several heads exploded within the Baron's company, accompanied by brief but, Anders felt, satisfying gasps of dismay. "*Had* Shapers, dead man, *had* Shapers."

Crossbow bolts flew and the knights charged. Anders said a word and the bolts disintegrated in mid-flight. He allowed the men to continue their approach. "Too many choices, too many choices," he said to himself, before drawing his sword and swinging it in a wide arc before him. The Baron's men began sweeping past on either side, in attempt to flank and surround him. An uncooperative bolt did find Anders' armor, only to disappear into it, as if it had been shot into a lake. There was a subsequent crackling of energies across Anders' torso and then everything returned to its previous state. The End-of-All-Things waited another moment to allow the knights to complete their circuit, then stabbed his sword into the ground at his feet, yelling a single, unintelligible syllable as he did. Immediately, the earth heaved and shook in great ripples, extending outward from Anders' sword. Knights were thrown from horses, others tumbled over, many simply stopped in their tracks. Hard on the heels of this action, Anders sent a sea of fire surging outward in all directions, raging through and over the knights, their horses and anything else in its path. He was sure the screams of men and beasts could be heard for some distance. Still, men battled through the inferno and drew closer. The End-of-All-Things was as impressed as it was possible for a man to be with an ant's feats of strength. But he was glad there were survivors, because he adored a little-hand-to-hand work.

To one determined fellow who stumbled up to him, heaving like an overworked ox, Anders said "Strong but stupid" and beheaded him in an instant. Three more men approached, crawling, limping, dragging themselves towards him. All had weapons raised. Anders allowed the first man to swing his axe, more out of curiosity than chivalry. It was a simple matter, however, to parry the blow and turn it forever aside. The poor man's momentum spun him completely around, and Anders reached out with the tip of his sword and almost gently touched the naked flesh of the knight's neck. That was enough to kill him, eventually. First, he ran off, howling, overcome with more mental and physical anguish than mortals were meant to bear. Inevitably, he would take his own life or, if not, wither, like last year's apples. It mattered not to Anders, as he always enjoyed either outcome. He also liked watching the first victim's effect on his former fellows-in-arms. The two men closest him stepped back and lowered their swords, struggling with fears and doubts.

"Damn you, tyrant!" a hoarse voice bellowed from the now smoking, seething mass of ruined horse and human flesh.

Anders didn't have time to play with these closest victims, so he exploded their heads, as well. He knew countless less gory ways to dispatch his opponents, but he favored the bloodier, more violent means for their shock value; more often than not, they stunned standers-by into permanent confusion and havoc. Anyway, he wanted to focus on the Baron, whose head, he knew, would make an excellent trophy.

"Rather stupid of you," he called to the man, "wasting all these loyal men in so pointless a manner."

"Not stupid," the Baron croaked, as he staggered into view, burnt and bleeding. "It was said that you annihilate without compunction, but many of my fellows refused to believe it." He turned his head ever-so-slightly to some nearby hills. "They've seen it now, though. They've no choice but believe."

Sending out a Questing Eye in that direction, Anders could indeed make out thousands more men watching the conflict from a safe distance. Interesting: he had thought them overconfident and under experienced pageant knights. Instead, they'd been bait, meant to tempt the End-of-All-Things into demonstrating his true powers and nature.

"It's naught to me," Anders assured the Baron. "I did all this alone, in the span of ten heartbeats. Imagine what I can do with my host by my side."

"I'll brook no more of your boasting!" the Baron spat and surged into striking distance.

This one, Anders thought, *I will enjoy playing with.*

The Baron came at him with long sword in his right hand and small axe in his left. His helm was gone, and his beard had been burnt to a shapeless mass. He needed neither, though, since he expected to die in this final fight. Awkwardly, he swept across Anders' midriff with his sword, while simultaneously aiming for the End-of-All-Things' head with his axe. It was a clumsy move, but a bold one, too. As Anders stepped back out of range, the Baron backhanded both weapons in a scissoring motion, which Anders smashed aside with his own sword.

"What's the matter, wizard? Out of spells?" the Baron snarled.

In this moment, Anders could almost respect his adversary's contempt for death. The man had no hope of winning, but he continued to press the issue as if he had. "I don't like to exert myself in that way for a single enemy. Besides," Anders said, "sometimes it's more fulfilling to ram a sword through a man's heart."

"I couldn't agree more!" the Baron yelled, lunging at Anders' chest with his long sword.

The End-of-All-Things parried the blow and spun to his left, adjusted his grip and swung at his foe's right knee. Anders, himself, had not seen more than a hundred such encounters, but his sword had experienced infinitely more, and it urged him to duck, just before the Baron's axe came whiffling overhead. Somehow the man blocked Anders' sword and stepped back, resetting his stance and switching his weapons from left hand to right, and visa versa.

Anders became aware that other survivors were staggering forward to form a rough circle around the two combatants. He might have to do this more quickly than he'd wanted.

The Baron came at him again, a whirling tornado of sharpened steel. It was all Anders could do to keep the man off him. He parried, he feinted, he dodged, he counter-attacked, but the knight would not be shaken off. Impossibly, Anders tripped and stumbled while moving backwards and the survivors laughed. Even the Baron paused a moment to grin at him. The End-of-All-Things had never been laughed at, never been so humiliated. He sent out another blast of fire that quickly silenced the survivors and dropped the Baron to his knees. Anders drew near the man, who appeared scorched into paralysis. Smoke and steam rose from the fellow's blackened scalp and armor. Only his eyes moved, following Anders' every move.

Anders took his time. "Your laughter has doomed your little band of witnesses in yonder hills. No one laughs at the End-of-All-Things. NO ONE!" he roared.

The Baron seemed to be trying to say something, but his lips were gone.

The End-of-All-Things considered his sword for a moment, then sheathed it. He reached out and put his hand atop the Baron's raw scalp. "Ah!" he said, his eyes closed, "you have a wife and three young children!" Anders cooed. "I will, of course, torture them to death. Slowly, so, so slowly. They will…what is it I want to say…? *Marinate* in their agony." This was much better than taking the man's head for a trophy.

Anders turned to leave and realized he had inadvertently killed his own horse, as well. He looked back at the Baron and sighed, as if to say "What's to be done?" and slowly lifted into the air. At last, he winked at the dying man and flew into the sky.

The Baron of Eemonfeld felt no pain. No physical pain, anyway. His eyes brimmed with tears as he thought of his family and waited to die.

Mocked because of a pebble. Anders still seethed when he thought about it, and even the destruction of the witnessing army in the hills, as well as the capture and torture of the Baron's family didn't alleviate his fury. He refused to consider any fault on his own part; a being of inestimable power ought to be able to engage a fantastically inferior foe without mishap. If he could pulverize every pebble from here to far N'Dare, he'd—

A voice tickled at his ears. That could only be Wims, using the Scaldean head to communicate, as ordered. Anders retrieved its twin from its hawthorn-wood chest and set it on his work table. The thing had once been the actual head of a Scaldean priest, years before Anders was born. The End-of-All-Things claimed it, along with its mate, after sacking a temple to the south east.

"Speak to me," he commanded.

"Lord?" Wims' voice asked from desiccated lips.

"Don't try my patience, Wims. I have none to spare today. Of course it's me."

"Yes, my lord."

"What have you learned?"

"As you suspected, the Virgin Queen is mustering her troops."

"I'll need to know more about her, Wims. What other news?"

"They say her army will be led by a man named Tarmun Vykers. Men call him 'the Reaper'."

Anders paused. "The Reaper. I like that. It's...eloquent."

Wims spoke again. "I mean no disrespect, my Lord. No one alive can best in you battle. But this Reaper is...a legend. He is also called Scourge of Empires."

"Tarmun Vykers, the Reaper," Anders repeated, almost to himself. The Questing Ear worked much better when it had something specific to listen for. And he was almost excited to learn more of this Reaper.

"My Lord?"

"Continue on to the Capital as planned and infiltrate the Queen's inner circle," the End-of-All-Things instructed. Which was impossible, he suspected, but it would undoubtedly test his servant's abilities and loyalty. When and if Wims returned, he would at last have earned his master's trust.

"As you command, my lord," Wims' voice responded, before the mummified head went silent. Anders considered it for a moment. He could send out a pair of Questing Ears now, one from himself and another from Wims' Scaldean head. If anyone had anything to say of this Reaper, Anders would hear of it.

Vykers, On the Trail

So, tell me, Arune began, *is this story of you defeating two hundred and fifty men single-handed an utter fable, or merely an exaggeration?*

What do you think? You're the one poking around in my thoughts.

It's like a labyrinth in here, Arune lamented. *Too many doors, too many dead ends. And you're getting better at obstructing me.*

Vykers broke open the bone he'd been gnawing on with a rock and sucked at the marrow. *Why do I feel like you're lying?*

Arune groaned. *Fine, I'm lying. Happy? I simply asked you about the two hundred and—*

It's true, as far as it goes.

As far as it goes...?

I was carving 'em up pretty good and, at some point, the rest just thought 'fuck it' and took off. They fired off a few half-hearted shots from their crossbows once they got outta range and that's the last I ever saw of 'em.

So...how many did *you kill, then?*

I dunno. Five, six score.

A hundred and twenty? You ARE the Reaper, Arune said, impressed.

Huh, Vykers shrugged indifferently, as he threw the remains of his meal into the fire.

Still, it sounds like this End-of-All-Things character destroys entire civilizations.

And that's why he's got to die. Besides, what's left for me if he wrecks the whole world?

Good old Vykers: a moment of selflessness, followed by absolute selfishness.

What else is there but ourselves?

Philosophy, Vykers?

The Reaper stood. *I gotta piss,* he thought and wandered into the underbrush.

SIX

Vykers, At Morden's Cairn

In fairytales, the land always grew dead around the haunted places, as if the spirits of the underworld bore malicious intent against rabbits, mice and shrubbery. As the party drew nearer Morden's Cairn, however, Vykers could see this wasn't the case. The hills, forests, marshes and streams all seemed perfectly normal, if admittedly less welcoming. And what did that mean, exactly? The Reaper couldn't say, except that he wouldn't feel comfortable sleeping in the open without a fire and someone to stand guard. Even the Five were acting a little skittish, or as skittish as they ever acted, anyway.

"What's up?" he asked Number 3.

"There's an...odor here."

That's centuries of dead, Arune offered.

"That's centuries of dead," Vykers said.

Nice.

What do you want, credit? You want me to tell my little pack of monsters that the ghost in my head is giving me directions?

Point taken.

"I thought so," said Number 3. "How do we proceed?"

"Well, a cairn is a...uh...big heap 'o stones."

"Yes, I was aware."

Sometimes, Vykers wanted to haul off and belt one of the chimeras right in the snout. They were, by turns, sycophantic and condescending, and Vykers couldn't tell if that was due to their strange origins or their lack of exposure to and experience with 'normal' people.

"Right," he finally said. "So, that's what we're looking for."

It's centuries old, at least, Arune said. *What if this hill we're on is the cairn?*

Be a hell of a big cairn.

Might be a metaphorical cairn.

A what?

I still think it's this hill.

"Could be this whole hill we're on," Vykers said to the Five.

"In which case," Number 17 said, "we just need to find an entrance."

"Right," Vykers said again. Long as they took his orders, he guessed he didn't much care about decorum and all that. He looked around and ahead. It was an enormous hill. Was it even possible that it was also a cairn, or had been at one time? He continued walking.

After some time, Number 3 said "Menhirs."

Vykers just looked at him.

"Standing stones," the chimera clarified. "In the distance."

Vykers didn't see them, but he'd learned to trust the Five's senses. "How far?"

"A quarter hour, perhaps."

Damn big hill. "Alright, then. Let's see what we see."

Ten minutes later, Vykers could see the stones for himself, arranged in some sort of pattern, with a few even stacked atop one another. "That looks promising."

Arune teased him, *Promising*?

Vykers didn't respond. He wasn't in the mood for banter at the moment.

Five minutes out, he stopped and surveyed the area for potential threats. Seeing none, he nodded to his companions and resumed his approach. The stones were definitely placed in a great, triangular configuration, framing a gaping hole in the earth. Less obvious in purpose were several outlying stones that had fallen or been placed in various positions and distances from the triangle.

"Reminds me of home," Number 12 said.

Vykers had no idea if he was joking or not. He looked at the chimeras. "What kind o' sense are you boys getting about that place? Are we walking into an ambush?" he asked. And then, to Arune: *Any magic we need to know about?*

*Gods! Magic? Plenty of it. None recent. Some of it...*Arune trailed off.

Yes? Vykers prompted impatiently.

When Arune spoke again, her voice was almost a whisper in his head. *Some of it goes back farther than the Awakening. Some of it...is of a type I've never seen before.*

"Great," the Reaper muttered, aloud. *Is there any immediate danger?* He clarified.

I don't think so.

Vykers about shit himself. *You don't think so?*

Do you know everything?

What in all hells has that gotta do with anything?

Do you know everything?

No.

Right. And neither do I, Arune scolded.

Number 17 spoke up. "If you're uncomfortable going in, I can enter and tell you what I find."

Leaders lead. "I'm going in," Vykers responded, a little too brusquely. "You wait here."

Number 17 bowed his head ever-so-slightly and stepped back amongst his companions.

Vykers looked up. The day was overcast, but rain didn't seem likely. There was still a bit of frost in the shadows, too. On one side—the north side—the menhirs were mottled with lichen and moss. Facing the hole, however, they were bare and dry, revealing a faint blackening here and there that told of exposure to fire at some point. The mouth of the hole looked to have been burnt, as well. *Well,* the Reaper told himself, *now or never,* and he climbed down into the hole.

Long, On the Trail

They had been riding for a day and a half and seen no sign

of the enemy's scouts. In many ways, though, Long reflected, searching was better than finding. Finding meant possible battle; battle meant potential casualties, even death. Death did not sound appealing. He thought of his dearest friend, Short Pete, fading away in a puddle of his own blood on the cold ground of that unremarkable campsite in the middle of nowhere. He wondered what Short would make of their latest predicament. Probably, he'd be delighted, in his element. Crazy son-of-a-whore. Crazy dead son-of-a-whore. Spirk started singing again and brought Long back to the present.

"Nessno!" he spat in an urgent whisper. "How many times I gotta tell you not to sing, you Mahnus-be-damned idiot? You're makin' a target of us!"

Long could tell by their eyes that the rest of his squad were in complete agreement. Spirk's mouth clapped shut abruptly.

"Sorry, Sarge," Spirk said, for the twentieth time that day, at least.

"Listen to me, boy, and listen good," Long said, pulling his horse alongside the younger man's. "Next time, I'm gaggin' you, and you'll stay that way, except for meals. Do you understand me?"

"Yes, sir."

Long growled, "Not good enough. Say 'I understand you'll gag me if I sing one more time.'"

Spirk glanced around and saw that everyone was staring at him. "I understand you'll gag me if I sing one more time," he repeated.

Long slapped him on the back and rode back into position. Things were not going to end well for the boy, Long told himself. It was a mantra he'd been repeating with increasing frequency the closer the squad got to actual combat. The kid was as sharp as polished river rock and possessed absolutely no martial skills whatsoever. To make matters worse, he appeared to have no talents of any other kind, either. Oh, Janks had assured him the boy's blandness was some sort of talent, but so far Long hadn't seen it. Quite the contrary, he'd—

Up ahead, one of the twins motioned the squad to stop. He jumped down from his horse and examined something in the dirt. Long dismounted more carefully and walked over to his point man. He didn't see anything on the ground.

"What've you got?" Long asked.

The man held something small and round between his fingers. "Button," he said.

Long whistled, quietly. A button? The man had spotted a button in the grass? That was impressive. Long gestured for the rest of the squad to stay put, stay mounted, while his point man looked for more signs of their elusive prey. After a while, the man wordlessly showed Long places where taller grass had been broken or shorter grass had been trampled. There were even a few impressions in the hard earth that might have been hoof prints.

"So, what do you think?" Long asked the twin.

"What it looks like: scouting party. Three or four riders."

"What kind of scout wears buttons?"

"Well, Sergeant," the man said, "they do say the enemy's host is made up of all kinds, with a lot of civvies pressed into service."

Long sucked his teeth, thinking. "Any idea which way they went or how long ago?"

"Looks like west, to me," the man replied. "Sometime today, too."

"And this isn't a trap of some kind? Trying to bait us into following?"

"There's ways around that."

"Of course," Long said and walked back toward the rest of the squad. "Listen up. Here's what we're gonna do," he said, keeping his voice low. "We'll split into two smaller groups. Spirk, D'Kem, Bash, my twin and I will follow along to the north of these signs. The rest of you do the same with Janks to the south. Sundown, we'll try to meet back up in the middle, if nothing else happens. It's important we camp together."

Left unsaid was the fact Long had assigned Mardine to Janks' group, while taking the biggest liability, Spirk, into his own. Long felt awkward, never having mastered the twins' names. It just hadn't been long enough, he told himself, but that was no excuse. For identical twins, they really looked quite different from one another. It was easy to tell them apart. Still, Long had taken to calling them "you two," "the both of you," or "you and you." When they were separate, as now, he called one "my twin" and the other "Janks' twin." Wasn't a good way to earn the twins' respect, but he figured that would have to wait. He'd given Janks the A'Shea—mostly to ensure Mardine wasn't killed—and he'd have to be satisfied with the old Shaper.

Mardine stared him down as she filed past with the rest of her team, but Long pretended his crossbow needed sudden inspection. He knew she wasn't happy, but he couldn't be seen to be coddling her, not if he wanted the others to follow him anywhere. Finally, Janks' group split off to the left with Janks' twin in front. Long's twin led the sergeant's group north, and he followed. Worst came to worst, the two groups would only be a few hundred paces apart, with the twins ranging back and forth between them.

It was truly a weird fire, warm as usual, but completely subdued in brightness. It simply did not shed light outside the small pit in which it sat.

"Campaigner's Fire,' we called it back when." D'Kem explained. "It's meant to give off all the heat, but not attract attention from unwelcome eyes."

"I ain't seen Campaigner's Fire since..." Janks scratched the crown of his head, "forever, really. Must've been a boy, then."

"It's a nifty little spell," D'Kem said, pleased with himself.

"Do you think you could teach me?" Spirk asked with his typical enthusiasm. "I love magic! I'd be a great magician. My ma always said..."

"Magic's not to be trifled with!" the A'Shea said.

Bash snorted; he didn't have much respect for those who used magic and even less for those who used it while warning others not to do so.

"I don't wanna trifle with it," Spirk complained. "I want to...explode...evil and summon demon kings to do my bidding!"

"Hush, you fool boy!" the A'Shea cried out. "Alheria forgive and protect you!"

"What? Why?" Spirk sputtered. "I'd be a great magician! Better than Pellas, even."

"Better 'n Pellas, is it?" Janks echoed. "That's some tall talk, Nessno. If the stories be true, Pellas was the greatest of 'em all."

Long could see where all this was leading from a mile away, but it broke the predictable fireside routine of overblown legends about the Reaper or frightened musings about the End-of-All-Things, so he was content to sit and listen. Besides, unlike the other two men, Pellas was not rumored to have been a heartless, amoral bastard, but was rather a true and noble hero. And the story of his death was one of the most heart-breaking tales ever told. Long hoped Janks wasn't heading down that road.

"The High Wizard Pellas was the finest example of a man you could hope to find." Janks began.

Long heard a rustling off to his left, and turned in time to see D'Kem fumbling his flask out of hiding, take a long pull and secure it back within his robes. For an instant, the two men exchanged glances, and then Janks was talking again. It was clear he had the squad's attention and assent to continue.

"He was born a slave, so they say, in the Southern Kingdoms and was trained from birth to be tutor to the children o' the wealthy or of royal heritage. But he quickly outstripped his own tutors, so he was sent to study under the Emperor's own Shapers, the wisest and most knowledgeable men in the land. In the Emperor's court, though, Pellas was troubled by the difference between the way slaves were treated and the nobility were treated. The more he thought on it, the more…"

The sound of snoring interrupted Janks' narrative, and everyone turned to see D'Kem leaning against Mardine, fast asleep. One of the twins reached over and gave him a good poke. D'Kem woke, flustered and disoriented.

"We're talkin' about the greatest of your order," Janks scolded. "You'd think you'd have some respect."

D'Kem stood, inadvertently (perhaps) broke wind and wandered off toward his sleeping kit.

Bash chuckled under his breath.

Janks sighed in exasperation. "Some people just ain't worthy," he lamented.

"What happened next?" Spirk asked eagerly.

"Well," Janks continued, "as I was sayin', Pellas was real bothered-like by this unfairness he saw, so he bided his time and he studied. Oh, how he studied. Pellas read books and scrolls and tablets and the like that few if any even knew existed. He learned the locations of magic…things…"

"Artifacts," Long put in.

"Right, right: artifacts. And he learned spells no one had used or even attempted since the Awakening. Pellas thought and thought and planned and planned. Then, when the day came for his final testing, he cast a spell turned the Emperor, his family and all his Shapers into glass."

"I heard it was gold!" Spirk protested.

"It was glass," Janks countered.

"No, no. It was gold, 'cause Pellas wanted to say if the Emperor was worth so much more than his slaves, he oughta at least look like it."

"That's a nice twist, boy, but it was glass. He meant to show 'em all how fragile life is." Janks insisted.

"He turned the Emperor's whole family and all his Shapers into glass?" one of the twins asked.

"So they say."

"What happened to the Emperor then?" the other twin asked.

"Ah!" Janks laughed, "the soldiers and slaves joined in smashing the Emperor and his family. I heard a story a while back that his daughter still exists in glass in some rich merchant's bedroom in Cabrede, but it's prob'ly just that, a story."

"The soldiers and slaves joined together, did they? Now that's what I call a fairy story," Bash interjected.

"You miss the point, Bash. Pellas toppled a tyrant and his closest mates and freed them as couldn't free themselves. Most o' the time, when you hear a tale of some great person, he's out for himself and none other. Just look at Vykers, as a for instance."

Long was enjoying this break from Vykers, so he quickly cut in to insure the group stayed on Pellas. "I remember a tale of Pellas," he announced rather loudly. Because Long didn't tell many tales, the chattering stopped and everyone looked his way. "Understand, the tales of great ones are all inevitably filled with loss and betrayal. There's nary a legendary man or woman who didn't lose the love of his life in some cruel way or another. Pellas, though, Pellas was forced to murder his own true love." Long glanced around the circle, the faces of his companions barely visible in the non-glow of the Campaigner's Fire. "Imagine that," he challenged the group.

"They say Pellas eventually ended up in the service of the Virgin Queen's grandfather, Harduc the Second, working alongside his other Shapers to secure a lasting peace between the various smaller kingdoms, fiefdoms, and city-states throughout the middle lands. And it was in this service that he met and fell in love with fellow Shaper, Maille. Now, on the surface, Pellas and Maille had little in common; he'd been born into slavery and she was the daughter of a wealthy noble. In fact, story is, they hated each other at first. You know how it goes: he thinks she's an over-privileged princess and she thinks he's an arrogant prick, that sort of thing. Anyway, over the years, of course, they fall for each other, and Pellas is happier than he's ever been. They go through a lot together—wars, natural disasters, political shit. Then, one day, his Highness asks them to go battle some sort of demon in one of the outlying provinces. The King tells them this demon has defeated every other attempt to destroy it and is now ravaging the countryside, threatening to cause mass panic in the King's subjects. So, Pellas, Maille and a large force of stout knights head off to kill the demon, who turns out to be the biggest, ugliest, nastiest fucker anybody's ever seen or even heard of. The battle lasts for days and days. Some say a fortnight, some say a month. Point is, it went on and on, taking a terrible toll on Pellas and Maille, to say nothing of their knights. Finally, Pellas had the thing on its knees, its life-forces rapidly ebbing away, when it unexpectedly took possession of Maille."

"What's that mean?" Spirk asked.

"It means he abandoned his own body and got inside her somehow. Pellas was devastated. He couldn't stand to lose Maille—or even the image of her—but he couldn't afford to let the demon go on living inside Maille, with access to all her additional knowledge, abilities and memories. They say Pellas incinerated her, and they say you could see the pillar of fire over half a world away. The demon inside her screamed horribly, but they say Pellas' cry of despair was heard the whole world over."

Long finished and the squad lapsed into silence, some thinking on how they'd loved and lost, others regretting the fact they'd never known love in the first place. The sergeant was unable to meet Mardine's eye, but he could feel it on him nonetheless. He was no Pellas, to be sure, and she was certainly no Maille. And yet...he stood, walked over to the giantess, and took her hand. Nobody smirked or raised so much as an eyebrow.

From all appearances, D'Kem had returned to his old ways, army-be-damned. Although everyone else was already packed and ready to resume the chase, D'Kem hadn't emerged from his tent. Long figured he was either dead at last or sleeping off more of his drink. When the sergeant finally poked his head into the Shaper's tent, he found the latter was true: D'Kem lay in a heap, snoring loudly and drooling continuously. Fed up, he grabbed the older man's feet and dragged him out into the morning air. D'Kem scarcely stirred, but Long did spy the man's treasured flask lying just inside the tent, half-covered by a ratty old blanket. How could such a limited quantity of liquor consistently leave the Shaper so smashed? Long unstopped the flask and took a tentative sniff. Whatever it was smelled bitter and vaguely metallic, but nothing like liquor. Bemused, he held the flask to his lips and began tilting it back.

"Don't..." D'Kem groaned, eyeing the sergeant with one bloodshot eye.

Which only made Long more certain than ever that he absolutely should, in order to get to the bottom of the Shaper's behavior. Without another thought, he upended the flask and took in a mouthful of the stuff. Before he could get a proper sense of its taste, his mouth went numb and he swallowed—or thought he did. He felt an odd, overpowering weightlessness overtake him moments before he collapsed. *Am I dying?* He wondered. And then he thought no more.

There was something massive on his forehead—Mardine's hand. Slowly, details of his surroundings and situation became clearer to him. He took a deep breath and smiled, sheepishly, up at the giantess, who frowned most mightily back at him.

"What kind of idiot drinks from an unfamiliar bottle?" she rumbled.

"I reckon I'm the answer to that one," Long answered. He'd expected to feel hung over. Instead, he simply felt as if he were "filling in," as he thought of it. Mardine tried to hold him down, but he gently if firmly brushed her hand away and sat up. "Well?" he asked Mardine. "Obviously, I scotched our chance to continue our pursuit..."

"No," Mardine replied. "Janks took his half, plus the other twin in my stead."

"That doesn't make any sense!" Long complained. "How are we supposed to find them?"

"We'll find them," said a voice behind the sergeant. So, D'Kem was alive.

Long turned to him. "So, you're not a drunk, after all. You're just some kind of addict."

"And you are lucky to be alive," the man replied. "How much did you ingest?"

"You mean swallow? I don't know. A mouthful, maybe."

"A mouthful," D'Kem repeated. "Beggin' your pardon, Sergeant, but that was the stupidest thing I've ever seen."

"So I've been told," Long answered, glancing over at Mardine. "Anyway," he continued, looking back at the Shaper, "what are you doing with the stuff if it's so dangerous?"

"Trust me in this one thing, Sergeant," D'Kem intoned, "you wouldn't want to know me without it."

"I'm not sure I want to know you now."

D'Kem regarded him with a stare a thousand years old, devoid of emotion but fraught with mysteries Long could never hope to decipher.

"So," he said aloud to no one in particular, "who have we got here in camp?"

Predictably, it was Spirk who answered. "You got me, Mardine, D'Kem and yourself, sergeant, sir."

Long looked at Mardine. "You know you're in Janks' half," he scolded as gently as possible.

"And I wanted to stay with you, in case..." Her eyes finished the sentence: in case he died.

"Well, we've lost the day, then," Long said.

"Three," Mardine corrected.

Long was poleaxed. "Three? I've been out for three days?" And then he was hit by an even more disturbing realization. "And Janks hasn't been back?" Long sank back onto the ground. "Damn me," he said.

And then the war party showed up.

Aoife, In the Forest

The abandoned little farmhouse in which Aoife had given birth had, itself, given birth to a burgeoning forest. Enormous trees sprouted from its foundations and fantastic waterfalls from its windows. Aoife scarcely recognized the place and found it even more difficult to recognize her children. Some, it was true, had stayed minuscule; most, though, had become gigantic in stature. The forest trolls were all but as tall as trees themselves. She loved them all—or wanted to believe she did—but she felt most comfortable with those closest her size and shape. It was these she sought out when it was time to go.

"You leave?" the satyr looked up as she approached.

"I do. I feel...I must, now."

"Yes, yes. More to do. More to be done," the satyr chortled. "Mother-Sister must go...create."

"Er...yes," Aoife replied, uncertain how to continue. "I'm just not sure..."

The satyr winked. "Your brother is now west of us. Find him. Surround him. This," the satyr said, "is the easternmost oasis. Now, go make the others."

"More?" Aoife ventured.

"Indeed."

The A'Shea was stupefied. She could not imagine going

through this experience, however magical, an untold number of times. And her feelings must have shown on her face, because the next thing the satyr told her was "You must." Aoife bowed her head in resignation; then, a new idea occurred to her. "You believe Anders can wait, then?"

"He will have challenges of his own," the satyr assured her.

Aoife regarded him, quizzically.

"The forest has been and would be forever. The old gods tell me what is like to be, and I tell you. If you listen, you will hear them without my help."

Aoife closed her eyes, concentrated, heard nothing.

"Then I will accompany you," the satyr said.

"Is that…wise? You can hardly be mistaken for…" But even as Aoife spoke, the satyr's appearance changed, until he looked credibly manlike. "I should have guessed," the A'Shea said.

The satyr-man smiled. "Your forest and children will supply you with a few things for the journey, and then we set out."

Always traveling, Aoife thought, *never staying*.

By mid-afternoon, Aoife and her companion had walked an impossibly long way, during which time she learned a great many things, including her escort's name, Too-Mai-Ten-La, or Toomt'-La for short. The A'Shea discovered, as well, that if she sat anywhere—a stone, say—for more than few moments, moss began to sprout and grass to take root.

"You are seeding the Great Forest anew," Toomt'-La told her.

"Yes, but…on a stone?"

"A stone, a fallen log, a sandpit. The Great Forest cares not."

The one advantage to this situation was that even if Aoife was not comfortable when she sat or lay down, she was invariably made comfortable by the growth beneath and around her.

"This won't happen indoors, will it?" she asked Toomt'-La.

"Indoors?" he laughed. "Now you're being silly."

Oh, okay. *Now*, she was being *silly*. It was good to know this greening magic had boundaries and limitations. She hated to think she might be holding a sick person someday, only to see him sprout leaves and blossoms. Something else had been on her mind, as well, and so Aoife said, "What does magic mean to you? How do you...perceive it?"

"Magic?" Toomt'-La repeated, thoughtfully. "That is a good question, Mother-Sister. You humans encounter it much differently than we fey folk, that is true."

"For instance?" Aoife prompted.

"Your Shapers—ah, poorly named!—consume it in order to channel it. You A'Shea do, too, but to a much lesser degree. Your Shapers burn the wood of the tree to fuel their efforts. You A'Shea burn the leaves. We fey consume the energies given off by the tree and its leaves. Do you see? Humans destroy the thing they most desire; we live off its beauty."

"But Shapers are so powerful!" Aoife observed.

"You call it power? They cannot heal," Toomt'-La paused. "They can only destroy."

"But they shape! They build!"

"Only by first destroying. And this is all-the-more reason to eliminate your brother."

Aoife jumped at the mention of her brother. "And this is yet another thing I do not understand: how was Anders able to raze the Forest of Nar in the first place? Can his power truly be so great?"

Toomt'-La grimaced. "Yes, his power is great. Perhaps unparalleled amongst your kind—but no, that is not accurate, either, since he is not truly of your kind anymore."

"Not of my kind?"

Toomt'-La exhaled deeply. "One question, then the next." He leaned back against the bole of a massive oak. "Your brother is strong, but we were...half-asleep, over-confident, complacent? All of these. By the time we realized the threat he presented, we had sustained too much damage. Ironically, his actions may result in the regreening of the world."

"Because I'm spreading the forest?"

"Just so. As to your second question, your brother was once as you are. You know this. Something entered and changed him. You know this, too. This something is very old, though not as old as my people."

"And what is this old thing?"

The satyr laughed. "Much I know, but I do not know that."

He stood and stretched. "We may well find out, though, before all is said and done. Come, let's continue on our way."

Aoife rose less enthusiastically. More walking.

The End, In Camp

He felt an unfamiliar thrill that have might been, what, anxiety? Doubt? Fear? Impossible. Sitting on a makeshift throne inside his tent, the End-of-All-Things listened to each and every tale of this Reaper that he could find. His face wore a pinched expression indicative of intense concentration. He had to learn the truth of this adversary. How was it possible that one man, without an army at his back or any sorcery at his disposal, could eradicate an entire city in his rage? Why had no one ever slain him with an arrow or even poison, for that matter? Here was another tale of this Vykers engaging an army by himself. This story was widely circulated and varied so little from village-to-village and town-to-town that it had the inescapable air of truth about it. One man against an army? Anders caressed the hilt of his sword. With his magic, his sword and Vykers' martial prowess, he could crush the whole world like an egg. Alas, things were rarely so easy, and he suspected he'd have to exterminate the Reaper. He sensed Shere in his peripheral vision.

"Yes?" he intoned.

"Forgive the interruption, my lord, but the latest group of recruits is ready for their induction."

Anders opened his eyes. "And how many, this time?"

"Nearly five hundred."

"Nearly?"

"Four hundred, eighty-two, and it please you."

"It does not please me. When I ask for a number, I want an *exact* number the first time I ask." Arcane energies burst into life on his fingertips, and his general quailed ever-so-slightly at the sight. "You cannot imagine what I will do to you if you fail or betray me."

"No, my lord," Shere responded, all humility and obedience.

"Let us go, then" Anders said.

Outside, several soldiers patrolled around the perimeter of a large, roped-in circle, inside of which were the aforementioned four hundred and eight-two "recruits."

The End-of-All-Things addressed a nearby officer. "Soldier," he called out, "tell me of this latest collection. All peasants again, are they?"

"No, my lord," the man replied, frightened to his marrow to have been addressed by Anders at all. "Some there be, that's certain. But there be craftsmen and local militia 'mongst the mob, too."

Anders nodded. "As you were, then," he told the man. To Shere he said, "Let us proceed."

On one side of the circle, there was a small gate of sorts, manned by four guards—two on either side of the rope. One at a time, another group of guards forced the captives to approach the End-of-All-Things, who reached into a nearby chest, retrieved an odd nutlike object and fed it to each in turn. At sword point, none resisted, though many had a look in their eyes that said they would if they could. As nothing dramatic happened immediately after swallowing these nuts, the mood in the roped-in enclosure remained reasonably calm. And because the nuts' magic only took effect during sleep, most of those in the pen would never see what was coming.

By morning, any who had slept would be little more than automatons; those who resisted sleep would fail, eventually. And once they succumbed, they would act with absolute obedience to their master, the End-of-All-Things. They would march endlessly, fight tirelessly, ignoring hunger, thirst or pain for as long as their bodies would sustain them. It was a dark marvel, really, to field such a force, a force that knew nothing of fear or fatigue. On this particular evening, Anders' host numbered well over a hundred thousand such soldiers. Tomorrow, it would have four hundred and eighty-two more.

Once again, Anders sat on his (latest) charger, on a ridge overlooking his host. This was a ritual he dearly loved, the testing of his power over his automatons. They faced him in perfect rows and columns, stretching almost out of sight to the East, West and South. The End-of-All-Things didn't believe there were so many stars in the sky. If there were, he would snuff them out, too, given time.

Anders raised his hands over his head and said "kneel." No one could have heard him more than twenty paces away, but his host felt his command nonetheless and kneeled in one thunderous motion. "Stand!" Anders commanded, and they did. "Roar!" he yelled, and they roared. Anders had no doubt that could be heard to the horizon line in any direction. He grinned. "Say 'Vykers must die!'" he commanded. "Vykers must die!" the host bellowed. "Again!" Anders laughed. "Vykers must die!" "Again!" "Vykers must die!"

"Did you hear that, Tarmun Vykers?" Anders asked the wind.

The wind howled in response.

Janks, On the Trail

Janks and his crew were pulled up short by the strangest noise any of them had ever heard, which sounded, to Janks' ears, like all the people in the world yelling at once from a distant mountaintop.

"Truly, my liege, that's a most fearsome clamor," Rem offered.

"Lay off the 'my liege' crap, eh Rem? I can't tell if you're supportin' me or mockin' me, but I ain't comfortable with it either way."

"As you say."

The corporal was not happy. His half was supposed to have returned to Long's camp three days ago, but their quarry had led them in circles until they were all but lost. The twins were supposed to be good at this kind of thing, but even they seemed flummoxed.

"Might be there's magic involved," one of them allowed.

Janks tossed his cap in the dirt and slid off his horse. "Well, that's fuckin' wonderful, lads, fuckin' wonderful."

"Corporal," Long's twin whispered urgently, "been an army up ahead, and recently."

"What'd you see?" Janks asked.

"Whole lot of hoof prints and no particular effort to hide 'em. But they look half a day old or more."

Slowly, the whole team crept in the indicated direction, scrutinizing the ground and keeping their hands near their weapons. After two hundred paces or so, the group emerged into a small clearing, their former campsite.

"Alheria's frigid tits!' Janks cursed. "This ain't good, no matter how you look at it. Either somebody came by and nabbed Sarge, or our own army's moved on without us. Mahnus be damned to the last of all hells!"

"There's no blood, if that helps," the mousy A'Shea said. "I'd know if there were."

Janks walked over to the fire pit, which one of the twins was busy investigating. "How long?" he asked the man.

"Couple hours. Maybe three."

The other twin came over and poked around in the ashes. "Yep. Two, three hours. Right enough."

Did they ever contradict each other? Janks would almost pay to see that.

"What's the order?" Janks' twin asked.

"We…follow, looks like. At least 'til we get a sense of what we're up against. If it's trouble, we head back to base. If not, maybe we join up with 'em."

Bash spat into the muddied grass.

Wordlessly, Janks' half pulled themselves together, made a quick check of their gear and supplies and headed out after the twins.

Vykers, At Morden's Cairn

The hole opened into a tunnel. A creepy fucking tunnel, of course. Why did this kind of stuff always play out exactly as expected? Vykers wasn't asking for half-naked dryads cavorting around an underground fountain of rum, but this? He clenched his teeth and looked around. Maybe he'd been a bit premature in his assessment. Whereas he might justifiably have anticipated a square or rectangular passageway, this one was completely round. Its walls had been thoroughly scorched by the same flames, he guessed, that had burnt the stones above. Must've been a hell of a big fire. Or maybe a lot of fires. Or both. Anyway, there'd been a battle here, at some point.

Vykers became dimly aware of an approaching headache. To a man who had experienced the amputation of both hands and feet, though, a headache was nothing.

What are you getting? He asked Arune.

Same as you: evidence of numerous battles at the entrance. Some of this is arcane damage, some of it's more conventional munitions. Arune paused. *Do you hear the screaming?*

What screaming?

Apparently not.

What screaming?

Ever since we passed underground, there's been a constant, distant screaming.

Let me guess: souls wailing in torment?

How can you be so cynical all the time without fracturing into a million pieces?

I have no idea what you just said.

I'm saying, what if it is *souls wailing in torment?*

You don't happen to hear any giggling dryads, do you?

<???>

Never mind, Vykers said, finally. He put his fingers to his lips and whistled back the way he'd come. Before long, he saw the familiar forms of the Five in silhouette against the daylight outside the hole. In another minute, they stood before him.

"Old magic," Number 17 said.

"Do any of you hear screaming?" Vykers asked.

Four of the five answered "no." Number 17 replied in the affirmative.

Thinking aloud, Vykers said, "So, it's magic of some sort…"

Number 17 cleared his throat. "Master…if I may…" he began awkwardly, "how is it that *you* hear the screaming?"

Vykers smiled at him. "Because I'm the Reaper."

Again, the Five exchanged looks of utter bewilderment.

Well done, Arune muttered.

"Awfully black down this tunnel," the Reaper observed. I can probably make a torch or two, but those won't last long.

"Darkness is no trouble to us," Number 3 said.

How well do you trust these five? Arune asked.

Not at all, Vykers answered.

That's what I wanted to hear. Anyway, I can take care of your vision problem.

I don't have a vision problem.

In here, you do. Or would have. Now you won't.

What—? Suddenly, Vykers could see quite a ways down the tunnel. *Ah,* he told Arune, *so you are good for something, after all.*

Arune never knew how to respond to these jibes, so she chose silence.

"Why don't you boys take the van," Vykers prompted, "and I'll bring up the rear."

"Yes, good." Number 3 responded.

It seemed the gods never tired of needling Vykers for his arrogance. He'd scoffed upon entering this hole, feeling it too much like every other warren, abandoned mine or catacombs he'd fought his way through. Typical, he'd thought it, and predictable. But it was neither. Where he had expected some sort of labyrinth, this tunnel ran impossibly straight and true for what seemed forever. There were no side passages, dead-ends, cave-ins or any of the other features that made underground exploration simultaneously so frustrating and fascinating. On the contrary, the sheer monotony of the place was enough to drive anyone crazy. Whoever had dug this tunnel was at once singularly focused on reaching his goal and shockingly incurious about anything he passed on his way there. Vykers saw no evidence of prospecting, interments, or military intent: it was, from all he could see, a smooth, round, unending hole. Which was far worse than he'd been expecting.

"The sun has gone down," one of the Five finally said, as the group stopped for a brief rest.

How do you know? Vykers wanted to ask. In the end, he supposed it didn't much matter. "Unlikely place to make camp," he said, "but it'll have to do. I don't see any change in this tunnel for a while."

"No, you're right," Number 3 said, a kind of awe creeping into his voice, "It does go on, doesn't it?"

Vykers sat, and the Five followed suit.

Any idea how long this thing runs? Vykers asked Arune.

Oh, I'm sorry, she responded, *did you say something?*

Bad enough sharing his head with someone else, but a woman? The gods hated him, all right. *Aren't we past the courtin' phase, yet?* He challenged her. *I just want to know, can you see an end to this damned tunnel!*

No, she replied, curtly.

No? Vykers felt a brief moment of something like panic. *What do you mean 'no'? How's that even possible?*

These walls are a lacework pattern of spells and spell wards, hundreds if not thousands of years old. I couldn't cast a spell in here if my life—or yours—depended on it.

So…?

So, I can't see beyond what you see. I can't hear beyond what you hear.

Vykers looked over at the Five. "Hey, is there anything you fellas can tell me about this place?"

Why do you always do that? Arune demanded.

Number 3 said, "Not a great deal."

What? Vykers practically shouted back.

Run to them every time I don't give you an answer you like!

You've never been in charge of anything, have you?

Arune was silent, but he felt her fuming.

Look, a commander, a leader—whatever you want to call it—he's got to get as much information as possible, from as many difference sources as possible. I'm not trying to slight you. I'm trying to keep us alive.

And so am I.

Good. Then, let's both keep doing our jobs. He turned back to Number 3. "I mean, you boys don't get a sense of how long this tunnel runs, or who else might be in here with us…?"

There are no Svarren, if that's what you're worrying about, Arune interrupted.

Svarren would be a treat compared to this endless slog. 'Least I know how to deal with them.

There may be worse things in here.

There's nothing on earth likes a sword shoved up its ass.

Poetry.

I'm gonna get some sleep, Vykers said.

Oh! Then I'll take first watch, Arune answered, wryly.

Then, he surprised her. *Thanks, Burner.*

They walked another day and then another. The Reaper finally had to shut everything out—fatigue, boredom, worry—and push himself forward like some sort of herd animal, driven before the whip. Unexpectedly, the group reached a fork in the tunnel.

Vykers stood and stared, stupidly, at his two choices. Left, right, left, right. "You boys gotta preference?" he said to the Five.

"Right," they all said in unison.

Vykers blinked. In unison? "Okay, left it is, then," he announced. Can't let the chickens rule the roost, and all that. Of course, these were some damned nasty chickens. Still, a leader had to be a leader. And the chimeras seemed to take no offense, as they forged off down the left tunnel.

After some time, Arune intruded on the Reaper's thoughts. *Did you notice the walls?*

He had. For the past hundred yards or so and continuing into the darkness ahead, the walls were inlaid with a mosaic of...human teeth. Vykers had seen some pretty weird shit, but this was especially unusual. He'd never been good at numbers, but it was clear even to him that thousands of people must have contributed to this...artwork, if that's what it was. The only question was whether the contributors had done so voluntarily and during their lives, or otherwise. Vykers found, not surprisingly, that he didn't much care either way. The dead were dead, and the living soon would be.

I was in a catacomb once in which the walls were lined with skulls, Arune recalled. *Teeth, though—that's a new to me. Why teeth?*

I once walked on a rug, I guess you'd call it, made of severed—

Don't finish that sentence! Aoife warned.

Flowers, Vykers said. *What'd you think I was going to say?*

You know bloody well what.

Vykers paused. *How do you know what I meant?*

You've got a rather gruesome image rattling around in here with me.

Ah, well, they're 'flowers' to some, I've no doubt.

Ugh, Aoife responded.

The teeth continued for hundreds and hundreds of yards.

Have there really been so many people in all the world? Vykers asked.

Seems rather excessive, doesn't it?

"Corpse!" Number 4 called out.

Vykers pushed through the Five and looked for himself. A figure in rusted chain mail and helm slumped against the left wall. His feet—one of which was bare—splayed out across the group's path. There was a battle-notched axe across his lap and an empty wineskin on the floor next to his right hip.

Arune? Vykers said. *Why haven't I been thirsty?*

Now, he asks! She sighed, melodramatically. *It's one of the many things I do for you.*

What do you mean?

It's complicated.

All the same.

Another sigh. *Very well. I extract moisture from the air—and that's getting harder and harder to do down here, by the way—and give it to you magically. I can also blunt or forestall your hunger, but…*

But?

I can't extract food from the air, so you need to eat, eventually.

Vykers nudged the body with the toe of his boot. "What do you figure? He died of thirst?" he asked the Five.

"Mmmm," Number 3 replied. "There is a faint odor of corruption."

"Huh," Vykers said, before kneeling to examine the floor. "Hard to say which direction he came from, he's been here so long. "Corruption? Might be. I don't see any killing wounds."

You recognize this armor? He asked Arune.

A brief silence, and then, *I don't know much about military history, arms, armaments, that sort of thing.*

"Well, he's old, you can say that for a certainty," Vykers muttered, mostly to himself.

Yes, hundreds of years, perhaps.

The Reaper dusted his hands off, took a final glance in the direction they'd come and said "Might as well keep moving."

Without another word, the Five moved off.

Vykers heard a soft clinking, followed by Arune's cry, *Look out!* But his sword was already sweeping in a great arc behind him, crunching through the dead warrior who had somehow risen and chosen, unwisely, to attack. By the time Vykers' whole body had turned to face the creature, its torso was toppling away from the waist, which, in turn, teetered sideways in opposition. Before the thing hit the ground, the Reaper's long sword chopped through the skull from the tip of its helm to the bottom of its lower jaw. It fell in a writhing heap on the ground, and Vykers stepped back to admire his handiwork. Misinterpreting the stares of his companions, he said, "Lotta men like to cut through the neck horizontally, taking the head clean off. I've always liked cuttin' vertically, though. Dunno why. Guess it just seems more...violent."

As Vykers and the Five continued to ponder the still-moving remains, Arune set them afire. In short order, there was nothing left but bits of charred armor.

"Never seen that before," Vykers observed.

"Fire?" Number 3 asked.

"Dead men walking around."

"Ah, of course."

"If there's more of those, this could get interesting right quick."

Number 3 nodded in acknowledgement and gestured to his brothers. Again, they all moved out.

The mosaic of teeth continued, a staggering monument to... what, exactly? After several hours, Vykers had to stop thinking about it, altogether. It didn't seem possible, and yet, there it was, all around them and seemingly always with them. Like the tunnel itself, it went on without end.

Except the tunnel did end. Just as the group was about to camp for the night, Number 12 spotted a wall: they'd reached a dead-end.

None o' this makes any damned sense! Vykers complained to Arune. *These walls are as smooth as you please—not a stone out of place, not a crack, no rubble to speak of. I've never seen anything like it. What's the point?* He drew his sword and started lightly tapping on the wall with the pommel.

You looking for a false wall, a hidden passage of some sort?

Yes.

Don't. There's nothing here.

"I fuckin' hate wasting time!" Vykers growled aloud.

"I don't understand," Number 3 admitted.

"We should have gone right back at the fork, like you said."

The chimera was wise enough to say nothing in response.

Almost a day later, they were back at the fork. This time, of course, they took the tunnel first chosen by the Five. Vykers was expecting some kind of comment, but his companions remained as inscrutable as ever, and Arune, as silent. As a younger man, Vykers would have been full of piss and vinegar about the incompetence of any leader as stubborn as he had been just twenty-four hours ago (and old Hobnail would've kicked his ass for it). He had expected the same from his "men," but it seemed such was not in their natures. Or maybe it was that Vykers had been kicking himself for the past day and merely wanted someone else to take over for him. He was painfully conscious of the time lost in following that dead trail; now all he wanted was to find the alleged sword, get back out into the open air and on the march towards his meeting with the End-of-All-Things. Mahnus forbid that whoreson wizard a single extra minute to build his host.

The most frustrating thing was that this new tunnel showed evidence of heavier and more-recent use, if only Vykers had taken the time to scout ahead. As the group progressed, they found bits and pieces of clothing, armor, abandoned weapons and more. Once, they found something scrawled on the wall, but no one—including Arune—could read the cryptic message. A few hours later, they found signs of an ancient camp fire, or, more accurately, an ancient attempt at a camp fire. It was time to sleep, but Vykers felt driven, certain their destination was scant moments away.

He was wrong, again. The tunnel continued for three more days, and although Vykers was faring reasonably well on travel rations, the Five were becoming noticeably irritable in the absence of fresh meat.

"I just wanna get this out," Vykers announced one morning—or what he assumed was morning. "If any or all of you try to eat me, it'll be the last mistake you ever make."

The immediate looks of umbrage and hurt that greeted him shocked the warrior into silence.

Strong and brave you may be, but you'll never put the diplomats out of work, Arune chided.

Vykers might have felt embarrassment, if he'd been capable, but a doleful blue light up ahead swept his mind clear of self-examination. Outside of a little fire now and then, light was something they hadn't seen in days.

Long, Captured

On those rare occasions when he'd had reason to imagine himself with a noose around his neck, his current predicament never arose as a possibility. Granted, this was probably the least lethal scenario of the lot, in the short term; still, Long was not comforted or mollified in the slightest. For one thing, even setting aside the noose (as preposterous as that was), the virtual forest of weaponry bristling around him assured Long's delivery to a fate that was almost guaranteed to be worse than strangulation. The End-of-All-Things would inspect him, torture him for information and then, Long had no doubt, kill him slowly. And he'd been bored of the gigolo's life!

For a moment, he stumbled. The noose, held by a man on

horseback somewhere behind him, tightened mercilessly. Long stopped moving in order to create some necessary slack in the rope and was rewarded with a smack on the back of his head by a different rider.

"Move your carcass, worms' meat!" the man yelled as he rode by.

Long moved his carcass. His tether allowed him just enough range to catch intermittent glimpses of Mardine, D'Kem and Spirk through the stream of warriors on his left and right. They, like him, struggled to remain upright and ambulatory at the end of their own ropes. Mardine, he noticed with a mix of anger and shame, was bound with multiple ropes and one chain.

He blamed himself. Of course he blamed himself! He'd known it was folly the instant Janks and Short first proposed this harebrained adventure. The world had changed—if, indeed, the world of his youthful fantasies had ever existed in the first place—and everything and everyone was a good deal less forgiving than Long had ever hoped or supposed. Even the weather seemed hotter, colder or wetter than at any time in his past. And evil? Evil had gone from abstract concept to something very, very real.

Gods, he was tired. His feet were killing him, his legs ached, his neck was chafed raw, and, unable to hold it any longer, he'd pissed himself a few hours ago. Such was his misery, he didn't even notice when his captors slowed to a stop and began setting up camp for the night. Although he was no hero, Long was no coward, either. He might have wished for death to find him in his sleep, but he still felt the need, the responsibility, to see his giantess free of this nightmare, one way or another.

A week later, Long and his friends were, miraculously, still alive. In fact, the closer they'd gotten to the End-of-All-Thing's host, the better they had been treated, as if their captors wanted to deliver them in the best possible condition. During that week, that eternal week, Long had learned a number of things just by keeping his ears open, despite being only semi-conscious most of the time.

For instance, he had learned that the enemy's host was

composed mostly of thralls of some sort—farmers, peasants, craftsmen and the like who had been ensorcelled to obey their master's every command. A much smaller percentage of the wizard's host was made up of professional soldiers, mercenaries and other men of experience and ill reputation. At the very top was a small collection of Shapers, renowned warriors and the End-of-All-Things, himself. Long's immediate captors were some of the enemy's mercenary troops. They were a motley bunch, to be sure, sporting armor and speaking tongues from all over the continent; fortunately, most relied on the Queen's tongue to communicate with one another.

When he wasn't listening, Long was thinking. Strategically, he and his friends were of no value to the Queen and thus could not be ransomed, and this End-of-All-Things would realize that pretty quickly. No, he would mine them for every last scrap of information they possessed, no matter how small and then... That part didn't bear too much consideration. The question was whether Long would find the time and the means to free Mardine while Spirk or D'Kem was being interrogated. Long realized he could—and would—die to buy her a little extra time to flee. But try as he might, he couldn't force himself to believe she could outrun or outfight a battalion of mercenaries on horseback.

"You! Come!"

One of the mercs stood over him with his sword drawn. Long got to his feet and glared at the man. Nothing wrong with a little last minute bravado. The man glared back. He was potbellied and missing several teeth in front. Long wasn't sure he could best the man in a fight, but he was fairly certain that attempting to read a book would kill the fellow outright.

"That way," the man grunted, pointing to a corralled-in area some fifty paces away.

Long noticed with no little shame that his companions were being shuffled into line behind him. To her credit, Mardine was noticeably defiant, which bolstered Long's spirits considerably and rekindled his pride. D'Kem, though, was his usual unreadable self. And Spirk? The young man was in the worst shape of them all—haggard, frightened, literally and figuratively at the end of his rope.

"Buck up, lad," Long said to him. "They can only kill you once." He'd meant it as a joke, but forgotten that Spirk had no gift for intentional humor. The boy looked back at him as if Long had stuck a knife in his ribs.

The corral was packed with people, most of whom looked a lot like Spirk in appearance and demeanor, a rag-tag collection of terrified nobody-in-particulars, waiting, it seemed, for their imminent executions. Men, women and children of all ages stood shoulder-to-shoulder, some in roughly catatonic condition. Here and there, Long heard weeping. One unfortunate merely babbled to himself incoherently.

"Get in," the merc growled at Long, prodding him in the back with the butt of a spear.

"They goin' to eat us?" Spirk asked, as he passed into the corral.

"Who? Our captors or these people?"

"The bad guys."

Long was about to assure his young friend that their captors would never eat them, when it suddenly hit him that he really had no idea. Maybe they would. Finally, the guards had pushed all four into the pen. Some of the other captives stood back and looked up at Mardine in awe; a rare few were completely oblivious of her presence. In some ways, Long envied them. Looking over at D'Kem, he noticed the old man's lips moving, ever-so-subtly. Casting? Praying? Gibbering? It made little difference. He doubted the burned-out Burner had anything left in him.

And so, they waited. Long was amazed at the paradoxical feelings of terror and boredom that consumed him simultaneously. Who'd have guessed such was possible? He also smelled shit. The captives had been standing here so long that some had lost—or surrendered—control of themselves. He himself reeked of urine, and he wondered how long it would be before he likewise smelled of shit.

As the sun went down, a skeletal man in travel-stained robes approached the corral, holding a small, pewter casket in both hands. D'Kem pushed through the crowd and fixed on the casket, mumbling more audibly than he had all day. The skeletal man's chin went up, as if he were listening to something. Abruptly, he opened the casket lid. From his vantage point, Long was unable to determine the casket's interior, but he again observed that his Shaper companion seemed unusually focused upon it. A strange, prickly sensation began to course through Long's body and inexplicably subsided before he could make head-or-tails of it.

The rest of the captives grew restive and then suddenly silent as a figure in odd, colorless armor appeared on the outside of their prison. Long found his eyes were drawn to the man's face, unable to look elsewhere. This was the End-of-All-Things. Of all the people in the pen with him, the man's pale blue eyes seemed locked onto his and his alone.

Well, that's it, Long thought. *I am going to die. Past due, really. I'm not afraid to die, either; it's the pain that frightens me.*

Inexorably, the other man's arm rose to chin level and he pointed at Long, calling out "That one. Bring him to my tent."

Long took a final glance at his companions, only to feel utter bewilderment as D'Kem winked at him surreptitiously. Confused, he looked over at Mardine, who smiled grimly in his direction. Strong to the last. Finally, he looked over at Spirk, who had tears trailing down his cheeks. Long nodded at him, as if to say "you're a good man, Nessno." It was a tiny, pathetic gesture, but it was all Long could manage in the moment. Rough hands grabbed him and dragged him away.

Deda, On the Road

The positives in murdering a monk so greatly outnumbered the negatives that Wims Deda couldn't honestly come up with any negatives. Oh, it was sacrilege; everyone knew that. But, in some religions, innocently enjoying oneself was heresy. In this particular case, Wims enjoyed killing the monk, and the monk, in turn, was given the means to meet the object of his lifelong adoration. It was, in Wims' mind, a win-win situation. Admittedly, the monk probably would have preferred to go in a somewhat less violent and painful manner, but those accepting the charity of a quick death should not gainsay the quality of said death.

Apart from killing a useless fuck, though, Wims found the monk's robe quite the opposite of its former owner: it was delightfully useful. Nobody questioned his purpose, anywhere he went. No one cursed him, as folks often did the homeless and unfortunate. No bandits tried to rob him, guessing, perhaps, that being a monk he had nothing of value, anyway. Wims fantasized briefly about joining the brotherhood after his current business blew over. A monastery, he suspected, would be the perfect base of operations for his golden years. First, though, he had to survive the End-of-All-Things and his plans.

It had been more than two weeks since he'd left his master, with orders to infiltrate the Queen's court at Lunessfor and obtain as much first-hand information about her plans as possible. Originally, Wims had thought this a suicide mission. Now, wearing his almost-magical monk's robes, he began to feel he might succeed; he might get in and out with the desired specifics, placate the End-of-All-Things and win his freedom—always assuming, of course, that his master didn't intend a literal destruction of the world. Freedom in a void did not sound very attractive.

Vykers, At Morden's Cairn

An enormous cavern opened before Vykers and the Five, a cavern so large that it dwarfed the remains of the ancient city housed within it. The warrior was able to comprehend either thing on its own—the cavern or the city—but seeing the two in juxtaposition made his head hurt.

"What in the endless hells?" he muttered.

The chimeras stood patiently, as if waiting for him to elaborate.

So, he tried. "It's a city, in a cavern. Don't you find that amazing?" He waved his arms for emphasis, to no avail. The Five just blinked. "Well, I find it amazing."

Tough crowd, huh?

Yeah. Pause. *What about you? You unimpressed, too?*

No, Arune admitted, *not unimpressed. Anxious—a little—but not unimpressed.*

Anxious. Alright. What can you tell me?

Why don't we do this the other way 'round this time?

Vykers grimaced. *What do you mean?*

Why don't you tell me what you *sense?*

He spoke aloud, "Right. I don't see any lamps or torches, so either the place is empty, or whoever lives here has learned to get along without light." He waited. Arune said nothing. "I don't hear anything, either. No livestock, no running water, no tradesmen working. It's quiet as a grave."

It is *a grave. There's nothing alive in there, bigger than a bat. But there are a lot of those.*

You gonna sulk if I ask the boys what they think?

<Sigh.>

I'll take that as a 'no.' "Well, fellas, what else can you tell me?"

Number 36 said, "Something is moving around in there."

"Bats?"

"On the ground. Something on the ground is moving in there," the creature clarified.

Vykers had a gut feeling. "Ready for some fightin'?" he asked the Five.

Slowly and with utmost caution, the group proceeded towards the ruined city. Here and there, tremendous cracks in the earth had set various sections on a perilous slant in one direction or another, as if something unspeakably massive had struck the city from below. Those towers that weren't broken or toppled entirely leaned like drunkards in random alignments. Walls were breached and others had been spontaneously created out of the rubble. The whole effect was of a children's toy wrecked by an angry god. Bold as he was, Vykers was not prepared to fight a god.

Some...power...is pushing at me, Arune said.

Heh. Now you know how it feels, Vykers told her.

Arune seemed not to have heard him. *It's like the rolling of the ocean. Not something I could ever push back for long.*

It had to be the thing he'd come for, the sword. *Which way?* He asked.

Somewhere on the other side of this city and…down.

Vykers groaned. *Down! Why is it always down!* He addressed the Five. "Well, boys, looks like we've gotta go through those ruins to find what we came for. But let's stick together. I still think we're in for hostilities, whether there's anything alive in there or not."

About thirty or forty paces in, Vykers' gut feeling was vindicated when some rubble shifted off to his left and a new dead warrior rose to its feet. Number 3 was about to charge, when another rose nearby. And another. Vykers watched with an almost amused air as a small army of the dead assembled before him. He noticed the apparitions were most numerous in the direction from which he'd come, as if they were blocking his retreat. Having come this far, though, he had no plans to retreat. Besides, it wasn't his way.

Okay, Burn, it's time to show me what you can do. You able to cast again, yet?

Tell your pets to stand back, please.

Vykers did. An astonishingly loud musical tone burst from his chest and the dead in front of him collapsed in heaps and piles. In the silence that followed, Vykers was greeted by the five chimeras with looks of confusion mingled with awe. He knew how they felt.

That wasn't fire.

Oh, I'm sorry. Was I supposed to use fire? Arune answered a hint of mischievous pride in her voice.

What did you do?

I shattered their bones. Pulverized them, actually.

There were still a few of the creatures lingering on either side of Arune's blast, but they wavered and swayed uncertainly, apparently stunned by the loss of their ghastly fellows. It was so comical, Vykers laughed aloud.

"Lose your taste for a fight, did ya?" he bellowed at them.

And then he heard the sound of countless undead feet approaching, and he knew he'd fucked up.

"Where are they coming from this time?" he called over to the Five.

"Everywhere," Number 17 replied.

"Pick your ground, but stay close. Sounds like this could get messy." *Can you do any more of those pulverizing things?* He asked Arune.

Not for a while. Takes a lot out of me. Especially here.

Well, you'd better come up with something. I doubt these dead bastards'll take to their heels if things turn against them.

The dead came pouring out of every alley, street, ruined building, doorway and window.

"How many you reckon?" Vykers asked no one in particular.

"Hundreds," one of the chimeras—he didn't see which—said.

"Yeah. I figured."

He took them all in and saw every conceivable kind of sword, axe, mace and spear. Some were equipped in full battle armor, others were little more than skeletons with odd bits of armor. The armor, though, was not of one style or era, and it occurred to Vykers that many of those before him must have been tomb raiders who had come here at various times and been claimed by the army before him. Although he would have thought they didn't possess the necessary anatomy, they screamed of a sudden and rushed him and his companions.

Vykers felt fantastic.

In seconds, an unbroken wall of howling dead was upon him and, as always, Vykers knew where in space to avoid their weapons and where to find their bodies with his own. And again, Arune played witness to his genius, still unable to believe or comprehend that anyone mortal could move with such prescience and magnificence. Clearly, Vykers had recovered from his ordeal In the Forest; he'd gotten stronger and more confident with each conflict. What would it be like to see the Reaper at the height of his powers? As it was, he was already a supernatural blur. The dead dissolved before his sword in a rain of dried flesh, broken armor and shattered bone. And all the while, he laughed.

Not that it was an easy thing, however much Vykers made it seem so. His adversaries knew no fear or exhaustion, and there appeared no end of them. They attacked with the single-mindedness of army ants tearing into a beetle. In his peripheral vision, Vykers caught glimpses of his chimeras tearing, smashing and battering their way through wave after wave of dead. For all the remains that now lay scattered about their feet, though, they didn't seem to be making any progress. *Hundreds?* Vykers thought. *This feels like thousands!*

At last, Vykers felt a twinge as Arune launched an incendiary barrage at the back of the attackers, decimating their force and severely weakening their assault. Through the smoking wreckage, Vykers was finally able to catch fleeting hints of open space behind the dead, welcome evidence of a limit to their number.

I think I'm startin' to like you, he told the Shaper.

And all I had to do was demonstrate a talent for destruction, she responded, coyly.

The Reaper continued whirling, hacking, and dodging. *How does one reap the already dead?* He wondered. *Might be time for a new nickname...*Gradually, he heard less and less of the clattering and clanking of his foes and more and more of the snarling, grunting and breathing of his friends, until the moment came when he realized nothing opposed him or his chimeras. The six of them—and Arune—had prevailed. Vykers kicked at the mound of dead in front of him, tossing various pieces away from the central pile.

"Some o' this shit's ages old. Might be it even goes back before the Awakening. Anybody recognize this?" He picked up an axe-like weapon and held it out before his face. In general, it looked like a mace, except for the long and sharp projections jutting from one side of its head.

The Five shook their heads.

That's an old Ntambi war club.

A what *war club?*

Ntambi. From across the Southern Sea.

Vykers was flabbergasted. *How do you know that?*

His Majesty had a small museum of arms and armor—souvenirs, relics, archeological finds. He had two or three of these things.

You're telling me somebody in this pile crossed the Southern Sea?

You asked if I recognized the thing. Its name is all I can say for certain.

Never occurred to me before, but I might have to go visit these Ntambi people once we're finished with old what's-his-name. Vykers sheathed his sword and tucked the war club into his belt. "Now," he said aloud, "about this magic sword..."

It's up ahead; I can still feel it pushing me. This'll take some getting used to.

There was a subdued groan, and Number 12 sank to his haunches.

Vykers crossed over to him. "You get hit?" he asked, giving the creature a quick once-over.

Without replying, Number 12 lifted his left hand from his stomach, revealing a bloody hole. Studying the other four, Vykers saw numerous cuts, scrapes and piercings. Number 12 had taken the worst of it.

"You gonna make it?" he asked the chimera.

It did not answer, but fell backwards into the dust and debris. The other four rushed to attend to it.

Can you do anything for him?

The only thing I can do to stabilize him is to occupy him, but I'd have to leave you to do that, and you'd lose your hands and feet.

"Can you do anything?" Vykers asked the four upright chimeras.

"Mmmm. Possibly," was all Number 3 said.

Gently, delicately, the four cleared the area around their fallen comrade and made him as comfortable as they could. Next, they all placed their hands on his torso, as near the wound as they could get without hurting him further. Vykers might have expected murmuring, spell-casting, praying. But there was none of that. The four healthy chimeras simply surrounded the fifth in a deep and prolonged silence.

Any idea what's happening?

I have no—

Number 3 turned to Vykers. "We have done our best, but we cannot save him."

"Well," Vykers began.

"There is more, master."

Vykers waited.

"We have to eat his remains once he passes."

The Reaper's jaw popped open and hung like porch swing.

"In this way, our friend will continue and the four of us will be strengthened by him."

Silence.

"Master, in respect for our friend, could we have some privacy in which to complete our...observance?"

Vykers shut his mouth, nodded and turned away, walking several paces in the direction of the sword he sought. Behind him, he heard a quick, meaty thud, followed by gruesome sounds of flesh being rent. This lasted only a few minutes before the more routine, if momentarily more meaningful, sounds of the chimeras eating took over. A normal man would, of course, have been put off by such things; Vykers had seen and heard worse. He'd been waist-deep in steaming entrails and bathed in blood and bile. The chimeras' consumption of their companion was awkward and strange, but they would all survive it. Excepting Number 12, naturally.

In time, Number 3 spoke up. "We are ready to proceed."

The Reaper waved them forward without looking back. "Lead the way," he said.

Continuing towards the heart of the ruins, the group encountered a great chasm that looked to have swallowed half the city at the very least. Broken columns, foundations, statuary and other masonry formed a talus into the chasm's depths.

Down there, Arune said.

I figured, said Vykers. To the Four, he said, "Looks like maybe we can pick a path through the rubble. If dead men can do it, shouldn't be too hard for us, either."

Now that he actually looked at them, Vykers noticed the Four had gotten slightly larger, and their various tusks, horns, claws and pincers, more menacing. If that's how it worked, the Reaper'd have to make sure one of them didn't eat the other three. The resultant beast would be something even he wouldn't enjoy meeting in combat.

It was rough going, but after nearly an hour, Arune announced, *It is here.*

Number 17 was oddly contorted and fixated on a nearby boulder, the once-upon-a-time marble cornerstone of a massive building.

Addressing both, Vykers said "I'm not seeing anything."

It's under that stone, I think.

What? Vykers asked in disbelief. *How am I supposed to move that fucking rock? Mahnus-cursed thing's as big as a…*Suddenly, he understood. *Shaper,* he said. *Do some shaping.* He paused. *Please.* He felt something like glee welling within Arune.

Brace yourself for the burn, o mighty one, she warned.

A wave of invisible energy surged from Vykers' chest. The surface of the cornerstone became blurry and ethereal. Number 17's head whipped around to regard Vykers. The creature nodded, as if acknowledging something, and then extended his hands to the stone, causing it to blur even further. Vykers was not in significant pain, but his body was definitely aware of the cost of Arune's spell casting. In moments, the Shaper and Number 17 had rearranged the stone's volume, so that its perimeter had reduced considerably, and its height increased, accordingly. On the ground where the stone had been, Vykers spied flattened plate armor filled with a dust he assumed had once been bones…and a sword, a sword that was not damaged. Vykers' discomfort subsided as Arune finished her spell.

How come I didn't feel that when you blasted those dead warriors?

You might have been a little preoccupied. Maybe you don't feel pain when you're fighting.

Vykers took a deep breath, exhaled through his nose. *Guess it's time to grab this thing, then…'less you've got any last words o' wisdom…*

Arune said nothing for a moment and then, *Good luck.*

He walked to the sword and stood over it for several seconds. It was not a gaudy thing, not decorated with elaborate runes and other etchings, not finished with gold in the hilt or jewels in the pommel. It was not of unusual design or unrecognizable material. In fact, on visual inspection, given the choice between this sword and a thousand others, the average man might pick five hundred before landing on this.

"I like it," Vykers proclaimed aloud. "I think."

Damned if you do, damned if you don't. He knelt down to pick it up.

SEVEN

Janks, On the Trail

"What's 'at look like to you?" Janks asked the twins.

His team stood on a ridge, overlooking a vast valley. In the distance, miles away, was an immense shadow that spread across the valley and off into the horizon.

"The enemy's host?" Long's twin guessed.

"That's it," Janks' twin agreed.

Janks, a veteran—if sometimes reluctant—campaigner gasped. "Biggest damned army I ever seen."

"That doesn't look good, I must say," Rem interjected.

"What it looks like," said Bash, "is the sergeant's dead. And so are we, if we don't turn around but fast."

For the millionth time, Janks inwardly cursed himself. They'd have never left that little town if it hadn't been for him. Long would still be telling tall tales about all the women he had to please. Hell, maybe he'd even been doing it. And now, he was dead, or would be shortly. The corporal glanced over at his troops, people he barely knew. He'd gotten them into this fix—he'd gotten them *all* into this fix. Whatever other plans or desires he might have, he had to see those still alive back to the relative safety of the Queen's army.

"We head back," he said.

"But..." the little A'Shea objected.

"Shut it," Janks ordered, in no mood for argument. "The only way you're gonna live is to turn tail and rejoin the Queen's army." He could see tacit agreement in the eyes of the twins, Bash and Rem. Only the A'Shea seemed resistant to the idea.

"We'd best get outta here, 'fore their scouts catch sight of us," Janks urged.

Everyone turned back they way they had come, including the healer.

Long, In the End's Camp

It was dark inside the End-of-All-Things' tent, and the air had an unpleasant, unidentifiable odor to it. The owner of the tent sat on a makeshift throne, before which Long had been brought in shackles. Two huge guards stood on either side of him, bristling with weapons. The End-of-All-Things was enjoying a meal of some sort of live, newborn rodents, which he dangled over his mouth like grapes before dropping them in and chewing. Long was both disgusted and terrified, which, he supposed, was exactly what his captor was aiming for.

"Care for one?" the man said.

"Hardly," Long managed in response.

"You don't enjoy fresh meat?"

"Seems overly theatrical, if you ask me," Long replied, his heart hammering in his chest. There was only so much fear a man could take. Maybe his heart would fail him before this damned wizard could touch him.

The other man stopped chewing abruptly, swallowed and set his bowl aside. He wiped his hands on a napkin draped across his lap and leaned towards Long.

"You have no idea of the horrors I can visit upon you. You think you're brave? I could have you wallowing in a mire of your own filth in seconds if it pleased me."

Long said nothing.

"Fast learner," the End-of-All-Things said. "Good. Maybe you'll outlive this day after all." Anders rose from his seat and walked to within inches of Long's face. "You are an officer of some sort, and as you're not one of mine, I must assume you work for the rancid Queen."

Long remained silent.

"Now, there is any number of ways I can extract what I need from you—you know that, I can see—and I'd just as soon have you dispense with all the posturing and tell me straight out what you know of the Queen's plans, the disposition of her troops, etc."

Long remained silent.

"I'm disappointed to find the officers of my enemy so lacking in logic and…foresight. You believe you can withstand whatever tortures I can devise. You cannot. You would not last five minutes. But as I don't want to break you unnecessarily…a little test of your loyalties, then. I am going to torture one of your friends to death. It will be slow, humiliating and of course agonizing. Whom should I choose? The young man?"

Long remained silent, though he found he was sweating profusely and his legs were trembling uncontrollably.

"The broken down Shaper?"

The sergeant struggled mightily to keep a calm veneer, though inside was all chaos.

"The giantess? Ah! Don't deny it, I can see it in your eyes. You would not have her hurt, so of course she will be. The only question is, how many fingers and toes will she lose before you submit to the inevitable? How much pain might you have spared her if you had only relented sooner?"

That was it, that was all it took—no magic, no torture, just the threat of hurting Mardine in any way made him crumble like a sandcastle in the surf. "You win," Long blurted, on the verge of weeping.

His inquisitor broke into a large, feral grin. "Ah, you poor people with morals, honor and integrity." He spat these words out as if they'd somehow soiled his tongue, an odd choice for a man who'd just dined on live rodents. "You're really hamstrung from the start, aren't you? You could stand all the flaming hot tongs in the world, but let someone mention those same tongs in conjunction with a loved-one's name? You're not fun at all, really." Anders spun and returned to his seat. "However, since I have more interesting ways in which to amuse myself, why don't we just get down to business?"

Again, Long remained silent.

"What is the Queen planning? And be specific. I'll know if you're lying."

"She's assembled a large force to block any advance you might make on her kingdom."

"And?"

"This force is meant to be led by a man they call 'the Reaper'."

Anders sat back in his chair, apparently delighted. "Ah, yes. Tell me of this Reaper."

Long felt defiance surging within his bosom. "You don't want to meet him in combat; I can assure you of that."

His captor actually giggled. "Oooh, he's big and bad, is he?"

"You have no idea."

The End-of-All-Things suddenly grew impatient. "Then *give* me an idea, or I bring your giant wench in here right now and start slicing."

"It's said he once destroyed a whole city, by himself."

"Yes, yes, I've heard all that—defeated five hundred men by himself, killed an army with a toothpick. What else? Why the fascination with this fellow? Surely he's more than a gifted swordsman."

The man wanted theatrics? Long decided to deliver them. "He is oblivion with a sword. No man, no army, no nation can withstand his onslaught. He is the Reaper, and there's no soul in the wide world he will not or cannot take. Including yours."

The End-of-All-Things grew still, dangerously still. Without warning, he cackled loudly and broke into vigorous applause. "I like it! I cannot wait to meet and annihilate him!" He paused to drink from a nearby goblet. In response to some expression on Long's face, he explained, "Oh, it's nothing untoward, I assure you. Water, in fact. I find it goes well with fresh vermin." He took another gulp. "Now, soldier, your name and rank?"

"Sergeant Long, sir."

"Sir?' No, no, no. You must call me 'lord,' or 'master'."

Not much of a choice, there, Long thought. "Yes, lord."

"Now, I tell you what, Sergeant Long: you are going to come to work for me. You'll join my army, work with my troops. Meantime, I will keep your paramour safe from harm. If at any time you think to betray me in any way, however, well, let's just say it will go poorly for the giant. Are we understood?"

The End-of-All-Things had him by the balls. "Yes, lord," he responded.

Spirk and D'Kem, the End's Camp

The throng was moving, slowly rotating towards the entrance, where the villain, as Spirk thought of him, was feeding something to the captors one by one. Spirk was frightened witless on a number of counts: first, he was so afraid of meeting this End-of-the-World fellow, he feared he might shit himself, which very well might be worse than death; second, he thought they might sense and steal his magic stone; finally, he hadn't seen Long in some time and was pretty sure they'd killed him. Spirk could do nothing about the first and third issues, but for the second, the matter of his magic stone, he had formulated a plan. Taking it out of the inside pocket of his ragged leather vest, Spirk held the stone in his hand a moment. "Don't let 'em kill me," he whispered to the stone, before putting it into his mouth and swallowing. And swallowing again. And again. It wasn't going down as well as he'd hoped, and his eyes began to bulge out as he staggered around the pen, bumping into other prisoners and feeling a rising panic. One of the guards outside the pen reached over and bashed Spirk on the back of the head, knocking him to his knees. He shook his head violently in attempt to clear the cobwebs and discovered he'd successfully swallowed his stone at last. "If I'm still alive on the morrow, I hope to see you again," he breathed.

Spirk watched as D'Kem was herded in front of the villain. If his imagination hadn't gotten the best of him, it appeared the man was spending more time with the old Shaper than he had with anyone else. He even seemed to be staring into D'Kem's eyes, as if searching for something. Apparently satisfied, he held out a small nut or some such and D'Kem ate it. For a moment, nothing happened, and then a nearby guard ushered the Shaper aside so that next prisoner could be fed. To Spirk's eyes, D'Kem looked like he was in the same stupor as any and everyone else who ate the nut. Spirk wondered how the nut would get along with the magic stone, already in his gut.

As he approached his turn to meet the villain, Spirk felt an odd, tingly sensation throughout his body. Then, in his mind, he heard a voice—D'Kem's voice: "Stay calm." He looked over at the Shaper, but the man still seemed out of it. Surely, this was the work of his magic stone!

Magic stone? Spirk asked.

He thought he heard an irritated sigh and then, *Yes, fine. It's me, your magic stone.*

What...what do you want?

What I just said: stay calm. When the End-of-All-Things feeds you, nothing will happen. Only, you must pretend that it has. I don't know that these pellets take effect immediately, but you'd best pretend anyway.

Pretend?

Yes, pretend. Pretend you've become as witless and lifeless as the rest of these prisoners. That first part shouldn't be hard for you, the stone concluded.

If Spirk didn't know better, he might have thought the stone had just insulted him in some way. But that didn't make sense.

A guard prodded Spirk into position.

And then what happens? He thought.

And then, you're still free to think and move as you like. But don't. You must wait until D'Kem gives you further instructions.

Spirk looked into the eyes of the villain. If the stone said anything else, he didn't hear it. The pale blue eyes transfixed him, so cold and without feeling were they. Spirk felt fingers on his jaw and then a small, cold lump landed on his tongue. Instinctively, he swallowed, feeling a slight spasm of pain as the nut followed the stone's rough passage down his gullet.

Now move, boy, move! The stone commanded rather harshly.

Spirk felt somewhat put out, but he complied nonetheless. Gradually, he found his way over to D'Kem's side.

That's right. Now, stay put until you hear different from me.

The young man sighed. He loved his magic stone, of course, but he didn't enjoy being pushed around by it.

D'Kem stole a glance at the boy. Magic stone, indeed. Well, whatever worked. The two had only each other anymore, since the sergeant and then Mardine had been led away. Spirk wasn't much to work with, but he was easily fooled into compliance. Perhaps, just perhaps, D'Kem could find a way to free them both without tipping his hand to the enemy. On the other hand, working from inside the End-of-All-Things' host provided opportunities, as well. The old Shaper would have to think on it.

Aoife and Toomt'-La, On the Road

Toomt'-La was the strangest satyr Aoife could have imagined; only, he was real. As he matured, his coloring became more and more fantastical, suggesting he was not merely "of the forest," but actually *made* of the forest. At any point where bone might have jutted against the skin—at elbows, knees, shoulder and the like—fringes and tufts of moss grew in abundance. Parts of his skin took on a bark-like appearance, while other areas assumed the waxy gloss of various leaves in summer. Without effort, Toomt'-La was able to blend into any wooded surroundings and become effectively invisible. When Aoife remarked upon this, the satyr reacted with surprise.

"But we are all like this, we children of the forest. In this way, we remain invisible in plain sight."

"But I've never seen your like before."

"Just so; we have been there, notwithstanding."

The satyr had become Aoife's closest companion and greatest teacher in a matter of weeks. His was the experience and knowledge of the ages, tapped in or connected, as he was, to the world's ancient forests, reaching back to the beginning of time. Yet, there were many seemingly obvious things about which he knew nothing. His knowledge of city life, for example, was outdated at best and completely inaccurate at worst. Aoife took some satisfaction in correcting these little misconceptions whenever she could; she knew they were poor compensation for the vast store of wisdom Toomt'-La had imparted to her.

Sometimes, though, the information she desired was much simpler.

"How far until our next birthing site?" she asked her companion.

"I have already inquired of the moon," he replied. "Four days, I think. We must be settled in three, then."

Aoife was nervous. She had come through the first experience with ease and now knew what to expect, but she had still not gotten quite used to the idea of birthing the old gods, their forests and their servants. She was not entirely sure of her role, beyond that of vessel or perhaps portal. While her first "children" had seemed to revere her, what would become of her when she had completed her task? And what would her fellow A'Shea make of her actions? Lastly, she wondered almost without cessation about what her final confrontation with her brother would be like and whether she and the rest of the world had any chance.

As was often the case, the satyr appeared to be reading her mind. "You worry about your brother, again."

"Yes, my friend."

"He caught us unawares before, as I've told you. He will not be so lucky, this time."

"I hope you're right."

"Mmmm. And there are many others arrayed against him, do not forget, from the fearsome Tarmun Vykers to the long-lost Sorcerer, Pellas."

"What? You haven't mentioned Pellas before, I would have remembered that."

"Did I not? So, so. He has reemerged, reappeared, from the shadows and fog of history. We sense his presence, but cannot tell his precise location."

Pellas. And Tarmun Vykers. Legends, mythical figures, and they had come forth to fight her brother. If the coming conflict did not result in cataclysm, there might be hope for the world yet.

"What can you teach me of Pellas?" Aoife asked the satyr.

"Ah," Toomt'-La sighed, contentedly, "a worthy human, most worthy. He spent a mortal lifetime healing in our forest after the death of his beloved."

"A lifetime?"

"Pellas has plumbed the depths of mysteries most mortals do not guess at."

"And after this lifetime, he left the forest?"

"He did."

"And what became of him?"

"Alas, I do not know. I hear only that he tried, briefly, to rejoin his community, found it too much changed, and disappeared."

Aoife ruminated on this for a moment. "He is one I'd love to talk to."

"I feel the same. What a fascinating creature he must be."

Coming from a fascinating creature in his own right, this made Aoife laugh with delight.

"This amuses you?" Toomt'-La queried.

"It is a funny old world," Aoife responded.

The satyr inclined his head, quizzically, and added, "And a dangerous."

The End, In Camp

The war map was almost disturbingly realistic, augmented with details from the End-of-All-Things' Questing Eye and rendered with sorceries none of his generals could even pretend to comprehend.

Shere surveyed the map and his fellow generals, who had gathered around it for their lord's latest briefing. His gut told him some kind of action was imminent.

After several minutes of uncomfortable silence, Anders stalked into the tent and right up to the map. He passed his dead eyes over each of his generals. Unlike some tyrants of legend, the End-of-All-Things demanded eye contact. He wanted to be able to stare into each man's soul and—what?—judge its worthiness for consumption? Shere really had no idea, but he obeyed just the same, despite the fear he always felt in doing so.

"The Rancid Queen is sending a portion of her host forth to forestall or prevent our advance on her kingdom." Anders pointed to a particular spot on the map. "Meantime, she holds the larger portion in reserve, to be commanded by some fairy tale named 'the Reaper'."

There was muted mumbling all around the table.

"Fear me and none other. That is your duty here." The End

continued. "We will crush him in the fullness of time. First, however, we will test him, play with him. I cannot find him at the moment, but when I do, we shall send forth a small force of our own to challenge him, see what he's made of." He looked around the table. "Thus, we shall have one force to counter the Queen's, one in reserve for this Reaper fellow, and our main force behind this range of hills," he indicated a spot on the map. "If needed, the three can reunite or surround a foe at any time. And, of course, we shall continue to press the locals into our service whenever and wherever we find them." Anders paused for questions, but there were none. "Good, then. Shere, I'm putting the entire Fourth Army in your hands. You'll be the first to wrangle with this Reaper, if ever he shows his head."

Shere just about bit his tongue off when he heard that. The End-of-All-Things was sending him against a legend? And if he failed, which was likely, his master would do something unspeakable to Shere's son.

The other man smiled at him, as if reading his thoughts. "Think of your son as insurance against failure or treachery," he said, all but confirming Shere's darkest fears. His master then turned to another of the generals, "Chuala," he began, "to you go the Sixth Army and the task of testing the Queen's resolve. I may well drop in on you from time-to-time to see the action for myself." Again, Anders paused and again, his generals were quiet. "The rest of you shall remain with me, continuing to build and train our forces in preparation for the outcome of these other engagements. That is all."

With that, the End-of-All-Things turned on his heel and disappeared into the darker recesses of the command tent. His generals knew better than to say anything to each other as they departed.

Janks, the Queen's Camp

Major Bailis was pissed. He ranted and yelled at Janks for a full ten minutes before the corporal could make a word of sense out of it. Finally, the major took a series of long, deep breaths and stilled himself.

"In essence," he said, "You lost your C.O. and a full third of your squad chasing phantoms. That about it, Corporal?"

"Yes, sir."

"I should bust you down for this, and I would, too, but...we're gettin' a might scarce on experienced officers. Ironic, wouldn't you say? I should kick you, but because of the scarcity you've just exacerbated, I have to keep you."

Janks didn't know what 'exacerbated' meant, but he could guess by context. And he did know enough to keep his mouth shut.

"Look, we're getting new recruits all the time. We'll scrape something together this afternoon and find you a new sergeant. Seeing how you treat your friends, though, I'm going out of my way to find someone you won't like."

Janks nodded.

"You can take your mates and pitch over by the southern latrines. I want to make it clear you're being punished."

"Aye, sir."

"Dismissed."

The corporal saluted and headed off towards his squad. Putting him near the latrines, that was funny, that. He wasn't just near the shit, he knew, he was in it, now.

Shortly before sundown, a hulk of a man in full mail approached from the direction of the nearest mess tent. The fellow was a hair over six feet, but more than half as wide, as well. To Janks, he looked like nothing so much as a poorly made statue of some forgotten hero, propped up in the town square of nowhere special. The stranger was a flesh-and-blood exaggeration.

"Which wunna you fuck-buckets is Corporal Janks?"

Bailis had been as good as his word: Janks hated the new man on sight. He stood up and greeted the stranger.

"Corporal Esmun Janks, at your service, sir," Janks said, saluting. The rest of his squad leapt to their feet, too.

The hulk got right in Janks' face. "I hear you got your last CO killed. That ain't gonna happen with me, missy. I decide when you move, where you move, whether or not you sleep, eat or take a shit; I even decide how often you get to breathe. Got that, Corporal?"

"Sir, yes sir. Beggin' your pardon, sir...?"

"What?" the other man bellowed.

"Would it be okay to tell us your name and rank, sir?"

The man ground his teeth for a moment. "Sergeant... Kittins."

Before Janks could even think of grinning, the sergeant had a hand at his throat. As expected, his grip was dismayingly powerful. "I've killed men for grinning at my name, missy. So, you wanna smile, smile. I hope it's worth the slow, painful death I give ya."

Janks found he could not even nod in response. Eventually, Kittins let go.

"Break down your campsite and find my pennant on the western perimeter. It's a flaming boar against a red background. You'll set up there and await further instructions."

"Yes, sir," Janks wheezed. He had never missed Long so much in his life.

Vykers, In Morden's Cairn

Nothing happened. Nothing that Vykers could see, anyway. He lifted the sword off the ground and held it before his face. It had a nice heft to it, felt fairly well balanced. The edge remained impressively sharp, which to Vykers was the surest sign of the blade's magic. Who knew how long this thing had been lying under that stone? And yet, it seemed almost new-forged. Still, he'd expected to feel...something.

Burn? He asked.

And got no response.

Hey, Shaper! Arune!

Still, nothing. But he had his hands and feet, so she had to be there, somewhere. He tried a few cuts with the sword, while the Four looked on, curiously. "It's a good sword," he announced. "A good one. Worth the effort? Remains to be seen. Wasn't much help to its previous owner," he said, gesturing down at the ruined armor.

After a few minutes, Vykers began to feel awkward, standing in one spot, hoping to hear from Arune. "I guess we'd best head back, then. Time to go dance with the enemy." He nodded at the Four as he strode by and into the lead. He'd gotten what he came for; if the thing was as powerful as he'd been led to believe, he had no reason to avoid the vanguard.

A strenuous climb and lengthy hike took the warrior and his escort back out of the chasm and through the ruined city. They saw occasional signs of movement, but it seemed, now that they possessed the sword, that the dead were uninterested in challenging their passage. At odd intervals, Vykers thought he heard a strange keening in the back of his mind, but whatever it was never responded to his inquiries. Eventually, he chose to ignore it.

More walking brought the group to one of its previous campsites, which Vykers decided to make use of again.

"Might as well rest here for a few hours," he told the Four. "We can't get out of here in a day, anyway, and there's no sense in exhausting ourselves tryin' to." What he didn't say was that he was increasingly agitated by Arune's silence. She'd been with him, a part of him long enough now that he missed her when she didn't speak for long periods of time. And this absence, he knew, coincided with his touching the sword for the first time. As uncomfortable as he'd been with the arrangement he'd reached with Arune, if it came to a choice between having her around or keeping the sword, he knew he'd be hard-pressed to decide. Arune had proven her worth; the sword? He'd seen nothing so far to indicate it had been worth the trouble of acquiring it.

The Four didn't talk much, and, at last, boredom set in and Vykers fell asleep on his side, cradling the sword in his arms as he slept. When he woke up, the chimeras were seated in roughly the same positions, although Vykers could clearly see one of them, Number 17, dozing.

That was painful.

Vykers became instantly alert and awake.

Arune? He asked tentatively.

You're using my name, she observed. *My real name. I take it you missed me?*

Missed you? Right. I get a boil on my ass once every few moons. I miss that when it's gone, too.

Some things aren't meant for sharing, warrior.

Not that I care, mind you. But where've you been, Burn? Vykers inquired.

It's the sword. The moment you picked it up, it grabbed me and took off. It was like...like riding a wild horse during an earthquake, if you can imagine.

So, you've been—what?—wrestling with the sword all this time? Then, I guess you came out on top, huh?

I wouldn't say that, Arune cautioned. *But we've reached a sort of agreement, if you will.*

Vykers coughed. *Well, I'm glad you're back with us. We've got some bloody business ahead of us.*

We have, Arune agreed solemnly.

It is the way of things that return journeys often seem to take less time than the initial journey towards a destination. This wasn't the case for Vykers, however, as he was keenly aware of the time being lost in travel, time he would rather have spent getting acquainted with his new host, his officers and their capabilities. When he and his Four finally emerged from the hole at Morden's Cairn, he felt as though he'd been travelling in darkness for weeks. He was relieved and excited to be back in the open air. But something had changed, too. The scenery somehow appeared sharper, clearer to him. The scent of the earth and air practically assaulted him. He took a deep breath and felt like he'd inhaled an entire forest.

It was almost night when Vykers and his chimeras climbed from the hole. He was sorely tempted to press on immediately, but he knew it made more sense to do a little hunting, have a real fire, take extra care of himself and his companions. They still had a ways to go before they returned to Ahklat, and he wanted to be ready for whatever came his way.

"You boys feel like restin' up a bit?" Vykers asked the Four.

"We are very hungry," Number 36 replied.

"You n' me, both," Vykers said. "Why don't I go see what I can scare up outta the bushes?"

"Master," Number 3 said, "you are a warrior without parallel, truly." The creature composed his thoughts. "But we are...slightly...better hunters."

Vykers laughed. "Not slightly, Three. You're much better. Go ahead and see what's out there. I'll start us a nice..."

But Number 17, the spell caster of the group, had beaten him to that, as well.

"Alright, then," Vykers surrendered, "I'll go find water. Any old fool can handle that job, right?"

In short order, the group had a roaring fire going, over which Vykers was able to roast his choice of hare, raccoon, pheasant, quail or deer—the chimeras had been very thorough in their jobs. Whatever he chose to decline, the Four consumed raw and with their typical gusto. Since his companions were already aware of his strange, ethereal hands and feet, Vykers decided to pull of his boots and warm himself by the fire. When he discovered his feet and hands fully restored to him, he almost fell over backwards and down a small ravine. So excited was he, that he jumped to his feet and began howling and dancing an ale house jig he'd learned in his youth. "Yes! Yes!" and "I'm whole again!" he cried, over and over, to the alarm of the chimeras. Finally, tuckered out, he plopped back into the dirt near the fire, content to examine his hands like the face of a long-lost loved one, completely unaware that he'd also regained the tooth he'd lost shortly after his hands and feet.

You don't need to thank me, Arune said, once he'd quieted down.

What? Oh, yes, er...thank you, thank you, thank you, Vykers responded.

I said you don't have to thank me; I didn't do it.

Vykers thought for a moment. *So, the sword, then?*

Yes, the sword.

When Vykers next spoke, there was awe in his voice. "I didn't believe it, wouldn't have believed it in a million years. There *are* enchanted swords. They're real." Looking over at his freakish comrades, though, it all began to make sense—the chimeras, sharing his body with a ghost, the walking dead, a magic sword. The Queen had mocked him for his know-it-all manner, when he clearly, clearly did not know it all. He'd been too proud in the past. One might think this revelation would embarrass Vykers, but, in fact, he was thrilled by it. There was so much more to the world than he'd imagined, so much more was possible than he'd experienced or attempted. A blind spot was vanishing, a weakness, disappearing. He'd be damned if this End-of-All-Things would catch him off guard.

It took a while, because of his highly energized state, but Vykers finally fell asleep—a better, deeper sleep than he'd known in a long time. He was awakened by a light snowfall. The chimeras had kept the fire burning, but it failed to keep flakes from adhering to Vykers hair, brows and lengthy beard stubble. Still, he sat up feeling refreshed and excited about facing whatever lay ahead. Again, he examined his hands in disbelief. The many scars he'd earned in battle were gone, the calluses he'd developed from swinging a sword or axe, non-existent. He picked up a stone and began worrying it with his right hand and then his left. He didn't mind the loss of scars, but he needed the calluses. He might find himself in some scrape, swinging his sword for hours. He needed those calluses.

"You four 'bout ready to hit the trail again?" he asked the chimeras.

"Yes, master," Number 3 said. The other three nodded in agreement.

Vykers looked into the sky. He had no particular love for snow and hoped it would disappear as soon as they reached a lower altitude. How people lived in this shit, he had no idea. Gathering a few things and slinging his sword across his back, he kicked dirt into the fire until he'd buried it, took a last look around and started the long trek back to Ahklat.

A few nights later, the group was again hunkered down around the camp fire when a disembodied voice called out of the woods, off the hillside and all around them. "Tarmun Vykers!" it crooned in a way that was both playful and sinister. "Tarmun Vykers! I know you're out here somewhere!"

<???>

Say nothing, Arune warned.

She should not have wasted her time. Vykers wasn't a man to hide from threats. "Right here!" he yelled, getting to his feet and taking his sword in his hand.

"Where? Oh! *There* you are!" said the voice, coming nearer. A huge, phantasmal head formed out of the mist and hovered and bobbed just outside the firelight.

The Reaper taunted it. "Afraid 'o fire, are ya?"

The head moved into the light, but only barely. The size of a small cottage, it was boiling in dark vapors and strange, spectral lights. Only its eyes were clear, and they were a cold, lifeless blue.

"Tarmun Vykers!" the head sighed with child-like pleasure. "The man who is meant to vanquish me!"

"That's the plan," Vykers admitted.

The apparition laughed. Vykers watched its eyes take him in and then scrutinize his companions, as well. "Charming little pets you've got there. What are they?"

This time, Vykers laughed. "I'm afraid that's—what do you call it—privileged information."

The eyes moved to Vykers' sword. "A man with secrets," the head said at last. "I've got a few myself, but I'll give one away for free, Tarmun Vykers. I hear you've done miraculous things with a sword, so I'm sending one of my armies to kill you! Even if you survive, I will have learned something, will I not?"

The smug self-satisfaction in the thing's voice rankled Vykers' nerves. "Just one army?" he asked as nonchalantly as possible. "I typically kill an army before breakfast!"

"Indeed?" the head responded. "I shall look forward to seeing that, then." With that, it vanished.

I kill an army before breakfast? Arune griped.

Seemed like the right thing to say to a giant, floating head.

Look, Vykers, whatever spell he was using just then, I have never encountered before. That means our enemy is one powerful and deadly son-of-a-bitch.

That makes two of us.

Point taken.

Number 17, not privy to Arune and Vykers' conversation, offered his assessment, "The wizard who wields that magic is fearfully strong. That apparition was the result of multiple spells cast simultaneously."

Vykers regarded him. "Does he frighten you?"

"I would be a fool not to be frightened."

"Good," the Reaper said, "then you know what we're up against." Vykers sat back down.

Number 3 spoke up. "What do you make of his threat to send an army after us?"

"I'm sure he was telling the truth; he is said to be insane, after all."

"Forgive me," the chimera said, "but you don't seem especially concerned."

"I'm concerned," Vykers corrected, "I'm concerned. But this is a test of some kind, and I mean to give our enemy reason for concern, too."

"What are your thoughts?" Number 36 asked.

"We can't make solid plans until we see the size of this army of his. We don't even know what his military hierarchy is like, so when he says 'army,' that could mean anything between a couple hundred soldiers to several thousand."

I think I can help, there.

How so?

By using the same spell he used to find you, I suspect.

One of the chimeras started to ask a question, and Vykers had to silence him for a moment, in order to complete his conversation with Arune.

Gotta learn how to have two conversations at once, Vykers complained.

I had a mentor once who could do it.

Great. What's this spell you spoke of and how do we use it?

It's called The Questing Eye. The more specifics you have, the better it works, the faster it finds what you're looking for. The End-of-All-Things just gave us a 'what'—an army. And we know it's somewhere between his host and here.

His host is in the East.

Exactly. I just have to search in a line between here and there. Something as big as an army shouldn't take too long to find. Arune hesitated a moment. *It would go faster if Number 17 and I worked in tandem. That, of course, would mean—*

"Okay, look," Vykers said to the chimeras. "The truth is, there are two of me in this body, and one of 'em's a Shaper."

The Four did not seem terribly surprised.

"And a strong one, at that. We saw what you did to the dead warriors in Morden's Cairn," Number 17 said.

"Uh...yes." Vykers agreed. "Anyway, she wants to work with you," he pointed at Number 17, "to seek out this army and get a good look at it."

The chimeras twitched in various ways that Vykers had come to understand meant they agreed.

"Once we know more about this alleged army, we can make a plan." The Reaper looked into the fire. "And believe me, the End-of-All-Things ain't gonna like what we come up with."

Every night, Arune expected the End-of-All-Things' specter to reappear and taunt them, but he did not. Every morning, Vykers joined hands with Number 17, so that Arune and the chimera could collaborate on their search. They sent a pair of Questing Eyes eastward, weaving back and forth across a central tack. So far, all they had discovered was that the enemy's army was not within three days' march.

"I want you to look for something else, too," Vykers said one morning without preamble. "Find some Svarren. As many as you can. Tell me where the biggest gathering is and how far away."

That's your plan, Svarren? Arune asked, skeptically.

Part of it. Depends on how many you scare up. Then, I need to find the right valley...

Ah! And they won't be expecting an ambush from a party of five.

More 'n likely, they'll be expectin' us to try and sneak by on either side.

So, what kind of valley are you looking for?

Steep—maybe cliffs—on one side, climbable slope on the other.

And how will it work?

Vykers balked. *I'll let you know when the time comes.*

That day's search, however, was complicated by torrential rain. Rather than slog on in the muck and mire, Vykers ordered the Four to join him, huddling in the lee of a large boulder.

Can either o' you get a fire going in this wet?

Nothing will burn in this weather.

Shit, Vykers spat.

I didn't say I can't help, though.

Vykers began to feel a familiar and mildly unpleasant prickling—the burn—throughout his body. Moments later, he noticed the boulder was giving off heat. Within minutes, it was well and truly hot to the touch.

"Ahhhhh," the warrior sighed. "'Least we won't freeze our asses off, now."

In the deluge, there was nothing to do but wait. Arune and her spell partner could see nothing through the endless sheets of water. She decided to learn more of her host.

Vykers?

Eh?

Who were your parents?

He chuckled. *So, I've still got a secret or two, have I?*

So, you're keeping that hidden from me?

The Reaper pondered his knuckles for several breaths. *Be nice if I was keeping that secret. Truth is, I got no idea.*

You've got no memory of a mother or father?

Nope. He bit at a loose piece of finger nail.

But you must have come from somewhere...?

I expect so.

What's your earliest memory?

Burner...Arune. What's the point of all this? It ain't like we're goin' to get hitched now, is it? You ain't fixin' me up to meet the in-laws, are you?

It was the Shaper's turn to laugh. *That'd be an awfully awkward wedding ceremony, though, wouldn't it?*

Vykers grinned.

Silence. Two of the chimeras dozed off; the other two became even more alert.

I'm asking, Arune continued, *because the things you do with a sword—even a plain old army sword—aren't possible.*

Did you see me do 'em? Vykers countered.

I did, but—

Then they're possible.

They're not, though. Not for anyone human.

His hackles up, Vykers protested, *You sayin' I'm not human?*

Arune tread carefully, *I'm saying, Tarmun Vykers, that you may be* more *than human.*

The End, In Camp

Tarmun Vykers was more than he seemed, of that the End-of-All-Things was certain. What bothered him was that he couldn't determine what else was involved. The man travelled with four monsters, the like of which Anders had never seen, but nevertheless admired. They would make excellent pets in his personal retinue, if he could manufacture the means to capture them alive. Of more concern was the man, himself, and the strange sword that cloaked him in a mysterious vortex of crackling energies frustratingly unfamiliar to the sorcerer. Anders had meant to call lightning down upon his adversary, but somehow the sword's aura had thwarted the attempt. In fact, the whole encounter had been much less satisfying than he'd envisioned when he conceived of it. Fortunately, the End-of-All-Things had a contingency plan—an army of 20,000 faithful, led by General Shere—that would wipe the smirk off Vykers' face, smash the swagger right out of his body. And if for some reason Shere failed, there was always the rest of Anders' host.

He reached out with his mind and found his general, doggedly proceeding towards the region Anders had described to him. The End-of-All-Things would like to have used the Scaldean Heads, which would have allowed for a two-way conversation, but he'd given one to Wims and they only worked in a pair. Instead, he sent the Whispering Mouth and spoke instructions in his general's ear, reminding him that he, Anders, held the man's son as insurance against any treachery or incompetence and telling him, with as a much detail as possible, where he might expect to cross paths with the Reaper.

Shere, for his part, was not happy to hear from his master and pathetically clumsy at hiding that fact. But it amused

Anders to see the man's extreme discomfort and discontent, along with his inability to do anything about it. In four days—five at most—Shere and his troops would face the legendary Reaper. From the End-of-All-Things' perspective, there could be no greater or more enjoyable act of theatre in the world. He viewed his general and troops the way a small boy looks at ants, as things to be fed, tortured or squashed, according to his whim. At the same time, he knew fresh troops were increasingly hard to come by, and he wanted Vykers dead. Whatever the outcome, Anders was sure it would be thrilling to witness.

Spirk and D'Kem, In the End's Camp

The eighth army and, D'Kem suspected, the larger host of which it was part featured the most bizarre command structure he had ever encountered: a general oversaw a band of mercenaries, all of whom had the rank of captain. There were no officers between the general and his captains. Each captain roused and motivated a specific number of troops—a battalion, essentially—in much the same way a shepherd's dog managed a flock of sheep. And what sheep they were. After consuming the End-of-All-Things' offerings, these former peasants, craftsman and soldiers had become little more than animals, filthy, ravenous and apparently without freewill. Tragically, to the Shaper's way of thinking, he noted countless women and children in the mix, every bit as mindless and primal as their adult male counterparts. These women and children would go to their deaths just as willingly and probably with greater ease than the men, never knowing...well, never knowing. The Shaper assumed that any unassigned mercenaries formed what served as the host's cavalry and scouting parties, but as they hadn't seen any combat since D'Kem had joined, it was only a guess.

As dire as the Shaper's situation was, he hadn't been idle. Two could play at this mind-control game, and, after insuring his own and Spirk's immunity to the End-of-All-Things' magic, D'Kem set about capturing the mind of the captain assigned to his group. It wasn't a difficult task, as it turned out, since the man was barely more than Svarren himself. "Ugh," as

D'Kem thought of him, was an immensely fat, slovenly and foul-smelling brute who did most of his work with the toe of his armored boot. He would quickly lose weight under D'Kem's control, however, as the Shaper made the man do endless circuits around the perimeter of his charges, cursing at random to add veracity to his actions. Thus engaged, Ugh left his troops alone, which gave them a little more peace and rest and D'Kem time to think than they'd known in ages.

Spirk continued to pepper the Shaper with questions, until the older man had to threaten to silence the younger's vocal chords for good and always. One problem that Spirk did point out, though, was that because he was not ensorcelled, it was a good deal harder to ignore his hunger than it was for the other troops. And feeding the troops didn't seem to be a priority for the End-of-All-Things. As the saying goes, "Even a blind squirrel finds a nut once in while," and D'Kem realized Spirk was right: they needed to eat. Thus, the Shaper directed Ugh to temporarily leave his patrol in search of food. Given the man's girth, this wouldn't surprise his peers in the least.

After some time, the man returned with a poorly roasted haunch of boar, charred on one side and little more than raw on the other, and a bottle of awful but strong wine. Given what he knew of the Shaper, Spirk was worried the older man would keep the whole bottle for himself and was surprised when D'Kem passed on it entirely. In no time, Spirk was drunk and laid down for a nap, which pleased the Shaper no end; it was much easier to think without having to worry about the boy and his antics.

Long, In the End's Camp

On the other side of the host, Long Pete was as miserable as he'd ever been. If it was possible to die of misery, he expected to find out, soon. In the meantime, he was charged with corralling a throng of witless and frightening peasants and keeping them organized until the order came to break camp. He thought often of Mardine, worrying incessantly and helplessly about her whereabouts and current condition. He wondered, too, what had become of D'Kem and the lad, Spirk, though he expected they had probably succumbed to the End-of-All-Things' sorceries. Somewhere in this horde, they were likely drooling and stumbling about, just like the rest of the "troops."

Troops! That was a laugh. Sleepwalkers was more like it. These troops had been rendered completely devoid of self-awareness and free will. The End-of-All-Things had a seemingly endless supply of them; he would throw them at the Queen's army in wave-after-wave, utterly unconcerned for their survival. And that was bound to have some kind of negative effect on morale on the Queen's side.

Long meandered through his charges, making sure none were absent-mindedly fornicating, injuring themselves or otherwise creating a nuisance he'd have to deal with later. When he heard his new master's voice, he froze in his tracks.

"Sergeant!" the End-of-All-Things said behind his back. "You're a man of many surprises!"

Long turned, carefully, met the other man's gaze as briefly as he could manage, and bowed his head ever-so-slightly. He didn't speak; he knew the End-of-All-Things would get to the point, sooner or later.

"Your...*girlfriend*...is with child," the sorcerer said. "Did you know this? Aha! I can see by your expression you did not. I don't blame you for being surprised, of course. I myself didn't know such a thing was possible. Indeed, I would have sworn otherwise, but there it is nonetheless: you're an expectant father."

The End-of-All-Things paused, savoring Long's confusion and despair.

"Of course," he continued, "there's no question of your being able to raise the child; you're my slave now, after all, which makes your child my slave, as well. Not to worry, though, I've become something of a surrogate parent myself of late, and your spawn shall not lack for company."

He paused again, studying Long's face.

"Oh, little insect," he sighed condescendingly, "do you hate the mighty sun? What on earth are you going to do about it?" And with that, he withdrew, laughing not-so-quietly to himself.

Yes, Long thought, *I am an ant.*

Vykers, On the Trail

It was time for a heart-to-heart. Vykers sat on an old stump and faced the Four.

"I guess I haven't been fair to you," he confided. "What I've got in mind's probably suicide, but there are other options."

The chimeras listened without comment, waiting for Vykers to continue.

"We could run some other direction, for instance. Or we could try to sneak by the advance scouts, though I reckon he's planned for that. Hells, we could even go back into Morden's Cairn. It'd take 'em centuries to dig us outta there."

Finally, Number 3 spoke up. "Your pardon, master, we are confused. A full-on assault seems to be your preference, yet you say it is suicide. Surely, you don't intend to die?"

"I don't think any warrior intends to die...but it happens. And if the information that you and Arune have given me is correct, we're outnumbered a thousand-to-one and more."

"Excuse me, again, master, but if that is so, why even attempt it?"

Vykers ran his hands over his scalp, exhaled. "Let me put it to you this way: how'd you feel if you were this End-of-All-Things and you just saw one of your armies routed by five men?"

Being rather literal in their thinking, the chimeras took some time in considering this question and conferring about it. At last, Number 3 spoke again, "We would be profoundly concerned, afraid even."

"Just so," Vykers agreed.

"And how do you rate our chance of success?" Number 4 asked.

"Not good, but that depends upon how many Svarren we can locate and attract. And there's always a chance that if we create enough havoc, we can escape in the confusion."

"We will stay with you," Number 17 said.

"Some of you might get killed," Vykers pointed out.

"We will stay with you," Number 3 said with finality.

"Good. Happy to have you." *Arune?*

Mmmm?

You having any luck finding Svarren?

Are you kidding? Turn over a rock and fifty'll jump out at you, Arune quipped.

How are you plannin' to get their attention?

Do you remember that wild pig back in your cave, or the oursine on the way here?

Yes.

Like that, only much, much bigger and much, much worse. I put a buzzing in their brains they can only stop by killing me.

You mean me.

Well, yes, you too.

You figure they'll get here in time.

Some will, some won't. Don't tell me the Svarren are your whole plan.

Vykers scoffed. *Hardly. Soon's we find the right kind o' valley, I'll tell you the rest. Only, we'd best find it pretty quick. We're running outta distance between us and them*

You think I'm unaware of that?

Just wanted to be clear.

As it happens, Number 17 thinks he's found a crease in the hills ahead that might serve. We should be there before sundown.

If it suits our purpose, we'll camp there and make our stand tomorrow.

Aren't you even a little worried? Arune asked.

What's the point? You can only die once.

That's what you think.

Deda, At Lunessfor

His master had warned him that he could not enter Lunessfor while carrying the Scaldean Head on his person, but Wims knew that he could not discard it, either, without incurring the

End-of-All-Things' wrath. It was the work of an hour to find a suitably hollowed out log in a nearby copse and stash the head within so it would never be found by accident. Such was the relic's aura, Wims very much doubted even scavenging animals would take much interest in it.

Once free of the Head, Wims joined the train of traffic travelling into the Queen's Capital. He had been here before, years ago, but found the place even more spectacular than he'd remembered. Most of the cities he frequented in the past few years were either slowly crumbling into ruin or hastily erected without much thought to posterity. Lunessfor, on the other hand, had been built as both a statement of man's potential and a defiance of his mortality. If Wims' life had unfolded differently, if he'd made different choices, he wouldn't have minded settling down in the Capital, acquiring a position of power and perhaps even angling for the throne, itself. If he was going to dream, he reasoned, he might as well go the whole hog.

He arrived at a mammoth gate—he'd forgotten its name—and was surprised at how closely the guards inspected him. More than surprised, really, he was taken aback. No one he'd thus far encountered had shown the slightest skepticism about his identity, and yet, all of a sudden, these guards were suspicious. Wims felt a trickle of sweat run down his neck and between his shoulder blades. He decided to give his monk a nasty cough, in hopes the guards would be anxious to move him along. The guards were well-trained, though, because no matter how thick Wims laid it on, they took their time in asking his particulars—his name, where he'd come from, why he was visiting, where he hoped to stay and for how long. Fortunately, Wims was a skilled liar, elsewise, he'd have been detained for sure. At long last (or so it seemed to Wims), the guards lost interest in him and focused their attentions on whoever was next in line. He took that to mean he'd passed muster and was free to continue on his journey.

Once inside the gate, he determined to get as far from those guards as he could. Better safe than sorry, Wims told himself. What he needed now was a dive, the sort of place where a fellow reeking of poverty and the road could blend into the crowd, take in the latest gossip and maybe make an arrangement or two that could bring him one step closer to his goal. Fortunately, despite its magnificence, Lunessfor boasted an impressive array of taverns, pubs and inns to suit any taste or budget, but especially those without either. It took Wims no time at all to find what he wanted, a dilapidated three-story inn by the name of "The Fretful Porpentine."

Stepping inside, his eyes took a moment to adjust from the bright outdoors to the smoke-hazed gloom of the inn's main room. Against the right wall, a narrow staircase ascended to the second and, one presumed, third floors. A bar of sorts occupied the left wall, and large fireplace stood in the wall straight ahead. Tucked neatly into the room's corners on either side of the fireplace, doors led off into other parts of the inn—the kitchen, perhaps or the jakes. Wims would have need of both, eventually. In the meantime, he scanned the room, made note of the few men who seemed the likeliest threats should anything untoward develop and plunked himself down at an open table. Then he remembered: it was his job to initiate untoward developments.

Wims needed to find someone of low station who worked inside the Queen's castle—a stable boy, a chambermaid, a cook—or, alternatively, someone from the town's criminal element who knew the old and secret ways into the castle, private tunnels the Queen's ancestors had used to slip out for midnight assignations, or to flee the city during outbreaks of the plague. Its occupiers pretended they didn't exist, but every castle of size had them. With patience, Wims would find one.

Patience, however, was his greatest challenge. How long had he been away from his master? Weeks? A month? More? He enjoyed his separation from the End-of-All-Things, but felt sure his master was expecting an update soon. And one did not keep the End-of-All-Things waiting. Even at this distance, Wims was certain the man could kill him in a heartbeat. Of course, it wouldn't take a heartbeat. The sorcerer liked to draw things out, especially when they involved others' pain. No, his master would take an eternity to kill him, if Wims ever gave him cause. The funny thing, to Wims' mind, was that he could easily kill his master but for his spells and his sword. *But that's all one,* Wims thought, *I can't so I won't.*

Spirk and D'Kem, In the End's Camp

The boy was missing. D'Kem was so preoccupied with other matters, he hadn't seen Spirk go, but go he had. The question was whether he'd been taken or had somehow managed to exit the enclosure of his own free will. Even as the old Shaper puzzled over this mystery, however, Spirk reappeared. D'Kem was not amused.

"Fool boy!" he growled in an urgent whisper. "Where in Mahnus' name have you been?"

"I had to go get my magic stone," Spirk explained defensively.

D'Kem blinked. "Your what?" Then he remembered. "What do you mean go get it?"

"Well, I didn't want them to steal it, so I had to swallow it. And just now I needed to go collect it again."

D'Kem took in the surrounding prisoners. In general, none were allowed to leave the holding pen for any reason and many absentmindedly shat themselves. The Shaper had arcane alternatives, but the boy...

"Do you mean to say you walked out of here and over to the pit latrines?" D'Kem asked, amazed.

Spirk flushed, guiltily. "Yeah," he admitted.

The older man was flabbergasted. He'd seen evidence of Spirk's strange gift before, but he'd never given it much credit. He remembered how Janks had once boasted that Spirk did indeed have something to offer their once-upon-a-time adventuring party, that the boy was so unremarkable as to be invisible. D'Kem had dismissed the idea at the time; now, he was reconsidering. In the back of his mind, too, he felt he should be disgusted by the boy's purpose outside the pen, but it was all he could do to come to grips with the fact Spirk had *gotten* outside the pen.

"Have you been outside before?" he queried.

Spirk shrugged. "Sure. Couple-a three times."

"Three times?" the Shaper said, almost raising his voice.

"Yeah. I think so."

"And nobody saw you or said anything to you?"

The young man thought about it for a moment. "Lots of people saw me, I reckon. They just—I dunno—didn't care?"

"I need to think on this," D'Kem declared and sank to the ground in one motion, pulling his cloak down over his eyes and muttering to himself.

"Only," Spirk ventured, "only, I'm gettin' pretty hungry again..."

The Shaper blew his lips out in exasperation. "Well, don't go walking out there again. Let me..."

"They were making huge pots 'o stew, though," Spirk interjected.

D'Kem shot out an arm and pulled the boy down beside him. He whispered a frantic word or two, and Spirk found himself unable to talk.

"I need you to be silent. And, more to the point, *you* need you to be silent." The Shaper's eyes locked onto Spirk's with desperate intensity. "Have you noticed they don't feed us prisoners much?" Of course, the boy didn't answer. "That's because this is one Mahnus-cursed enormous horde. There will never be enough forage to feed this many mouths, and winter's coming. So..." D'Kem's voice took on a hard edge. "What do you think's in that stew, boy? Or should I say '*who* do you think is in that stew?'" He gestured around the pen using only his eyes, and by the terror in Spirk's gaze, he knew he'd made his point, which was some kind of miracle as far as the Shaper was concerned. "The fears you expressed our first night in this pen have proven to be spot-on."

D'Kem took a moment to collect his thoughts before he spoke again. When he did, Spirk gave him his undivided attention.

"There are worse things than dying, boy. And if we don't get out of this camp, we're like to be seeing a bunch of them. Now, I want to try something," D'Kem pointed at the nearest guard. "See that ugly brute over there?" Spirk nodded. "I want you to go over and try—yes, actually try—to get his attention. Don't touch him. Just, you know, wave your arms a bit and jump up and down in front of him."

Spirk gave a look like a whipped dog.

"Don't worry," D'Kem added, "I won't let him hurt you. My word on it." He shooed the boy off and focused his thoughts on the guard.

Spirk advanced to the man like the condemned approaching the chopping block. He stopped a couple of times as if he'd lost his nerve and looked back to find reassurance in D'Kem's countenance. The Shaper bobbed his head almost imperceptibly, and Spirk continued. Finally, the young man arrived within five or six paces of his target and raised his hand. The guard scratched at his beard and looked terribly bored, but gave no sign of noticing Spirk. Flustered, the young man tried again. He raised both hands above his head and waved them back and forth. The guard sucked his teeth. Spirk jumped up and down. D'Kem had forgotten to remove the spell that silenced him, so Spirk tried whistling instead. That didn't work, either. Finally, foolishly, he hauled off and punched the man in the upper chest. The guard blinked, curiously, and his eyes slowly settled on his assailant—not with anger, but with the look of someone emerging from a particularly strong daydream.

"'Ere, you. Wot you doin' over 'ere? Get back over there," he ordered with no discernable animus towards the prisoner.

As he turned back to face D'Kem, Spirk rolled his eyes melodramatically, as if to say "talk about dumb, eh?" The Shaper winked back. It was almost funny.

By day's end, Spirk had repeated the procedure three more times with three other guards, all with the same outcome. At last, D'Kem removed the enchantment that kept the younger man quiet.

"I believe," he began, "I believe we may be able to escape this predicament."

Spirk, unfamiliar with the word, adopted his usual strategy of bluffing his way through the conversation. "That's a relief," said he. "I've never been in so grubby and foul-smelling a pre-dic-a-ment in all my life. Maybe 'cause it's so big, eh? I mean, a smaller predicament might be a bit tidier. D'you think the Queen's predicament is this big by now?"

D'Kem quickly replaced the spell of silence upon Spirk.

"Listen, lad," the old Shaper confided, "no offense, but you don't really need to talk for what's coming. Just follow my instructions." He searched the shuffling multitude surrounding them and found no immediate threats. "Come nightfall, we're just going to walk out of here." Spirk's eyebrows shot up in surprise and concern. "If they don't see you right in front of their noses in broad daylight, they're not likely to see you in the dark, either. And I'll make damned sure they never spot me." He paused. "Time comes, I'll pat you on the shoulder and point you in a direction. You start walking and I'll be right behind you." The young man remained skeptical, but D'Kem had an answer for that. "Unless, o' course, you want to sample a bit of that stew first…"

He was dreaming of home, of simpler times, of his mother's bread and his siblings' lame-brained roughhousing. He even thought fondly of his father, who'd never had much use for Spirk. And he dreamt of his old cat, Maunce. The fleabag had only one ear remaining after years of scrapes with other toms in the neighboring meadow, and his meow was more like a bullfrog's croak, but Spirk had loved him all the same. He wondered whether Maunce was still hanging on back home—he felt a thud on his shoulder and opened his eyes. D'Kem prodded him with his boot.

"Up, lad. Time to go, if we're going at all."

Spirk stumbled to his feet, sleep still heavy in his limbs and between his ears. The old man grasped him from behind by both shoulders and shoved him off amongst the other prisoners and into the dark. Although all light had drained from the sky and their enclosure offered no fire for light—or warmth—Spirk was painfully aware of the location of the various guards charged with keeping him and his brethren captive. As D'Kem had suspected, the guards remained inexplicably blind to Spirk's presence and passing. *Must be the magic stone,* Spirk told himself. *Has to be my magic stone. Magic stone. Magic stone.* He chanted the words over and over inside his head until they became a mantra of sorts or a benediction. It was undoubtedly the longest walk of his life, and yet, inevitably, he found himself ducking under the ropes that had been strung up to contain the prisoners and moving off into the camp proper.

Spirk passed dozens of pens like the one in which he'd been imprisoned. Each of these pens held anywhere from fifty to five hundred of the ensorcelled thralls who had once been townspeople before they'd encountered the End-of-All-Things. Now, they were fodder, battering rams of flesh and bone, to be used once and replaced. Or served for dinner. Spirk's gorge rose at the thought of it. But he was curious, too. Funny how things worked like that, sometimes.

At last, he found the courage to glance behind himself, interested in knowing how far he had walked and was startled, instead, to find no sign of the Shaper. In a panic, he took two or three quick strides in the direction from which he'd come and ran smack into…air. Falling onto his ass in the mud, Spirk was only slightly relieved when he heard the old man's voice growling at him from the empty air in front of him.

"Idiot boy!" D'Kem hissed. "Trying to get us killed?"

Fortunately, Spirk was still under the Shaper's silence spell, or, the old man was certain, his companion would have let loose with a litany of foolish questions and observations. "Turn around and keep walking until we're clear of this camp," D'Kem commanded. "I should think an hour will suffice." He could well imagine the complaints and protestations this would have brought on and was beginning to wonder why he hadn't silenced the boy weeks ago.

Mercurial though Time often is, in this instance it crawled at a pace much, much slower than a frightened and somewhat dimwitted young man could walk, so that even Spirk was aware it travelled considerably faster on other occasions and thus must somehow be angry with him that it moved so reluctantly at the moment. And it was in wracking his brains—such as they were—for answers to this conundrum that he finally achieved D'Kem's directive and wandered free and clear of the enemy's host.

A visible hand appeared on Spirk's shoulder, and the Shaper's voice urged him to stop.

"I think this will serve for now." The old man paused. "I

suppose I should remove the enchantment," he said to himself more than Spirk.

Suddenly, Spirk found he could talk again. "D'you think Time is mad at me?" he asked.

Of all the damn-fool things D'Kem might have expected the boy to say, this was by far the most baffling. "Time? What in Alheria's...never mind." He was, he decided, too tired to expend further energy on nonsense. "Let's see if we can find a small copse of trees or a pile of boulders or some such. That should give us enough shelter for decent rest."

Spirk frowned. "But...what about the sergeant? And Mardine?"

Aoife and Toomt'-La, In the Forest

Aoife's second birthing went much the same as her first, except that Toomt'-La was there to act as her guardian and mid-wife. As before, she produced an array of eldritch creatures, the likes of which she had only heard of in folktales and children's stories. And yet, they were real and had been born of her body. If she thought on it too much, the whole thing frightened her witless. At such times, Toomt'-La emitted an alien, musky odor that immediately calmed her nerves and filled her with a profound and patient peace. When she asked him about it, the satyr typically smiled, shrugged and responded, "Toomt'-La does what he can, as he must. You understand this, no?" And she did. She, too, did what she could, as she must.

Watching the rapid growth of her latest brood, Aoife wondered aloud how her first born must look after so many days of growth.

"Aha!" the satyr exclaimed. "Let us go and see them, shall we?"

The A'Shea regarded him with gentle skepticism.

"Come, come," he urged, "take of my hand, and let us be off!"

Did he mean to retrace their journey over the past several weeks? Or was this some sort of fey humor, previously unknown to her? Aoife could not tell, nor was she prepared to leave her young so soon. But Toomt'-La was insistent.

"Come, come," he said again. "It is here-there, you will see."

"Here-there?" Aoife asked.

"Just so. Come."

Clearly, her guardian/son was not going not let the matter drop, so Aoife relented, took his hand and followed him. But where their little clump of trees should have ended, they stepped back onto the woodsy farm where Toomt'-La had been born. At least, the A'Shea thought it was the same farm. Now, it was surrounded by enormous—and apparently ancient—trees. The structure itself had gone riotously green with a lush carpet of bearded mosses and sword ferns sprouting from and covering every surface. Aoife heard a peculiar clucking sound and, looking around, realized the satyr was laughing at the look of wonderment on her face.

"It's grown so much!" she gasped.

"Aye, and will do, for as long as the moon sings to us."

"The moon…?"

"It is a saying amongst our people."

"And how did we get here from…there?"

"It is here-there, do you see?"

Aoife shook her head.

"Anywhere you give birth to the forest is here-there to you, Mother-sister. Any grove you wish to see, is here-there."

"And outside, too? Cities?"

The satyr frowned, as if he'd suddenly discovered something most unsavory in his mouth. "Pah!" he said. "Only forest. Only *your* forest."

This, Aoife understood, was an amazing gift. If she continued birthing the fey folk and their forests, she could cross the world in a breath.

"But…where are my…children?" she asked.

Toomt'-La seemed to delight in her confusion. "Look, Mother-sister. Look around you. They are everywhere!"

And it was true. Slowly, the things she'd thought were trees, bushes and stones became animate, gradually resolving into the trolls, goblins and other creatures she'd known before. In short, her children were both of the forest and the forest itself, until it became impossible to tell plant from animal and visa versa. This epiphany explained to her, at last, why it was that so few mortals had ever seen any of the fey in person: they simply hadn't known what to look for or how to look for it. Aoife took the time to stroll amongst her offspring, reaching out to touch each in gentle acknowledgement of their existence and worth in her life. The larger ones murmured so deeply, their voices thrummed in her chest. The smaller ones whispered their love in her ears. And the A'Shea found she was loath to leave them.

"Mother-sister," the satyr ventured after some time, "we must resume our journey. These here have flourished in our absence and will continue to do so. They shall grow powerful. But we must continue to spread the forest. That is the purpose of your blooming."

Aoife bobbed her head in agreement. "Yet, much of this confuses me."

"Say," the satyr urged.

"How can I be your mother? You seem so much older, wiser than I."

Toomt'-La grew still, somber. "It is true I am older. Thousands of years older. The End-of-All-Things destroyed my body, but I have been reborn through you, as have many of my brothers and sisters. As you are gradually being reborn through us."

"What...what does that mean?"

"We shall see!" Toomt'-La said, pleasure evident in his expression. "There has never been one like you. Even your children-siblings cannot say how you will grow." Aoife must have looked frightened, for the satyr reached out and placed a calming hand upon her shoulder. "But it will be...wonderful," he assured her.

In truth, Aoife did not always understand her companion's words. Not literally, anyway. But she understood their essence, and that was good enough. Toomt'-La had never led her astray. She would follow his lead in all things unless and until they encountered her brother. At that point, she suspected, emotions and her need for vengeance might get the best of her.

She took the satyr's hand, and they strolled back into the

second grove and from there, proceeded to walk in search of a third suitable nest.

Vykers, On the Trail

"If I didn't know better," Vykers beamed, "I'd think Mahnus and Alheria are actually smiling on me. Look at this valley! Exactly what we wanted."

Yeah, Arune intoned. *It's a wonderful place to kill yourself.*

The warrior snorted, looked around. He and his companions stood at the western end of a small valley. Its northern slope was steep but not dauntingly so; its southern slope was almost cliff-like, impossible to scale in a panic and topped with outcroppings of broken rock. Perfect.

"Here's the plan," Vykers told his chimeras. "Nobody in his right mind would take an army into this valley. But our enemy is overconfident. And why not? Twenty thousand, give-or-take, against five? They'll barge right in here after us, and we'll spring the trap on 'em."

The trap? Arune asked.

"We still need a little luck, here, but once the bulk of their forces have entered, the Svarren will sniff 'em out and come shrieking down that northern side. Arune says we'll only get a few thousand, but, coming out of nowhere, those ugly bastards should offer an unwelcome scare. That's when my Shaper friend starts blasting away at those outcroppings on the army's left flank. We'll have 'em pinned between a rockslide and the Svarren. 17, your job is to fire up the eastern end of this valley, to the enemy's back, if any of 'em try moving that way. Most'll want to run out our end, and that's where you other three fellas and I come in."

Much to Arune's surprise, she was getting good at reading the chimeras' expressions. "You...you want us to stop them?" Number 3 asked, dumbfounded. "Twenty-thousand soldiers?"

"Won't happen like that. Their leader'll figure they need to move up the northern slope to escape the rocks. That, and they have to deal with the Svarren. As I said, we need to, we'll seal that eastern end. Some'll try to come our way, too. Those, we cut to pieces." He studied the sky. "Looks like rain. That'd be good, too. Nobody wants to be caught in a valley in a downpour. Like I said, Mahnus and Alheria must be on our side, for once."

This is all conjecture, Arune protested. *We could just as easily get butchered. In fact, that's almost certain.*

Well, Sunshine, Vykers responded wryly, *you're forgetting one thing: if this works, we might just put an end to the coming war before it even gets going. This End-of-All Things is gonna figure if he can't take me and the chimeras down with twenty thousand men, how's he gonna fare when I've got the Queen's army at my back?*

Arune snorted. *That sounds grand. But now you're the one forgetting something: this tyrant is mad. A normal person might respond as you say, but a madman?*

Then I guess, Vykers concluded, *it's just a question of which of us is more mad.*

That is the stupidest fucking thing I've ever heard Arune wanted to say. But she knew it would make no difference. The Reaper was in his element.

Vykers made a large campfire atop a hillock near the valley's eastern entrance and sprawled leisurely in front of the flames, to Arune's mounting distress.

"This smoke will bring them to us all the faster," Vykers informed the chimeras. "And we wanna make sure they enter the trap, rather than wandering off to either side."

Incredibly, he rolled onto his back and closed his eyes. "Wake me if you see anything, huh?" To Arune he said, *Your Svarren still coming to the party?*

They are.

He began snoring, lightly.

Tarmun!

In an instant, he was on his feet with his sword in hand. The chimeras regarded him curiously. Dust clouds arose from the valley's far end.

Don't call me that, Vykers warned for the hundredth time.

It's the only sure way to get your attention, Arune replied. *And I've just discovered something you should know—*

Vykers waited.

That army out there, it's mostly slaves of some sort. Peasants.

And...?

They've been pressed into fighting, somehow. They've been... altered.

So? Vykers watched the dust clouds increase in size.

So? Arune cried. *So? So, they're being compelled to fight, Vykers. They may not even be aware of what's happening!*

Can you get to the point sometime in the near future? I've a battle to fight.

But you can't! Those people, they're innocent victims. If you kill them, you'll be no better than the End-of-All-Things.

Never said I was better, Vykers said dismissively.

That shut Arune up. He hadn't. Quite the contrary, the man hadn't come by his reputation by building hospitals and orphanages.

Only way to free them, Shaper, is to free them, he said finally, in a way that left no room for doubt as to his meaning.

In life, she would have fought him tooth-and-nail on this point. Now, she found it disturbingly easy to relent. *It's Brouton's Bind,* she told herself in horror. *I've got bloody Brouton's Bind.*

Where's my Svarren? Vykers asked, interrupting her panic.

Arune reached out. *A few miles north.*

They won't get here in time. That army won't take thirty minutes to reach us. Vykers was silent a moment, thinking. *What can you do to slow 'em down a bit?*

17 and I can throw some fire in their path. It won't stop them for long, but it should be enough.

Do it, Vykers commanded. In seconds, he heard dialogue bouncing around his skull that he took to be communication between the Shaper and chimera. And then the familiar but never welcome burning coursed through his body, a first sign that his order had been executed. At the valley's far end, huge gouts of flame leapt from the ground in the path of the advancing army, the second sign Vykers' order had been carried out. Without warning, the burning sensation became an order of magnitude stronger, forcing the Reaper to growl, *What in the infinite hells is going on?*

Arune's voice, fraught with tension and effort, responded, *They've got Shapers, too. You didn't think otherwise, did you? We're struggling with them now.*

Vykers stole a glance at 17, who stood rooted in his tracks, facial muscles twitching with strain and eyes fixed determinedly on a point about twelve inches in front of his forehead. Not Vykers' kind of battle, to be sure, but he was glad he had those who could handle it.

The distant flames surged and died away, surged and died away. At last, with a great whoosh, they died altogether, and the army continued forward.

They beat you?

Arune laughed weakly. *Tactical retreat.*

Uh-huh, Vykers replied dubiously.

Have to save some energy for the other chores you've assigned me...

Svarren?

Still coming.

"Well, shit!" Vykers said aloud. He eyed the chimeras and said, "I'm gonna go buy us some more time." Without waiting for a reply, he added, "You stay here. I'll probably be back in a few minutes."

"Probably?" Number 3 questioned.

Vykers smirked. "Yeah, I'll be back." The warrior adjusted the angle of his sword hilt, tightened his belt a notch and, satisfied, strode down into the valley proper.

What in Mahnus' name are you doing now? Arune demanded.

You just focus on getting those savages down here as fast as you can. I don't mind impossible odds, but don't mind improving them even less.

The Reaper walked confidently towards the approaching army and didn't stop until he was just out of bowshot. Abruptly, the enemy stopped, at which sight Vykers broke into a crooked grin.

Well, well, well. They're not so mindless after all. Or at least their commanders aren't.

And what does that signify?

I'll tell ya later. If it works.

"Hello, the army!" he yelled across to his adversaries.

From within the throng, a voice bellowed out in return, "Tarmun Vykers! We arrest you in the name of our Supreme Ruler, Grand Torzine, High Priest and Arch Sorcerer, End-of-All-Things, Last of Mortals and First of the New Gods, Anders Cestroenyn."

Grand Torzine? The fuck is that? Vykers asked his Shaper.

Never heard of it; I'm pretty sure it's made up.

"That's quite a name." The Reaper called out. "I knew a whore once who always said men with the biggest titles have the smallest pricks." In Vykers' experience, most armies would have been enraged by such taunting. This one, however, stood slack-jawed and drooling, awaiting its leaders' commands.

"Tarmun Vykers!" the voice called out again. "You are under arrest. Submit and live or resist and die!"

The Reaper laughed. What else could he do? The whole situation was ridiculous. "Big man, you are, whoever you are!" he shouted back. "Hiding inside your fortress of flesh. Why don't you come out here and arrest me yourself?"

The air around him grew so still, Vykers could hear the army's individual fighters—if that's what they were—breathing through their mouths and shuffling restlessly in place. After several minutes, someone within the enemy ranks issued a muffled "forward!" and the horde stumbled back into motion. A flash of motion in Vykers' peripheral vision attracted his attention. Glancing up the northern slope, he caught a glimpse of Svarren bursting out of the tree line and making for the valley floor. The Reaper didn't even wait to see the number of his unlikely allies, but jogged back towards the chimeras, chuckling to himself all the way.

"This'll be interesting," he said, to no one in particular. When he reached his companions, he turned to watch both the army and the Svarren advance. As the misshapen savages caught wind of the army, they went into a rabid frenzy and fairly threw themselves down the slope into its right flank.

Hit those outcroppings, Shaper, if you've got anything left to offer! Vykers thought urgently at Arune.

Great bolts of white light exploded from Vykers' chest and lanced towards the cliff tops to his southeast. He winced for the briefest moment at the internal searing such shaping brought on, but was immediately gratified to see showers of rock cascading down onto the army below. And then he scowled. A normal army composed of normal men would have spooked at the sudden appearance of Svarren and the equally unexpected avalanche. This army—or the bulk of it, anyway—continued forward as if these twin perils were no more annoying than gnats.

"More rocks!" Vykers yelled, forgetting to issue this order internally. "And 17," he added, "change of plans. Hit 'em in the face with everything you've got. They're not backing off like I thought they would, so we're gonna have to push 'em."

The army drew nearer, within three hundred paces. Svarren could plainly be heard hissing, snarling and ululating as they fell upon their prey, while their opponents merely grunted or made strange keening sounds in reply. Vykers also heard more composed voices yelling within the force's mass, along with the sound of war drums beating a steady rhythm and whips cracking to inspire continued movement. The army's right and left flanks buckled inwards to some extent and bodies began to pile up on either side, but the majority of the enemy trudged forward unabated. Once more, an enormous wall of flame leapt up in its path, stalling the enemy's advance at last.

Number 17's face was a mask of tense concentration, and Vykers noticed the other three chimeras rocking or swaying from foot to foot in anticipation of the coming clash. Behind the wall of flame, the shrieking of Svarren and thrall reached a fever pitch, even as boulders and smaller rubble continued to rain down from the valley's southern cliffs. The army's forward edge stumbled onward, into and through the flames, while the strange keening of the thrall intensified.

Vykers felt rather than saw 17 collapse on his right,

thoroughly drained from his efforts. Shortly thereafter, Arune withdrew, too, and became decidedly quiescent. The Reaper surveyed the enemy a final moment before engaging. His plan had worked—to some extent—but fully three-quarters of the enemy's force remained on its feet and in motion, despite the mounds of wounded or dead. Vykers hefted his sword, passed it from hand-to-hand.

"Can you boys run and still carry him?" he asked Number 3 while pointing to the unconscious 17.

It was the first time he'd ever seen his strange comrades look relieved.

"We can!" 3 answered, a little too enthusiastically.

"Then let's get the hell out of here!" Vykers commanded as he turned and ran, not bothering to wait for a response.

Eager though it was, the enemy's army could not maneuver around its own casualties fast enough to pursue. Secretly, General Shere was grateful for that. He'd just lost an impossibly large portion of his army to...what, exactly? He wanted nothing more than to make camp and discuss the day's debacle with his Shapers and his fellow officers. He did not possess the kind of troops necessary to chase his quarry down and, clearly, might alone was not going to get the job done, either. Somehow, some way, Shere would have to outsmart the Reaper. He wondered if he should just fall on his sword now and get it over with.

EIGHT

Long, the End's Host

"Care for a bit o' firewater?" A voice asked behind him. Turning around, a bone-weary Long found himself sizing up the first truly human, sympathetic face he'd seen in…he didn't know how long.

"Name's Yendor. Yendor Plotz, though I'm s'posed to say 'General Plotz.' Them as have fought before's automatically made general in the High So-and-So's Host, don'tcha know." He held out a water skin at arm's length.

Long stared at it, in a near-stupor.

"It's good stuff, honest." Plotz said, then seemed to reconsider. "Well, it tastes awful," he amended, "but it's got more than enough kick to calm your nerves for hours. Try a pull."

Slowly, Long extended his hand and took the proffered skin. He couldn't afford one more enemy, and the man might prove helpful in the future, though Long couldn't imagine how. Uncorking the brew, he sniffed it and nearly retched, causing the other man to laugh. Gauging the unhappy look on Long's face, Plotz retrieved the skin and took a swig himself.

"See?" he asked Long, shivering from the apparently loathsome flavor. "Tastes just this side 'o the grave, but—sweet Sister Mumfreckles!—what a kick!" Again, Plotz offered the skin to Long. Again, Long accepted it. He'd swallowed D'Kem's strange elixir. How bad could this be?

Very, very bad, as it turned out. The stuff brawling its way down his throat was by far the worst thing Long had ever tasted. And he would have thrown up, if he hadn't temporarily lost control of his nervous system, sending him into shuddering spasms of disgust that occupied his every conscious thought. After several minutes, the sensation passed and Long felt an utterly unholy warmth spreading from his stomach into his limbs. "What in Alheria's name is *that* shit?" he bellowed.

"Skent," Plotz shrugged. "It's made from fermented Baleerian urine."

Long was poleaxed. "Here's what I wanna know," he said, "what in the countless hells was wrong with the first man to try this stuff? I mean, what possesses a man to even consider something like this without knowing anything else about it?"

"The kick, you mean?"

"Aye, the kick. Not knowing that part even exists, why would someone get near this stuff in the first place, much less put it to his lips?"

Yendor Plotz laughed as he thought of it, and Long joined him.

"Yep, that's some right nasty shit."

"Oh, mate, it's that and then some."

"But, again, there's that kick."

"Yes, yes." Long found himself feeling rather light of limb and somewhat mischievous.

"Care for another taste?" Plotz inquired.

Uncharacteristically, Long giggled. "Don't mind if I do!"

It was an epic struggle just rising into a kneeling position and Long felt, not for the first time, that maybe he had a drinking problem. Oh, he didn't drink often. But when he did drink, the results were practically always catastrophic. Witness his current condition, a hangover worse than any he'd ever felt, worse than the mead that brought him into Mardine's bed, worse than D'Kem's fell potion, worse than anything. He might've come up with a suitable metaphor, if only he weren't so devastated.

"Urmphllll..." someone groaned nearby.

Long was assaulted by the horrendous howling of the muscles, tendons and vertebrae in his neck as he turned his head to seek the source of that groan. His temples pounded like

Mahnus' own war drums. Two paces off, Yendor lay in a pool of his own creation, though Long was unwilling to ponder the substance of that creation.

"Ffffffuck. Me." Yendor managed.

"Mind if I wait 'til I'm not dead?" Long retorted sourly.

His new friend actually laughed. It was a painful, sickly sort of laugh; still, the bastard must have been superhuman.

A stretch of minutes passed, during which Long felt breathing was the most difficult task he'd ever undertaken. Finally, he said "I'm guessing the point of this little picnic was to teach me there are some things worse than the End-of-All-Things' wrath…?"

Yendor laughed yet again.

Long did not. "I'm gonna hafta kill you when I feel better."

"Fine by me," Yendor moaned, rolling onto his back like some great, beached sea creature.

Long gave in and crashed back onto his back, as well. "The fuck drinks fermented piss that makes you yearn for death?"

More croaking laughter from the other man. "I knew I was gonna like you, General Pete, the moment I saw you."

"Can't imagine what you'd do if you hated me…"

"Prob'ly make you drink *fresh* piss!"

This time, even Long started laughing until his tears carved streaks down his filthy cheeks and made a sodden mess of the hair on the back of his head.

Time passed, and Long slowly became aware of the thrall, still shuffling to-and-fro to no apparent purpose. He sat up, surprised at his own resilience. Yendor had fallen asleep, snoring lustily despite his circumstances. Long battled his way to his feet and was reminded of the way toddlers do the same in their first few attempts.

The sun was setting. He'd wasted a whole day or, rather, wasted a wasted day. Didn't that mean he'd redeemed it? He was still too muzzy to sort that out. What Long did know was that no one had come by to check on him or his charges all day, except for Yendor. Strange army, this was. A light breeze wafted through the camp and, setting aside the stench of his thralls, it felt rather pleasant on his face. The sound of purposeful footsteps approaching cleared his head in an instant.

"You General Fendesst?" a rather non-descript soldier in battle motley asked (battle motley, as experienced campaigners called it, was whatever mismatched assembly of armor and weapons a fighter could scrabble together in the field).

Long sighed. "Guess so."

"The End wants to see you."

'The End?' Long thought. *Cute nickname for a monster.*

It was a long, deeply depressing walk through the host's maze of camps until Long and his guide reached their destination.

"In you go," the other man said. "I weren't invited, and I ain't following."

"Lucky for you," Long replied.

The man turned without a word and disappeared into the gloom. Long entered the tent.

"General Fendesst," an unwelcome voice crooned, "how are you enjoying your new...assignment?"

The-End-of-All-Things was in a distant corner of the huge tent, reclining on a large bearskin rug, next to the infant Long had glimpsed earlier. When Long failed to respond, the End prompted, "Come closer, man. It is difficult to have a civilized conversation when yelling across so much space."

Absent other options, Long obeyed and drew nearer. Even spread out on the floor and playing with a small child, there was something ghastly about the sorcerer.

"Good," the End said, "Good. Now, you didn't answer my question: how are you enjoying your new assignment?"

Perhaps it was the lingering effect of the Skent, but Long felt unafraid of answering honestly. "I go by Long, and I am not. Enjoying it, I mean."

The End nodded. "Well, then, you're not completely stupid, are you? Nor cowardly, speaking your mind like that. To me."

Long wasn't sure what was expected of him.

"That lack of stupidity and cowardice might make you valuable to me. But I must have your complete loyalty."

The silence that followed, though it must surely have been no more than a few seconds, seemed in Long's mind to last an eternity.

"If you will turn to your right, General Long, you will find reason to prove loyal to me."

The shock was almost overwhelming. Stepping out of a darkened corner Long hadn't inspected on his way in were three guards pulling the chained form of...Mardine. A single second of eye contact and then she refused to look up at him, so miserable and ashamed was she. Long wondered if he could reach the End-of-All-Things and actually do any kind of damage to the man before being killed himself.

"I know what you're thinking!" the End intoned in a sing-song voice. "I wouldn't try it, if I were you, but I admire your pluck."

Long watched in horror as the End passed something dead to the child to play with.

"And here's why you'll never betray me, General..."

"I'm no general."

"But you are. Interrupt me again, though, and I'll tear your lady love's ears off and make you eat them. Where was I?" The End gazed at the child, as if expecting him to answer. "Ah, yes. Your loyalty. I believe I mentioned earlier that your giantess is with child. I wasn't convinced you quite believed me, so I've brought you together so you can see the truth of it for yourself."

Oh, he saw the truth of it. One look at Mardine's defeated body language told him everything he needed to know. He felt as if he'd gone completely hollow and was slowly being filled up with ice water. The End broke into weirdly musical laughter at his discomfort.

"Amazing, is it not? I'm terribly curious to see the thing, of course. I'll probably add it to my menagerie when it comes. I do so love a good curiosity. At the same time, you know, children are so malleable. Truth to tell, I've been getting a mite bored of this one," he said, gesturing to the child by his side, "and the get of a man and a giant, well! Thrillingly bizarre!"

"You're insane," Long managed at last.

And found himself flying through the air and out of the tent, unable to breathe as if he'd been kicked by a score of horses. As he lay on his back, disoriented and in agony, the End came and stood over him.

"You will obey me, General. You will accede to my every wish and whim, and you will address me with respect, or I will rip your child from the womb and immerse it in molten iron. Then, I will beat your love to death with the smoldering result and make you watch."

Long dared not even inhale.

"Do you understand me, General?"

Long nodded.

"You are mine, now. Mine. And when we go to fight the Bitch Queen, you will command and fight and die for me." The End's eyes seethed with a fury the like of which Long had never seen or imagined. "That is all."

Vykers, On the Trail

I don't believe it! The great Tarmun Vykers—the legendary warrior—ran away from a battle! Arune said.

If it hadn't, I'd have been legendary for my stupidity and not my fighting, Vykers countered.

Still, I don't know whether to be disappointed or relieved.

I'm not done, yet.

Oh?

Whoever's commanding that shambles they call an army seems bent and determined to waste every last body they've got in pursuit of us.

Of you.

Yes. Down south, I could lead them into a desert and watch them all die of thirst and exposure.

Ah. But there are no deserts up here, are there? Too rainy and cold by half. We...Arune paused, chuckled. I think I've got just the thing, she said finally.

Shere, In Pursuit of Vykers

His fate had been sealed in that last engagement, Shere realized. The only excuse for losing his grunts on such a massive scale was in capturing Tarmun Vykers. But Shere had not done so.

He'd never even come close. In fact, it was now painfully evident he hadn't the right resources for the game of cat-and-mouse his quarry proposed. Overwhelming numbers alone were not the answer; guile was, and Shere had precious little of that.

One of the other "generals" approached, but Shere thought of the man as little more than a glorified sergeant. "What's the damage?" Shere asked him.

The other man shook his head, sneered at nothing in particular. "Over five thousand dead, another three-or-so going to it shortly."

"That's more than a quarter of our army," Shere said, more to himself than his confederate.

"What do you want to do?"

Shere became angry. "Want? What do I *want* to do?" Flecks of spittle sprayed the other man as Shere heated up. "Want's got nothing to do with it, has it? We fucking press on. We catch that bastard Vykers and bring him back in chains, or the End'll make us howl for it!"

The target of his outburst saluted weakly and walked off. Shere would like to have been ashamed of himself, but he hated everyone and everything associated with this pathetic army and the greater host to which it belonged. He was damned, and he knew it. The only question that really bothered him was why he hadn't the courage to kill himself and be done with it.

Vykers, In the Moors

Having skirted the moors days ago, the chimeras were of course mystified to be returning and actually entering them now. But inquiries as to the purpose of such action were always greeted with Vykers' enigmatic grin and an equally cryptic "you'll see" or something similar. Normal men might have received such a paucity of information with predictable trepidation. Not being normal, however, the chimeras were only perplexed. They had even learned to adopt Vykers' characteristic shrug, as if to say "It makes no difference to me, one way or the other." The very fact they were asking, however, told Vykers that it did. In straights as dire as theirs and surroundings as bleak, these little games were sometimes the only things that kept them sane.

The hard, reliable ground they'd all been used to gradually gave way to tussocks and clumps of softer soil, floating in mossy bogs.

How far'd you say this thing is across? Vykers asked the Shaper.

That depends on your speed, of course, but days and days, by anybody's measure.

Days and days, is it? I like it.

I thought you might, Arune answered wryly.

A dense, almost tangible mist began to seep up from the mire, reaching knee and sometimes belt height, making the search for solid footing evermore difficult. To Vykers' surprise, the chimeras seemed possessed of some instinctive knowledge of such things and had no difficulty scouting the path for him.

"Where'd you learn how to do that?" Vykers wondered aloud.

"Here and there," Number 3 said, smiling sheepishly.

Vykers laughed: they were giving his own back to him. "But can you lead us to the center?" he asked, seriously.

This time, it was Number 17 who responded. "I believe we can, Master. Yes."

"Good," Vykers nodded. "Good."

It got dark so early, the Reaper felt a tinge of uncertainty.

That's the mist, Arune assured him. *We've only just now passed mid-day.*

Huh. I guess you and the boys'll have to tell us when to camp, then, 'cause I can't tell my ass from my elbow in this soup.

Arune sighed. *Ah, the quips we forego in the name of friendship.*

Friendship?

Stranger things have happened.

Vykers glanced ahead to the dim shapes of the chimeras. *Truer words were never...whispered in someone's head by a ghost.*

In full health, the Reaper was not a man to get tired, period. But he'd never slogged through an endless marsh before, either. The good news, as he saw it, was that it would be a worse hell for his pursuers. It had to be. After some time, Vykers was ready to bed down for the day.

"Where's a good place to make camp?" he asked aloud.

"There's a small island just off to the left a few hundred strides. It should be sufficient for the four of us," Number 3 replied.

"Five. Five of us," Number 17 reminded him, "counting the other Shaper."

Wading through the muck, Vykers slipped, sank and had to be rescued more than once.

"This does wonders for a man's self-image," he grumbled.

I'm sure your self- image will be just fine, Arune answered.

The promised island was little more than a glorified clump of moss and roots, but Vykers was glad to finally climb ashore and get off his feet. The whole island settled a bit deeper into the water once the others joined him and bobbed ever so slightly with their movements.

"One more man and we'd likely sink," Vykers said, giving voice to everyone's thoughts, and then "Can anyone get a fire going?" This was something he'd done himself countless times, but with two Shapers in their number, he had no qualms in passing that frustrating chore along.

"I will do it," Number 17 replied, as Vykers had suspected he would.

If you want me to do something, why not just say so? Arune asked.

What, the fire? No, I want you to do that thing you do, scout the surroundings for potential threats.

Uh-huh. And what are you going to do?

Vykers stretched out on an especially lush patch of moss. *Sleep.* A sullen silence greeted him. *Look, Burn, I'm a fighter. Show me something to kill, and I'll kill it. This other stuff? Scouting, hunting, starting fires? You four are better at that, and we all know it. So: you do what* you're *good at. Time comes, I'll do what* I'm *good at.*

You're pretty good at giving orders, Arune quipped.

But Vykers was already asleep.

Vykers awoke with a painful frost on his tongue and a roaring susurration in his ears. Hundreds, thousands of minute swatches of darkness swirled about him, diving at his face as if seeking entrance to his body. He could feel them leaching at his warmth, sucking the heat right out of him. So numerous were they, Vykers had trouble seeing the four chimeras, though he could hear them struggling well enough.

Arune!

Working on it!

Vykers felt blindly, frantically for his sword. A blade would be useless in this situation, but maybe…He found it, ripped it from its scabbard and was instantly greeted with a sound like a chorus of midsummer firecrackers, multiplied by a thousand. All around him, the little specks of darkness exploded in showers of sparks. The few that escaped that fate raced, hissing, off into the moors.

"Anybody wanna tell me what that was all about?"

The chimeras shrugged. Or at least Vykers thought they did.

Would that I could.

That's helpful. I thought you Burners knew everything.

Arune snorted. *Hardly. The more you study, the more you realize you don't know anything.*

Then why study, if the results the same either way?

I didn't say the result was the same. Only that there's so much more to learn, to discover.

Think I'm gonna puke. You sound like a bleedin' A'Shea.

We're not so different.

Right, right. A'Shea are always runnin' around settin' shit on fire…

Arune went silent, as he knew she would, with the now-familiar sensation of a door being closed elsewhere in the building. Just as well. He needed time to think.

Oh, yes, their pursuers were going to *love* this place.

Deda, In Lunessfor

The Queen's castle had stymied Wims' best efforts to sneak in. He'd tried for a fortnight and had gotten nowhere and learned nothing—except that Lunessfor's upper crust was damned serious about its security. Between the city watch, the Queen's Swords and various privately contracted entities, the castle was clamped shut tighter than the thighs of the newest A'Shea initiate. A man couldn't even go for an innocent stroll in the city's sewers without attracting unwelcome attention.

It was over a mug of cider one night that Wims finally caught a break. During his brief stay in Lunessfor, he'd developed a powerful appreciation for the city's particular brand of pear cider, and of all the places he'd sampled it, the Farmer's Daughter had by far his favorite vintage. By sheer coincidence, the Farmer's Daughter was also the tavern of choice for members of House Radcliffe, one of the more aggressive families wheeling and dealing for the Queen's throne after her hoped-for death.

Eavesdropping on the Radcliffes, Wims first thought of killing one and assuming his victim's identity in order to gain entrance to the castle. He soon dismissed the idea as unlikely to deceive anyone. Listening to the Radcliffes' venal and duplicitous chatter, he realized a more direct approach might be best. Perhaps some sort of deal could be struck between these vultures and the End-of-All-Things, an agreement of sorts—although he knew full well neither side would ever honor it. And he only needed it to hold long enough to get him inside. Wims' ace-in-the-hole was that he knew these were Radcliffes, and they would think him unaware of that fact.

Without another thought, Wims jumped right in. He began muttering to himself in barely audible tones. Halfway through a third (or fourth?) mug of cider, his mutterings got louder and began to annoy those sitting at nearby tables. Success! One of the Radcliffes leaned towards him and said "Keep it down, old sot!"

"I won't!" Wims replied. "If I don't like Her Majesty, ain't no one can make me speak well of her!"

Immediately, the other man's gaze took on a furtive, conspiratorial quality. "Easy, then, easy," he urged. "I'm just looking out for your safety and welfare. Not everyone is as understanding and open-minded as my fellows and I. Speak such thoughts too loudly in the wrong crowd and you're minus one head!"

Wims made a big show of scanning the room for spies and continued under his breath, "Yes, well, it's time the old hag went to it, is all I was saying. Her brains have turned to mush! Let someone younger and fitter take the reins."

"Indeed," the other man said, hushing his tablemates and sliding a fresh flagon of whatever he'd been drinking in front of Wims. "Trouble is, Her Majesty isn't in a cooperative mood." He sighed, "What's to be done, eh?"

Taking an enormous swig of the proffered beverage—which turned out to be a surprisingly tasty brown ale—Wims belched, "I can think of a thing or two. Unfortunately, there's no way in to the castle." He pretended to lose himself in his drink long enough to give his new friend time to confer in urgent whispers with his cohorts.

"Well," their leader said at last, "I think there may be a way we can get you in to the castle. But…er…what are you planning once you get inside? You'll never be able to get near Her Majesty, and even if you did, her Swords'd cut you down before you laid a finger on her."

"I s'pose you're right," Wims agreed, acting defeated. A moment later, he feigned epiphany. "But if I was to sow enough mischief around inside—foul the food stores, poison the wells, spread gossip, discreetly damage important items, that sort o' thing—I'm guessing I could make hanging on a lot less appealing for the old bitch." Of course, it was a stupid plan. The question was whether or not the Radcliffes would find it—and Wims—sufficiently stupid for their *own* plans.

Once more, the other man and his associates whispered amongst themselves. Wims made out the name of House Gault and quickly understood that, yes, his new friends had taken the bait: they would get him into the castle under the Gault name, and Wims, supposedly none-the-wiser, would seriously embarrass House Gault with everything he attempted. Plainly, the Radcliffes expected him to die, but in the process they believed he'd knock the Gaults down a peg or two.

Naturally, they were generous with the ale.

Come morning, Wims—who was nowhere near as hung over as he should have been—stood at the appointed rendezvous, just outside a tinker's on Shale Street. The Radcliffe fellow sauntered up as arranged and pretended to ask directions to a local apothecary. During this charade, he successfully passed a small parcel Wims' way without attracting a moment's notice from passersby. That done, he thanked the "helpful citizen," and wandered off in the direction Wims had pointed. Wims, then, spent half the morning meandering through various back alleys before returning to the inn he had called home for the past two weeks. He enjoyed a rather large meal and then headed up to his room, to sleep off the last of the previous evening's alcohol. The truth was, he was simply putting as much space between himself and House Radcliffe as possible. The next morning, when he approached the castle with his newly acquired credentials in hand, no one would be able to connect him with the Gaults' nemeses. At least, Wims had convinced the Radcliffes that was so; he had yet to decide for himself whom to damage and whom to spare; if he could contrive to bloody everyone's nose, so much the better.

That evening, Wims concluded that he'd exercised enough patience and finally opened the parcel the Radcliffes had supplied him. Inside, he found a letter from House Gault, introducing him to the castle guards as one Merius Quendl, and requesting his admission in order to "Bring physic to our beloved uncle Konr, resting in hospice in Her Majesty's east wing," etc., etc., etc. Apparently, this Konr Gault had fallen ill some time ago during a feast in the castle and been deemed too ill to travel back to the Gault estates. Her Majesty would not hear of endangering his life further by letting him leave until he was fully recovered...which, as the ensuing months had proven, seemed less and less likely every day. It was a reasonably cunning ruse on the Radcliffe's part, Wims thought, but the paperwork would be the deciding factor. Along with the letter—stamped with the official seal of House Gault (or something wickedly similar)—was a silver ring, boasting the Gault crest in miniature and another, sealed letter for Konr. That last was a nice touch, Wims felt, because it implied a desperate optimism, when in fact everyone knew Konr would never be able to read it.

The following day, Wims was actually excited to see how well this subterfuge would work. He was not disappointed. After only a few minutes' interrogation, the guards ushered him right into the castle. Evidently, the easiest way to accomplish evil goals was by pretending to do good. In that regard, a little false concern for others was a much deadlier poison than open rancor. Wims determined to remember that for future reference.

Janks, the Queen's Camp

"That the best you got, Wanks?" Sergeant Kittins jeered. "My old nanna hit harder than that and she lost both arms to the plague!"

Another day, another beating disguised as sparring with Sergeant Kittins. Say one thing for the guy: he enjoyed his job. "Come on, ya simpering flower girl!" Kittins yelled again. "I've given you the bleedin' mace, and I'm unarmed! Ya need me to wear a blindfold, too?"

Not a blindfold, Janks thought. A gag would sure be nice, though. The inescapable truth, however, was that Janks would never score a solid hit on his sergeant. The other man lived to inflict pain—he even seemed to enjoy receiving it, on those rare occasions when someone else connected—but ever since Janks had lost Long, he just couldn't bring himself to care anymore, about Kittins, the war or his squad mates. Part of him even hoped Kittins would kill him, hit him a touch too hard one day and stove his skull in. Janks just didn't give a shit.

"Ah, you're hopeless!" the sergeant roared. He then stepped into Janks, ripped the mace out of his hand and smashed himself on the head with it. "See that, girly? That's how it's done!"

If only he'd have hit himself harder.

"Yes sir," Janks said.

Kittins threw the mace down in disgust. "You'll never be a soldier, Wanks. How you've managed to live this long is beyond me." After a long, uncomfortable silence, Kittins finally walked away.

Rem's voice invaded Janks' moment of peace. "He's smarter than you take him for, you know."

Janks said nothing, moved not a muscle.

"If you're trying to get him to kill you, I mean."

Janks looked over at his newest old friend. Was it that obvious?

"He'll find a million trivial jobs for you, he'll run you ragged and belittle you forever. But he'll never let you win," Rem concluded.

"I've made a right ruin o' this squad," Janks breathed. "Got my best friends killed. The fuck do I care what Kittins does or doesn't do to me?"

"I believe you assume too much."

Janks looked wearily over at the actor.

"We don't know Long's dead—or Spirk or Mardine or D'Kem, for that matter. Fears ain't facts, as my old da used to say."

A burst of raucous laughter caught both men's attention, and Janks turned in time to see Kittins and Bash, blood streaming from their faces, arms thrown across one another's shoulders, stagger back towards the tents.

"It appears Kittins has found a worthy playmate, at last." Rem joked.

"Much joy may it bring him," Janks murmured.

Spirk and D'Kem, On the Trail

"D'Kem! D'Kem!" the young man yelled at him. "Wake up, will ya?"

The Shaper rolled over and cracked one eye to see Spirk standing over him, hopping from foot to foot. "Mmmm?" D'Kem groaned.

"I have to piss!"

D'Kem exhaled mightily and rolled back to his previous position, trying to recapture the warmth he'd felt only seconds ago.

"I'm serious, D'Kem! I have to piss."

"So piss."

"Yeah, but I need to know if it's safe."

"It's never safe," the old Shaper said.

"It's not?" Spirk's voice rose an octave, at least. If he'd had the presence of mind, he might've noticed the faint trace of a smile that graced the old man's lips. "Really? What am I supposed to do? When will it be safe?"

D'Kem rolled onto his back and stared into the sky, his smile completely gone. "What's all this about, anyway?" he asked, rather irritably.

"The End-of-the-World might have spies looking for us. I don't wanna get killed taking a piss!"

"Is there a better way to die?" D'Kem asked.

"Well, that's just it: I don't wanna die!" A moment, and then, "Leastways, not right now and not right here."

D'Kem sighed and sat up. Again, an astute observer might have suggested the old man looked less...old, less worn. There was a new clarity in his eyes and a sense of growing strength. Spirk saw none of this. D'Kem climbed to his feet, stretched, looked about. He and Spirk had slept amongst a small grove of Synlaeys bushes, their citrusy scent permeating everything in their vicinity and cloaking the men's odors from predators and search parties. Without a word, the Shaper began picking leaves from the bushes and secreting them on his person. D'Kem was almost shocked when he turned and found Spirk still standing nearby.

"Can I piss now?"

D'Kem waved a hand and the boy's bladder let loose, drenching his trousers and leaving him utterly gobsmacked.

"Better?" D'Kem asked, dryly.

"You! You...you made me piss m'self!"

"But I thought you wanted to piss! Isn't that what you said, over and over?"

"Not in my own pants!" Spirk yelled, stamping his foot.

D'Kem said something under his breath, and the boy's pants began to dry quite rapidly.

Spirk wasn't quite mollified. "I'm still gonna stink to high Desnar!"

Gritting his teeth, D'Kem grabbed a handful of Synlaeys leaves, walked over to his companion and roughly shoved the lot down the kid's trousers. "Now, let's hear no more about your piss, your pants or your problems!" He told Spirk forcefully. "We've got bigger fish to fry."

"Well, I am kinda hungry, now you mention it."

D'Kem stalked off.

"Hey! Where are you going?"

"I don't think this is a good idea," Spirk warned later, as D'Kem prepared to attract the attention of a scouting party.

Did you just use the words 'think' and 'idea' in the same sentence? The Shaper almost asked in irritation. The young man had been babbling since they'd awoken that morning, and his constant chatter was driving the older man to distraction. But there was nothing for it: the boy was what he was, whatever that was.

"Look, Spirk," he began. "Each of us has his role to play...I haven't yet discovered what yours may be, although doubtless it's of paramount importance. My role at the moment seems to be returning our host's hospitality by stealing a few of his troops, just as he's taken our sergeant and giant."

Spirk stared at him, open-mouthed.

D'Kem shook his head. The scouting party drew nearer. The Shaper tried again, "Spirk."

"Yes?"

"The End-of-All-Things captured us, did he not?"

"'Course he did! You was there."

"Yes. And now I'm going to return the favor and capture a few of his men."

Instantly, the younger man grew anxious. "We gonna torture 'em?"

"That's for the Major Bailis to decide."

Spirk nodded. "But what about Long Pete and Mardine?"

D'Kem put a hand on his shoulder. "I'm sure they're being held in or near the command tent—where the End-of-All-Things spends most of his time. In a host that large, there's simply no way we could locate and free them without getting them both—and ourselves—killed. Better to trust in Mahnus and accomplish what good we may from the outside."

"I don't like it," Spirk concluded after a lengthy pause.

"No," D'Kem agreed, "nor do I. But there it is, nonetheless."

There being nothing more he could say to the boy by way of reassurance, the Shaper turned his attentions to the approaching scouts. There were five of them, lightly armored for speed and distance of travel. They were looking for signs of the Queen's army, not two lone men on foot, so it was entirely possible they would ride right on past, unless...

D'Kem cupped his hands on either side of his mouth. He felt a moment's uncertainty as to how best to draw them in, through flattery, an appeal for help or outright belligerence. Since he was past pretending anything other than contempt for anyone working for the End-of-All-Things, he decided upon insults.

"Cowards!" he yelled lustily. "Cutthroat dogs! Filthy, inbred, mercenary scum!"

In his peripheral vision, he could see that Spirk was becoming alarmed, so he hissed "Stay back!" with all the intensity he could muster. To his relief, the younger man obeyed.

The scouts came on, confident in their numbers, ability and mounted advantage. They spent not a moment pondering the peculiarities of the situation but silently agreed that whatever the old bumpkin's motives in abusing them might be, he indisputably needed to suffer for such disrespect. At one hundred paces, their confidence bloomed, and they spurred their horses into a gallop.

D'Kem felt Spirk's hand on his upper arm. "Not now!" he yelled at the boy.

At twenty-five paces, D'Kem did a quick, almost furtive series of gestures. By fifteen paces, the horses had slowed to a trot, their riders equally slow in reacting to this development. Spirk let out a startled yelp, but the Shaper remained focused on his adversaries. When they finally came to within arm's reach, mounts and riders alike seemed barely awake. One man listed sideways, and gravity pulled him to the ground with a thump. He didn't even wake up.

"We'll leave him behind, then," D'Kem said, "Unless you fancy lifting him back into his saddle."

Spirk, goggle-eyed, could only shake his head in response.

D'Kem made a dry, chuffing noise that sounded like it might evolve into laughter in a couple of years. "You needn't worry, lad. They're asleep. I'll keep the men that way and rouse the horses when we need to go."

"But how do we...?"

"We'll each climb up and ride behind one of these scouts. From a distance, it'll look like we're their prisoners, or perhaps part of their party. At any rate, I can deal with anyone who gets too curious."

Spirk believed it and was uncharacteristically silent.

"Nothing remains, but we take these bastards back to Major Bailis."

Spirk's thoughts drifted back to Long Pete and Mardine. He hated abandoning them like this.

Long, the End's Host

He was talking to Yendor when he saw the man's eyes go wide and the color drain from his face. The other man even took a step backwards and lowered his head in submission. Without turning, Long knew the End-of-All-Things was behind him. Steeling himself, he did turn. The sorcerer frightened him, anyway, standing a mere foot from Long's face. Now, it was Long who took a step back.

Without introduction, the End-of-All-Things held up a familiar flask and asked "Where is the Shaper who made this elixir?"

How to reply? "I've not seen him or the boy since you summoned me from that first holding pen." Long said.

The End-of-All-Things was silent, ruminative. He looked around as if seeing his surroundings for the first time. "Tell me everything you know of this Shaper," he commanded.

Long didn't hesitate. "He's an old burn-out. I didn't even want to travel with him at first, truth be told. Didn't see how he could help the squad."

"The fellow's name?"

"D'Kem. Anyhow, that's what everyone calls him."

"How long have you known him?"

"Well," Long hedged, "I've known *of* him for a couple of years. But *known* him? We've only been working together a scant two months."

"During which time, you witnessed him doing what, exactly? As a Shaper?"

Long laid it on. "Not bloody much. Set a guy's beard on fire once when a friend's life was a stake. The friend died and the Shaper fell back asleep. 'Nother time, I saw him kill an archer with an exploding arrow. He mighta started a campfire or two. Things like that."

The End-of-All-Things frowned, held the flask up again. "Do you know the purpose of this elixir?"

Now, Long could share without reservation. "It's nasty stuff. I was stupid enough to try some once..."

"You tasted this?" the End asked, astonished. "Whatever possessed you to do that?"

"I dunno. Thought it was some sort of special liquor."

The End considered Long with an appraising eye. "I'll have to reassess both your physical strength and your intelligence. The one's much better than I'd assumed; the other, much worse. This...*stuff*...is meant to disable the ability to Shape and blunt the desire to try. Presumably, then, it alleviates the burning that most Shapers feel constantly, to one degree or another." He paused. "If your D'Kem drank this regularly and was still able to walk and converse—to say nothing of casting minor spells—he's much, much more than you took him for." Another pause. "How does it feel to have been deceived for so long, by one so close to you?"

What he did not say, Long deduced, was that D'Kem had somehow escaped and the End, remarkably, felt threatened by the old burn-out. Long tried a different tack. "And the boy? Is he still...?"

"I have no interest in the cretin." the End responded. "But I do have one other item of interest to you: my scouts have located a village a day's ride to the northwest. As you may have surmised, it has been my practice to raze villages and press the most-able of their citizens into my host. Tomorrow, you and I will travel to this village and, in order to make myself thoroughly understood, I will kill every last man, woman, child or animal I find. This, I do on your behalf, so that you will know I have both the will and the means to do what I say."

Long about collapsed in horror. "That is not...necessary. I believe you. I believe you are, as you say, the 'End-of-All-Things'."

The sorcerer smirked. "You would have me spare them?"

Long nodded.

"Beg."

Long sank to his knees, bowed his head. "I beg you...master. I beg you not to do this thing."

"Kiss my feet."

Inwardly, Long wept. If he produced any real tears, he was too shaken to notice. He leaned forward and kissed the End's left boot. Before he got to the right, the End erupted in laughter.

"You may as well entreat the night not to fall. I will see you bright and early tomorrow morning, my slave."

Long fell back onto his haunches, stunned. There seemed no bottom to the misery, the despair he was capable of feeling in the End's company. Every day brought something worse, and yet Long's heart continued to beat.

The End

Predictably, he got no sleep that night. And he hoped his newest general hadn't, either. The End-of-All-Things did not require as much sleep as most men, but when he got less than he wanted, it was bad for his officers and worse for everyone else. He was vexed and beyond vexed when he pondered the escaped Shaper, D'Kem—if that was even his real name. The "old burn-out" was clearly nothing of the sort. What he was for a certainty was a troubling and troublesome mystery. How had he resisted the compulsion, the magical nutlike pellet the End had literally fed him? Anders couldn't compass letting the man flout him in this manner. And quite apart from that problem, he had learned that General Shere hadn't fared well in his first brush with Tarmun Vykers. He hadn't expected immediate success, but, from everything he'd seen, it didn't appear Shere laid a finger on him, while sustaining massive casualties himself. Finally, Anders hadn't heard from General Deda in too long. He understood the man had stashed the Scaldean head somewhere outside of Lunessfor, as instructed. But Anders had not reckoned on weeks and weeks going by with no word whatsoever, and the myriad spell-wards on the Queen's castle made it nigh impossible to gain any further information.

In short, things were not going as well as they ought, and Anders was more than ready to take his frustrations out on a few thousand hapless peasants. Yes, yes, it was akin to pulling the wings off butterflies, but the End-of-All-Things would take his little pleasures wherever he could find them. And, anyway, the best part of the carnage would be laying it all on General Long's head. One way or another, he would break the man to his will, while still leaving him just enough sanity to insure he remained useful. For someone who bore a more than passing resemblance to a barnyard chicken, General Long had proven surprisingly resilient.

Long, the End's Host

The End-of-All-Things got his wish: Long also got no sleep that night. Awaiting a village's execution, he decided, could not have been much different from awaiting his own. The only distinction, as he saw it, was that with luck—bad luck—he'd survive the day and have to live with the guilt and horror of it. Before he went completely mad, however, Long found himself distracted in thinking about D'Kem. What did he really know of the man? They'd lived in the same town for a couple of years, yes, but Long had never seen him as anything more than a wastrel, a has-been, or perhaps even a never-was. Now, somehow, the Shaper had managed to escape the End-of-All-Things' host and had taken the boy, Spirk, with him. That, at least, was good news. He'd never thought much of the young man's ability or prospects, but, strangely, had grown somewhat fond of him anyhow. Or maybe the desperate nature of Long's situation had made him maudlin. It was all one: he would have relished *anyone's* company—save the End-of-All-Things'—in the dark hours before dawn. When nothing emerged to distract him further, he considered suicide. For one heartbeat, maybe two. The fact was, he still felt an unquenchable and inexplicable spark of hope that somehow he and his would emerge on the winning side of this catastrophe; he felt an equally stubborn thorn of responsibility, pricking his conscience on behalf of Mardine, their child, Spirk, D'Kem, Janks and all the others. And Short. Always, Short.

There's no night so long that self-torture can't devour it in time.

For someone so unquestionably evil, the End-of-All-Things had proven surprisingly spontaneous. He was actually singing when he arrived outside Long's dismal little pup tent in the morning.

"There be a young maiden in Fallaree
Whom all the young lads want to bed
But lacking a suitable dowry,
There's nary a one she will wed."

He might have been accounted a fair singer were it not for the disconcertingly sadistic gleam in his eye, which made it impossible to enjoy his voice.

"Still abed, you sluggard?" the End teased.

Long felt goose bumps rise on his arms and neck. He climbed to his feet.

The End studied him for a moment before speaking. "You don't look well, General. Have you been eating?"

Oh, that's rich. "I'm having a little...difficulty adjusting to... life...in your camp."

"Yes, well, it's not life in the camp we're concerned with this morning, but death in the village," the End reminded him.

Long tried a final time. "With all respect...Lord...this ain't... isn't...necessary. I fully believe you are in earnest. Only a fool would seek to test you."

"Well spoken!" the End beamed, clapping his hands together. "But, as I've rather been looking forward to this, I'm afraid I can't possibly change my plans now. Are you ready to leave?"

It was hopeless. "Do you mind if I...that is, would it be alright if I...er...relieved myself before we go?"

The End blew his lips out in irritation. "If needs must. Be

quick about it. Do not try my patience."

Long limped off in the direction of the pit latrines, too weary even to talk to himself along the way. Every day was worse than its predecessor. Every new moment brought fresh horrors and indignities. Surely, there was a limit to how much a man could endure before he imploded. Perhaps creatures like the End-of-All-Things existed solely to test that limit. Finished with his business, Long returned to his tent.

"Time to go!" the End roared, as he reached out and grabbed his general by the left shoulder.

There was a sudden collision of sound, light and darkness, a furious rushing of winds, and then Long was thrown to the ground, where he indulged in a few moments of dry heaves before his nemesis yanked him to his feet again. They were elsewhere. The grass was longer here, not having been trodden into the mud by the tireless feet of countless thralls. In the near distance, the thatched roofs of the doomed village peeped over a small hill. Smoke crept upwards from two or three chimneys, and Long caught the scent of bacon.

The End must've read his mind, because he turned sharply to his prisoner and said "You'll never want bacon again after today. Come."

Long was powerless to resist. To his horror, the village was sizeable, which meant more death than he'd imagined at first glance. The End led him into a central square, pleasant and quaint by anyone's standards. The charm of the place was killing the old soldier. Snug in their cottages, the locals, Long thought, were blissfully unaware that the End was nigh. *Ha!* Calamitous choice of words: the end was nigh because *the End* was nigh.

The sorcerer looked at Long. "Now," he began, "I can't have you mucking this up for me, playing the fool and attempting to warn these people. The greatest purpose they will ever achieve is in serving as the instruments of my lesson to you. They await my pleasure, and before this hour is up, you will see that I am all that will ever matter to you for the rest of your life." In a flash, his hand snaked out from his sleeve and his forefinger brushed ever so gently against Long's brow, completely immobilizing him. "Watch, wonder and learn."

The sky, which had been brightening with the advent of dawn, began to reverse course and grow darker. The End shot both arms over his head, and the heavens began to rain fire upon the thatched rooftops all across the village. This was followed by the first sounds of alarm within those cottages nearest the square. Now, the End reached towards the earth, making an eerie keening sound, and a deep rumbling shook the ground beneath Long's feet. Huge cracks opened between the cobblestones of the various paths leading to and from the square. A figure burst from a smoking building, but was unable to escape the End's attention. In the next moment, the luckless fellow dissolved in a mist of blood and bile. Across the square, another two peasants emerged from their cottage, only to be dispatched in like fashion. By this point, fire had taken hold of every structure in town, whilst great, thundering tremors toppled walls and tore enormous holes in the earth. An angry red cloud emanated from the End's open mouth, spreading eagerly as it searched nearby windows and doors with an unholy hunger. Where it found life, the red mist grew until Long felt sure there was nothing left in the world but blood and fire. In the distance, screams rang out with ever greater frequency and emotion, desperation and terror plain in their discordant melodies. On top of the horrific sights and sounds, the odors that began to assault Long's nostrils threatened to snap his tenuous hold on sanity. The End had been correct, though, in saying Long would never want bacon again.

For a brief period, the beset villagers came to recognize the source of their misery and attempted an armed response. A few of them on every side took up swords, axes, farm tools and anything else that came to hand. But it was all for naught: the End was not to be bested today, not by such as these. He exulted as he drew his sword: nothing was more fulfilling, more exhilarating than sword work, especially with this sword. The thing eagerly leapt from its scabbard at the promise of bloodshed, racing from target to target, as if the more it fed, the hungrier it became. The End seemed merely an extension of his blade, instead of the other way 'round, an anchor in space from which it could lash out without danger of becoming lost or embroiled in actions too far from home. It was a fell and foul thing, to Long's eye, an unlovely shard of steel that seemed to grow uglier and more vicious with each swing of its master's arm.

Forced to witness this endless butchery, Long found himself praying to Time, that it might quicken its pace for mercy's sake. But Time had never been merciful. There was nothing she could not, did not reduce to dust in the end. And therein lay Long's only solace, that even the End-of-All-Things would know an end, some day. Alas that Long would not be there to see it.

The massacre continued around him, as, at last, his mind began to drift.

Aoife and Toomt'-La, In the Forest

Despite all the magic and the ever-rejuvenating effect of Toomt'-La's company, Aoife was growing genuinely weary of her new destiny. She had birthed several broods and could not fully embrace the notion of continuing to do so endlessly. Toomt'-La, always alert to her moods, reached out to her.

"You are…anxious?"

"I do not think I can do this forever."

The satyr's eyes twinkled with unspoken mirth. "You cannot, no. Yet, no one is asking that of you."

Aoife pushed a strand of hair from her eyes. "It does feel that way, sometimes."

"Ah, but look what you have accomplished!" Toomt'-La beamed. "You have done much to return the forest to the world. And in so doing, you have established a wall against your brother's retreat, should he be so foolish."

"Tell me."

"His army remains to our west. To his south lies the mighty kingdom of your Virgin Queen. She, in turn, has wisely sent a portion of her forces to your brother's southwest, although I do not think they will plant themselves there. With luck, we shall have him surrounded.

"But…"

"Yes, but. Always but." Toomt'-La laughed. "There are those others I spoke of, as well. Do not underestimate them."

"And be sure you do not underestimate my brother."

For a moment, Aoife thought she'd gone too far. The satyr's expression darkened dramatically and he sneered at the ground. "Not again, no. Never again."

Neither spoke for some time, and then Toomt'-La said "But a few more birthings, Mother-sister. This brother of yours grows impatient. Whatever we achieve must of force serve our turn."

Aoife took the satyr's strangely rough and smooth hand and resumed her journey.

That night, she dreamt of her past-self, of her childhood and her parents. Curiously, there was no trace of her brother. Later, her dreams dragged her again through her failed marriage, the many occasions she felt she could almost love Bres, and the hollow, desolate feeling she'd known when at last he left her. She then saw herself entering the Sisterhood and reliving the many trials she'd endured on her way to becoming A'Shea. She watched herself travelling a dark road, as tendrils and roots reached up from the earth and snatched at her robes and leggings. They wound about her torso and sought entrance into her eyes, ears, nose and mouth. Struggling, dream-Aoife screamed, vomiting leaves into the sky. Looking down, she saw her skin shifting and cracking as it turned into tree bark. An explosion, an eruption was coming.

Aoife cried out in earnest and sat up, awake and trembling.

Toomt'-La was nowhere to be seen.

Shere, In the Moors

Damn the man. He had gone into the moors. Of course he had.

"Your will?" one of the captains asked.

Shere took his time in answering. He probed the edges of a broken tooth with his tongue. Well, it was suicide, was what it was. Following Vykers into the murk and muck was absolute suicide. Shere rubbed the back of his neck, thinking.

"You can't be thinking of going in there!" one of his Shapers protested. "With real soldiers, we might have a chance. This lot will drown within the first mile!"

Shere ignored the man, started pacing.

"General!" the Shaper complained.

"What would you have me do?"

The man sputtered.

"Uh-huh. I thought as much. Leave me." Shere commanded.

The Shaper sniffed petulantly and stalked off, muttering to himself just loudly enough for Shere to note the man's disapproval. The general pointed his chin at the sky and arched his back, stretching the soreness out of his muscles. *Bookish types!* He'd never had any use for them. Still, the question remained: what *was* he to do?

He couldn't make camp and lay siege to the moors, hoping to wait Vykers out, because Vykers might exit at some other point and melt into the wilderness. And Shere couldn't very well attempt to go around the moors and cut Vykers off, because, again, there was no way to know where he'd emerge. It might be possible to surround the moors with the End's entire host, given another few months. But merely suggesting this to the End was unthinkable. In short, Vykers had outplayed him: Shere had no options that wouldn't result in abject failure. Which meant Shere was already a dead man.

He pondered this for several minutes. Shere had no future in the End's service, whether the sorcerer won the coming war or not. On the one hand, if his master triumphed, it would mean the end of anything worth living for; on the other, if he lost, Shere would become a pariah at best and a wanted war criminal at worst, to be run down eventually and put to death. And there was the issue of his son. Son? Whatever he might once have been, he was no son now. Shere doubted he was even human, anymore. He sighed, flexed his hands. Well, *what was* a dead man to do in these circumstances? When the answer came to him, he laughed out loud, alarming some of his mercenaries who'd been loitering nearby. Shere didn't care. This was brilliant: he would follow orders.

Yes, following Tarmun Vykers into the moors *was* suicide, for him and everyone else in his army. But what better way to strike back at the End-of-All-Things than damaging the larger host's strength by doing as he'd been told? Who could the End blame but himself? In addition, should any of his mercenaries survive, this effort might rehabilitate Shere's reputation, dying in one last, heroic pursuit of the legendary Tarmun Vykers. Finally, on the off-chance Shere succeeded, well...surely, the End would find some way to reward him. But that last was foolishness: Shere and his army would die in these moors. He only wished he could see the look on the End's face when the bad news arrived.

Bolstered by this paradoxical act of compliant defiance, Shere signaled his captains. "We're following him."

His men exchanged worried looks.

"Now," Shere clarified.

Vykers, In the Moors

"They're coming after us," Number 17 said.

"Huh," said Vykers, shaking his head. This was going to be an obscene waste of lives, but if that's how the other side wanted to play it, the big man wasn't going to complain.

Arune couldn't argue, which brought her back, obsessively, to Brouton's Bind. Time was, she'd have ranted at Vykers—or anyone like him—for his lack of humanity. Now, though...

"What shall we do?" Number 3 asked.

"Keep moving," Vykers replied. "Cover as much territory as we can and hope the whole damned army sinks into the quicksand."

Arune gave it a try, anyway. *No misgivings about sending twenty-thousand slaves to their deaths?*

No. It's the only freedom I can offer them.

The Shaper would like to have said he was wrong, but couldn't find the words.

Life in the moors knew no morning, noon or nightfall, but existed in an everlasting twilight that fluctuated from nearly dark to almost light, depending upon the mists, fogs and other vapors that reigned there. The myriad pools, bogs and sluggish sloughs that snaked throughout each had their own attributes, their own personalities, which only intensified the unpredictability, the unknowability of the place.

Yes, there were things that lived in the moors, things of shadow, things of scale, some infinitesimally small, others—from the sounds they made in the distance—unimaginably huge. Without exception, they feared the sword, which gave Vykers an unsettling feeling of invulnerability—unsettling because he knew it wasn't so, couldn't be so. The siren call of hubris had killed many a legendary warrior in the past; Vykers would not join their number if he could help it. He was no Burner, for sure, but neither was he stupid.

"Gotta be honest," Vykers said to break up the eerie silence, "I *am* sorta itchin' for a fight."

One of the chimera—he couldn't see which—grunted in agreement.

They all slogged deeper into the moors.

Arune looked out Vykers' eyes onto the pitiful campfire she'd started hours earlier. At the moment, the Reaper and three of his chimera were sleeping. Or so she'd thought.

Out of nowhere, Vykers asked, *Hey Burn, what's 'Brouton's Bind'?*

If she'd had a body of her own, she would have gasped in shock.

Come on, Arune, I know you're there, her host prompted.

Where did you hear of Brouton's Bind?

You've been fairly shouting it at me these past few weeks, 'specially when you think I'm sleeping.

She took a moment, composed herself. *Aries Brouton was a Shaper, and a rather renowned one, at that. He discovered that on occasion the prolonged possession of a subject—*

Like me.

Yes, like you. The prolonged possession of a subject can lead a Shaper to lose sense of himself and to…sympathize so greatly with the subject that he, in effect, ceases to exist as a separate being.

Vykers sat up sharply. The lone chimera on watch turned towards him, inquisitively, but Vykers ignored him. *Which means what?*

The Shaper sees himself as the subject, essentially becoming absorbed into the host's personality forever.

Vykers broke a nearby stick in half and tossed it into the fire. He didn't know how to feel about this. There were a million things he could have said, perhaps should have said. He chose, *And if we try to get you out right now?*

I would cease to exist.

Because you need a body. Wouldn't the same thing happen all over again?

With a living body, yes. I need a newly dead body, someone who is seconds from having passed.

We'll find plenty of those on a battlefield.

It's not that simple.

Vykers threw another stick into the flames. *It never is.* He cast about for scraps from the evening meal, found none. In his sleep, one of the chimeras, Number 4, kicked his feet and murmured something that sounded like, "The jaws that bite, the claws that catch."

So, what do you need to make it work? Vykers asked Arune.

I need to be with the body before, during and immediately after death for maybe an hour on either side.

And how soon we gotta make this happen?

The sooner, the better.

Not bloody likely, in these moors, Vykers said to himself, being careful to shield the thought from Arune. Wouldn't do to get her any more riled up than she clearly already was.

He pulled out the sword—he didn't yet think of it as *his* sword—and began moving through an exercise so old he knew neither its name nor its origin. Sometimes, exercise was the best distraction.

Long, the End's Host

Yendor approached his newest (and if the truth be told, his *only*) friend. General Long or General Pete or Sergeant Long Pete—whatever he called himself—sat on the ground in a heap, legs splayed and head bowed. Yendor knew what that meant: he'd been broken to the Master's will. Well, had to happen sometime or other. He just hoped there was enough left of the man to talk with when the tedium got unbearable.

"Glad to see you made it back!" he offered, though he knew his friend would be unresponsive. "There's some as don't."

To his surprise, Long Pete rolled to his knees and wobbled unsteadily to his feet. Against all reason, the man began dancing what appeared to be some sort of jig. In short order, he was whooping, laughing and kicking dust into the air. Aye, broken indeed.

It began to rain.

"Ya prob'ly don't wanna be doin' that," Yendor cautioned, looking around to make sure no one else was watching. "One o' the other generals catches you, who knows what he'll tell the End?"

Long stopped instantly and completely. It was hard to tell he'd even been moving.

"That's more like it!" Yendor said.

Long started whistling.

Yendor rolled his eyes. "For the love o' Mahnus, man! Are you tryin' to get us killed?"

Again, Long stopped, stared hard at Yendor. "If only it were that easy," he answered tonelessly. "But I'm doomed to see this through to the end, come what may."

The rain fell harder.

"You there!" a gravelly baritone called out.

Both men turned to see a rough and solidly-built soldier squinting at them through the deluge.

"Get your units ready to move. The End's gotten tired of rotting in this hell hole and wants the whole host out of here by dawn," the man said.

Yendor halved the distance between them. "What's the word, though? We foragin' or fightin'?"

"You'll have to ask the End that; he's not told me."

"Ask the End," Yendor muttered to Long under his breath. "And why don't I goose him while I'm at it?"

The soldier yelled over again. "Up and out by dawn. Make

sure of it!"

As the third man walked away, Yendor continued his lament. "That's the problem with this fuckin' army! Too many generals and not enough privates."

Long glanced at the pitiful thralls that comprised his unit. No matter how many times he looked at them, their vacant-eyed, slack-jawed demeanor never got any easier to accept. They were *people*, for Mahnus' sake, or had been. Now? Swine had more presence of mind. How the End-of-All-Things would provoke them to attack an enemy was beyond Long, and he found it increasingly hard to care, either way.

"I guess I'll head back over to my unit, yell at a few o' these mouth-breathers and get some shut-eye," Yendor said.

In the morning, Long attended his first official briefing as a member of the host's command. As before, the End stood near his uncanny map of the local terrain. His generals were in a tightly-packed clump some ten-to-fifteen feet away, clearly apprehensive about their master's seemingly buoyant mood.

"Change of plans!" the End announced abruptly. "I see no point in waiting any longer to assert our will upon this region, nor do I see any value in allowing the bitch Queen and her little hero more time to assemble and organize their forces. Indeed, a quick, decisive strike now could well cripple the Queen's ability to interfere with our plans forever. And without her in our way…" the End trailed off.

Long's new colleagues dared not a word; he followed their example.

"In moments, we shall begin our advance on the enemy's force to the southwest. I am quite confident we'll find them woefully unprepared to deal with us. They may even take to their heels when they see us coming. But we *shall* get them running, inevitably, which time we can either cut them down or augment our own numbers, as occasion permits." The End paused, surveyed his officers. "Come now, I know you have questions. Show a little courage and ask them."

A hulking figure near the front of the group cleared his throat. "You mentioned the Queen's hero, milord. What of him?"

"Ah, yes, the legendary Reaper," the End crooned, "destroyer of nations, bane of empires, and first pastry chef to my lady's cuckold!"

Polite laughter, Long thought. Then, *politically necessary.*

"This fearsome being, this demigod ran—ran!—from General Shere's army and even now hides himself in a glorified mud puddle."

Forced laughter.

"It seems the reports of his valor were somewhat over-exaggerated. The man's a barbarian, little more than a brute, really. If he joins with the Queen at all, it will be far too late to be of any help."

The hulk spoke again. "That is reassuring. And, master, how many days' travel do you estimate before we catch sight of the enemy?"

The End shot a look at another general—Omeyo—who instantly replied "a week. Ten days at the outside."

"Excellent," the End breathed. "A final word, then, generals: your responsibilities in my host are few. You know this. I direct the thralls, the Shapers and the A'Shea. You have only to keep the whole of it moving in the right direction and motivate the mercenaries when the time comes. Everything depends upon our numbers and the ferocity of our thralls. If the host is not at strength and in condition to fight when the battle is joined, we shall all suffer for it, and none more than you."

The last was said in Long's direction, but he hadn't the nerve to meet the End's eyes today. He had no trouble imagining the threatened torment.

"Yet, I am not an unappreciative ruler. Obey me in act and in spirit, accomplish everything I ask of you, and the spoils of this battle shall be yours and yours alone. Now...let us march!" the fiend yelled, and they were dismissed.

NINE

Long, the End's Host

Normally, Long loved the sound of an army on the move. It made something stir in his chest, affecting him more than the sound of crashing surf, music, wind in the trees, or a woman's sated sigh. The thunderous cadence of thousands of booted feet marching in unison, along with the hooves of horses and oxen, as well as the rumbling of supply wagon wheels never failed to make Long feel a part of something bigger, grander than himself. The additional noises of armor clinking, leather creaking, and pennants snapping smartly in the breeze simply enhanced the experience.

But the noise made by the End's host was nothing like that. Where there should have been the rhythmic pounding of feet, there was instead a titanic cacophony of shuffling, staggering and stumbling that overwhelmed all other sounds, save the occasional crack of a whip. It was an eerie, foreboding roar that set Long's already too-frayed nerves on edge. And it continued to rain, which didn't help matters.

Still, Long was at least glad they were finally leaving the Mahnus-forsaken cesspool the host had made of this valley. Armies always left land worse than they found it, of course. It was just the unavoidable consequence of forcing so many people to live in such a confined space on a temporary basis. But the thralls—gods!—they were little more than drooling, pissing and shitting machines. It was probably possible, Long mused, for a determined (if perverse) person to cross the entire valley without ever stepping out of the muck left behind by the thralls. And there didn't seem to be a hint of vegetation, even a single blade of grass that had survived the host's passing. A more loathsome, foul-smelling and blighted place, Long could not envision.

"My generals ride," an all-too familiar voice said from Long's right.

He bowed his head and swiveled his eyes towards the End, who sat atop a beautiful black stallion. In his gloved hand, he held the reins to another horse that trailed a few feet behind.

"And besides, there are things we must discuss before we engage the Queen's forces." The End extended the reins in his general's direction, and Long accepted them without comment. Slowly, carefully, he hoisted himself into the saddle. It was the first time he'd seen the host from this height; the sight left him even more frightened and depressed than before.

The End must have sensed his mood, for he declared "an unconventional force, to be sure. What it lacks in training and experience, it makes up in single-mindedness and fearlessness. These...*people*..." he indicated the thralls with a sweep of his arm, "would assault a lava flow with their bare hands and feet if I so commanded. Your Queen's army will never be able to undermine their morale or break their focus. And, of course, I have an inexhaustible supply!"

Long nodded, afraid that going too long without some sort of response would anger the volatile sorcerer. It seemed adequate, as the End continued speaking.

"Nevertheless, the enemy will have advantages of its own that must needs be countered. Your task is to anticipate and explain these things to me, so that we are not caught off-guard." The End smiled blithely and seemed to speculate on a bird that flew by. "I know you've wondered. It is for this purpose I have kept you alive." Unexpectedly, he reached over and gave Long a hearty pat on the back. The incongruity of the act shook the old campaigner to his core.

Vykers, In the Moors

Has there ever been anyone mortal who didn't wax reflective when staring into a campfire? As much as he liked to pretend otherwise, Tarmun Vykers dreaded that moment when the evening's small-talk died away and left nothing but silence and the eventual onslaught of memories, questions and other musings that proved his mortality, and thus his vulnerability. Some there were, he knew, who could block out all distractions, external and internal alike, and focus solely on a single breath, moment or idea. Vykers was not of their number; he was too impatient. But impatient for what, exactly? What was the rush? Where was he going except the grave—if he was lucky enough to actually receive one? And, just like that, his mind wandered down paths he'd sooner have avoided. Where had he come from, really? Why did it seem as though he lived at the mercy of forces outside his ken? Not long ago, he'd been living in a cave, stewing in his own filth, struggling to survive without hands or feet. Now, he lay next to a fire he shared with creatures unlike any he'd ever seen or heard of before, in possession of a sword whose nature defied belief, and equally possessed—that was the bare truth of it—by a Shaper he'd never seen in the flesh. Why? There was a plan here, somehow, if only he could see it. And who was the author of this plan?

Vykers didn't believe or disbelieve in the gods; he simply had no use for them. He'd never said their names except when cursing. He'd built no temples in their names and never would. What were they to him, and what could he possibly be to them? He'd seen and caused far too much death to believe in either divine favor (for either side in a conflict) or divine providence. So who or what was guiding his destiny?

It couldn't be the Queen. Yes, she'd orchestrated certain events and even manipulated Vykers to some degree. But she hadn't created The End-of-All-Things. If the Reaper succeeded in defeating him, he would probably have enough subsequent momentum to topple the Queen, as well. She must have realized that, but had given him the reins to her army nonetheless. It made no sense.

And if he failed...

So, you're human, after all...

Arune! Vykers groaned. *Can't you give me a night's peace, just once?*

She laughed. *That was peace? You're welcome to it—*

No, no, you're right. I've got too much time to think on this slog. I need to be fighting and killing. That's what I do best.

It's sunrise, Arune said, a propos of nothing.

Huh. Coulda fooled me.

We need to get up and moving soon or you'll have that fight you were yearning for.

Well, they're determined fuckers, if nothing else. How many of 'em still behind us?

They're losing men—or whatever they are—by the score. Those in charge don't seem to care, though.

Somewhere out in the moors, the sound of something roaring interrupted their dialogue. Hard on its heels was the shouting of multiple voices and the noise of muffled explosions, followed by more roaring.

They're closer than I thought.

Hard to tell in this soup.

Vykers stood. "Time to go, boys."

The four agreed.

It was slow going, of course, trying to pick a path through the puddles, ponds, bogs and larger bodies of water, trying to determine which floating clump of weeds was dense enough to support weight and which would sink when stepped on, trying to guess if the ground in front of oneself was actually solid or instead quicksand. But as hard as it was for Vykers and his crew, he knew it was taking its toll on those who pursued him. So far, he hadn't lost anyone, while—

Something massive shot out of the water and across his path, taking Number 12 with it. A barrage of arcane energies followed in its wake, as the other three chimeras responded without thought in attempt to kill or at least injure the beast that had taken their brother. A searing sensation in his sternum told Vykers that Arune had joined the fray. Soon, the very water was on fire with the group's efforts and great geysers of froth and mist shot into the air, but there remained no sign of their attacker or the missing chimera. After several minutes, Vykers yelled "Stop! Let the smoke clear! Let's see what we're shooting at!" In truth, he was also concerned the noise was helping his pursuers zero in on his location. He looked over at the chimeras. Was it his imagination, or was there not a hint, for the first time, of hurt and resentment in their eyes? He hoped not. That would make things immeasurably more difficult. Unable to sustain his companions' gaze, he looked down at the water again; they followed suit.

It was still. And because the magical bombardment had burned away all the algae, it was also relatively clear. What it revealed was a deep blackness that stretched who knew how far down. Vykers was just about to turn away when bubbles began to rise and burst on the surface. The chimeras tensed. More bubbles, something was rising towards them and fast. Number 17 stepped forward, ready to renew hostilities. One of the others held out a hand, restraining him. In a rush of sound and spray, the lost chimera erupted from the water and landed in his brothers' outstretched arms. Gently, gingerly, they laid him down on the moss, staring at him with looks of evident stupefaction.

"That was…exciting," he managed. But there was something wrong.

"Er…Number 12…" Vykers began.

"Yes, Master?"

How to say this? "Your…eh…head…is on backwards."

Number 12 sat up, got his bearings. "Why, so it is!" He said, amazement in his voice. "One moment…"

The Reaper was not squeamish. He may have had other weaknesses, but that was not among them. And yet, when Number 12's head slowly rotated back into the proper position, making a slight grinding sound throughout, Vykers could not help shivering.

"How long have you been able to do that?" He asked the chimera.

"I don't know," the creature answered. "I never tried before."

It was then Vykers realized Number 12 hadn't been gasping for air when he reappeared, either.

"Can you breathe under water?"

"It appears I can."

I don't like this, Vykers told Arune.

They're full of surprises, aren't they?

And where we're going, I can't have any surprises. I need to know my troops' capabilities and liabilities.

Why don't you ask them?

The group all clearly heard the enemy drawing nearer.

No time for that now. We need to get outta here.

Aloud, Vykers said "Let's go!" in his best no-bullshit voice. The Four complied, moving to scout the path ahead with no complaint. There was no trace of anything in their eyes or body language other than soldierly obedience.

Much later, after they'd again increased the distance between themselves and their pursuers, they stopped to rest. As per habit, the chimeras sniffed out and obtained more than enough for everyone to eat, although Vykers wasn't always sure what it was or even which end to put in his mouth. The chimeras, it seemed, would eat anything. Which reminded the Reaper of his earlier misgivings.

"What happened today?" He asked pointedly of Number 12.

The other chimera paused in their eating, exchanged glances and settled back, apparently ready to hear the story.

Number 12 swallowed whatever was in his mouth, inhaled and said "We were scouting the way forward. I sensed something coming moments before I was hit, but I couldn't discern the direction. I tried to brace, myself, but..."

"The damned thing was fast," Vykers concluded.

"Just so. I felt its teeth all along my left side as it pulled me down." 12 ran a hand over his torso and, indeed, there were a number of seeping wounds Vykers hadn't noticed before.

"Sorry I missed those," he said.

"It's of no importance. They are not overly painful. Anyway, the thing took me down into the depths without damaging me any further, which proved to be its fatal mistake. After some struggle, I was able to get my claws inside its gills and pull its innards out."

The other chimera growled their approval.

I'll have to remember that, if I'm ever attacked by a monstrous fish, Vykers thought. "I'm glad you survived," he said. "This whole thing would have been much harder without you."

Number 12 nodded humbly. His brothers seemed to agree.

"But I'm not real happy to be finding out just now that you can breathe underwater and…that thing with your head. I need to know what you boys are capable of before things get desperate."

It was Number 3 who spoke up. "Sadly, this is a consequence of our creation, Master. We do not entirely know these things ourselves."

"Are you alluding to trust, Master?" Number 17 asked, "Do you still question our loyalty?"

Careful, now, Arune whispered.

Vykers took his time in answering, finding, in the end, he had nothing to say, nothing that would make matters better or more clear. Instead, as was his wont, he swung around and moved off into the moors. It was an act of trust—of faith—to turn his back on the chimeras as he had done. He didn't exhale until he heard their footsteps joining with his own.

And what footsteps. It seemed this particular expanse of bog had no solid ground to speak of; what passed for ground was soft, spongy, and—

The ground! Arune shouted.

"Down!" one of the chimera yelled.

The earth below the group's feet shuddered and heaved as if it had a life of its own, as if—

Gods! Vykers had just enough time to unsheathe his sword and bring it round in a sweeping arc, severing two of the leg-like things that emerged from the still-growing hill beneath his feet. Again, Arune and the chimeras blasted away with mystic energies. With a thunderous quaking, the earth resolved into the gargantuan shape of…something. Something insectoid, but also vaguely amphibian. Vykers would think on it further when it was dead. Assuming he was able to defeat it.

The huge thing twisted around and revealed row upon row of pincers, inside of which was an even larger number of black, glistening teeth. Down its sides and back were countless limbs, making it quite clear that the two Vykers had managed to shear off would never be missed. If he wanted to hurt this thing, he'd have to do ten times as much damage. A head the size of a farmer's wagon swooped down upon the chimeras, scrambling them into the surrounding water and temporarily blunting their attacks.

Damn it all, Arune, can't you set that thing on fire or something? Vykers demanded.

Easy for you to say! Maybe you hadn't noticed the monster's water-logged?

Then blind it, for Mahnus' sake! Vykers charged towards the head and took a vicious hack at it, but he was used to fighting humanoid creatures and this beast moved in unexpected ways, so he missed. There were advantages to being Tarmun Vykers, though, and one of those was that he never missed twice. In the same breath, he reversed his grip on his sword, continued to spin in the direction he'd gone and caught the thing under the jaw as he came back around. Vykers expected a roar of pain; instead, a loud shushing sound emanated from all along the monster's body that was immediately followed by thick, yellow-green clouds of vapor spurting into the air all around. Instantly, Vykers felt his eyes, nose and throat begin to burn and also felt something raking across his chest, trailing fire as it went. He did hear a roar, then, but it did not come from the creature. Vykers ducked and rolled several feet to his right, hoping to buy time to clear his head. A sonic blast he hadn't heard since Morden's Cairn smashed through the air and, at last, the creature wailed. It was a much higher-pitched and plaintive sound than Vykers would ever have imagined possible from such a monstrosity. He might have laughed at it, then, had not it grasped him with its legs and pulled him into the muck and under. On the one hand, Vykers reflected, the water was clearing his vision somewhat; on the other, he was going to drown, if he wasn't torn to pieces first. Submersion seemed to be the kill-tactic of everything in this accursed place. Frantically, Vykers wedged his sword between his body and the thing's legs and began pressing outward, in attempt to loosen its grip.

Strange, to suddenly realize the sword was ecstatic. The more Vykers hacked, the more exhilaration poured from the sword and into his arms and chest, rejuvenating him. The monster, however, was decidedly not exhilarated, as the sword sliced through its armor like so much paper. Underwater, its cries of rage and distress sounded even more bizarre than above. The Reaper thrilled, desperate as he was for air, to ram his sword deep into the creature's side once, twice and a final, third time. Something grabbed a hold of his jacket and pulled him away and up. All he could see was his sword, ablaze and pulsing with victory. His gaze lingered on it, even as he was pulled from the water and tossed unceremoniously onto a floating clump of weeds.

Tarmun...Tarmun...Tarmun! Arune called.

Vykers shook off his bemusement and sat up. A short distance away, he saw three of his companions standing over a fourth. Another chimera had fallen. Cautiously, he worked his way over to them. Number 4 was lying in two pieces about four feet apart. The remaining three barely glanced at Vykers as he came to stand near them.

"You will excuse us, Master, I hope. You know what we must do," Number 3 said quietly.

What could he say? Vykers nodded and walked off, pretending to look for signs of the beast they'd killed. The noise of feeding set his nerves on edge, but he found ways to occupy himself until the chimeras had finished. Or essentially so.

"Master," Number 3 said. "You are not...comfortable with us. Still." He held up something that looked like beef liver. "If you would know us, trust us, you must eat."

There were a million things he could have said. Instead, Vykers took the offering and bit into it. He did not balk, nor gag. Keeping his eyes on the three chimeras, he succeeded in eating the whole thing. When he was finished, he said, "Experience has taught me that I am alone in this world." He looked in turn at each of the chimeras, stared into their eyes. "I expect to die alone, too."

Again, something unspoken passed between the chimeras. At last, Number 3 said, "Then let us all die alone...together."

Which made no fucking sense, but pleased Vykers immensely.

"Good," he said.

Shere, In the Moors

They'd not even met in battle, and already Tarmun Vykers had found and exploited a weakness in the End-of-All-Things' designs. While Shere's army of thralls worked perfectly in open terrain or against civilian populations, it foundered and suffered tremendous losses in the moors, where the ability to move forward without difficulty could not be taken for granted. Hundreds of thralls died in the first day, drowning in deceptively deep puddles, disappearing in the mire or borne away by stealthy predators heard more often than ever they were seen. With every mile, Shere's Shapers and his handful of mercenaries protested, offered alternate plans or just plain cursed him when they thought he wasn't listening. Or perhaps because he was. At all events, the general didn't care: he was going to catch Vykers as ordered, or die trying, as ordered.

There were moments, tantalizing and torturous, when Shere and his men thought they'd heard something just ahead, or seen flashes of light through the murk, only to arrive at the approximate location and find more of the same featureless green-grey nothingness they'd left behind. At times, Shere wondered if he wasn't already dead and these moors weren't some sort of hellish afterlife. But, if that were the case, wouldn't he have encountered a few of his former employers by now?

He wanted to resent Tarmun Vykers, to well and truly hate him for leading Shere and his army into this mess, but that was a dodge and he knew it. He'd followed of his own accord, against all reason and the strident protests of his advisors. In a rather perverse twist, the general found he actually admired Vykers' actions and thinking on this matter. He—

Out of the corner of his eye, he caught sight of his most obnoxious Shaper, Manders, approaching with a determined gait. Gods! The man was insufferable.

"What now?" Shere grunted.

"You know full well what. You are wasting this army chasing a ghost through a graveyard, and graveyard it will be if we continue."

Shere punched the man in the face and knocked him onto his ass in the mud. The other Shapers and nearby mercenaries fell silent. To Shere, each looked as if he was counting silently to one hundred in his head. Manders gathered himself and rose unsteadily to his feet, wiping a trickle of blood from his mouth with the index finger and thumb of his left hand. He never took his eyes off the bigger man.

Quietly, he said "I could incinerate you where you stand."

"Then, do it," Shere urged.

Manders stayed still.

"Then shut the fuck up!" Shere commanded. He was about to turn away when he changed his mind. "I have had it with you cowards. The man we hunt is worth more than all of you combined."

Incredibly, Manders spoke again. "He runs away."

Shere barked a laugh right into the Shaper's face. "Runs away? You imbecile! If he'd merely wanted to run, he could have outrun us easily in the open. There's but a few of them, while we drag an army of angry vegetables behind us! He's using our orders against us!"

"But..." Manders began, a light coming on.

"Yes, he's trying to cripple the End-of-All-Things and humiliate him at the same time. *That* takes courage."

The Shapers and mercenaries started muttering amongst themselves.

"Look, I don't give two shits for the lot of you. You all wanna leave? Leave." Shere said. "That's an order. I'll continue on myself."

One of the mercenaries started to say something but Manders cut him off with a gesture. Then, with a very sly and self-satisfied look, he said "As you command, General."

Shere wasn't going to wait around for them to leave him. He grabbed a nearby water skin, adjusted his belt and walked into the mists without a word or backward glance. After a few hundred paces, he was completely alone, isolated from his former army by a dense, swirling fog. Somewhere behind him his men were venting at one another. Shere grinned. Then he heard the sound of his army moving away and felt a brief twinge of fear. He was committed now. He would succeed or die in the next few hours.

Deda, the Queen's Castle

It was the largest building he'd ever been inside in his life. There were also probably more people in the castle than in most towns he'd visited over the years. As a result, though there were plenty of guards and elite Queen's Swords at important junctures, it wasn't especially difficult to blend in with the regular traffic rushing hither and yon, or hard to find directions to the ailing patient he was allegedly visiting. Wims' real purpose, of course, was finding a corner, a room, perhaps, in one of the less-frequented parts of the castle, in which he could hole up for a while and from which he could scout the territory, so to speak. His gut told him the place had far more rooms than tenants, despite the stampedes on business in one direction or another. All Wims needed was to find such a room and wait until Soul's Midnight—the best time for reconnaissance, he'd found.

Hours of searching, however, brought him no closer to his goal. Finally—and against his better judgment—he stopped a cleaning lady, an ancient crone so stooped she surely needed never bend down for her bucket.

"'Scuse me, mum..."

She cocked her head in his direction, and Wims could see she had cataracts in both eyes. A blind cleaning woman? Plainly, standards were not as high as he'd imagined. "Yes?" she croaked.

"The...er...steward assigned me to a room 'round here, but I can't seem to find it."

The old creature cackled. "A room around here, did he?" She laughed again.

Wims began to grow impatient. "And why is that amusing, woman?"

"There's naught but jakes this whole hallway!"

Infuriating, to be sure, but also useful information. "Bah! The old trickster's having a laugh at my expense, I see. Where *should* I be, then?"

"Y'can stay in my room," the crone said with a disturbing leer, "It's big enough."

Wims fought the urge to crush her skull then and there. "Uh, yes, well I'm sure it is. But I'll be needing privacy to entertain business on his lordship's behalf," Wims bluffed.

"His lordship!" she spat. "May Alheria visit kibes upon 'im!"

"Which way must I go?" Wims fairly shouted in exasperation.

"Turn 'round. Take the second hallway, left, then…let me see…the third right. Try any o' them doors on yer left."

As he started moving away, Wims heard an odd sloshing sound, and turned back towards the crone just in time to catch her slop bucket on his jaw. The world spun before his eyes and he fell to the floor.

He felt a peculiar tension in his arms, legs, shoulders and hips. Even before opening his eyes, he understood the severity of his predicament.

"Come now," a vaguely familiar voice said to him. "We both know you're awake, so why pretend otherwise? You're only embarrassing yourself."

Sound logic, Wims thought, and opened his eyes. As expected, he lay chained and spread-eagled on some sort of table in a mostly dark room. The one source of light came from behind the figure leaning over him, the only other figure in the room, as far as he could determine.

"And thus ends the last source of suspense in our relationship."

He recognized the voice: it was a stronger, clearer version of that used by the crone in the hallway.

"Your Majesty," Wims said, a statement of fact, an acknowledgment of her station.

"I have many enemies," she responded. "More than I can count and probably more than I'm aware of. Can we dispense with the gamesmanship and the torture? Tell me what I wish to know, and I shall let you live, largely unharmed and free to return to whoever it is you serve."

Inwardly, Wims had been bracing himself for prolonged torture and a slow death. "I don't believe I can accommodate you," he said. Something about chatting with the Virgin Queen elevated his speech, or at least his desire to speak well.

"You do understand, don't you, that I have the means to compel you to tell me, whether you will or no?"

"Undoubtedly. But I suspect the…one I serve would visit worse upon me than you're capable of."

"Then the only way to spare you that torment is to kill you."

What could he say to that?

"I am unspeakably old, for a human," the Queen said. "Surprising enough in itself, but when one considers how many assassination attempts I've survived—not to mention the more mundane things like the plague, food poisoning, accidental injury—you'll begin to see just how resourceful and determined I am."

"Yes," Wims agreed, "I would never have guessed you'd roam your own halls in disguise."

"Don't try to flatter me, boy," the Queen snapped, "Your life has just gotten an order of magnitude worse. I will have what I want from you, if I have to reduce your body to a quivering pile of offal. However, I was hoping you would not be stupid enough to force my hand in that regard."

Wims heard little of that; he was still reeling from the fact she'd called him "boy." He hadn't been called boy in decades.

"Now, I have an army of well-trained and highly paid torturers. And, of course, I have an equally large number of Shapers, Alchemists and suchlike. The fact of the matter is, we don't even require you to be alive in order to extract the information we want. It's just as easy to kill you now and interrogate your captive shade. But…" she paused for dramatic effect, "I've been feeling a little bored of late. I was hoping you might amuse me by trying something novel, like cooperating."

For a moment, Wims wondered if the Virgin Queen and the End-of-All-Things might be related, such was their mutual penchant for flamboyant threats. He'd once heard someone say "Absolute power corrupts absolutely." What hadn't been noted was that it also made rulers bat-shit crazy.

"Well?" the Queen asked, expectantly.

Then, Wims heard himself say something he couldn't quite believe, "I'm afraid you'll have to torture me, your Highness."

The Queen groaned in irritation. "Men! And they wonder why I've remained unwed. Fine!" she spat, "Torture it is! Much joy may it bring you!"

The light grew brighter for a second before it went out altogether. The door opened and shut again with authority. Wims wondered what sort of torture they'd try first.

"Ah, there you are!" a weirdly alto but undeniably male voice said. "I was beginning to fear that Her Majesty hit you a touch too hard with that old bucket of hers."

Wims rolled his eyes toward the speaker and discovered a man of middle years with an absurd mop of hair that could not possibly have been his own. Watery blue eyes gazed at him from either side of a nose whose size was only surpassed by the owner's Adam's apple, both of which were magnified by the man's complete lack of a chin. "Now that I know you're again amongst the living, I shall resume my reading of scripture for your benefit," the fellow said.

This had to be a trick, a jest of some kind. Wims readjusted his head and shoulders as best he could under the circumstances and took a better, closer look at his visitor. He was dressed in the ragged homespun of friar—not unlike the disguise Wims himself had been wearing just days earlier—and had brought nothing with him Wims could see other than the massive tome he now had perched on his lap.

"This is torture?" Wims asked aloud.

"Pardon?"

"I understood I was to be tortured," Wims replied in an almost disappointed tone.

"Torture?" the man said, clearly mystified. "I know nothing of torture. I was asked to minister to your spiritual well-being."

"Ha!" Wims laughed. "Waste of time."

An eternity later, the man droned on, unabated, never changing his tempo or volume, and Wims Deda would happily have climbed the smooth stone walls with his fingernails if given half a chance. *She was diabolical,* Wims thought. The Queen was utterly diabolical. Somehow she'd known he could endure his measure of physical agony and then some, but that he had precious little patience for prattle. Still, this couldn't possibly be the torture he'd been expecting. Easiest thing in the world to shut the man out.

Except that it wasn't. The man never tired, never changed, and the unusual pitch of his voice seemed to cut through whatever barriers Wims threw up. Now, Wims just wanted to throw up, period. The endless litany was making him ill, he was sure of it. Just when he was about to surrender, the other man closed the book and stood.

"We've made tremendous progress today…through Volume One. It's fortunate you're lying down and able to rest, as the remaining twenty-seven volumes can be a bit taxing."

Before Wims could yell in protest, the other man doused his candle and left the room.

Twenty-seven more volumes and not done with this one? Diabolical!

Janks, the Queen's Camp

"Wanks!" Kittins bellowed. "Major wants to see you. This minute!"

Bailis hadn't wanted to see him since the major had ripped him a new one. Janks had been convinced Bailis had washed his hands of him, but now, out of nowhere, a summons. What could it be? Had they found Long's corpse somewhere? Janks' chin sagged to his chest as he stumbled off towards the major's tent. What new misery was in store?

He reached Bailis' tent just as the major popped his head out to check on Janks' status. Unexpectedly, Bailis smiled upon seeing him.

"Ah, there you are. Do come in."

Janks wished he'd refilled his flask before coming. He could do with a good pull right about now. Short of alternatives, he ducked, followed Bailis' retreating form inside...

Where he immediately spotted D'Kem and Spirk sitting at a table, finishing what from all appearances had been a hearty meal. As he made eye contact with D'Kem, the older man stood up and Janks rushed over to embrace him.

"By the gods, you're alive!" Janks shouted, emotion welling up in his voice.

"And so am I!" Spirk pointed out.

Same old Spirk. Unable to control his excitement, happiness and relief, Janks just laughed. "So you are, lad, so you are! But tell me, how did you manage it? And Long, is he..."

"One thing at a time," Bailis interrupted. "These two've been through it, Corporal. Give 'em a moment to breathe, eh?" He pulled out a chair and gestured for Janks to sit, join his friends.

"You're right, of course. As you say."

D'Kem wiped his mouth with his napkin and spoke. "I won't keep you waiting, Janks. We don't know Long's current... situation. He and Mardine were both alive last time Spirk and I saw them. We survived the enemy's initiation rites, for lack of a better term, and spent the first several days together, until they dragged Long away."

"But...did they drag him away to kill him?"

"I don't believe so."

"But you don't *know*?"

D'Kem sighed. "No, I do not know. But I have reason to believe he's still alive."

"But he could be dead?" Janks asked, in a rising panic.

D'Kem regarded him sternly. "Hadn't you reconciled yourself to that, already?"

"Well, yes. Seeing you again, though...I mean...I was hoping..."

"Tell him the rest," Bailis urged the old Shaper.

"Yeah, tell him the good part!" Spirk chimed in.

This time, the Shaper wheeled in his seat and glared at the younger man, as a father might a mischievous child. Turning back to Janks, he cleared his throat, composed his thoughts. "I believe our friend is still alive, because the End-of-All-Things needs his assistance."

Janks looked from D'Kem to the major and back, searching for any sign they were joking. "His assistance?" he repeated, at last.

"Whatever else may be true of him, the End-of-All-Things does not possess a particularly military mind. His entire plan seems to be to crush everyone he encounters with superior numbers and firepower. So far, his methods have worked. But he's sharp enough to recognize that this won't work forever or in every circumstance."

"And how do you know all this?"

"We captured some scouts!" Spirk answered brightly.

"We?" D'Kem asked.

"Well, I was there!" Spirk protested.

"And what did these scouts tell you?"

Clearly, it was Major Bailis' turn to speak. "This End-of-All-Things goes through generals at an alarming rate. Seems he has a very short temper. And he needs his generals to formulate strategy, counter his enemies, all of that. The thing is, his command structure's a botch-up: he's got several generals on top, and all other officers are sergeants, essentially—he calls them 'captains'—whose job is to herd the horde one direction or another and keep it more or less in fighting trim."

"But how does he maintain order?"

"Mahnus knows. The whole thing's like an army run by an angry child."

"You think he's forcing Long to advise him, then?"

Before Bailis could answer, a soldier was ushered into the tent and came over to stand before him. Saluting, he said, "Enemy's on the move, sir."

This caught everyone's attention.

"He's moving?" Bailis asked, not certain he'd heard correctly.

"Yes, sir."

"Direction?"

"Comin' right at us, sir," the soldier answered.

"This enemy's out of his mind! Nobody starts a war this late in the autumn. We'll be up to our knees in snow at any moment. Both sides'll lose more men to the cold than each other!"

The soldier coughed. "They respectfully request your

presence in the officers' mess."

"I'll be there straightaway," Bailis said. To D'Kem, Spirk and Janks he added, "You'd best get back to your unit. Tell your sergeant we may have to mobilize quickly."

Frightened as he was by the coming conflict, Janks smiled. At last, he'd be one-up on Kittins. "Yes, sir, Major!" He saluted and led his companions out of the tent.

Back at the campfire, Sergeant Kittins leaned with feigned indifference against the wheel of a nearby supply wagon. Janks could tell the big man wanted to know why the corporal had been called away, but was too proud to ask.

"We gotta get ready to move."

"Says who?"

Janks was in a great mood. He walked right up to Kittins and smashed his fist into his sergeant's face with every ounce of strength he could muster. Kittins did not go down, but there was a satisfying crunch in his nose and a subsequent geyser of blood that redeemed every miserable moment Janks had spent in his company. For a few heartbeats, he was afraid Kittins would kill him on the spot, until he saw the big man's eyes drift over to D'Kem.

"Who's this, then?" he growled, wiping his nose and upper lip with the back of his hand.

"Company Shaper," D'Kem answered curtly.

Kittins spat an enormous gob of bloody phlegm into the dirt at Janks' feet. "'Nother fuckin' magicker, eh? Just what I *don't* need."

Unbelievably, Spirk had something useful to say. "Maybe you should worry 'bout the major's order, huh?"

A look of confusion came to Kittins eyes as he suddenly became aware of Spirk. "The fuck? Where'd *you* come from?"

"You're wasting time, Sergeant—sir. Word is, the enemy's moving this way at speed." Janks made up that last, of course, but he felt entitled to a little artistic license after all he'd been through. "We gotta break 'er down and pack 'er up."

Kittins shot him one last vicious look and started yelling at his unit. "Okay, fuckers and fuckees, I know you all heard that. Let's get moving!"

Long, the End's Host

Try as he might, Long could never get over the sheer size of the End's host. It was like watching the countryside move along with his horse. The thralls and their mercenary tenders stretched from horizon to horizon on either side, while reaching nearly the same distance in front and in back, though Long guessed he was closer to the van. The End must've subjugated every man, woman and child on the eastern half of the continent. Every day, Long rode over scores of the fallen, but it never seemed to make any difference in the host's basic size. Of course, he knew the End was adding new thralls every day, as well. Human fodder, as the End saw them, was virtually inexhaustible. So, too, were the carrion fowl that followed the host—crows, vultures and worse, things out of legend, things out of nightmares, things that were drawn by the stench of putrefaction and despair. Long did his best to keep his eyes forward and down. Best not to know too much of what surrounded him.

But he had plenty of time to think, between visits from his new master. In many ways, it was a laughable army...except for its size. If a way could be found to neutralize that...Then, it occurred to Long that the End's host had one other advantage: the Queen's army—or whoever the End fought next—might be reluctant to battle enslaved peasants, no matter how fearsome the End's influence made them. Who in his right mind wants to butcher milk maids, stable boys and innkeeper's wives? There was no honor in that and no satisfaction, either, especially when the enemy looked like the folks back home.

Long heard a rider approaching from behind, forcing his way through the throng, and he turned as best he could to see who it was. One of the mercs, a messenger of some sort.

"What news?" Long called out, to save a few of his thralls an unnecessary trampling.

"River up ahead. Shallow enough we can ford it dead-on. The End says we're to water and soak our thralls, clean off some 'o this filth."

How nice of him, Long thought sourly. *Soak the poor bastards outdoors in winter. That'll reduce our numbers for sure. And so much for that river, while we're at it. Probably never recover from the damage we're about to do.* "Will do!" Long yelled back.

The merc veered to his left and began forging off in a new direction. So, too, did Long's thoughts. In his mind, Mardine had a strange gravity all her own, and no matter how hard he tried, he could not avoid thinking about her for long. And thoughts of her inevitably led to thoughts of their unborn child. The babe was a miracle, surely, but was the world worthy of him (already, Long thought of the child as "him")? Would he even be given a chance to find out? For the millionth time, Long struggled to find a way out of this mess, for himself, for Mardine, and for their child. He was not an especially brave man, he knew, but he could not altogether abandon hope, as it seemed his master would have him. Which might have been bravery of a sort.

The promised river appeared up ahead, a vast silver-grey line that constituted the largest body of water Long had seen in years. It was a mile across, if it was an inch. Still, the front of the host would be able to enter and exit before the center reached the near shore. A crossing like this could take all day, which was just fine with Long; he'd absolutely no desire to begin the next battle. The first thralls hit the water. Many went down, struggling to adjust to the sudden current. Most got back up and continued onwards; some few never rose again, but were carried southward by the surging flow. Long wondered if that might work for him, as well: dismount and pretend to help one of the beleaguered thralls, only to be conveniently swept away himself. He looked over at the nearest merc, who was eyeing him rather intently. So much for that idea. The sound of a whip cracking brought his attention back to the shoreline, where the thralls were being herded into the water like nervous sheep. Long had to admit the mercs did their jobs efficiently, if perhaps without much imagination or enthusiasm. He'd oft heard it said that mercenaries would swing swords for whoever paid the most, regardless of their employers' intentions or prospects. He very much doubted, though, that mere gold would convince these mercs to abandon the End, such was their fear of him. Their only hope was also Long's, that somehow, some way, the

End would fall. Would they ever admit it, even in their cups? Not in this lifetime.

"Thinkin' o' goin' for a swim?" the familiar—and welcome—voice of Yendor asked from a few horse-lengths away. The man looked terrible, but Long was happy to see him just the same.

"What happened to you?"

A dry chuckle. Yendor was missing a few more teeth. "The other officers, is what."

"You been passin' that fermented goat's piss around to them, too?"

"Nah. 'S too good fer the likes 'o them. Nah, they don't like me talkin' to you."

Long was taken aback. "They what now? They don't like you talking to me?"

"Fuck 'em all."

"Why don't they like it?"

"They're afraid I'll bring the End down on 'em, somehow."

"Alheria's tits! Is that all anyone ever talks about in this damned army? The-Bleeding-End-of-All-Things? Tell you one thing, even in Tarmun Vykers' army, there's talk o' women, there's cards and boasting of battles past. There's camaraderie. It ain't all about the leader, no matter who the fuck he is!" Long was on a rant now, and Yendor was clearly amused.

"You sayin' there's no brotherhood here?" he goaded.

"Are you fuckin' kidding me? There's brotherhood, aye. The brotherhood of cattle being led to slaughter. The brotherhood of orphans being whipped by an unruly and unreasonable master." Long gestured down to the river, to the merc with the whip. "There's precious few in his host in possession o' their right minds, and those that are don't side with each other for shit!"

Having finally brought his horse alongside, Yendor reached out and slapped Long on the back. "That there's why I like you so much: you ain't given up."

"Oh," Long sighed, "I talk a big game..."

"Come on, now. The End's either gonna kill us outright or get us all killed, eventually. We know this. But there's nothing says we can't have a laugh or two along the way."

Long eyed him askance, provoking gales of laughter from his companion. "Plotz, were you ever kicked in the head by a horse when you were young?"

"Twice," Yendor beamed. "Horse came up lame the second time!"

Aoife, On the Road

Without the calming influence of Toomt'-La's company, Aoife lost focus, wandered, became worried and then depressed. Before crossing the ruined remains of the forest of Nar, she'd intended to travel to Lunessfor, to...to...she could not fully remember. Something about finding an ally in her endless quest for vengeance against her brother. Well, she'd found one. In losing the satyr, though, she'd lost the means to communicate with and understand this ally. What was she supposed to do next? What did it expect of her?

A bell tolled somewhere in the fog ahead of her, startling her from her trance. Unwittingly, she'd drifted back amongst her own kind, amongst people. A rush of emotions and sensations besieged her: she was hungry, yearned for a hot bath, craved the sounds of singing and laughter, ached for an environment and interaction she intrinsically understood. She wanted to be human again, if only for a short time.

Fifty paces brought her through the fog and within sight of a village. The bell, she surmised, belonged not to a church but the town square. It rang out the hours between dawn and dusk, measuring the working day for those who lived here. Drawing closer, Aoife found what she'd been looking for, the largest building in town. Nine times out of ten, this was the inn, and so she hoped to find it today.

It was early morning. Funny, she hadn't noticed that until now. Any moment, the locals would emerge from their homes to work, tending the livestock, stoking the forge, chopping the firewood, kneading the dough—whatever it was they did to contribute to the town's continued survival. As the bell's chime faded into silence, a rooster leapt into the void, crowing for all he was worth. Shortly, Aoife heard the lowing of a single cow; she would have expected more from a town with so many buildings. Still, no one appeared. Reaching the perimeter at last, Aoife gasped. Much of the town was in ruins. The shapes she'd taken for whole buildings were instead their gutted shells, their skeletons. In the streets lay the broken remains of wagons and vendors' carts, along with other things far less recognizable.

Anders had come through. But not recently.

A furtive, shuffling sound off to her left put the A'shea on alert: she was not alone. Looking up, she saw, in the bones of a nearby home, a small boy, perhaps four years old. She knelt, to diminish her size, make herself appear less threatening. She expected to have to coax him out of the shadows, to prove her harmlessness. "It's okay," she began, "I'm not..."

The boy ran to her arms. As he got closer, he began to weep. By the time he reached her, he was sobbing. Aoife had no words, hoping her embrace would say what needed saying. In her peripheral vision, she saw other shapes moving into the clear, other children. Five, ten, fifteen, seventeen. Seventeen orphans, dressed in rags, filthy as the ground they stood on, perilously thin and broken. But not beaten. Aoife felt hot tears of her own roll down her cheeks.

"You're an A'Shea?" one of the girls asked, her voice unusually husky.

Aoife nodded vigorously, still unable to speak.

"Can you help us, then?"

Aoife rose, sweeping the boy up into her arms. He weighed nothing. Or she had gotten stronger. The two were not mutually exclusive. The boy buried his face in the crook of her neck and continued weeping quietly.

The children stood in a semi-circle in front of her. A few were younger, even, than the boy in Aoife's arms. The oldest, a boy, was perhaps twelve or thirteen, almost old enough for conscription in desperate times.

"Is this all of you?" the A'Shea inquired.

"Nah, nah." One of the older boys replied. "Terce's in the tower-top with the baby."

On the far side of the square, there was, indeed, a three-story tower, attached, it seemed to the ruin and rubble of the town's inn, declared as such by a rickety sign that still dangled from the charred framework: "Shreds and Patches." Now, *that* was an ill-fated name.

"How is it you all survived the…the…?" She could not find the words.

"When our folks saw 'em coming, they hid us all in a root cellar outside o' town," said the girl with the burly alto. She stepped forward. "They call me 'Meeps'."

Aoife nearly grinned. Nearly. "Meeps?"

"'S a nickname!" the boy on Meeps' left said. "On account o' she meeps when she snores."

The A'Shea looked down at the children's feet, bare on the frost-crusted cobblestones. "Let's get you all inside, shall we?" she suggested. "I can help you better if we're not all freezing to death!"

The top of the tower consisted of one large room, apparently used for meetings of the town's council. Now, the entire floor was covered in mattresses in various states of decay and dishevelment. The room itself reeked of sweat, urine and worse. But the children, who sat along the room's perimeter, were alive, which was a miracle in Aoife's mind. Terce, the oldest of them (having recently flowered into womanhood), sat cross-legged near a window, holding a baby not her own, though you'd never have known it by the way she held it. As much as she wanted to believe in Aoife's benevolence, experience had taught the girl to be wary, wary and above all, wary. Aoife wondered if her name wasn't spelled "Terse."

"So, y'can help us, then?" Terce began.

"Some." Aoife answered. "Much. But I cannot solve your central problem, which is that you all need…adults, a community, to…protect you."

Terce snorted, derisively. "Yeah, we've seen how well *that* works."

"You need a bigger community," Aoife clarified. "Or one further from harm's way."

"And how far is that, pray?"

"We can find one."

"Don't lie to us!" Terce yelled. "We seen 'im, the one calls himself 'The-End-of-All-Things'." Some of the younger children began to cry again. "We heard 'im speak, we know what he plans for us!"

Without knowing why, Aoife rose and extended her arms. A soft golden-green light radiated from her and filled the chamber. Before Terce could even cry in alarm, she relaxed, and the anger drained from her face.

"What...what 'ave you done?" she asked, lazily.

"I understand why you don't trust adults. But you must trust me. You simply must. I am an A'Shea and...and more. Now," Aoife concluded, "sleep." And every child in the room drifted off into peaceful, healing slumber.

It was hard to keep all their names straight, but a few stood out: Meeps, of course, and Terce. There was Danty, the oldest boy, and Will, the one who'd first run to her arms. There were Lisbeth and Moll, twins. And there was Tadpole, the Irrepressible (as she thought of him), whose goodwill, mirth and sense of mischief seemed completely unharmed by the chaos and suffering around him. He was the kind of boy her brother might have been, if. And she feared she was getting too attached to him.

"When y' go about your travels," he said to her one day while helping her bathe one of the younger children, "can you take me with you?"

It was a serious question, she knew, and Aoife gave it the attention it deserved. She sat back and regarded Tadpole in silence for a moment. He was a charismatic young imp, that was certain. With his nut-brown hair and sparkling blue eyes, his quirky smile undiminished by a missing tooth in front, a light dusting of freckles across his nose and cheeks and, lastly, the hint of a brogue, Tadpole was an undeniable and captivating character, the sort who could probably one day find an apprenticeship in any trade he chose to study. He was, in short, the little brother she'd always wanted.

"Mine is a dangerous path," Aoife started.

"Dangerous?" Tadpole laughed. "Are you kidding me, Miss Aoife? Have you not noticed the scenery?"

Aoife laughed in return. Then, solemnly, "Things are not likely to end well for me."

"I won't let no one nor nothing hurt you!" Tadpole swore.

"Mmmmm," Aoife nodded, seriously. "Even if my fight's with the End-of-All-Things himself?"

Tadpole's face took on a stony aspect. "'Specially then."

"You're a fine young man, Tadpole." Aoife said. "But you're still a young man. A boy, in fact."

In a flash, Tadpole's arm shot out, and Aoife heard a thud in the wall across the room. A small skinning knife juddered inside a circle that had clearly been used for such before. "The right boy can kill as well as any man," Tadpole said, quietly.

Aoife was not reassured. "The End-of-All-Things is no circle on the wall. He's an unimaginably powerful sorcerer with an impossibly large and ruthless host at his command."

Tadpole wouldn't give an inch. "And for all that," he retorted, "he still puts 'is breeches on one leg at a time, don't 'e?"

Aoife let out a long, slow breath. "I can't," she said. "I just can't."

Tadpole grinned. "A battle of wills, then, is it?"

Irrepressible, indeed.

"We need to speak of more pressing matters," Aoife said.

"More pressin' than the End-of-All-Things? That don't sound good."

"We need to find you and the rest of these children a home."

Tadpole was ready. "First," he said, "you ain't getting rid o' me. Second, the rest o' the kids have a home and this is it!"

"You've done well for yourselves, that's a fact. But you can't live here alone forever. It's not safe."

"Not safe?" Tadpole protested. "We wasn't safe when the town was whole!"

"Right. So we'll find you a bigger town, a city."

The boy exploded. "You are not ditching me in some stupid city. You're not gonna do it! You're not gonna leave like the others. I'm not gonna let you!"

The child in the washbasin began to cry, and Aoife pulled her out and wrapped a blanket around her, pulling her close. "And you," she said sternly to Tadpole, "are not to yell at me, nor issue orders. The A'Shea are no one's slaves."

"But you can't..."

"I can. I might wish things were otherwise, but I have a duty that's larger than either of us." Aoife hesitated, watched the boy's anger drain from his face, to be replaced by fear and loneliness. "Now help me get the smaller children to bed, and then you can help me take stock of your food stores."

True to his nature, Tadpole helped begrudgingly at first and with greater and greater enthusiasm as time wore on.

On the fifth morning, Aoife was startled as she awoke by the appearance of a silent, shadowy figure in the nearest corner. It was watching her, she could tell, but the fact it hadn't moved on her eased the rhythm of her pounding heart.

"Is there something you wish of me?" she whispered.

"It is time to return to the road, Mother-sister," Toomt'-La replied, his voice raspier than she remembered.

"But..."

He stepped forward into the light, and Aoife gasped. He was horribly burnt over most of his body. His skin was covered with sores that wept a fluid more like sap than blood. His right eye was closed or gone—the A'Shea couldn't immediately tell—and the other was terribly discolored. The satyr swept an arm before himself and said "The children will sleep a while longer."

"What happened to you?"

Toomt'-La's chuckle in response had an angry edge to it that Aoife had never heard before. "Something there is that doesn't love a forest."

"The End-of-All-Things again?"

The satyr scowled. "Not this time. Just men. Ordinary men. I must confess, I have no love for your kind."

"My kind?" Aoife felt umbrage rising within her. "My kind? Am I not, as you have often called me, your Mother-sister?"

It seemed she'd outflanked him, for Toomt'-La would only repeat, "It is time to resume our journey."

Aoife took in all the children, curled up around the room. "Our journey, or yours? You disappear without warning, are gone for days and days, and upon your return abuse me with dark insinuation. Tell me, what is it you would have of me?"

The satyr fixed his lone eye on the A'Shea. "But you already know the answer to that: you are the mother of the forest's rebirth, the mother of forests yet to be." He scuffed a cloven hoof impatiently upon the floor.

"And what of these?" Aoife demanded, gesturing to the children.

"What of them?" Toomt'-La retorted. "Countless thousands more will perish if you abandon your duties now."

"My duties?" Aoife snapped. "As an A'Shea, I have a duty to these children."

"You have a duty to your *own* children!"

"But a moment ago, you implied I was not of your kind. Now, you would own me. And for what purpose?"

"You know we have a mutual enemy."

"Not a very appealing basis for a relationship."

"You need us."

"You need me."

Toomt'-La fell silent for a long time. Finally, he said, "Forgive me, Mother-sister. I am...damaged. More seriously than you would guess. I need to...sleep, myself, if I am ever to heal."

In the second Aoife bowed her head to acknowledge his apology, the satyr disappeared again. She had bought a little time, she knew. A very little time.

Vykers, In the Moors

"Master," Number 3 said, "a man approaches. Shall we kill him?"

Vykers stood up from the clump of moss he'd been resting on. "No. I'll hear what he wants, first." *Probably just wants out o' these fuckin' moors.* "Which way?" he asked the chimera.

"There," Number 3 said, pointing off into the mist.

"How far?"

"Near. He should appear right...about...now."

A large, shadowy shape emerged from the swirling vapors. As he became clearer, the man stopped. "Shit," he muttered. "Wasn't expecting four o' you."

"And I wasn't expecting just one o' you. Life's full o' little surprises, ain't it?" Vykers responded.

"Bad ones, mostly," the man observed.

Vykers laughed. "Aye. Can't say as I disagree. You here to kill me, then?"

The stranger shrugged. "Thought I'd have a go at it, yeah." He paused. "That is, if your…er…whatever-they-are don't mind."

"You boys mind?" Vykers asked the Three.

Number 17 beamed. "It is fine with me!"

"Thanks," the Reaper said, sourly. To the stranger, he said, "Well, ya might as well come closer, eh?"

"Appreciate it. Kinda hard to kill you from twenty feet away."

Number 3 spoke up. "I think you'll find it equally hard to kill him up close."

Vykers grinned at him. "I always knew you were the smart one," he joked. Then, he turned his attention to his adversary. He was a big man, even bigger than Vykers. A little younger, perhaps, but a lot more scarred. "What's your name?"

"Hargen Shere. *General* Hargen Shere, as it happens," the man said, rolling his shoulders to loosen up.

"And now you're here to *shear* me in two, is that it? Too bad your name ain't 'Victor.' So, you work for this End-of-All-Things?"

Shere smiled ruefully. "That I do."

"Must be a right bastard, to send you after me like this."

"He ain't my favorite," Shere confided.

"What kind o' general fights without an army?"

"Kind that doesn't wanna see his troops die for nothing."

"Troops? You got a funny definition o' troops."

"Yeah, well…what can ya do?" Shere hefted his sword.

Vykers considered. "You don't have to die here, you know."

"Nah, I think I do. You don't kill me, the End will. Between you n' me? I'd rather it was you."

"I understand. Any last words?"

"Could you maybe let me parry a few before you end it? I'd kinda like to die feeling I was good at something."

"As you wish." Vykers said, drawing his sword and holding

it before him. The chimeras stepped back several paces.

*Vykers...*Arune interjected.

Later, Vykers shot back.

Shere came at him with a roar and a sweeping blow to the crown of Vykers' head, which the Reaper parried with ease. It was a traditional sort of opening, and Vykers could have killed the man then and there, were it not also traditional to accept such a blow as an acknowledgement of the opponent's worth and gauge of his strength. He found Shere had plenty of strength.

"Bet you've killed more 'n your share over the years, eh?" he asked the general as he leapt backwards and reset his feet.

"More 'n I can count or remember, but nothing like you, if the tales be true."

"Tales?" Vykers scoffed, "Bullshit's more like it." He feinted at Shere's right shoulder, then, impossibly, turned it into an uppercut for the groin. Shere tumbled backwards out of range.

"No going after the jewels, alright? I'm here, facing you fair and square. There's no need for that!" he protested.

"Just keeping you on your toes. You wouldn't want me going easy on you, would ya?"

Shere advanced again, raining a series of blows—two right, one left, one high, one low, two high, one lower left—trying to keep his pattern unpredictable but also keep Vykers busy. As long as the other man was on the defensive, Shere figured, he might have a chance. Then, out of nowhere, Vykers' sword sliced a nasty gash into his left forearm.

"Dammit!" Vykers grumbled to himself.

"Hoping for better, were you?" Shere taunted.

"I wasn't trying to touch you at all!" Vykers complained. "Damn sword's got a mind of its own, wants your blood sooner than later."

Shere thought he saw an opening and lunged for Vykers' midriff. Somehow, the Reaper parried and turned his sword into the general's shoulder.

"Fuck!" Shere howled. "That hurts like a bitch. You got poison on that sword, Vykers?"

"Hold!" the Reaper yelled back. "This ain't gonna work."

To Shere's surprise, the Reaper sheathed his sword, though somewhat clumsily.

"What's this, then?"

Vykers undid his belt. "Three!" he said, "hold this for me."

"Certainly," the chimera answered, stepping forward to take it.

"I still have to fight you," Shere reminded Vykers.

"Right. But let's do it the old way; otherwise, I won't be able to keep my promise."

Shere understood. "Magic sword, huh? The End's got one, too."

"So I hear, which is the one and only reason I've got this."

"Makes sense. Still, I wouldn't have figured you'd need one."

A vicious grin came to Vykers' face. "I don't. Now, drop your sword and let's see what you're made of, General Shere."

"Happy to oblige!" the general bellowed, dropping his weapon and bull rushing at Vykers' chest.

Again, the Reaper could easily have dodged aside. Instead, he took the full brunt of Shere's head and shoulders in his chest, dropped to his haunches and used the man's forward momentum to heave him over his head and into the air behind him. A second later, he heard a loud thump as Shere crashed onto the ground. Vykers was already spinning to meet him.

Shere grunted. "Nice move, that. Where'd you learn it?"

"I dunno. Just seemed like the thing to do," Vykers shrugged.

Shere stood, fists up and ready, and stepped forward. He faked a jab at Vykers' head that came nowhere close to the target, then swung a wheeling hook from the other direction that was equally unsuccessful. He faked another charge. Vykers didn't budge. "Well, this is…" Shere saw a flash of movement and his head snapped back. He tasted salt in his mouth. Shaking the cobwebs away, he realized he'd been punched in the mouth, splitting a lip and cracking a tooth in the process. "There's the Tarmun Vykers I was expecting," he said, wiping his mouth with the back of his hand.

Vykers stood just out of reach, his hands on his hips. "Why not switch sides? Man like you could tip the scales in our favor."

"He's got my son," the general answered sadly.

"Ah," was all Vykers could say in reply.

"Anyway, you can't imagine how brutal the End can be with traitors. There's no limit to the suffering." Shere began circling again.

"And dying here is better?"

"Getting killed by the legendary Tarmun Vykers is a pretty fair end, far as I'm concerned." Shere said. "Still, I woulda liked to have landed one lousy blow!"

"Alright, then. Make it count," Vykers said, as he stepped into a massive fist. His vision exploded in stars and he felt himself falling, landing hard on his seat. He expected the other man to follow up on his success, but, instead, sensed him moving off. "Why do I feel like you're not giving me your best?"

"I wanna earn what I get from here on out." Shere said.

For close to a half hour they fought, back and forth across the small clearing, both men sweating profusely, Shere bleeding profusely, too. Try as he might, he could not connect, but Vykers indulged the man, anyway. He gave the larger man ample opportunity to test every skill, theory and idea he'd ever had about combat. In the end, Shere simply collapsed, unable to mount one more offensive.

"I guess that's it, then."

"You sure about this?" Vykers asked one last time.

"Mercy from the Reaper? You're destroying all my illusions."

Vykers couldn't help laughing. "It ain't mercy, friend. It's mercenary. I'm offering you a chance at revenge!"

Shere sagged even further to the earth. "Can't do it, Reaper. I've got no feeling for it anymore."

"So."

"End this."

"You fought well," Vykers said and hit him as hard as he could on the left temple, cracking the man's skull and breaking his neck in a single blow. The general fell sideways into the dirt. The Reaper rubbed his knuckles, which were bleeding at last.

What's this, Vykers? Empathy? Arune asked.

Vykers ignored her, turning instead to the Three. "No point in staying in these moors, now. Can any o' you lead us out?"

TEN

Janks, the Queen's Camp

Some people have a peculiar manner, when speaking to others, of looking any and everywhere else but into the faces of those they're addressing. Lord Marshall Ferzic was one of these hapless folks, and it made taking him seriously more difficult than necessary, especially under the present circumstances.

"The bastard's on the move!" he declared in the general direction of the officers assembled before him. "A sane man waits 'til the weather favors warfare." There was some laughter and some grumbling at this. "A sane man doesn't cede the choice of battlefield to a more-seasoned force!" One or two polite chuckles, a lot more murmuring. "And a sane man doesn't challenge Her Majesty in her own territory!" A scattering of "Hear! Hears!" "But the End-of-All-Things is *not* a sane man and, as such, is all the more dangerous." Silence. "Yes, he has a vast host of apparently deranged peasants and desperate mercenaries. But those who have underestimated him have all died. We shall not make that mistake."

To Janks' ear, this was just about the worst speech he'd ever heard; if it had been meant to inspire, it had failed miserably.

"General Branch," the Lord Marshall called out.

A tall, iron-haired knight with a nasty scar across his upper lip stepped forward. "Yes, Lord Marshall?"

The Lord Marshall swept his eyes near the general. "To you, the honor of selecting the precise terrain of our stand. We have two days, three at most, before the enemy's host appears. General Lescoray."

Another knight stepped forward, with flaxen hair and passing good looks, but for a rather weak chin. "Lord Marshall?"

"Once Branch here has chosen our battlefield, you'll be in charge of camp fortifications and front line defenses. General Darwent?"

The meeting went on and on, making Janks thankful he'd been of too low rank to attend others like it. All he knew was that the end—or "The End"—was coming, and his fate would most likely be decided within the fortnight. The long list of appointments and assignments wore on, until Janks heard Bailis' name come up.

"I want you right in the heart of it," the Lord Marshall told Bailis. "I know I can rely on you and your men should the front line falter."

Great. Fucking great, Janks thought. Coulda been placed on the flank. Or guarding the baggage train. Somebody's gotta do it. But nope. No. I've gotta wind up in the absolute shittiest shit. For a moment too brief to be properly called a moment, Janks thought of deserting, high-tailing it the hell out of camp and the army first chance he got. Then he thought of his buddy, Long Pete, whose predicament was undeniably worse. Janks couldn't even imagine what his old friend's daily existence was like, living amongst and working for the enemy, while his sweetheart—Janks couldn't help grinning at the thought of it: Long had fallen for a giantess!—his sweetheart was held hostage. In all probability, Long, Mardine and Janks would die in the coming fray, and never see one another again. Janks needed a drink.

Deda, the Queen's Castle

By the time the Queen finally returned, Wims was desperate to surrender his secrets, his freedom, even his life to escape the endless droning of his torturer.

"I'll talk!" he shouted when Her Majesty entered. "I'll talk!"

"Oh," the Queen said, her tone dripping acid, "*now* you'll talk?" She let the question hang in the air a moment before continuing. "Now, you'll talk," she repeated, almost to herself.

"Sadly, your secrets are no longer secret and turn out not to have been worth the trouble you went to keep them, or my friend here," she indicated the friar, "went to extract them."

Wims gaped at her, unable to fathom this apparent turn of events. "What?" he said, at last.

"My friend not only makes an excellent spiritual...advisor, but he's a world-class painter as well. With the portrait he's made of you in his spare moments and which we subsequently showed to various *merchants of information,* call them, we've been able to determine a great deal about you."

Ah! This was some sort of gambit. She had to be bluffing. Anyway, he fervently *hoped* she was. The next words out of her mouth convinced him otherwise, however.

"And so, Mr. Deda, you are less than worthless to me."

He braced himself for a death sentence.

"Unless..." the Queen said, playfully, "you're worth something to the rest of the infamous Deda clan."

Wims doubted it. "Of course I am!"

The Queen laughed. It was a hard sound, like that of a smith's hammer striking his anvil. "Of course you are! We'll fish around a little. See if there's anyone willing to pay your ransom." She turned to leave.

"So...you don't want my head, then?"

More hammer blows. "If you've no use for it, what in Mahnus' name would *I* want it for? No, no. I'll take gold over vengeance every day, especially when I've got a war to fund."

"The End-of-All-Things'll just kill me, anyway."

"Perhaps in the next life, you'll be more careful in your choice of employers."

"Unless you'd like to employ me in this one?" Wims didn't know what made him say it; maybe after all he'd been through, he'd developed a death wish.

"You've got some cheek, haven't you?" The Queen spoke to her torturer. "Do you think you can manage another twenty-four hours, as a favor to me?"

The torturer nodded. "It would be my pleasure."

Twenty-four more hours of this torture? Wims felt panic rising in his chest.

"Survive this with your wits intact, and we'll talk," the Queen said with finality.

Time slowed to a stop.

The Queen's Camp

General Branch had chosen well. The battlefield-to-be was a meadow that sloped gently downhill between a heavily forested drop on the left and another, smaller woods on the right. The enemy would be unable to flank the Queen's host, condemned, instead, to approach dead-on and uphill all the way. Janks might've seen a better battlefield somewhere, but he couldn't remember it now.

"We'll trench, left to right, across the slope," Bailis was explaining to Sergeant Kittins and others, "and line the uphill side with sharpened stakes, caltrops, anything that'll do some damage and slow them down. Of course, we'll set our longbowmen near the top, where they can rain death down on the bastard enemy all day long. Eventually, even his own dead will make a formidable obstacle for his infantry. We'll station a division of heavy horse on either end, so they can sweep out behind any given wave and ride them down from the back."

"And the pikemen?" one of the other officers asked.

"The usual: we'll intersperse them with the bowmen. If the enemy gets too close, our bowmen will be able to withdraw without too much difficulty."

"And we're behind that, are we?" Kittins asked.

"Just so," Bailis replied. "Meanwhile, the bowmen get behind us and resume firing downhill."

"What about the Shapers?" someone wanted to know.

Bailis pointed uphill, where a large group of soldiers was busy building platforms. "They'll be up there, naturally. They can't help if they can't see what's going on." Bailis looked pointedly at Janks. "Your friend D'Kem will be up there with the rest of them. I'm sure you were counting on his help down here, but the fact is we need him to help coordinate the, uh, *arcane* response."

"But but but we gotta have him with us!" Spirk complained,

completely surprising Janks, who hadn't even known he was present.

"I understand your…attachment…to the Shaper. You've been through an ordeal together that most of us cannot imagine. However, he's needed elsewhere. You're just going to have to trust the rest of us—all sixty thousand of us—to keep you safe." Bailis again addressed himself to the larger group. "Questions?"

There were none.

"Very good, then. About your business. Dismissed."

Janks stood for a moment and watched his breath rising into the cold air. He thought of the way blood and entrails steamed in winter battles. Better that than flies, he supposed. Still, a disturbing image nonetheless.

"You worried?" Bash had snuck up beside him and stood staring down the slope.

"Hell yes. You?"

Bash was quiet a long time, long enough for Janks to divine the answer. "Yeah, maybe a little bit. Mind, I'm not afraid of anyone one-on-one or even three-on-one. It's the magic and arrows and shit flyin' through the air I don't like. No telling what's gonna land where. You could be the best brawler in the world and still catch a spear right in the back o' the head."

"Don't seem fair, does it?"

"That's what I'm saying!"

"From what D'Kem was telling me, though, the enemy's host is mostly built for straight-on, eat you alive kinda stuff. Not a lot of subtlety."

Bash seemed reassured. "Good, then. If they play it like that, I ain't worried at all."

They weren't friendly, but Janks didn't have the heart to tell him the End-of-All-Things would never play it straight. The truly evil ones never did. Bash sauntered off to go sharpen his weapon, Janks supposed, so he looked around for the rest of the old unit. The twins would be on the hilltop, preparing to join the ranks of the longbowmen. Rem, meanwhile, had taken Spirk aside and was regaling him with some bullshit story undoubtedly intended to bolster the younger man's confidence. Janks' own confidence could sure as hell use some bolstering.

He'd never been in an army as big as the Queen's, and yet, word was, it was dwarfed by the End-of-All-Things' host. He couldn't conceive of sixty thousand men losing to anyone, but if they were truly outnumbered two, three or even five-to-one, what hope did they have? How long could they withstand the inevitable?

"Shouldn't you be sharpening stakes?" Kittins growled at him.

And there was another worry. The sergeant didn't like him, had never liked him, and was just as likely as not to "accidentally" kill him during the melee. Janks had seen it too many times before. Unless, he killed Kittins first. "Yessir!" he said, keeping his head low and rushing off to the nearest woodpile. The sound of axes and swords hacking at stakes blossomed all around him.

The End, In Camp

"You've told me of the different units and their functions. Let us move to the battle, itself."

Long cleared his throat. "Well, er, as we're the ones attacking, they'll have their choice of ground. Most likely, they'll place themselves on a hill. Maybe they'll find the ruins of an old fort or some such. The important thing is, they'll try to limit our options, make us work for every inch."

"You serve me well. They have indeed chosen higher ground. What else?"

So, it was another test. Every day, every moment in the End's service was a test. "They'll want to dictate who outflanks whom."

"There'll be none of that on this battlefield—too much forest on either side."

Long nodded. Good. But he said "I don't like it," adding "master" almost a breath too late.

"They challenge us, they *dare* us to a full-frontal assault," the End sneered. "The fools. Now, let me guess...we charge right at them and they hit us with an endless barrage of arrows, stones, et cetera. Correct?"

"From their position, that would seem the thing to do."

The End laughed. "And when their arrows run out and my thralls keep coming?"

"Then we go hand-to-hand," Long answered, dutifully. "No question we have superiority in numbers, master, but the Queen will have more mounted units."

"Overrated."

Overrated? "As you say," Long responded.

"You haven't mentioned their Shapers..."

"I expect our Shapers will engage them."

"And annihilate them," the End smiled. "I have a few surprises they will not have seen before. And the weather?"

Long lifted his head, scanned the clouds. "It's cold. Don't think it'll snow, but cold makes a difference."

"How?"

"Well, er...it makes the ground harder, for one thing. If there's frost, there could be ice. That ain't...that's *not*...good. Especially climbing uphill."

"There won't be ice, then."

"If I may ask..."

"How long 'til we arrive?"

Long never got used to the End's uncanny prescience. "Yes, master."

"By this time tomorrow, we'll be in sight of their force."

One more sleepless night.

Long, Before the Battle

Yendor was sharpening his sword when Long approached. "You look like you're actually going to fight," he told the other man as he hunkered down by the fire.

"Fightin' *somebody*. 'S all I know."

"Somebody," Long repeated. "Meaning?"

"Might be, in the chaos, a man could get himself lost. Disoriented, like."

"Probably safer in a battle than trying to drift away down a river, that's true."

"I figure the End'll have his hands full. For a while, anyways."

"O' course, if he catches you..."

"Aha! But I'm planning to switch clothes with one o' the Queen's dead," Yendor whispered and winked when he'd finished. "You wanna come along?"

"Do I!" Long exclaimed. "But..."

"You can't leave the missus," Yendor said, shaking his head sadly.

Long was about to protest that Mardine was not his wife, but a wave of guilt stopped him. "No. No, I can't."

"I understand. I wish I had someone to die for."

"Anyone ever tell you you have a way with words?" Long asked sarcastically.

Yendor seemed to contemplate the question earnestly. "Nope. Don't think so."

"Well, don't hold your breath."

Both men fell silent, while Yendor continued to sharpen his blade. Then, Long said, "You've been with this outfit longer'n me. What do you reckon tomorrow will be like?"

"Pretty much what you'd guess. The End likes to overwhelm with numbers and savagery. He'll lose more troops than the Queen's got in her entire army. And he'll still have enough left to take Lunessfor."

"Yeah," Long sighed. "That's what I was thinking, too. I keep hoping I'm wrong, though."

"Don't hope, and you won't be disappointed."

"But there was some talk about the Reaper coming in on the Queen's side. Have you heard anything about that of late?"

"Just what the End's been telling everyone: the Reaper ran off and hid in a mud puddle somewheres to the north."

"Which means, if we engage the Queen's army tomorrow and they're able to stretch this out a while, we could have Vykers at our backs."

"What'd I just say? Don't hope, and you won't be disappointed."

Long wriggled his toes in his boots. They were damp and cold, and the fire felt good on the soles of his feet. "You got any o' that Skent on you?"

Yendor's smile was as radiant as a filthy man's smile could

be. "Never without it, old son. Never without."

"Pass it over, would ya?"

The two armies caught sight of one another around three in the afternoon, too late in the day, by the End's estimation, to begin an attack. And, anyway, he wanted to give the Queen's force a day to stare at the enormity of his still-gathering host and panic, stew in their fears and anxieties. Sometimes, anticipation was a soldier's worst enemy. By nightfall, the bulk of Anders' host had finally arrived and parked itself in the appropriate positions across the meadow's bottom. The sheer number of campfires alone had to be daunting to the Queen's men.

Yendor and Long Pete had been hung-over all day and decided the only suitable response was a little—or a damned lot—of hair of the dog. Secretly, Long expected to die on the morrow and didn't feel up to facing death sober. Yendor, the more fatalistic of the two, was paradoxically convinced his plan was destined to succeed. "Funny old world," he might have said, if he'd been capable of stringing that many words together without losing his train of thought.

Behind the Queen's line of trenches, barricades and sharpened stakes, Janks and Rem were sharing a drink as well, though their liquor was of infinitely better vintage.

"What is that?" Janks asked, as he passed the wineskin back.

"Blackberry wine, I'm told. Not half bad, really," Rem replied.

"Look at all them fires, would ya? Like looking at stars in a summer sky."

"They say the stars themselves are fire. Did you know that?"

"Fire?" Janks asked, disbelievingly. "How do they stay lit?"

Rem chuckled. "Mahnus knows."

"Fuckin' Mahnus!" Janks spat. "D'you s'pose he's watching this little conflict right now?"

"No question! We're only here for the gods' entertainment, you know."

"Well, least I didn't have to play the girl."

Rem chuckled again. "There is that, my friend, there is that."

"So, how's this compare to your plays?"

"Truth? I would I were still playing the Mad King for ten silver a night. At least when you die onstage, it's not permanent."

Janks bobbed his head in agreement. "This what stage fright feels like?"

"Can't say. I've never had it. But I'm about to soil myself looking out at the enemy's forces."

"That's the point. But you'll get over it."

"Oh, aye? When?"

"When you're dead!"

Rem made a sour face. "You'd have made a poor clown, you know."

"Tell that to Long Pete. If you ever see him again."

Aoife, In the Village

Once again, Toomt'-La came while the children were asleep. He looked much recovered, though he was still heavily scarred and mottled with odd grays, browns and yellows. "I mean no disrespect, here," he said, "but there is more at stake than the lives of these particular children. Your brother is moving towards battle with the forces of your Virgin Queen. This is far sooner than anyone anticipated and, should he prevail, he'll not be long in conquering the human capital."

"Where is he?"

"Far, far to the South and West."

"Where I have never been. So there can be no 'here-and-there.' We cannot get there in time to make any difference." Aoife said.

A strange light came to Toomt'-La's eyes. "That is not entirely...true," he said.

"No? Tell me."

"It is accurate that you cannot step between forests you have not birthed." Toomt'-La admitted. "But as a child of the forest, I can travel to any forest, anywhere in the world, with a thought."

"Why have you kept this from me?" Aoife demanded. She had no reason, she felt, other than the sense she'd lost control, somehow.

"We had no need to visit thriving forests. Ours was—is—the

task of planting them where there are none."

"And what has changed?"

"There is forest on either side of your brother's intended battlefield."

Which meant she and her children—no, the children of Nar, if she was honest—would be able to attack her brother when his focus was elsewhere, potentially helping to bring him down. Yet...

"I cannot abandon these little ones," she said. "I simply cannot."

The satyr tilted his head, as if something had just occurred to him. "There is another option."

It was by far the fastest of Aoife's gestations, lasting from roughly the time Toomt'-La had suggested the idea until moonrise of that night. But it was also the one she felt most needful of. It would turn this broken little village into woodland, disguising it, perhaps, from raiders and scavengers, while at the same time providing her collection of orphans with eldritch guardians. The resultant forest might even lead to a sort of rapprochement between humans and the children of Nar. Aoife could dream, if nothing else.

In the morning, Aoife felt apprehensive as she prepared to introduce her offspring to the village orphans, but she needn't have worried. Children are nothing, if not resilient. With the exception of Tadpole, every one of the kids seemed spellbound by the collection of goblins, fairies, imps and sprites. It was a smaller brood than usual, but, given the circumstances, Aoife was more than pleased. Perhaps she had planted more than a forest here; perhaps she had founded a new type of community.

Glancing over at Tadpole, her buoyant mood faltered.

"You're fixin' to leave now." It was not a question.

Aoife stepped near him and touched his face. She found she could calm him. "I am going to war, young one. All you have seen and experienced—horrible though it was—is a drop in the ocean of what is to come for me."

Calm, yes, but still irrepressible. "You need me."

"Aye," Aoife smiled. "That I do. I need you to protect my

young while they grow. Once grown, they'll protect you, in turn, until I can rejoin you."

Tadpole sniffed. "You'll come back?" he asked. "You mean it?"

"I swear by Alheria's light, by Mahnus' hammer and by the Forest of Nar itself. You will see me again."

"I'd better." And then he was off, eagerly stepping into the crowd of Aoife's children.

"Shall we go to battle?" Toomt'-La asked from a shadowy corner.

Vykers, On the Trail

Gods, it was good to see the sky again. Even if it was grey and threatened snow. "Damn me, if I ever go near a moors again," Vykers exclaimed.

We shook our pursuers, Arune reminded him.

And lost one of our number, too.

Ah, but you're still alive. That's what matters, eh?

"Master," Number 17 said, gesturing to the south. "Something comes."

Arune?

It's an Essuragh.

A what?

Before the Shaper could answer, a small bat fluttered into view.

It's carrying an Essuragh—a sort of lodestone for magic.

"Shall I destroy it?" Number 17 asked.

No!

"Er...no. No, let's wait and see what this is."

Without knowing why, Vykers extended his right hand, and the creature flew towards it, not a bat after all, but a tiny gargoyle. With an odd purring sound, it landed gently on Vykers' outstretched fingers. In its left foot, it gripped an iridescent purplish bead.

"Just when I think I've seen..." the Reaper began.

"Tarmun Vykers?" the creature croaked, in a voice several

times too large to have come from its body.

"Yes," was all he could think to say.

The thing chirruped. "Please wait."

Vykers looked over at his companions, each of whom was every bit as confused.

Burner?

It's a messenger of some sort, I'm guessing. The Essuragh in its claw drew it towards us.

Right, and?

I don't know. Wait, I suppose.

"I don't like waiting!" Vykers said aloud.

The creature did not respond, but climbed up his arm to sit on his shoulder.

"What am I waiting for?"

"Please wait," was all he got in response.

"Wait. That's fuckin' great." Vykers took a deep breath. "Boys," he said, "let's see if we can scare up a real meal, huh?"

The chimeras grinned and bolted off in different directions; the hunt was on.

"I guess I'll find some firewood while I *wait*," he said, placing special emphasis on the last word.

In no time, game was roasting over a small but serious fire, and Vykers was, again, lying back and relaxing. The chimeras wolfed down enormous chunks of raw flesh, occasionally tossing a tidbit or two to the gargoyle, who had found a new perch on Vykers' right foot. The Reaper pulled off his gloves and examined his hands. His fingers and toes had been tingling ever since he'd eaten the chimera's liver. Now he knew why: his nails had hardened and grown into sharp, mean-looking points. He sat up.

"Hey, boys, what am I supposed to do with *these*?" he asked, somewhat accusingly.

The three chimeras looked at one another, and Number 3 said "Retract them?"

"Retract? What do you mean 'retract'?" But almost as soon as he said it, Vykers understood. It was an odd sensation, but not entirely unpleasant. He started laughing. "I've got claws.

I've got Mahnus-be-damned claws!" The chimeras smiled sheepishly at him, as if he wasn't quite right in the head.

I always knew you were a beast, Arune added.

Yes, and be glad of it!

"The war has begun," the gargoyle suddenly said in an all-too-familiar voice.

"Your Majesty," Vykers said. "You're looking well."

"As you, alas, are not. You look like you've been living in a cesspool these last few weeks."

"You're not far off the mark. Tell me what's happened."

It was weird and beyond weird speaking to the Queen through the little gargoyle. The gravity of her message, however, overrode all other thoughts for Vykers.

"The lunatic—I will not call him the 'End-of-All-Things'—has surprised us by attacking at the onset of winter."

"Thought he'd wait 'til conditions were more favorable, did you?"

"A reasonable assumption, but a lesson learned notwithstanding."

"If the battle's started, I don't see how I can help you, magic sword or no."

"My Shapers have the ability to get you there almost immediately. But you won't have had time to meet the troops, structure your command, formulate strategy…"

A mischievous gleam came to Vykers' eye. "Please wait," he said and went inside to talk to Arune.

"Wait?" the gargoyle croaked. "This is no time for your cheek, warrior! I brought you down before and I can do so again." The Queen ranted for another minute or so before Vykers spoke aloud again.

"Can your Shapers get me behind the enemy, say, a league or so?"

The gargoyle stopped jabbering, its mouth hanging open. When the Queen spoke again, her voice was quiet, steely. "What are you planning, Tarmun Vykers?"

"You said the enemy surprised you. What do you say we surprise him right back?"

"I don't like asking twice: what are you planning?"

Vykers leaned forward, tore a piece of meat off the haunch in the fire. "You're gonna have to trust me, Your Majesty. Just like I have to trust your Shapers won't drop me into a crevasse somewhere."

"Fine!" the gargoyle-cum-Queen snapped. "You may as well eat your fill. This will take a few minutes' time to prepare."

Vykers, I wouldn't...

Oh, leave me be. I'm hungry, and I'm gonna eat.

Suit yourself, Arune retorted.

Vykers was on his hands and knees, vomiting so violently, he felt sure he'd bust a rib.

I tried to warn you, Arune protested.

Fuckin' Shapers. Don't think I've ever been so dizzy in my... Vykers puked again. At least, he noted, the chimeras weren't faring much better.

A half hour later, he sat on his ass on the frosted ground and stared at a fixed spot between his knees. "I think I can stand now." And so he did.

All hail, the mighty Vykers!

There was a haze across the southern horizon that could only have been the enemy's host. *'S a big fuckin' army, all right. You work things out with 17?*

We've already started, Arune said.

Deda, the Queen's Castle

Her Majesty looked disappointed. "You've survived," she said dryly.

"Only just," Wims admitted, finally allowed to sit up on the table to which he'd been chained. All his joints ached as if he'd been stretched on the rack; perhaps there had been a physical element to his torture, after all.

"I've decided to accept your offer," the Queen said. "You now work for me. Times being what they are, I believe I can use someone with your lack of...convictions, shall we say."

Wims wasn't completely brainless. "What do I have to do?"

"I like the way you put that—'what do I have to do'—it shows an accurate assessment of your situation. You *have* to do as I command. And what I command is for you to return to your former employer and pretend to resume your...whatever it was you did for him."

"I won't be welcome if I come back without having done, er, some damage to Your Majesty."

"Which is precisely why my staff have already begun spreading rumors of horrible crimes perpetrated against me and my inner circle by an unknown assailant. We've even come up with a few sadly unidentifiable corpses to lend veracity to the claims. Try to stand now."

Slowly, Wims pushed forward and slid his legs down onto the floor. Excruciating pain shot up both legs. After several deep breaths, He hobbled across the room in order to work more blood into his legs. "Don't know as I can ride a horse in this condition."

"Who said anything about you riding? Time is short. My Shapers will have to send you."

If there was one thing Wims didn't like, it was magic. The End used it of course, so Wims swallowed his fears and suspicions. "Yeah, well, about that..."

"This is not negotiable. Remember where you are and to whom you are speaking."

"Yes. Your Majesty." Then he had a thought. "There is one other thing, though. Something I'm supposed to bring back to the End-of-All-Things."

"You refer to that mummified head." Not a question.

Wims was flabbergasted. "Is there nothing you don't know about?"

The Queen smiled a brief, secretive smile and changed the subject. "You'll need to bathe and change your clothes. We can't have you returning to your former employer smelling like a jakes."

"Nor a lord, neither, Your Majesty."

"Just so." She turned to the friar. "Take Mr. Deda to the room we've prepared. See him washed, fed, and dressed appropriately. Make sure he doesn't leave before our Shapers arrive." Without another word, she stepped towards the door.

"Eh...Your Majesty..."

The Queen went rigid, turned back at glacial speed. "Something else, Mr. Deda?"

If a man didn't stand up for himself, who would? "I was just wondering what sort of, uh, pay I might get for this job?"

The response was a while in coming. "I am unclear as to how it has escaped your notice that I have your life in my hands." The Queen glanced down at those hands and wrenched one of the numerous rings off her fingers. Imperiously, she thrust it into Wims' face. "Take it. I'm too old to wear that particular gem, anyway, and it will lend credence to your tale. Now, do not speak to me again, Mr. Deda, or I will have your tongue out."

He could not meet her eyes, so he examined the ring she'd given him instead. A man could buy a farm with such a ring.

"Let us go," the friar/torturer said.

A hot bath and an abundance of sack put Wims in a better mood than he'd enjoyed in ages. Truth to tell, he couldn't remember feeling better. Oh, his joints and muscles still ached, but, on the whole, he'd have to argue he'd come out on top again. He experienced a brief moment of trepidation when two servants came in with his supper, because he worried it might be poisoned. But that made no sense: the Queen could have killed him any number of ways. Indeed, she seemed the kind of ruler who'd shove the dagger in your guts herself. Confident the enormous, diverse and tantalizing meal before him was not poisoned, Wims dug in with gusto.

Of course, it *was* poisoned.

Janks & Company, Before the Battle

It was colder than Mahnus' balls in a snow drift in Janks' opinion, and, judging by the mobs of men packed around campfires, he wasn't alone in that belief. But even had it been warmer, he wouldn't have been able to sleep. Within the hour, he knew, the eastern sky would begin to lighten, which meant—just being realistic—he had as little as sixty minutes to live.

A pair of tall, shiny boots appeared to Janks' left. He didn't need to look up to know who'd come calling.

"One of us'll be dead soon," Kittins growled. "But I promise we'll bury your corpse...after I'm done shittin' on it."

What has a dead man got to lose? Janks stood up, chest-to-chest with the sergeant. "Little confused about which side yer on, there, big man?" Kittins sneered at him. "I'm fighting for the Queen, myself," Janks said. "How about you?"

Kittins scanned the rest of the crew around the campfire; all eyes were on him. "I'm fighting for the Queen, too," was all he could manage. He spit on Janks' boots and walked away.

"One down," Janks muttered to himself, "hundred thousand to go..."

Somehow, Spirk heard him. "You really think there's a hundred thousand of 'em?"

"You tell me," Janks replied. "You was in their camp, right?"

"Right, but...I can't count that high."

Bash guffawed. "Fancy numbers don't matter, anyways. Only question in war is, who's got more troops, them or us?"

"Them," Spirk answered.

"There's your answer, then."

"Of course," Rem chimed in, "there are plenty of stories of smaller armies besting larger ones."

"Let's hear one, then!" Janks said.

"Ah!" Rem said, settling into a comfortable position nearer the flames, "one of my favorites has to be the surprising victory of the Desetorian Elites against the Jebuur Nation..."

Long, Before the Battle

"Wannanother?" Yendor asked.

"Nah. No thanks. Guess I'll die sober and defy the gods."

Yendor laughed good and hard at that one. "Not me," he said. "If I'm gonna die, I don't wanna feel it." He drained the last of the Skent and fished around in his coat pockets for more.

"Anyway," Long sighed, "I rather expect another visit from the master before hostilities begin."

"All the more reason for drinkin'!"

"Then I think I'll leave you to it, my friend. Best of luck in the battle."

Yendor snored in response.

Long Pete would be dead by noon, one way or another. He was certain of it. Well, and about time, he figured. Short Pete was probably tired of waiting for him to cross over. Long felt he should dedicate a few moments' thought to Mardine and his unborn child, but it all seemed so futile. No matter how hard, how loud or how often he prayed, the giantess would never hear him, would never know he was actually proud of their relationship and only ashamed of the end he'd brought her to. He hoped his son had a chance to be born, a chance to live and to grow. He hoped his son would become a better man than he'd been, leading a more purposeful, less self-indulgent life. He hoped his son never knew self-pity.

As predicted, the End-of-All-Things appeared, as if from nowhere, wearing his customary, otherworldly armor. "You fear your death," he said almost casually.

"I fear the pain of it, aye. I fear the things left undone," Long responded.

The End did not laugh, as Long might've expected. "And the pain of dying is less, somehow, than that of living? All you mortals ever *do* is complain about the pain of living."

Mortals?

"As for the things left undone, that suggests your kind is capable of more, of better. You are not. That is why your *world must be undone*."

"Perhaps you're right," Long murmured.

"What? No bold defiance? No brave last words?" the End scoffed. "You disappoint me."

The old campaigner knew better than to even imagine a retort, so he said nothing.

"Very well, then, General," the End sighed in exasperation. "Prepare your thralls for battle. Use your whip and horse to move them forward when the time comes and try not to get yourself killed in the opening skirmish; I may have need of you later."

Again, Long bit his lip, kept his head down. "As you say, Master."

"Do you recall your assignment?"

"Third line, fourth position."

"Correct. Right between Generals Daurits and Ni-Nmen."

"But..." Long stumbled.

"Yes?" the End asked, a hint of mockery in his voice.

"Normally, General Plotz' unit is on my left."

The End broke into a smile that did not reach his eyes. "Not today. Would you care to guess where I've placed him?"

Long had a sinking feeling. "First line, third position?"

The End nodded, approvingly. "You are learning. Yes, front-and-center. We have seen the last of General Plotz, I'm afraid."

Long hoped to hell his friend was still good and drunk.

Janks, Before the Battle

Some mornings, the first rays of sunshine give everything a pinkish hue, but even this small pleasure was denied the Queen's soldiers on the morning of battle. The sky merely went from black to grey. If a soldier has to die, he wants to do so with the sun on his face, gazing up into the infinite. This morning, though, the sky was low—a featureless, colorless blanket that did nothing to shore up the mood around camp, where men rose from their fires, shook hands one last time, and moved off to their final rituals before combat. Some fell to their knees and prayed, others oiled and sharpened their blades for the umpteenth time, and still others checked and rechecked the bindings and straps on their armor. Some visited the latrines, some drank. One crazy bastard kept bashing his forehead into a wagon wheel and laughing louder and louder after each blow. Whatever it took.

Janks had no rituals, but wished he'd had the foresight to create one. He'd just never been in a war he expected to survive. As he was making the rounds, wishing his comrades well, D'Kem showed up, brightening everyone's mood considerably. It was true Janks hadn't seen much of the old Shaper lately, but the man looked positively hale and hearty. The lines in his face had diminished, while color had crept back into his hair and beard. Strange to imagine the Shaper as a younger man, with a full head of auburn hair. He also seemed taller and more solid, somehow, than when Janks had seen him last.

Spirk was overjoyed to see him, too. "D'Kem! Good to see you! I knew you'd come!"

Just as Janks began to worry that Spirk's jubilant shouting might provoke a premature attack from the enemy, D'Kem reached out and placed a hand on the younger man's shoulder, whereupon he became almost somnambulant.

"Nice trick, that. Care to teach the rest of us?" Janks joked.

D'Kem laughed, a surprisingly deep, jolly sound. "Alas, I expect I'll be too busy, shortly."

A small crowd of D'Kem's former mates gathered 'round. "Seems you've been plenty busy already," Rem observed.

"Oh, aye, I'll not deny it. But how about you? Are you folks ready for this morning's action?"

Janks was amazed at the man's relaxed, almost easy manner. Suddenly, he had an epiphany. "You're him, ain't you?"

"I am…me," the Shaper said, coyly. "All I ever was or hope to be."

"But you can take him, right? This End-of-All-Things?" Janks asked.

"I don't intend to find out. It is, after all, our army against his army. And you all are a big part of that." D'Kem reached out again and patted Spirk on the back, reanimating him.

"And I've still got my lucky stone!" Spirk blurted out helpfully.

"Ah!" D'Kem intoned with exaggerated gravitas, "then we have little to fear!" He turned to the group. "I hope to see you all after the battle, whether it be tonight, tomorrow or the next full moon. Let us show this tyrant what the Queen's men are made of!"

Watching the Shaper stroll away, Janks felt something he'd never felt about his former companion before: awe. Glancing at his fellows, he could see they were all equally inspired. If this was magic, it was magnificent. Janks dared a peek towards the enemy's host, lurking to the north. He found he was no longer afraid of it.

Vykers, On the Battlefield

The ground behind the End's host was as blighted as any ground, anywhere, could ever be. The passage of upwards of two-hundred thousand feet, along with all the feces, urine and worse dropped by the owners of those feet, had churned the frosty turf into a loathsome mire. Once blood and bile were added...Vykers doubted any scavenger was that desperate, but time would tell, he knew.

Vykers?

Burn?

There's some movement a few hundred yards to the south.

Sure enough, someone or something was struggling along the ground in the wake of the enemy's host. Vykers made eye contact with the Three and said, "Care to join me?"

Of course they did! In two minutes' time, they stood behind one of the End's thralls, pulling himself along the ground with his forearms, because his feet had largely rotted off. And yet, he still fought to keep up.

That is one strong compulsion, Arune noted.

Disturbing, Vykers agreed. Drawing his sword, he rammed it through the thrall's back and into his heart.

"You are merciful and wise to have done so," Number 17 offered. "The man's mind was gone."

Vykers stared at the corpse, an emaciated peasant with matted blond hair and filthy, ragged clothing. His death wound hardly bled. "Mercy?" the Reaper asked. "I came here to kill these bastards; this one's just the first."

How's our little project coming? He asked Arune.

Hard to say. Obviously, the longer the Queen's force can engage the enemy, the better our results will be.

The old crone's cunning. She'll have some excellent officers, well-trained troops and plenty of arms and armor.

You hope.

I know. I've thought of taking her on myself a time or two. I've had her thoroughly scouted.

*Well, she did capture you…*Arune goaded.

And I'll settle that score one day, too. Right now, I've got to deal with the End-of-All-Things.

ELEVEN

Janks & Company, Before the Battle

Mid-morning came and went and still the enemy had not attacked. In the trenches of the Queen's army, frustration was mounting.

"Fuck're they doing?" Bash grumbled under his breath.

"My guess?" said Janks. "They're testing our patience, tryin' to see if they can provoke us into coming down there."

"That ain't gonna happen."

"'Course not. But they lose nothing by trying. And the longer they stand down there, the longer we have to look at 'em."

In that instant, the End's host began to scream in unison. It was the loudest, most intimidating and most awful sound anyone on the Queen's side had ever heard. Up and down the trenches, men grabbed their weapons and prepared for an assault. The unholy din went on for several minutes and then stopped abruptly.

Here it comes, thought Janks.

But it didn't come. The enemy became quiet and still again. More minutes passed. Just as the men of the Queen's army began to relax, the End's horde rumbled forward, screaming again. "To arms!" rang out all over the slope, more than enough to ensure every soldier got the message. In the distance, Janks could hear the longbow men being ordered to draw and take aim—not that aim was required in such a massive sea of targets. Given the incline and the intended storm of arrows, it would be two or three minutes, at least, before the first of the End's thralls reached the heavily staked front line. Behind that, an entire division of pikemen stood ready to repel any who made it through. The archers came next, but they would continually retreat behind successive lines of heavy infantry, needful of cover to carry out their jobs.

Janks watched the approaching flood with a mixture of terror and disbelief. If ever an avalanche rolled uphill, surely this was it. Fervent whispering on his left drew his attention away briefly; Spirk was talking or perhaps praying to his magic stone. *Another ritual.* Janks smiled grimly to himself, amused to realize that he wished he, too, had a magic stone. Anything to give him hope.

The sound of several thousand arrows being released simultaneously is unique and unforgettable. Normally, a foe would look up, however fleetingly, to track the progress of those arrows. The thralls did not, but barreled forward unawares. Just before the arrows were to find their marks, an enormous flash of light lit up the sky and reduced most of them to ash. This was followed immediately by a concussive blast of thunder at the rear of the enemy's host, resulting in more white light and tendrils of black, sooty smoke. The Shapers had begun their own battle. Another volley of arrows flew, and, this time, were not destroyed en route to targets. Dozens, hundreds of thralls and mounted mercenaries fell. It made no difference. The End-of-All-Things had an inexhaustible supply of replacements. From somewhere at the back of the Queen's army, trebuchets launched their deadly payload at the oncoming enemy.

Long, On the Battlefield

The End had given him a good horse, if nothing else. Long wouldn't have blamed the beast for bolting into the woods, after the horrific and prolonged wailing of the thralls, but it had stayed calm, unperturbed. Long would've given anything to feel the same, or maybe the horse was just a better actor than he. Either way, this was as frightened as the old soldier had ever been. When at last the End's thralls charged, Long felt almost relieved. *Won't have to endure this much longer, whatever the outcome.*

He kept his eyes peeled for signs of Yendor, astride his red pony. Somehow, the End thwarted the first flight of incoming arrows, saving countless lives. Or rather extending them, briefly. But a huge explosion to the rear of the host nearly caused Long to piss himself—an increasingly and distressingly common occurrence. Nothing but nothing was scarier, more unpredictable than magic. There was no effective armor against it, no telling where it would strike or what kind of damage it might do. And he took no solace in the fact his master was using it also. Fighting fire with fire was all well and good, if you liked living in ashes. Long did not. He lost sight of Yendor for a moment, and then the third line pushed forward, carrying Long and his unit with it.

Already, the bodies of the thralls were piling up and the first line hadn't even reached the enemy. Long had to maneuver his horse briskly to avoid trampling on fallen troops felled by arrows, boulders and smaller stones. For every step forward, he seemed to take ten or a dozen to either side, all the while trying to keep an eye on his only friend in the host and dodge anything coming his way. In selecting this meadow, the Queen's officers had chosen well; if he ever did reach their troops, he'd be too exhausted to engage them.

Not far in front of Long, a thrall went down with not one, not two, but three arrows through his neck and head. *Lucky bastard!* In that instant, Long lost his fear of arrows. "Do your worst!" he yelled up the slope, though he knew he'd never be heard over the clamor of battle. He pushed forward another ten yards and was at last within bowshot. "Hit me, you Midlands sons-o'-bitches!" Shafts hammered down all around him, taking out several more thralls. Long remained unscathed. Still, the surging horde pressed him forward, forward, ever forward. He searched the hillside for any sign of Yendor, but all was chaos, right up to the enemy's front.

Janks, In Battle

His new, army-issue armor was heavier than he'd worn in years and made him sweat something fierce. The chain hauberk and leather breastplate and greaves had a reassuring bulk to them, but were also more restrictive than the random merc's gear to which he'd been accustomed. Janks lamented not having had time to drill in his new armor for a few weeks—or months—before seeing action.

From his defensive trench, he had an all-too clear view of the enemy's advance. It was hard to believe there were so many people in the world entire, much less on one battlefield. Janks and his comrades had been warned the End-of-All-Thing's host was composed of enslaved and ensorcelled peasants. He'd thought himself prepared for the sight of them, but when they finally drew within a spear's throw, he was stunned, mortified by their frenzied, animalistic affect. Here was a girl—a girl!—leaping over the sharpened stakes and throwing herself at a pikeman, froth exploding from her lips. There, an old man, scrambling up the slope on all fours and cackling madly to himself. Another fellow about Janks' age inexplicably hurled himself on the stakes and lay there, twitching and writhing, while other thralls ran over him. A monstrous creature who must have once been a blacksmith batted several pikes aside and charged into soldiers behind them. Janks was amazed that he heard no panic, no dismay; personally, he could not have been more frightened.

All along the line, thousands of thralls were hurling themselves against the army's defenses. The Queen's men cut them down by the hundreds, but "hundreds" was not good enough by any measure. Soon, Janks knew, the wretched, desperate creatures would be upon him and his mates. He hefted the single-bladed axe he'd chosen from the armory in his right hand, drawing a long knife with his left. Some folks preferred the sword and shield; not Janks. To his mind, twice as many blades meant twice as much damage. The things coming at him weren't trained professionals, they were beasts. If needs must, he would cut them down like beasts.

On a platform above and behind the Queen's army, D'Kem had problems of his own. Whatever else he was, the End-of-All-Things was an obscenely powerful sorcerer. He had, on numerous occasions, overwhelmed one or another of D'Kem's colleagues and caused the poor Shaper's head to explode in a shower of blood, brains and bone shards. The effect on the other Shapers' morale was predictably devastating. But it just made D'Kem angrier. If that's the way the End-of-All-Things wanted to fight, the old Shaper was more than ready to answer.

Anders exulted in his superiority over the Queen's Shapers and was preparing to deal them a final, decisive blow when four of his own froze solid with an eerie crackling sound and slowly turned to crystal. The End-of-All-Things was not easily astonished, but a thrill of dread rippled through him as he stared, confounded, at the transparent statues of his former Shapers. One of the survivors let out a cry of alarm. Another took several steps backwards, as if considering flight.

"Hold your positions!" the End commanded. "I will deal with this threat!"

Two more of his Shapers froze and turned to crystal, and the rest fled in the variety of ways magic allows. The End bellowed with rage. Powerful as he was, he could not orchestrate the assault on the Queen's front and chase after his cowardly Shapers. He glanced around: a few stood strong. "I will protect you," he assured them and threw an ancient and elaborate spell upon them. A violet glow suffused the area, and the remaining Shapers felt no harm. "Destroy their archers!" the End screamed. "And let me deal with the enemy's magicians!"

"Gods!" Vykers roared. "I can't stand this waiting! I need to get into this fight!" From his vantage point, the Reaper could see clouds of arrows, flashes of sorcerous energies, vast boulders crashing down and sending bodies flying. It was as if the sight of warfare made him drool with hunger, the way a nice piece of meat will make a dog drool. *Burner! Arune!* He thought, urgently. *How's it coming along?*

Well, I've got both 17 and your sword working with me this time. Between the three of us, it's looking hopeful.

Hopeful? Hopeful? The battle's started, by Alheria's tits! This had best work, or the Queen's army's lost!

Which wouldn't be in complete opposition to your long-term goals.

Shit! Know why I liked that General Shere? He wouldn't take nothing he hadn't earned. That's the true warrior's way, and that's how I feel about the throne. I don't want it handed to me; I want to take it.

How long do you think they'll hold out?

Hard to tell from this angle. Maybe a day.

The longer we can wait…

I know, you told me: the better our results. Vykers looked over at the chimeras. "Three, think you can sneak around through those woods and get a better look at this fight, a sense o' how it's going?"

Number 3 grinned wickedly. "I would be delighted."

"Have a go, then."

Number 3 raced off into the forest on the left side of the field and disappeared amongst the trees.

"Sorry, boys, I need you two with me," Vykers told the remaining two.

Were it not for his magic stone, Spirk would have passed out from the sheer terror of watching the thralls' advance. He'd spent time with them, it was true, but he'd never seen them like this, so agitated and enraged. Once upon a time, his old man had been forced to put down a mad dog. The thing had been snarling and lunging at anyone who came near it, even its master. It had a festering wound on its hindquarters that was a sure sign of a run-in with something wild; that, and its erratic, aggressive behavior had been enough to seal its doom. These thralls reminded Spirk of that dog, only he didn't think his Da could put 'em down. Not with the world's longest sword.

Spirk gripped his mace. Well, it was the army's mace, but they'd lent it to him, along with a medium-sized shield that strapped to his arm and everything. Bash told him "Stay behind your shield and just smash, smash, smash with that mace. You'll be fine." Spirk hoped so, but he feared he might be smashing 'til he was an old, old man. He stole a glance left and right, to see how his mates were faring. Janks wore a look of grim determination that Spirk very much admired and attempted to mimic. On him, though, it looked more like his privates were itching. Bash was grinning like a bloodthirsty wolf, whereas Rem had a look a grave concern. Kittins' face was frighteningly devoid of expression, except for his eyes, which were very, very scary. The A'Shea—whose name Spirk had never learned—was huddled down in her robes, and the twins were, of course, off working with the rest of the archers. Spirk wondered how things were going for D'Kem and whether or not he'd see the old Shaper again.

The End-of-All-Things had switched tactics, forcing D'Kem and the rest of the Queen's Shapers to follow suit. The mad sorcerer abandoned the notion of trading Shaper-for-Shaper and had launched, instead, an all-out effort to eliminate the Queen's archers, which threatened to divide D'Kem's focus: he now needed to protect the bowmen, but he was also aware that, preoccupied as they were, the End's magicians would be less prepared for an attack.

A sinister, supernatural cloud formed over the archers, none of whom missed its arrival or doubted its provenance. As their fears increased and their courage waned, sergeants demanded order, while themselves looking to higher-ups for further instruction.

D'Kem nudged the man next to him. "I think I can handle this thing, if the rest of you will do something to slow the assault on the ground."

The other man curled his lip in contempt. "I hardly think..."

"We do not have time to argue. Attack the enemy, or join them!" D'Kem raged in the man's face.

A black, tar-like substance began dripping from the sky above the archers. When it fell on men, they gasped and shouted in panic, which quickly became terror, as their armor dissolved and the flesh fell from their disintegrating bones.

"Attack the enemy!" D'Kem commanded his colleague again, before turning his attentions to the noxious cloud. Stretching his arms high and wide, D'Kem recited a spell in a language the other Shaper had never heard before. Unfamiliar though it was, he could not question its power. A strange shrieking noise whistled through the air in every direction, and the End's cloud began to collapse in on itself.

Humbled and frightened, the other Shaper rushed to his nearest neighbors and began formulating a plan to attack the thralls.

Above, the cloud continued to shrink, its rain, to taper off. The cries of the wounded and dying below, however, showed no signs of letting up. Despite the cold, sweat streamed down D'Kem's face and into his beard, so taxing was the effort he'd undertaken. His arms trembled, his knees buckled. And the cloud grew smaller.

Far away, the moaning of the thralls intensified.

"What did you decide to do?" D'Kem yelled over to the other Shapers.

The man he'd reprimanded earlier responded, "We raised the water table to the surface, Shaper."

D'Kem grimaced at the cloud another moment or two and then laughed. "I like the way you think!" he exclaimed. Raising the water table would soften the ground. The countless feet stomping across it would soon turn it to mud. In no time, the End's army would be wallowing in a quagmire.

With a tremendous effort, D'Kem reduced the End's poisonous cloud to a dense black ball, perhaps three feet in diameter. Carefully, he lowered it to the ground. He might've yelled out that everyone should stay away from it, but that was clearly unnecessary. The Queen's troops regarded it with undisguised horror.

"What are you going to do with that, my lord?" the other Shaper asked.

"Obsequiousness suits you no better than arrogance. Call me D'Kem" the older man answered. "As for that thing," he said, pointed to the sphere, "I think we should load it into a trebuchet and send it back where it came from."

The other Shaper smiled. *And I like the way* you *think,* he wanted to say.

Unholy. The black shit was unholy, and that was all anyone ever needed to know about it. Janks had watched it raining onto the bowmen and some of the pikemen and could not have been more relieved that it hadn't reached his particular trench. "All praise to Mahnus and Alheria" he whispered to himself, though he'd never before said such a thing. The unholy black shit had stopped falling, uphill. Downhill, the first wave of thralls was almost upon him. Without warning, Bash let out a terrifying war cry, making Janks' heart pound an ominous tattoo in his chest. He decided he'd best yell, too, and let out a throat-rending scream. Not one to be left out, Spirk chimed in with a rather pathetic yelp. Rem alone remained silent.

Too soon, the thralls—a wall of shrieking, snarling fury—were upon them.

A ragged woman who had obviously once been quite fat threw herself at Janks and clawed at his eyes, while attempting to clamp her thighs around his chest. The stench she gave off just about toppled him, but he buried his axe in the base of her neck on her left side and plunged his knife into the copious folds of loose flesh at her midriff. The damage didn't seem to slow her in the slightest. She scrambled for better purchase and tried biting Janks' face. Withdrawing his blade, he brought it across the woman's right forearm on the backslash. Her hand flopped useless to the side. When she turned, confused, to look at it, Janks smashed her in the face with his axe and pushed her aside. *That's one,* he thought.

That was the last solo thrall he would see.

The battlefield had become a swamp. Impossibly, water leached up through the soil, where countless feet churned everything to mud in seconds. The crowd around his horse thickened, as well, because the thralls in front of him were no longer able to run up the slope, whilst the ones behind kept pushing forward. Had he not been mounted, Long suspected he might've been uncontrollably claustrophobic. He'd long since lost sight of Yendor; with everything else going on around him, he simply didn't have the time or energy to worry about his friend.

Long witnessed the arrival of the End's cloud and its aftermath with morbid fascination, in the same way it is difficult to look away from an execution. Yet, he was heartened by the response of the Queen's Shapers. Somehow, they'd managed to neutralize—transmute was a better word, an alchemist's word—the End's weapon until it fell from the sky in a small, black clump. He'd thought that was the last of it until he heard cheering from the Queen's army. Looking up, he saw the black stone streaking towards the heart of the End's host. Without thought, he forced his mount forward, desperate to create as much space as possible between himself and the stone's impact. Surging ahead, his horse smashed thralls out of his way left, right and downwards. Long didn't care. All that mattered was getting as far from the black—

He didn't hear it land, exactly, but he did hear the resultant hue and cry from thralls and mercenaries caught in its splash—a much different sound than that produced by the Queen's men. Long assumed it was because the thralls were less aware, so their cries held less horror in them and more sadness. It was a mournful noise, is what it was. Except for the mercenaries, who screamed in a more-familiar hysteria. Inappropriate though it was, Long found himself smiling as he imagined the End's reaction to being bombarded with his own evil.

"Push the attack!" the-End-of-All-Things snarled at General Omeyo. "If we fought for a thousand years, they would still be unable to match our numbers. We shall bury them in bodies."

Omeyo bowed his head and left without saying a word. It was a risky choice, but he knew his master's moods and knew, too, that the End was preoccupied as he'd never been in the general's experience.

To suggest that the End was vexed would be an understatement. His host was like an endless herd of Bospai, thundering across the plains. The Queen's forces were the stinging flies that harried them every step of the way: no threat, really, but highly annoying—especially the nameless Shaper. No matter. The End would deal with him sooner or later, as he'd dealt with all other threats to his designs. An unexpected voice roused him from his musings.

"Master?"

General Deda. About the last man he'd expected to see. "You have failed, then?" The End asked with more than a trace of irritation in his voice.

The man actually looked offended. "No, master. I would have thought...I mean, have you not heard the news from Lunessfor?"

The End swept an arm across the meadow. "You may have noticed I'm a little busy at the moment," he said sardonically. "What news?"

Naturally, Wims had rehearsed his report, but it came out awkwardly all the same. "Well, I, er, eliminated several of the Queen's inner circle...her closest advisors...as you instructed."

"And why do I feel you're lying to me?" the End asked with obvious menace in his voice.

Wims' hand shot out, opened. "Here's one of her rings, master. I'm sure you can tell it's genuine."

The End extended two fingers and lifted the ring as if it were something unsavory. Then, he brought it closer with both hands, staring at it intently. After several seconds, a cold smile came to his lips. "You are indeed a clever man, General Deda. I would feign hear the story of how you came by this." He paused. "Unfortunately, it will have to wait. I will not rest or meet with my commanders again until we've broken the enemy's front. Go and refresh yourself, General, and then report to General Omeyo. And take this with you," he added, tossing the ring back to Wims. "It stinks of rancid hag's flesh."

Wims had no great love for Omeyo, or anyone, really, but he was relieved to have escaped his master's presence so easily. He'd expected the End-of-All-Things to see through his lies and incinerate him on the spot. That he had not simultaneously pleased and troubled Wims. He was grateful to remain among the living, surely, but couldn't shake the feeling something was deeply, seriously amiss. Nothing for it, but a mug of wine, he supposed and headed off towards the mess.

The End watched his man leave with equal disquiet. The ring was genuine, of that he had no doubt. And experience had taught him Wims was a determined and resourceful killer. The timing and manner of his return, though, were highly suspicious. Were it not for that bastard Shaper on the Queen's side, the End would gladly have spent more time interrogating Deda. As things stood, the Shaper was clearly the greater and more persistent threat. Anders needed to find a way to negate him as soon as possible.

Several pairs of strong hands yanked him violently from the trench and dragged him backwards. Janks could not have been more thankful. The place had become an abattoir. He'd been chest-deep in blood, offal and other body parts with no hope of extricating himself.

"If anyone's gonna kill you, mate, it'll be me. Not these damned bewitched peasants," he heard Corporal Kittins say.

The next voice belonged to Bash. "Come off it, Corporal. We ain't got time for fighting 'mongst ourselves. Let's take care 'o them as wanna eat us first and then settle with each other."

Kittins grunted. "Let's get back to the next trench before they overrun us. And, look you," he snarled at Janks, "keep yourself *behind* the trench, not in it!

Janks lurched to his feet. Gods, he stank. He was drenched through with every kind of fluid a human body can produce; his arms and legs ached like the countless hells, and everything was sticky with blood, much of it his own, he didn't doubt. He took a second to look downhill. "What's going on in the middle, there? Looks like everything's turned to swamp."

"I figure that's the only thing slowing 'em down," Bash said. "That, and we fired their black poison back at 'em and it's eatin' a huge hole in their forces."

Kittins laughed. "Serves 'em right, the bastards. Let 'em all go down in that stew."

Somebody shoved a wineskin in Janks' face, which mercifully turned out to be full of water. Was there anything better in the whole, wide world? He took seven or eight swallows and reluctantly passed it back to the closest man, Rem. Good old Rem. Who knew actors could be such upright fellows?

Janks looked again at the enemy's struggles. That quagmire was the only reason he and his mates were getting this little breather. Otherwise, they'd see thrall after thrall 'til the end of time. Or the End-of-All-Things. And somewhere down in that mess was Janks' best friend, Long Pete. And Mardine, o' course. Hard to believe the gods were benevolent when they placed old mates in such terrible circumstances.

Major Bailis came by. It didn't look like he'd seen any fighting, yet. "Proud of you men!" he declared. "I've never seen the like of this enemy, but you've given that soulless wizard more than he bargained for!"

Words. Janks inspected his weapons, tried to work the cramps out of his arms and legs. His axe and long knife were the only things keeping him alive today. Assuming he stayed alive. Somewhere behind the clouds, the sun was nearing eleven o'clock, which seemed impossible.

It had taken a while—too long, really—but the End had finally managed to nullify the effects of his own nasty magic, which the enemy had thrown back in his face. The black slime gradually evaporated, and the hole in the center of the End's army was quickly filled by thralls pushed forward by angry mercenaries and generals. Slowly, too, the ground was firming up as it froze in the winter's chill. The Queen's men had had their moment, to be sure, and good for them. But Long's fiendish master would not be denied.

Long cast about for his unit, searching for thralls he might recognize, and spied some familiar (if vacant) faces a hundred yards or so to the northeast. He'd lost a few to the black ooze it seemed, but with luck the End would never know he had bolted. And now, what? The entire line he'd been a part of would likely reach the enemy's first trench within the quarter hour; arrows, spears, pikes and sharpened stakes aside, it would be tooth and nail, sword and mace within minutes. Mahnus and Alheria have mercy.

Overcast though it was, the sky was brightening. The liquid nature of time in a battle never ceased to amaze Long; sometimes a heartbeat lasted an hour, sometimes a day went by in a breath. And it didn't seem to depend upon which side had the advantage. Time was fickle: it did—or did not—as it pleased. Was it possible this fight could last a day? Long Pete would never have said so before this very moment. Now? He had no idea.

Back with his own thralls, Long half-heartedly cracked his whip (more for appearances than desire) and resumed steering his "troops" towards the hill. Somehow, he'd acquired bits and pieces of other units, probably demolished by the End's black ooze. It made little difference: they were going to the same end, anyway.

D'Kem had a ferocious headache, unquestionably a gift from his rival, the End-of-All-Things. The man had been battering at the old Shaper's defenses all morning, but it pleased D'Kem to know he occupied so much of the End's attention. He shuddered to think what the sorcerer might accomplish without him in the way. Not that he personally feared the End-of-All-Things. There was a time when D'Kem wanted nothing more than oblivion, but oblivion had not obliged. Now, the Shaper saw a world of things—human and otherwise—that did not deserve the fate the End-of-All-Things had planned. At the same time, D'Kem was intrigued. How was it possible he'd lived so long—several lifespans—and never encountered this enemy before? Who or what was the sorcerer? Whence came his power, and what did he hope to accomplish through the annihilation of all life? What would be left to him, in the event he succeeded?

Another blast of pain lanced through his skull. *If he's so fond of headaches, I'll give him one of his own!* Throwing his arms forward and yelling a single command, the Queen's first trench collapsed even further with a thunderous rumble, 'til the bodies inside sank out of sight into a newly yawning abyss, whose bottom could not be glimpsed by anyone nearby. The Queen's men had long since abandoned the trench, but now they scrambled back further, like crabs scuttling away from predators. D'Kem heard a gasp and realized, without turning, it came from one of his fellow Shapers. He had no time for their admiration or awe. He knew he and his foe would not both survive this conflict.

There was an earthquake. Or so it seemed to Long. The first trench abruptly caved in, not twenty-five yards from his unit. He watched with grim interest as one of the other generals drove his thralls into the chasm. Stupidity, or intentional suicide? Given the morale of the few conscious and sane members of the End's horde, it was impossible to tell. Long spurred his horse in circles around his thralls, driving them back from the trench. Why, he had no idea. It was evident most of the other generals were equally stymied. There was no way across such an enormous gap, not at the moment at any rate. The obvious thing to do was enter the woods on either side, hack down some suitable-sized trees and build portable bridges that could be thrown across the trench. Of course, the End was a sorcerer, not a tactician. If he—

A phantasmal vapor appeared directly in Long's path. He knew in an instant it was some aspect of his master. "And what do you recommend I do now, little soldier?" the End's voice inquired.

"I was just thinking we ought to go into these woods and build something to span this gap."

"Mmmm," the End mused. "There is something about these woods I do not like. However, since I won't be the one venturing into them, it's hardly my problem, is it? Gather a few of these generals in front, and I'll alert those near the back. Build your bridges. And do it quickly."

"I would not go too near the trees, Master," Number 3 said, upon returning from his mission.

"The enemy got an ambush in there, does he?"

"I do not believe so. But something..."

Arune?

He's right, now I think on it. There's something...poised...in those woods.

Poised? The fuck's that mean?

If I knew more, I would tell you. And save your hostility for the enemy.

I'm bleedin' tired o' saving it. I want to get out there! How much longer?

Nightfall. Perhaps a bit later.

"Nightfall?" Vykers said out loud. "I hope the Queen's

forces can hold that long." He faced Number 3. "So, what do you think's going on in those woods, then?"

Number 3 bowed his head, embarrassed or ashamed. "I…do not know. They feel…alive."

"Alive? Ha! Which side, left or right?"

"Both."

A third party, then. The question is, is it friend or foe? Arune asked.

Only one way to find out, Vykers replied and began walking towards the trees on his left.

Tarmun!

Don't call me that!

What are you doing?

What else am I 'sposed to do to kill time 'til nightfall? "You boys wanna come along?"

Sheepish looks, all around. "No," they answered in unison. "Unless you command it," Number 17 added.

"Nah. Stay here. Get some rest," Vykers said insouciantly. "Gonna be a big night!"

Before he'd even reached the forest, the sword on his hip began to throb—there was no better word for it. Vykers placed a hand atop its pommel, which seemed to placate the weapon somewhat. So: he'd had multiple warnings, from the Three, from Arune and now from his sword. But the Reaper had never been overly fond of others' advice. A hundred or so paces from the forest's edge, he felt a prickly sensation all across his skin and his pulse quickened. Still, he kept his sword sheathed and continued his approach. At last, he reached the tree-line. Without hesitation, he plunged into the verdant shadows and took a moment to let his eyes adjust. Before they did so, a voice spoke to him.

"Your battle is in the meadow at your back, Tarmun Vykers. Not within these woods."

At first, Vykers thought he'd been addressed by an old stump. As his eyes finally became comfortable in the wood's gloomy interior, he recognized it for something else entirely, something he'd heard of but never believed in. Well, it was no stranger than anything else he'd encountered these last few months.

"You know my name," he said. "And what is yours?" He thought he heard the creature sigh.

"Too-Mai-Ten-La."

"Well, Too-Mai…"

"Ten-La."

"Yeah. What I wanna know is, are you just planning to watch this fight or are you looking to get involved, and if you're looking to get involved…"

"Am I friend or foe?"

Vykers nodded.

"Neither," the creature said. "But at the moment, my people's dislike of your enemy is greater than our dislike of you."

Vykers bristled. "Your dislike of me, is it?"

"There's no need for hostilities between us," another voice said.

A'Shea! Arune whispered urgently.

A second figure stepped out of the underbrush and into view, a woman in deep blue robes. Vykers had known countless women, even countless beautiful women of every type imaginable. This one, this A'Shea, was not beautiful in any conventional sense, but she positively radiated…something. Lifeforce, Good…the Reaper had no words for her mysterious, captivating energy. In staring at her, he came near to forgetting about her fey companion.

"Your friend's answer's no answer at all, really," he observed, pointing his chin at Toomt'-La.

The two strangers exchanged looks before the woman spoke again, slowly, carefully. "We have come to witness—and perhaps aid in—the fall of the one who calls himself the End-of-All-Things."

Vykers was about to reply when she cut him off.

"But we will not take orders from anyone. If we act, we will act in our own time and fashion."

That sounded like something Vykers might've said, if a bit less eloquently. "I guess we're done here, then," he said and moved to leave.

"Tarmun Vykers," the A'Shea called out.

He looked back, questioningly.

"Do you truly believe you can destroy the sorcerer?"

"You just watch," he answered, and winked at her. He wouldn't swear to it, but he thought he saw her blush.

"That man is arrogant," Aoife said into the awkward silence that followed his departure.

"Is there any other kind?" Toomt'-La retorted.

"I've met a few humble ones over the years."

"Oh, yes, and I've seen cold fire."

"Sarcasm is beneath you, my friend, and I ask you to remember that I, too, am human."

"Yes, Mother-sister, but still not a man."

Aoife faced the satyr. "I loved a man once. Or thought I did."

"And, yet, see where you are today."

The A'Shea's eyes blazed in fury at her companion and, without another word, she followed the warrior out of the forest. Toomt'-La appeared in her path and she pushed past him. Again, he appeared; this time, she shoved him away with all her strength. Once she cleared the trees, Toomt'-La heard the unhappy murmurings of his siblings. It was just possible he'd gone too far, said too much. He was not human, after all, and could never fully understand.

Vykers, the Battlefield

She's following us now, Arune said.

I know.

You know, do you? Can you also tell me why?

I reckon it's 'cause she's a woman.

Because she's a woman? You ass! You self-satisfied, over-confident—

Not what I meant, Arune. Calm down.

She brooded a moment. *Alright, what did you mean?*

You saw that little goblin thing. She's been living with the fey folk. Gotta be dying for some human company.

Oh? And you think you qualify?

I was good enough for you…

I was desperate, the Shaper quipped.

Might be she feels the same.

Arune thought about it. *Might be you're right.*

Vykers grinned.

And stop grinning!

When he was well clear of the woods, Vykers stopped and waited for the A'Shea. No question, she was easy on the eyes. "Thought you were keeping your own counsel," he said.

She met his gaze. "I can make better decisions if I know what your plans are."

The Reaper laid it out for her. "You know my name; you must know my reputation. I kill people. Large numbers of people. Thousands and more. That's my plan, here, too."

The A'Shea pursed her lips, squinted at him. "Under normal circumstances, I'd have a problem with that…"

Vykers barked out a laugh. "Oh, but you got flexible beliefs, do ya? This killin's better than other killin'?"

Just under her breath, Aoife muttered "Why must everyone be so objectionable today?"

Although the comment wasn't meant for him, Vykers answered. "It's the war. It makes folks…irritable." He smiled.

In that instant, Aoife experienced a flutter of panic, as she felt the beginnings of an attraction to this man even as she loathed him. His smiled broadened, as if he could read her mind. "I see nothing amusing in any of this, warrior," she snapped.

"Missed it, did you?" Vykers asked breezily. "Here we are, a healer and a killer, having a friendly chat behind the biggest battle in ages. We've both got work to do, yet here we stand."

Aoife set her jaw. "You're right about one thing, Tarmun Vykers. I have work to do, most likely repairing the damage *you'll* do."

"What kind o' nonsense is that, A'Shea? You can't undo what I'll do. And what's more, you won't want to."

"The world would be better off altogether without your kind."

"Ah!" Vykers replied, "But then you'd have nothing to do. The world needs both night and day; the one without the other would be…unending boredom."

"I very much doubt that," Aoife scoffed. "At any rate, I've

heard enough." So saying, she gathered her robes and headed back towards the forest.

Such a way with words, you have, Arune interjected.

It ain't my words she's liking.

Sweet Alheria, save us all from men!

Aoife and Toomt'-La, the Forest

Toomt'-La held his tongue when Aoife reentered the woods. "That man is an animal," she said.

Oh, what he might have said in response. *You do animals a disservice*, or *aren't they all*, or *he's more of a monster, than an animal* were some of the things he considered, but kept to himself. The A'Shea was, after all and in truth, the Mother-sister. He could no more afford to lose her than he could lop off his own arms. "What will he do?" he asked meekly, already certain he knew the answer.

"He will wait until he thinks he has the advantage and then he'll attack the End-of-All-Things."

"Your brother," the satyr could not resist reminding her.

"Yes," she answered distractedly. Abruptly, she changed the subject. "What did you learn of my...of the End-of-All-Things in your last battle?"

"First, that there is very little of your brother left within that creature. The body that one sees is like...a snail's shell to the snail. It is his armor, yes, but it is also a disguise. The outer thing has no relation to the inner."

"I don't understand," Aoife admitted.

"The thing inside is very, very old and has occupied many bodies over the years. Your brother—Anders, you call him—is but the latest."

"Then is my...is Anders dead?"

Toomt'-La frowned. "Would that I could tell you so. Alas, some fragment of him still endures, along with bits and pieces of every other soul the creature's taken."

Aoife fought back a sob, remembering the night, long ago, when a loathsome being had burst in upon her family and died at Ander's feet, vomiting its vile essence all over the boy. "Then, the previous body was but a shell as well?"

"Just so."

"But where did this...monstrosity come from in the first place?" Aoife demanded.

"That is beyond my ken," the satyr said, gravely. "The world is larger than you dream and more is unknown than is known."

Aoife jumped back to Vykers. "What I don't understand is how he expects to defeat Anders without an army."

"Might this be some sort of ploy to lure us into his service?"

Aoife frowned. "I don't think he cares about us one way or the other, any more than a cyclone cares for the waves on the sea."

In hushed tones, Toomt'-La admitted. "I have never seen the ocean."

Aoife regarded him with renewed interest, a mixture of wonder and humor in her eyes. "Indeed? It is...magnificent. If we outlive this day, I shall have to take you."

Far away, the sound of her brother's host assaulting the Queen's trenches was not completely unlike the roar of waves crashing on a rocky shore. Only, the carrion fowl that haunted this battlefield sounded nothing like seagulls.

Janks & Company, In Battle

"They're pulling back," Rem announced to all and sundry.

"And well they might," Janks said. "Somebody's Shapers've split that trench right down to the endless hells."

"It was D'Kem, I know it!" Spirk chimed in.

Janks scraped some of the muck off his armor. "Aye," he allowed. "Might be." There was more he wanted to say, but what he suspected didn't seem possible. "Leastways, we can use this little—what's the word? Reprieve—to get ready for the next wave, whenever it comes."

Kittins spoke next. "Any fool can see they're off to fashion ladders and bridges. Our job is to knock the damn things down when they come."

"One o' my favorite parts of a battle!" Bash said. "You get

the timing just right, you can kill ten men with one ladder!"

Rem looked at his comrade, clearly unable to believe what he was hearing. "You…you find this enjoyable?"

Bash guffawed. "Damn right, I do! They wanna kill me. Why shouldn't I enjoy killin' them first?"

"I never thought of it that way."

Bash punched the actor in his left shoulder. "There's your problem, then. Stop thinking and start doin'!"

They all fell silent and looked north, across the still-smoking chasm. The enemy's host seemed to stretch off into infinity.

Long, In Battle

The mercs did not enjoy taking orders from Long Pete, whom they saw as both a Johnny-Come-Lately and an inferior fighter. The resentment fairly radiated off them, a palpable force as powerful as their rank body odors. But they obeyed him and the other generals who ordered them into the woods to fetch timber. Long waited just outside, of necessity. He had to keep an eye on his thralls, as well. Say what you will, it was impressive how well the End managed their moods, considering the distances and number of thralls involved. And at the same time, the sorcerer was waging war with the Queen's Shapers. It boggled the mind, really. Long reached down and patted his horse's neck. Poor beast. He wondered how long it would survive.

Several minutes elapsed and Long became alarmed by what he did not hear: the sound of axes chopping wood. Under his leathers, he felt goose bumps rise on his arms. He spun his horse, in hopes of sighting one of his fellow generals, found one just to the south. Long whistled. The fellow looked up and then pointedly ignored him. *Alheria's tits, was everyone in this host an asshole?* Long urged his horse into a canter and quickly reached the man.

"Seen any of your mercs lately?" he asked.

The man, a great, lantern-jawed oaf almost too big for his mount, frowned to himself. The woods were awful quiet. Without so much as a "how do you do," he drove his horse into the trees.

Long realized his mouth was hanging open. He shut it. He watched the other general travel deeper and deeper into the forest, heard the man's horse nicker briefly and lost track of him. The woods were lovely, dark and deep. And, suddenly, very frightening. What to do? Alert the End that the Queen's army had troops In the Forest, or simply allow events to unfold as they would. In warning his master, he would betray the Queen's men, amongst whom, he knew, were the few actual friends he had left in this world. Too, he'd have to abandon his thralls if he hoped to reach the End in time to make a difference. Failure to warn the sorcerer, though, might result in more punishment, and Mardine and his child were never far from Long's mind. Not much of a choice, when you got right down to it. He turned his horse towards the back of the host and set off.

It was an exhausting, frustrating and harrowing effort, taking far too much time, but Long eventually reached his objective: the command tent. Normally, a soldier dismounting from a horse wants to do so in style, or, at the very least, with minimal fuss. Poor Long, run ragged by his journey through the host, tumbled off his horse and landed in an awkward heap at its feet. *That'll impress the mercs*! He thought. Picking himself up, he staggered past two indifferent guards and into the darkened tent. The End's voice greeted him almost immediately.

"What are you doing here, General?"

Long dropped to his knees, which instantly rebuked him for doing so, and squinted into the darkness while his eyesight continued to adjust. "Our men have gone into the forest, as you commanded. But none have come out. I suspect the Queen's army has ambushed them."

"No. Not the Queen's army. Something else abides there."

Long dared a look at the End-of-All-Things. The sorcerer sat in his accustomed seat, apparently fidgeting with a length of string. "Then..."

"Yes, yes, I've known for some time. Your mission was simply the most efficacious means of determining the nature of the threat. Now we know."

Well, he couldn't say he was surprised by the End's response. Gods, he was weary. "What is your will?"

The End looked up from his string, looked directly into Long's eyes. "Why, return to your unit, of course. We shall be ready to renew our attack by sunset."

"Forgive me, *master*..." He still had trouble saying it without choking. "But..."

The sorcerer stood. "You want to know how," he said flatly. "I don't know which offends me more, your presumption or your predictability." He sauntered over into a corner, turned his back to his general. "You will be amazed, General. You have that, at least, to look forward to." The End said nothing more for such a long time, Long finally understood he'd been dismissed. Carefully, quietly, he backed out of the tent.

Deda, the End's Host

It was during this lull in the battle that Wims walked into what passed for the End's mess tent, looking for wine. He hadn't felt well for the past hour; wine was his life-long remedy for everything. Just a cup or two of red—or even better, a nice, crisp white—and he'd be better in no time.

He might've expected the place to be deserted, given that most of the host's officers were meant to be with their units. Instead, the tent was packed. Generals and mercenaries occupied every table, bench and stool in sight, all of them drinking and gorging themselves as if this were their last meal. Which, of course, it couldn't be. Wims had a better chance of sprouting wings and flying to the moon than the End had of losing this fight. Maybe that explained it: the men in this tent were having a pre-victory celebration, enjoying what was certain to be an easy and short-lived conflict.

If he'd been hoping for quick service, he was disappointed. The few slaves employed by the End's cooks were busy dashing from table to table, carrying trays of food, refreshing mugs of ale—essentially doing everything in their power to keep from getting whipped, or worse. Grumbling, Wims followed one of them until the fellow reached a makeshift bar in the back of the tent. Luck was still with him! A balding, sallow-skinned man behind the bar was busy breaching a small keg when Wims approached.

"What do you want, then?" the man asked insolently.

"Got anything white?" Wims asked.

"My backside!" the man quipped, "Other than that..."

Wims punched him hard in the mouth, knocking the man to the ground. Nobody seemed to notice. He waited for the fool to right himself. "This is General Wims Deda you're talking to, mate. You wanna be turned into one o' them thralls, you keep on with the fuckin' wisecracks."

The bartender's mouth was bleeding. Strangely, the sight soured Wims' stomach even further. The faster he got that wine, the better. "Find me some white."

"At once, General," the chastened man fawned. "I believe I have a special stash of it right here..."

Violent cramps wracked Wims' guts. He pushed away from the bar, confused. Something was wrong. More wrong than he'd ever experienced.

"I can find you some white, after all, General..." Wims heard the bartender say to his back. Sod the white. He needed a jakes and fast. Or a surgeon. His legs seemed to have a will of their own, propelling him into the thick of the tent's diners, giving out on him unexpectedly, so that he toppled over onto a nearby table. Cups, plates and all their contents went flying. Men reeled back in surprise and anger.

"What the fuck?" some bearded lout roared in Wims'face. "That ain't funny!"

"Get the hell offa there!" someone else commanded.

"You drunken son of a bitch!" a third yelled.

The pain and pressure in Wims' belly were unbelievable. To make matters worse, his vision and hearing were faltering, too. Gods, was he dying? He felt like nothing so much as a fish tossed onto a dock somewhere, goggle-eyed and gasping for air, thrashing about, unable to return to his element.

"I. Said. Move!" the second man shouted, before slamming a knife into Wims' stomach in a swooping, overhand blow.

Wims barely felt it, but he did have a split second to see his entire abdomen explode in a gory shower of entrails, changing the angry expressions around him to those of horror. Wims faded into oblivion amidst a chorus of terrified shouts and screams.

The End-of-All-Things heard panicked screaming, and then he was there, in the center of the mess tent, which now lived up to its name. With a word, he stilled everyone and everything in the room. Even the flames of nearby candles seemed to solidify at his command.

What had occurred, here? Scanning the gruesome scene, his eyes settled on the disembodied head and shoulders of General Deda. It was the work of several minutes to find the lower half of the man's body, half-buried under a table that had fallen over in the corner. The End examined every face, body and other surface in the tent. There was none without evidence of Deda's blood in the form of splotches, splashes and almost invisible spots.

Whatever had been done to his servant in Lunessfor, the results were impressive. The End had no doubt the whole tent was contaminated and, if left unmolested, would do considerable damage to the rest of his host. A ring of flames raced outwards from his body and soon the whole tent was on fire. Better to burn the whole thing to the ground than suffer one more loss from Deda's...illness. The End blinked outside again, to a distance of twenty-five yards or so and watched the mess reduced to ash. The Queen's forces had embarrassed him enough for one day. Or forever, in fact. If he was honest with himself, the End hadn't really been giving this battle his best effort.

That was all about to change.

Janks and Company, In Battle

"Here they come!" someone shouted. Everyone in Janks' vicinity sat up and looked downslope. It was true: the enemy approached in a massive, dark wave. And right at sunset, Janks observed. The men of the Queen's army rose en masse from the ground, reached for weapons and generally readied themselves for whatever the next few minutes might bring. But...they'd heard no sounds of wood chopping In the Forest on either side of the meadow. How did the enemy plan to bridge the chasm that separated the two armies? Janks saw confusion and worry on every face he inspected.

At length, the End's thralls achieved the very brink. In the growing darkness, he saw several push through to the front of the clamorous swarm and begin to convulse erratically. Janks happened to catch Kittins looking over at him, and for once there was no hostility in his expression. Plainly, the other man was every bit as flummoxed as everyone else as to what this new action might signify. It was common—typical, even—for the enemy's thralls to moan and mewl, but the ones in front began screaming, as if in rage or agony. If that was all they did, Janks thought, it was more than enough. The sound was as unnerving as he could imagine. One by one, the screamers erupted from their skin, like butterflies emerging from chrysalises. Their outer flesh dropped away, revealing sinewy, crimson creatures of muscle, bone and little else. They looked like hunger incarnate. Unconsciously, Janks took a step backwards and then caught himself. Ridiculous! Frightening as these new apparitions were, they could never—

One of them leapt the chasm. It was unimaginable, but Janks had just seen it done. The men around him, he saw, unanimously joined him in stepping back. Another creature soared over the chasm, and another. Kittins and Bash were having none of it. They rushed forward, weapons swinging, and engaged the fell creatures the moment they landed. The sky grew darker and so, thought Janks, did his prospects of surviving this conflict. A titanic, earth-shattering rumble knocked bodies to the ground on both sides of the crevasse. It was unclear whether the gap was growing or closing; no one could begin to guess which side was responsible. And Janks had his hands full, anyway, in helping Rem and Spirk fight off one of the End's ghoulish changelings. The thing was fast, far too fast to have ever been human, surely. With one swipe, it took a terrible gash out of Rem's arm, catching Spirk on the chin at the end of its swing. The eyes in its horrible, skull-like face fastened on Janks; it seemed he was next on the menu. He fought back, trying to match the thing's ferocity, hoping it couldn't cope with his long knife, his axe and the continued efforts of the Actor and the Idiot. More of the creatures landed on or near neighboring soldiers.

Janks heard an enraged bellow and saw Kittins lift one of the ghouls over his head before hurling it into the still-shifting fissure at his feet. "To the hells with you!" the big man screamed. It was then Janks noticed that half the man's face had been torn away. Too early to tell if that was an improvement or not.

In a blaze of light, D'Kem appeared nearby, tossing bolts of energy that disintegrated the monsters on impact. At the same time, he seemed in some fashion to be battling the rift between the two armies. Every time it managed to narrow, D'Kem's thunderous voice commanded it wider, chanting an unending litany of alien words and sounds.

Janks had never been so inspired. "For Pellas!" he yelled and smashed his assailant's skull in with his axe, before rushing to D'Kem's side. Here was a man for whom he would fight to the death. D'Kem gave only the slightest sign of having heard him, but was either too preoccupied to object or had finally chosen to reveal himself. Janks' companions, however, wholeheartedly agreed and took up the refrain: "For Pellas! For Pellas!"

"Corporal," D'Kem said, stress evident in his voice, "You have a choice, here. I can either eliminate these bloody creatures, or widen this gap for good and all. I cannot do both."

Janks understood. Right now, the ghouls were ripping the Queen's men to shreds. Better to face waves of normal thralls than any more of these things. "Kill the ghouls!" he replied, much louder than he'd intended.

D'Kem nodded and started revolving. In seconds, he transformed into a pillar of the purest, most-blinding light Janks had ever seen. Hastily, he looked away, afraid to be blinded for even a moment in the face of his enemies. There followed—how to put it?—a soundless explosion and the fighting instantly came to a stop. Left and right, Janks saw bemused fighters standing before smoking piles of ash. Janks searched out the Shaper, who had tumbled onto his seat in a dazed condition. "Somebody get Pellas to safety!" he shouted, then realized he trusted no one else with the job and rushed to D'Kem's side, himself. Cautiously, almost reverently, he bent down to lift the older man to a standing position. "I've got you, Pellas," Janks said softly.

"I never doubted it," the Shaper said.

Downhill, the gap shuddered closed. The sea of thralls advanced, urgently.

"I need to get higher up," D'Kem said. Before Janks could respond, he found himself standing atop one of the army's wooden towers at the very height of the meadow. D'Kem seemed surprised to see him at his side.

"Er...sorry about that," he said. "Still a little woozy from that last effort."

"No apology necessary. I quite understand." Janks paused. "Not really, o' course, but, you know." He looked down and out over the battlefield. From this vantage point, the seemingly infinite size of the enemy's host was even more apparent and dispiriting than from below, despite the almost complete arrival of nightfall. At least down there, he only saw his opponents a few hundred at a time. Up here—"I gotta get back down there," he muttered.

"Thank you for your help," D'Kem told him and whisked the corporal back to the front with a thought.

Janks reappeared not ten paces from Rem and Spirk, feeling more than a little nauseous. Rem, he saw, had managed to bandage his wounded arm; Spirk's chin bled freely, but he'd never die from the wound, unless it went septic. He pointed to the boy's injury. "You gonna have that looked at?"

"Rem says it's good."

"That right?" Janks asked the actor.

"Oh, we cleaned the hell out of it, if that's what you're after."

They all heard the next wave of thralls scrabbling closer.

"Back to it!" Janks said, with more confidence than he felt.

"Pellas?" the End screamed in Long's face. "Pellas?" As if it was somehow Long's fault. "You have my word, my absolute guarantee I will kill your giantess and your child for this treachery."

Long snapped. If death was coming, let it be now. "Kill me, instead!" he yelled back. "Enough of the threats, kill me already or tell me how I'm to blame for Pellas' reappearance."

"You brought him into my host!"

"You *captured* us!"

"You covered his escape!"

Gods, it was like arguing with a willful child. Exactly like it. Long narrowed his eyes.

The End glared back at him. "What is it you suddenly think you know of me?"

"You're a child," Long replied, his voice devoid of emotion.

He saw the backhand coming, couldn't quite muster the energy to duck it in time. "And you are an insect. We've been over this. I will not kill you, General Long. I treasure your suffering. You do it so well. It is, perhaps, the only thing you do well." Just as Long was about to respond, the End spoke again. "But I grow tired of your insolence, I weary of your voice. *That,* I *will* take from you. Forever."

Long felt an odd rustling sensation in his throat and knew he'd been rendered mute. He chose not to give the sorcerer the satisfaction of proving it.

The End continued. "My thralls will continue our assault through the night. At dawn, you will lead a very special charge into the enemy's center. I want you to be able to see all that transpires and know that I put you there." He blinked away again.

Although he'd lost his voice, Long realized he'd grown in power: he no longer feared the End-of-All-Things. Oh, he feared for Mardine and their child naturally. But the sorcerer himself and his infantile behaviors no longer frightened Long. He pondered how one goes about punishing an unruly, all-powerful brat.

The End-of-All-Things was as angry as he'd ever been. He'd been mocked by that worm, Long Pete, in the most inexcusable manner. And yet, Anders had allowed him to live. Again. He struggled to understand his inaction in this case. What was it about the fool that fascinated him so?

At the back of his mind, he became aware of a large force approaching his host from the north. His anger grew. He probed the mysterious army for details and was dismayed to discover the familiar blind spot that signified Tarmun Vykers and his damned sword. Of all the demons in every hell! He'd left his back vulnerable to the Reaper while he'd been unexpectedly distracted by the Pellas of legend. And he still had to reckon with whatever lurked In the Forest on both sides of the battlefield. He was boxed in! The End, who had never known fear, felt his first faint frisson of the stuff and found it unpalatable. This could not be so.

TWELVE

Vykers, the Battlefield

He'd never admit it, but the Shaper had impressed him this time. The swarm of Svarren raging towards his position was among the largest he'd ever seen. Vykers—the big, ruthless warrior, the ultimate basher—almost giggled like a child in his glee. And the funniest part was, the End had fallen for the same gambit twice! For an evil tyrant, the man was ridiculously overconfident—a mistake Vykers vowed for the millionth time to avoid himself. "Lads," he told his chimeras, "we'd best start running!"

And so they did. The four of them sprinted at the End's host (with Arune, as ever, along for the ride), struggling to remain in view of the Svarren, but just out of reach. In minutes, they knew, the savages behind them would shift their focus to the slower, more plentiful prey.

Explosions of fire and ice rocked the area around Vykers and his companions, but Arune, 17, and the sword somehow managed to keep them at bay. If the arcane barrage bothered the Svarren, it wasn't apparent: they came on like a storm, not to be delayed, diverted or avoided. Vykers viewed this as a potential weakness on the End-of-All-Things' part: if he truly believed in the overwhelming strength of his host, wouldn't he focus fire on the front lines and leave his thralls to deal with the Svarren? Interesting. In no time, the howling and shrieking behind him escalated in volume and urgency. The enemy's host had been spotted. Time to disappear.

Burner?

Done! She answered.

Vykers realized he could no longer see the chimeras. "To my voice. We'll clump together and let 'em run past. Once they're engaged, we're free to follow," he said.

"As you say," one of the chimeras—Number 3, Vykers thought—replied in hushed tones.

The air grew close and warmed up noticeably; they'd done as he asked. The Svarren came on in the only way they knew how: gibbering, jabbering, screeching and snarling. The carrion fowl would never eat better than what today's actions promised to produce. And still the Svarren ran by.

How many you figure? Vykers asked of Arune.

Fifteen, twenty thousand? At this rate, you're like to drive them to extinction.

Me? If they're too stupid to turn back, that's their own fault. I'm just standin' here, watching.

You'd better hope there are no truly intelligent Svarren out there somewhere. They won't forget this any time soon.

Bah! They've taken enough of ours over the years. You of all people should appreciate that.

She wouldn't say so, but Arune thought this a brilliant strategy and loved every second of it. *Brouton's Bind.* Her mood instantly darkened.

The End's thralls and their tenders were lethargic in responding to their master's pyrotechnical display against the onrushing Svarren. After all, the mercs and generals at the back of the host had not been expecting to see action so soon. And, some reckoned, the End would have warned them of any approaching threat. Whatever the mad sorcerer may or may not have failed to do, his soldiers knew to a man they'd be the ones punished for it. Their initial lassitude rapidly evolved into frantic determination: but five minutes earlier, they had been bored. Now, their lives were at stake. It was wake-up-or-die time.

The Svarren and thralls smashed into one another like opposing battering rams. The slaughter was instantaneous. Viscera flew through the air, bodies and parts of bodies fell to the ground with a dull thumping sound, which, sickening as it may have been was nothing compared to the constant noise of ripping flesh, snapping tendons and crunching bone. Not a few of the mercs vomited all over themselves, despite their years of battle-hardened experience.

Here, an enthralled young man ferociously gnawed on the shoulder of a Svarra who completed the loop by returning the favor on his assailant's opposite shoulder; there, two thralls attempted to tear the arms off a Svarra nearly twice their size. Elsewhere, a mob of Svarren pulled a merc from his saddle, whilst scores of thralls jumped on them from behind. In one spot, a Svarra with two heads shoved pieces of thralls into both his mouths as fast as his three hands could manage; in another, a fallen thrall chewed at the legs of a Svarra too busy clawing the eyes from an enemy to notice. It was all gruesome, senseless, insane. Even a pack of starved wolves or hyenas has more reserve, more respect for the sanctity of life. Whips cracked, teeth gnashed, combatants died by the thousands.

The world edged ever closer to the End's grand design.

Janks and Company, In Battle

Was there nothing in the world but his axe, his long knife, and those he fought with them? There'd been a break, he remembered, a time when the End-of-All-Things had been stumped by Pellas' actions. But he couldn't for the life of him recall what that break felt like, the sensation of laying his weapons down and stretching his sore and overly-tested muscles. The world was a palette of darkness, black shapes spurting blacker blood against an even blacker background. Occasional glimpses of torchlight ahead or behind did nothing to alleviate Janks' hopelessness and dread. Hack, slash, stab, duck, smash, duck, stab, bash. He'd become some sort of machine, a clockwork soldier of the sort he'd seen at festivals in his youth. Hack, slash, stab. He'd been injured, he knew, and tended to by the nearest A'Shea. Was that why he still stood, still battled? A toothless old man charged across the dead piled up in the second trench and lunged at Janks. Hack, slash, stab. It was clear: if nothing else, the Queen's men would die of exhaustion fighting such a monstrous horde. These thralls were ferocious, to be sure, but lacked finesse. Perhaps that was the only reason Janks still breathed. And how many had he killed, he wondered. More than in every other battle he'd ever been in, combined. The old man wasn't quite finished, yet, and two younger thralls approached. Janks worked a kink out of his neck, set his feet and resigned himself to more—more attacking, more defending, more death.

Sometime during the last hour, Bash had gone to it. Janks wouldn't have known but for Spirk's forlorn howl. When Janks looked over, a large mound of thralls lay atop the warrior and was greedily tearing into his abdomen. Kittins scattered them like crows on a rat carcass, but the damage was done. How had it happened? Janks was aware to his bones that Bash had been the better fighter, the better man. How had these feral imbeciles overcome the big man, while Janks remained more or less unscathed? But 'how' and 'why' were the worst enemies in war. They taunted, left a man internally crippled for life. You'd have more luck squeezing stout from a cow, than wrangling with such questions.

Janks was always a little unsettled when his mind wandered during a fight. While he appreciated the brief escape from the horrors confronting him, he feared inattention might get him killed. He returned his full focus to the foes in front of him and redoubled his efforts to annihilate them. Hack, slash, stab. Mahnus-be-damned monsters! Evil fucking bastards! To the hells with each and every one of them! Let the worms have their fill of 'em! Hack, slash, stab.

A short ways off, he could hear the boy, Spirk, sobbing. Damn, but it was hard to stay focused! He risked a glance over at the kid. Like him, Spirk continued to flail away, despite the odds, despite his terror, despite the utter and absolute destruction of his innocence. Once in a while, a pike would thrust out of the darkness on either side of the lad, impaling a would-be attacker. Janks wondered where his own pikemen had got to. Ah, well. Why should anything be easy?

He realized of a sudden that Rem no longer spoke in verse when chopping his way through waves of attackers. A while ago, he'd've said that was a blessing. Now, he kinda missed it.

The woods on either side were pregnant with malice—not the sort he enjoyed, either, but something clearly directed at him. There was an eerily familiar tang to the energies seeping from their boundaries, too, that reminded the End of his destruction of the Forest of Nar. But he had reduced that place and all its denizens to ash. How was it, then, that he felt its ghosts nearby, almost *poised*?

He considered his options. At the rear of the host, his thralls grappled tooth-and-nail with Vykers' Svarren. The End had added a little surprise since the Reaper had last pulled this trick and, sooner than his overconfident foe expected, this new skirmish would come to a close in the sorcerer's favor. So, the action behind him was a short term annoyance, at worst. At the front, his numbers were slowly, inexorably wearing the Queen's forces down, pushing them back, despite Pellas' interference. Thus, the front offered no immediate concern. Back to the woods, then. He'd sent scores of men in, knowing full well they might never return, and he'd been proven correct. How would these little forests respond to thousands upon thousands of thrall, though? Could a brief, overpowering action sufficiently stun whatever-it-was that awaited him in those woods, cause it to lose hope, abandon its plans? The End ruminated. If he temporarily withdrew from the front in order to assault the enemy—or enemies—on either side, might that not provoke the Queen's men to stage an ill-fated counterattack? Once they emerged from their network of bulwarks, trenches and the like, his thrall could swarm over them in numbers too large to be resisted. Anders smiled, leaned back in his chair, put his feet up. This mysterious threat in the woods might actually help him break the Queen's forces! What delicious irony.

Vykers, the Queen's Army

The last of the Svarren had finally run past, leaving Vykers and company again well behind the action. Nevertheless, the Reaper could clearly see something had changed since the last time he'd employed this strategy: now, whenever a Svarra successfully consumed any part of a thrall, the creature briefly became somnambulant before suddenly turning on its brethren. Eating the thralls was turning the Svarren into thralls, as well.

We need to get out of here, Vykers thought grimly.

*Funny you should say that...*Arune interjected.

The world turned inside out, along with Vykers' stomach, and he landed hard on a wooden platform, high above the battlefield. He'd joined the Queen's army, at last. A nearby brazier cast a ruddy light on Vykers' immediate surroundings. He noted that the Three were as befuddled as he. And visible, of course. Not ten feet away stood an older man in Shaper's robes. The stranger was surprisingly unsurprised at Vykers' sudden appearance, as if the Reaper had been standing there all evening. When the man finally spoke, his voice sent strange ripples through Vykers' mind, as of a stone tossed into a pond.

"For the longest time, I actually believed *you* were the greatest threat to this world," he said wryly. "And here we are." He indicated to the conflict below.

In Vykers' mind, Arune gasped.

What? Vykers asked.

Arune did not respond.

"And you are?" the Reaper asked the stranger.

"My name is D'Kem."

It's Pellas! Arune hissed in a frantic whisper.

"Or Pellas, yes. If you must." Pellas said, just as if Arune had spoken aloud. He placed his elbows on the platform railing and stared into the night.

Vykers grunted, "I've heard 'o you."

"And I, you."

"I thought you were dead."

Pellas chuckled, mirthlessly. "And I, you. Fine couple of ghosts, we are." He turned his gaze on the Three. "I must say, you keep interesting company."

Vykers put a hand on Number 3's shoulder. "That's puttin' it mildly."

"And your Shaper?"

"She ain't mine," Vykers huffed. "It's a temporary thing."

Pellas smiled enigmatically, nodded almost imperceptibly.

"So," the Reaper said, for want of anything more clever.

"So," Pellas agreed. "This End-of-All-Things means to crush the Queen's army by this time tomorrow."

"Things don't always work out like we plan."

"No, indeed. Your little ploy to the north, along with whatever's brewing In the Forest..."

"Oh," Vykers interrupted, "you know about that, then?"

Pellas simply regarded him in silence.

"'Course you do," Vykers muttered. "You were saying?"

"Those two actions and the impressive resilience of the Queen's men have made this battle considerably more challenging than our enemy expected."

"And your presence don't help him, either, I'm guessing."

"Nor yours. But we can't simply stand here all night exchanging pleasantries."

"Nah. I'm better at hostilities, anyway. What've you got in mind?"

Pellas pulled at his beard for a moment. "I believe the End-of-All-Things will have to address the threat to his flanks before he can fully commit to taking this hill."

"Makes sense."

"And I believe that will take him longer than he thinks. Which will give you the chance, at last, to reveal yourself and address the troops at dawn."

"And then, what? I'm not big on defensive actions."

"I don't believe it will come to that. I expect our enemy will not be able to resist confronting you—or both of us—directly. If he does, we'll oblige him. If he surprises us, however, and maintains his distance, I may be able to distract him long enough to get you through his defenses and within arm's reach. Then...you do what you were made for."

He's got a lot of confidence in you, Arune whispered.

Pellas turned directly toward the Reaper. "By yourself, you are, of course, formidable. But you also carry a gifted Shaper and a legendary sword. Yes, I have great confidence in you."

Vykers couldn't help himself. "And what of you?"

Pellas looked back towards the battle; his face became lost

in shadow. "I do not expect to survive this conflict," he said quietly. "Like you, the sorcerer is more than he seems, whereas I am only—have only ever been—human. This old Burner will likely spend the last of his fire in this fight."

Was that…? Had he just heard Arune weeping?

"Maybe," Vykers said aloud. "Maybe not. You speak flatteringly of me, but no one alive's ever seen the full scope of my…*talent*. You put me within arm's reach o' that bastard and even the maggots won't want what's left of him when I'm done."

Perhaps it was just the dance of light and shadow on the platform's top, but it seemed Pellas' posture straightened a bit, that he grew imperceptibly taller.

"I've never been a great lover of violence," he admitted, "but in this case…"

The End, In his Host

Thick-headed and brutish savages though they were, the Svarren were not entirely witless. Of the original group that attacked the End's host, only two or three hundred had turned before the remaining fifteen-to-twenty thousand grasped the problem and murdered their rebellious kin before taking one thrall more. When they resumed their attack on the thralls, it was with increased rage and bloodlust. Somehow, they understood what had been done to them; they meant for someone—anyone—to suffer for that treachery.

What had seemed certain victory became a worrisome, lingering problem from the End's perspective. And, weirdly, more Svarren continued to trickle in all the time, as if answering a summons only they could hear. If that was the case, the End knew its origin: Tarmun Vykers. The only thing he hadn't quite worked out was how to isolate the man so he could be dealt with. Anders shook off his scrying trance and walked outside his tent to clear his head. It was snowing. Lightly, but snowing nonetheless. He considered that for a moment, decided it made no immediate difference, either way. It was time to attack the presence in the woods.

"Omeyo!" the End yelled into the night.

"Master?" the general inquired, from a mere three feet away. The man had an uncanny knack for being in the right place at the right time, a gift which had surely kept him alive longer than almost anyone else in the End's service. But...it was also somewhat embarrassing. The End did not like to be surprised, would like to have thought himself incapable of it.

"What am I going to say next?" the sorcerer asked his general.

Omeyo bent slightly at the waist, the barest hint of submissiveness. "I wouldn't presume to guess."

"Wouldn't you?" the End asked, dryly. "I'm sure you've realized there's a threat to our host, lurking in the woods on either side of this meadow." Statement.

"I suspected something was amiss, but had every confidence that you would instruct me when the time was right."

The man's subtlety made the End more than a little paranoid. On the surface, Anders showed nothing. "Organize the third and fifth armies for an attack on both the right and left. We'll proceed as we did at Nar: flame arrows and flaming pitch into the trees, assisted by a few of my more aggressive Shapers. If it becomes necessary, I'll step in and insure those woods catch fire. At that point, I expect a response from our hidden foes, and all your mercenaries and thralls must needs be ready for a fight."

This time, Omeyo's bow was deep and likely sincere. "As you say, Master."

In seconds, he heard the man shouting orders left and right as he disappeared into the darkened sea of bodies that was the End's host at night time. Omeyo's orders were soon echoing around the meadow, followed by whip cracks and the neighing of startled horses. Within a quarter hour, a great clearing opened between the End's command tent and the thralls at the distant front line. His host had split approximately in half, as the third and fifth armies moved into positions along the left and right edges of the battlefield. The sixth army continued to struggle with the Svarren at Ander's back, while the first and second continued to engage the Queen's forces at the front. If only he still had the fourth army at his disposal. The End wondered if they would return in time to be of any help whatsoever. He wondered, too, if he oughtn't to finish what Tarmun Vykers had started and blast the survivors to the last hell for their humiliating failure. Bah! No time for such pointless musings! The End rose into the air and surveyed the battlefield. He sensed Pellas' mind out there, in the dark, probing, testing his defenses. He found the anomaly that signified Vykers. Not with the Svarren, where he'd spotted him last, but near the front line, amongst the Queen's forces.

The End frowned. He'd been hoping to provoke an attack by the Queen's forces, but that was before Vykers joined their ranks. This changed the equation in ways he'd of course considered but hoped to avoid. No matter, this action on the left and right would be over in less than an hour, he believed—too short a time for the Queen's men to overcome the first and second armies and reach the command tent. Perhaps the sight of the forest afire would even frighten those uphill. Men were such *fragile* creatures, after all.

The Fey, in the Forest

Fire streaked towards the trees, just as Toomt'-La had promised. The self-designated End-of-All-Things was such a destructive creature. But that also made him predictable. This time, the children of Nar were ready. An uncanny and practically invisible mist exhaled from the trees and everything hidden within them. As the attackers' arrows arrived, they were snuffed out, as surely as waxen tapers dipped in water. The bundles of flaming kindling dipped in pitch and launched from catapults met the same fate, and even the End's Shapers struggled with their magic.

"What sort of a thing burns a forest out of spite?" the satyr asked.

"My brother," Aoife replied, unable to think of a better answer.

"His thralls will have to enter sooner or later."

The A'Shea held her tongue. What could a human say, after all, that would make any sense, any difference?

The enemy himself intervened, repeatedly sending lightning and fire into the trees, finally managing to set them alight...before the fey folk extinguished the flames. Aoife could well imagine her brother's frustration; what she didn't know was whether it made him more dangerous or more careless. Too soon, his thralls and their minders pushed into the woods, so numerous that Aoife felt certain her own death was imminent. Crazed peasants trampled the undergrowth in search of prey. Mounted mercenaries reared up behind them, forcing the action inwards, ever inwards.

The Children of Nar were paradoxically merciless and elated to receive this chance at vengeance. They snatched the End's thralls in plain sight, strangling them in roots, burying them in thick humus. They tore them limb-from-limb, exactly as the End had done to their trees so many months before. Many of the thralls were swiftly carried into the canopy, where they were disemboweled or dropped upon other thralls. In the greenwood at night, the ensorcelled peasants were at a decided disadvantage. Some of the fey folk perished, to be sure. Perhaps even hundreds. Yet, the damage they inflicted upon the End's armies was ten times as bad, or more. Again, the End tried to set fire to the forest; again, he was repelled. An hour into the skirmish, he appeared at the forest's edge, to see for himself what the difficulty was.

Without knowing why, Aoife stepped from the shadows and revealed herself to him. Anders went as hard, cold and still as if he'd been carved from alabaster.

"I might have known," he said.

"You might have. But you did not. Surely you didn't believe there would be no price to pay for the crimes you've committed?"

Though the fighting raged around him, Anders existed in a bubble of calm. "I should never have left you alive. But then, I was young. Hardly more than a boy."

"And less than one, now," Aoife retorted.

"You misjudge the situation," Anders warned his sister. "It is true you have grown in power, though I know not how. But next to me, you are like a firefly circling a volcano."

"You should have been an actor," the A'Shea taunted. She

had no idea where this sudden surge in courage came from, but, at the moment, she dared not examine the question too closely.

"And you, a corpse. I plan to rectify that oversight immediately."

But even as the sorcerer raised his hand to attack, his sister disappeared, whisked away somehow, somewhere, by elements of the forest itself. Anders searched the night and found her, impossibly, beyond his reach. In his wrath, he sent earthquakes rattling through the woods and meadow and still the forest would not relent or retreat. With a thought, he blinked back to his tent.

Long minutes later, a series of horn blasts summoned his armies back to the center of the meadow, back to their previous positions. The End had been rebuffed.

Long, In Battle

Long's unit and the army it belonged to had been assigned to support the End's troops at the front and so, for the nonce, the old soldier found himself frustratingly uninformed about the massive troop movements just downhill of his position. The first army remained stalled at the second trench, neither gaining nor losing ground, so it didn't look like Long would be moving any time soon. Strange, to be bored while one's stomach was tied in knots. Long took the opportunity to gaze north again. He watched with interest as the End's armies tried and tried, unsuccessfully, to put fire to the forest that flanked their battlefield. This was followed by a prolonged engagement that gave no evidence of greater success. In fact, the End's forces eventually returned to the middle of the meadow. Those capable stared back into the trees with resentful or fretful looks, or at least that's what Long inferred from their body language. The thralls, of course, were largely oblivious—agitated, but oblivious.

Long searched again for any sign of his friend, Yendor, always making sure he stayed out of range of the Queen's bowmen, although he couldn't have said why if anyone asked him. Yendor had been on horseback, so the obvious thing to do first was look for a dead or lamed horse, struck, perhaps, by the same archers Long avoided. Wandering fifty or so yards to his right and then left, Long found a number of dead horses, but none of them looked like the one Yendor had been riding. Some still had riders attached, equally dead. Others had managed to gallop free of their masters, only to succumb to their injuries further on. The absence of Yendor's horse was a hopeful sign, though he might have been thrown from its back and lie, even now, in any of the myriad piles of human dead already being picked over by crows. When the sky lightened, he knew, it would be easier to search. Unfortunately, it would also be easier to see other things best unseen. And then there was the End's promise to make Long lead a charge into the teeth of the Queen's forces. It came to Long, then, that he was undeniably in the last few hours of his life. He would die fighting those he cared about on behalf of someone he abhorred.

He wished he could think of some way to go out a hero, to die a hero's death.

He was out of ideas and nearly out of time.

The End, In his Host

"Your thoughts?" the End demanded of General Omeyo.

"Those In the Forest derive their strength from the forest. I do not think they'll attack us in the open."

The End considered this. "Then, what is the point in their presence here?"

Omeyo shook his head. "To prevent our use of the woods either to attack the Queen's forces or escape them?"

"Why would we want to escape them?" the sorcerer thundered at his general.

"We would not, of course." Omeyo answered adroitly. "But those In the Forest may underestimate our resolve."

"And the Svarren to our rear?"

"Dead at last."

The End acquired a far-off stare. "Yes, that is my sense of it, as well." After a moment, he added, "I should like to have some of those creatures in my host some day. They might prove sturdier and even more ferocious than these human thralls. How many have we lost in that attack?"

Omeyo was again careful in answering. "Master, I do not wish to provoke your ire. I have noted time and again that you do not like bad news—and I cannot blame you. But I would not join the ranks of generals who have displeased you, especially when I can still be of help to your cause."

The End's eyes were black pools of malice, his thin lips practically invisible in their tension. "I understand your point, General. But I asked you a question, and I will not ask you twice."

"We are still counting," the man answered quickly. "But the Svarren killed at least twelve thousand of our thralls and perhaps twice that." Omeyo closed his eyes, waited. When he opened them, his master was gone.

Back in his tent, the End brooded. "Bring me the boy!" he said aloud, "And some red wine."

His servants had learned to stay alive by being as unobtrusive as possible. Despite Anders' magically-enhanced senses, he was barely aware of them most of the time. A skeletal, utterly hairless man in a rustic robe emerged from the shadows, carrying Shere's son. Without a sound, he set the boy down near the End's feet and backed away again. Anders heard the faint clink of a brass cup on the table near his right hand and was pleased to see not a trace of the servant who'd brought it in his peripheral vision.

"Boy," Anders said to the child. It looked up at him immediately. "Things have become decidedly more complicated than I anticipated. Have I made mistakes, you ask? I have not. I do not. But sometimes fate can be...*contrary*. What is my sister doing here? If she cannot attack and knows I would never retreat through the woods, what does she hope to accomplish? Surely, she cannot think to witness my defeat. At the hands of the Bitch Queen's army? Hardly! Any one of the armies in my host could crush those vermin, and I have *many* armies. But... this business with the forest and Vykers' Svarren, along with the sudden appearance of Pellas has been embarrassing. And that, of all things, I cannot have. I cannot have my generals and lower soldiers doubting me. I cannot have the enemy doubting me. It is time to push the whole host down the Bitch Queen's throat. Let her choke on it."

Aoife and Toomt'-La, In the Forest

"And now?"

"That depends upon your brother."

Aoife screwed up her mouth, as if she'd just bitten into something terribly sour. "As always," she said. "At least we got him to retreat."

Toomt'-La nodded. "That is curious. For whatever reason, he seems to believe we're not a threat to him or his host."

"Meaning he knows something we do not?"

"Or he assumes something that is not true."

Aoife tired of the cryptic nature of this conversation. "I wish Tarmun Vykers would do something more substantial than stare at Anders' host. He's supposed to be a legendary warrior, but so far, I have seen nothing to merit that reputation."

Once more, Toomt'-La cocked his head at an inquisitive angle.

"What?" Aoife demanded.

"Oh, nothing," Toomt'-La responded with exaggerated nonchalance.

"You don't fool me, you mischievous satyr! What's on your mind?"

The mischievous satyr grinned. "The real question is, what is on yours?"

"What's that supposed to mean?" Aoife asked, knowing full well what it meant.

Toomt'-La shrugged. "I just find your leap from discussion of your brother's plans for our forest to the subject of Tarmun Vykers rather...convenient."

Aoife fumed. "You are becoming too human!" she said.

To which, naturally, the satyr took umbrage. "Me? Human? Take that back this instant, or I'll..."

"You'll what? Turn me into skunk cabbage? My reference to Tarmun Vykers was about this battle and nothing more!"

"Indeed?" Toomt'-La asked in a knowing way.

"Yes, in fact, you are never to mention the warrior around me again!" Aoife said, fairly shouting now.

"But you are the one who brought him up in the first place!"

"And I'm the one who's dropping the subject, too. And I'd advise you to do the same."

"Excellent. I shall never again mention Tarmun Vykers in your presence."

Aoife frowned most severely at him.

"Question, though..."

"Yes?"

"Am I allowed to say the name Tarmun Vykers when you are not present? Is it acceptable if I refer to some other Tarmun or Vykers? How about 'the legendary warrior?' Is that allowed? May I still say 'the Reaper'?"

Aoife screamed in irritation. "Enough, Toomt'-La! Enough!"

After an extended silence, the satyr spoke. "We shall wait until your brother is at his most preoccupied, and then we shall give him a taste of the agony he visited upon Nar."

Vykers, the Queen's Army

"What's your assessment?"

Vykers looked at the old Shaper. Why did they always have to use words like 'assessment?' "Looks like the End got beaten back by our friends In the Forest."

D'Kem searched him. "And what makes you think they're our friends?"

"I gave 'em a chance to kill me a while ago, and they only sent some A'Shea to talk to me."

"Really?" the Shaper asked, clearly intrigued. "An A'Shea?"

"Yes. I was surprised, too."

D'Kem began pacing, talking to himself. "Even at this height, I can't see the whole picture. What's an A'Shea doing in a forest of fey folk?"

The Reaper rolled his eyes, but kept his mouth shut. Time was, he'd have mocked the old man for even mentioning fey folk. Then, he'd met the Five (now Three), battled the dead in

Morden's Cairn and come into possession of a bleedin' magic sword. "I thought you wanted my *assessment*," he reminded the other man. "I wasn't finished."

"Oh?" D'Kem asked.

"His host has quieted down somewhat, so I'd say he's killed the last of the Svarren chomping his ass."

"Now, there's an image," D'Kem said.

"Unless there's a magical shit storm still to come, I can't see what he's got left to him but an all-out attack. We play by those rules, I don't see how we can win."

"As I said, I believe this all hinges on our ability to get you within striking distance."

"Well, I wish he'd hurry the fuck up!" Vykers grumbled. "If we're gonna fight, I wanna fight."

"That's exactly why he's making us wait."

"Well," Vykers began, "that, and he wants the taste of losing to those woodlings outta his troops' mouths before tries us again. That's not good for morale, you know."

D'Kem was impressed. "I hadn't thought of that."

"Master," Number 3 interrupted, "Is there any chance of a meal before hostilities resume?"

"Mind if we hit the mess tent?" Vykers asked the Shaper.

"That could create quite a stir," D'Kem responded, "which, now I think on it, might be just what we need about now."

Vykers looked, found a ladder. "And, no offense, but the boys and I'll be taking the normal way down."

"Suit yourselves," D'Kem smiled.

"I always do," the Reaper replied. On the way down the ladder, he sought out Arune. *You're awfully quiet.*

I've been conversing with Pellas.

The whole time?

The whole time.

The old Shaper rose in Vykers' regard. Anyone who could carry on two conversations at once...amazing. *And, uh, the subject o' your conversation?*

Arune was coy. *Oh, this and that.*

I hate it when you do that.

I know, was all she said.

Long, In Battle

It was difficult to tell whether the eastern sky became lighter or merely less black. One might think that amounts to the same thing, but it did not feel so to Long Pete: lighter was cause for hope; less black might be an anomaly, an aberration.

Thinking of aberrations, the spectral image of Long's master again revealed itself. Evidently, the End wasn't comfortable appearing in the flesh so close to the front. "I am sending the entire host at the enemy within the hour. You will know when the time has come and assume your position in the vanguard of the assault."

There was nothing Long wanted to say, had he been capable.

"Cat got your tongue?" the End taunted. "If you feel nothing else as you die, know that I have, indeed, been the end of all things—at least far as you and yours are concerned. And do not think you can escape your fate by rushing into the Queen's arms. Your voice is not the only thing I have taken from you."

The sky was demonstrably lighter. Hope, then, in spite of his master's promises. Long saluted the specter in as ambiguous a manner as he could muster. *Let the fiend chew on that for a while.* Had he imagined it, or had the End's shade been scowling as it faded away?

A series of horn blasts shattered his reverie. Downhill, the various armies comprising the End's host began organizing themselves into a forward-attack configuration. Uphill and to Long's left and right, the second army did likewise. The clamor of battle continued unchanged at the front.

Vykers, the Queen's Army

Vykers stopped the first officer he saw and asked directions to the mess. The man recoiled in fear at the sight of the Three, but became excited as recognition dawned upon him.

"You're…you're the Reaper!" he breathed. "You're here!"

In less time than it takes to explain it, Vykers and his

chimeras were surrounded by a fast-growing mob of the Queen's soldiers, jostling one another as they tried to get closer and verify the officer's claim.

"Mahnus' balls, it's him!"

"The Reaper, himself!"

"I'da never believed this day would come!"

"The End's in for it, now!"

And suchlike over and over until Vykers had had enough. He drew his sword and everyone leapt back, some falling over each other in the effort.

"You're keepin' my friends and me…" Vykers gestured to the Three, "from a much-needed meal. I don't think you want to be doin' that." He let that settle in a moment.

"May I show you to the mess tent?" the first man asked deferentially.

Vykers grunted in the affirmative and followed the man away from the mob and further into the camp. As he walked along, he heard a gradually escalating commotion throughout the camp.

Fuck's that? He inquired of Arune.

They're cheering your arrival, you big idiot.

He might've been insulted, but her tone was playful and carried more than a hint of pride. *I ain't done anything, yet.*

But you have. You've bolstered their spirits.

Huh.

Have you thought about what you're going to say when you address them?

Nope. He waited. *You gonna suggest something?*

You're the warrior, not me.

Glad you remembered that.

They arrived at the mess tent, which had been mostly cleared out in advance of Vykers' arrival. Amazing how fast word travelled in a military encampment. At a long table in the back, a handful of servers stared at the chimeras with unmasked trepidation. For their part, the chimeras perused the food offerings with identical unease.

"Er…Master…" Number 3 said.

"You got any meat that isn't cooked yet?" Vykers asked the nearest server.

The man nodded silently.

"Well, that's very nice and all…" Number 3 continued.

"You got any meat that ain't dead yet?" Vykers clarified.

The servers exchanged looks of pure panic. The first server nodded again.

"Like what, fer instance?"

"Steer?" the man said, as if he were asking a question rather than answering one.

Vykers noticed the Three were beaming. "That'll do," he said. "Can one o' you fellas lead my boys to their dinner?"

None of the servers volunteered, so Vykers volunteered one. "You!" he said to the first server. "Show 'em the way and stay with 'em, so nobody gets spooked. As you can imagine, their dining gets a little messier than most folks are used to. Wouldn't want anyone in camp to get the wrong idea."

The server just about expired in fright, but he managed to lead the Three through the back of the tent.

"Now," Vykers said to the remaining servers, "whatta we got?"

A short, chubby little man answered. "We have smoked ham, bacon, capon, beef, salted herring, uh, Merual sausage, duck eggs—boiled or, uh, fried—mutton, uh, four or five kinds of cheese—though I'd recommend the Brisial—brown bread, corn bread, just about every kind of jam you can think of…"

It was clear the man meant to go on for some time.

"I'll take some of everything," Vykers interjected.

"Ev…uh…everything?" the man asked.

"My accent too thick for ya? Everything!"

He didn't need to tell them a third time. The servers whirled into action, stacking several trays with samples of absolutely every last item they had available, until Vykers felt positively dizzy at the sight.

"Why don't you just put everything over there?" he suggested, pointing to a table in the corner. "And what've you got to drink?"

The chubby server started, "Uh, we've got…oh, never mind.

We'll bring some of everything, and it please you."

It did. The first tray had barely touched down and Vykers had stuffed his mouth to capacity with…something…delicious. He groaned in inarticulate praise and offered his servers a hearty thumbs-up. Halfway through his third tray, the Reaper saw a large shadow fill the doorway, and he looked up from his meal to see three men—generals or some such, he guessed—he'd never seen before. From the looks on their faces, he could see they were no threat to him. He wiped his mouth with his forearm.

"One o' you in charge, here?"

The most ostentatiously dressed of them stepped forward. "Actually, you are, Mr. Vykers. As per the Queen's orders."

Still chewing, Vykers waved the men forward, offered them seats.

"Thank you, sir, but we've eaten," the ostentatious man said.

"Huh. You mind if I finish up here?"

"Not at all," the man replied, in a manner that suggested he felt rather pressed for time. "I'm Lord Marshall Ferzic. This gentleman…" he said, indicating the man on his right, "is General Branch, and this gentleman," he said, referring to the other, "is Major Bailis."

"Uh-huh," the Reaper said. "And you already know who I am."

"And your three…friends?" the Lord Marshall asked delicately.

"Gifts from Her Majesty."

"Ah…yes. Do you have any particular orders for us this morning?" the Lord Marshall asked. "The enemy shows every sign of preparation for a major assault."

Vykers stretched, belched. "Yeah. I wanna talk to the troops. All of 'em."

"Of course."

"I'm gonna need a wagon or something to stand on."

"That shouldn't prove difficult to arrange."

Vykers reached over to his pack and nudged it towards the Lord Marshall. "Have somebody keep this safe, will you?"

"Yes," Ferzic replied tersely.

"Good. Give me, say, half an hour and I'll be ready."

The three officers traded looks of confusion.

"Gotta finish eating and visit the jakes," Vykers explained. "Never know when your next chance is your last."

Janks & Company, In Battle

Everyone knew the final push was coming. The End kept thousands of thralls at the front just to keep the pressure on the Queen's men, but the bulk of his host was gathering into an enormous, dense, dark block in the meadow's center. Against the light dusting of snow that now covered the ground, the enemy's host looked somehow smaller—not the massive, unending sea of thralls and mercs that had threatened the Queen's army just a day ago, but something at once more familiar and pathetic. Still, there were enough warm bodies on the End's side to smother and rout the Queen's army. Nobody was thinking too far ahead.

Another unit had stepped in to spell Kittins' men for a while. These new troops were saviors and saints to a man, and Janks would've said so if talking hadn't required too much energy. Instead, he joined his fellows some fifty yards back of the fray and collapsed in a heap on a bale of hay meant, he supposed, for the cavalry's mounts. Conventional wisdom had it that sitting or lying down between stints at the front only made you more stiff, more sore. Janks didn't give a shit. Another five seconds and he'd've passed out from exhaustion and dehydration—there's only so much an A'Shea can do during battle, after all, to keep the men fresh; the real work came later—mending the wounded, releasing the dying. The corporal didn't need either of those, though he knew he'd acquired some new scars in this fight. One o' them thralls, for instance, had taken a sizeable bite out of his left ear. His mates'd be impressed, but his potential *mates* would be *dis*tressed. In war, men respect ugly scars, but women rarely found them sexy. Or maybe they were objecting to his body odor. Mahnus' balls, how he stank! A normal enemy might've been repelled by his stink. Not the thralls. It seemed to bring 'em on, the way fish oil attracts cats.

Someone dangled a water skin in Janks' face and he

drank deeply without pause or question. Much as he'd been a borderline drunkard, he'd swear, again, there never was or would be any drink better than pure, cold water. It almost made him believe in Alheria. Janks heard waves of cheering break out throughout the camp, and he twisted his weary torso this way and that to see what the excitement was all about.

"They're sayin' the Reaper's arrived," Kittins said in a voice raspy from too many war cries. With half his face torn away, he looked about as bad as Janks felt. Good to know the bastard was struggling, too.

"The Reaper?" That was Spirk, of course. Except for the gash in his chin, he looked surprisingly healthy.

Janks pulled himself up. Damn, but that was hard. He fought his way onto the hay bale. Sure enough, there was a crowd gathering a couple hundred yards uphill and, in their midst, a man stood atop a supply wagon. Suddenly, the old corporal felt a surge of nervous energy. "Let's get closer," he breathed. "I wanna see if it's true, hear what he has to say."

He got no argument from his comrades. Each and every one of them stumbled after him. From a distance, they looked like nothing more than besotted invalids, holding some sort of perverse relay race-of-the-damned. But they got where they were going.

It took several minutes for the cheering to die down, during which time Janks got his first good look at the legendary Tarmun Vykers. He was not disappointed. Though not as tall or as muscle-bound as rumor made him out to be, Vykers was still a head taller than Janks and appeared as solid as an anvil. He wore his hair and beard short in the style of the midland kingdoms, but couldn't have been more foreign to them if he'd been painted green. Janks wondered why it was he could not take his eyes off the man's face. The Reaper was neither handsome nor charming, but possessed of an animal magnetism that was close to spellbinding, in much the same manner that staring into the face of a caged lion was spellbinding. When the cheering began to subside, Vykers spoke.

"Morning, men," he said so casually that almost everyone laughed at the greeting. "I'm sure over the years you've heard your share 'o great speeches." He paused. "This ain't one o' them." Janks found himself liking the man more by the second. "Nope. All I've gotta say is, keep the End's puppets at bay long enough for me to get close to the bastard. By the time I'm done with that fucker, even the maggots won't want anything to do with him."

The Queen's men burst into cheering and applause so loud the End's generals must've quailed at the sound. That, Janks realized, was the power of legend. Scores of his fellows reached out to grasp hands with the Reaper, to touch his arm or shoulder. One of them touched the pommel of Vykers' sword and fell, twitching, to the ground.

"Curiosity," Vykers said, "meet the cat."

One or two of the fallen man's friends seemed offended, but everyone else shrugged it off. Vykers stepped aside with the Lord Marshall, a couple of generals and, Janks saw, Major Bailis. What he wouldn't have given to be in Bailis' boots for just five minutes. He'd love to know what the real plan was, how long the Reaper expected this battle to take, etc. Slowly, the crowd broke up and men went back to their assigned positions.

"Got anything left for the enemy?" he heard Kittins ask him.

Janks felt like the cock of the walk. "Plenty!" he boasted.

They continued talking as they walked towards the back of the Queen's camp, the furthest one could get from the front.

"We thought perhaps we might send the cavalry out both sides and down the enemy's flanks once the fighting got thick in the middle."

"Don't see a problem, there," Vykers told the Lord Marshall Ferzic. "I'm sure you've seen that, uh, buffer he's giving the woods on both sides since his failed attempt to burn them down."

"Ah, yes," Ferzic said, "the woods. The old Shaper..."

"Pellas," Vykers said.

The other man seemed uncomfortable admitting it. "Eh, Pellas. Just so."

"And who am I?"

"You?" Ferzic stammered. "Tarmun Vykers, the Reaper."

Vykers gripped the Lord Marshall's shoulder. "Yes, the Reaper. And the old Shaper, as you call him, is Pellas. And that nasty fellow across the battlefield," he pointed "is known as the End-of-All-Things." Vykers looked the Lord Marshall in the eyes, forced him to maintain eye contact. "Rise to the occasion, sir, or the occasion will bury you."

Ferzic was not used to being spoken to in such a manner and looked as if he wanted to argue Vykers' point. Glancing at his generals and Major Bailis, however, he concluded that might prove unwise and shut his mouth.

"So. Where were we?" Vykers wondered aloud. "You were gonna to tell me something about Pellas?"

The Lord Marshall cleared his throat. "Yes. It's rather hard to credit, but he says the woods are full of…fairies, I suppose you'd call them, for want of a better word. And, uh, these fairies, while not necessarily on *our* side, are almost certainly opposed to our enemy."

One of the generals chuckled softly to himself, but Vykers shot him a look and the man turned whiter than the snow at his feet. "Couple o' months ago, I thought as you do," he told the general. "But it turns out the world's a good deal darker and more mysterious than I thought, and I'll wager anything you like I've seen far more of it than you. You wanna laugh at the thought o' fairies, go ahead. Just don't come cryin' to me if you manage to anger 'em." Vykers turned back to Ferzic. "We gotta fight, soon," he said. "So, here it is: you'll have that alley on both sides of the meadow, between the End's armies and the woods. You wanna send your mounted troops out that way, that sounds like a good plan. I see you've got some siege weapons, trebuchets and such. Good. I'd use 'em to pepper the middle o' the End's forces. Pellas says the Shapers you've got left'll do the same. Make an obstacle of the enemy's bodies. Your foot will have to keep scrapping in the middle, 'til Pellas and I can work out our little surprise."

"And, em, if I might ask…" Ferzic began.

Long, In Battle

There were not a lot of drums in the End's host, but there was no shortage of horns, and when the final surge began, it was unquestionably clear to one and all. One moment, Long was sitting astride his horse, his eyes shifting in and out of focus, and the next, he was being pressed forward by thousands upon thousands of the End's thralls. There was nowhere and no way to go but forward. As always, Long was struck by the sheer noise of his master's host on the move. The entire world must have been at his back, minus the few unhappy souls they were about to trample into the snow.

Funny thing about snow, though: it makes slopes slippery, especially when it's been tamped down by countless feet, or iced over with frozen blood. Long's horse handled the icy terrain ably enough, but thralls to his left and right lost footing and were crushed by those behind. So, the host would climb this hill on the backs of its own dead. Long quailed at the pointlessness of such deaths. He imagined the lives these thralls had lived when fully conscious and free, useful, productive lives, some full of bitterness, but some full of hope, surely. To think they'd end up as mere footing for others of their kind was beyond appalling.

Arrows knifed down more of the thralls, but nothing stopped the press: forward, forward. Fire and explosions lit up the ever-brightening sky both before and in back of Long's position. The Shapers were at it, again. The familiar sounds of trebuchets, ballistae and catapults assaulted Long's ears. He knew in his gut this was truly it, the make-or-break battle of this little war. He would not live to see it, he knew, but by this time tomorrow, the world would either be free of the End-of-All-Things or completely fucked. Looking up, Long saw that he'd somehow managed to approach the first trench—yesterday's conquest—without injury or incident. Still, his horse was bullied, buffeted and bounced forward.

The first trench was entirely filled with the dead from both sides. How deep it went, Long dared not guess, but there were, undeniably, thousands of bodies here, a gelid stew of human remains. A less-experienced man might have puked. He wondered how the boy, Spirk, was faring, if he was still alive. Just beyond the trench, a huge crevasse split the hillside from west to east. The End-of-All-Things had clashed with the Queen's Shapers over this chasm; tragically, it appeared the sorcerer had prevailed. In spots, the chasm's rim had collapsed inward, creating earthen bridges that the thralls were only too eager to use. Long was nowhere near as anxious to cross, but cross he must if he hoped to avoid being pushed into the fissure. On the far side, a veritable wall of thralls grappled with the Queen's men in furious action. *Well, shit,* Long thought, *fall into an abyss or attack my friends? Small choice in rotten apples,* he'd heard a poet say once. *Small choice, indeed.* Long spurred his horse across a stony ridge and achieved the southern side.

Back it at. His arms felt like they weighed a thousand pounds apiece and ached like all hells. Funny how it all blurred together, to make separate shifts seem one endless nightmare. Janks was beyond hack, slash, stab. He was more like a windmill, arms turning mechanically, gears grinding the enemy to… what? Nothing worthwhile. He doubted they'd even make good fertilizer. Swing, swing, swing. Chop, chop, chop. Like threshing wheat, 'cept wheat didn't try to eat yer face off.

"Get that bastard on horseback!" Kittins shouted. "He's the one drives 'em. Take him out, they'll slow down!"

Janks caught a glimpse of Kittins, nearly buried in thralls. Obviously, his comment was meant for Janks. He stole a quick look-see past his immediate opponent and saw the horseman in question. Fuckin' coward with a sword at his hip and a whip in his hands. "Hey, shithead!" Janks yelled at the man. "Wanna fight someone who fights back?"

The horseman rode closer, recoiled.

Good fortune, at last! In all the teeming thousands, to run into his old friend Janks was nothing short of a miracle. Long shouted greetings to his friend, only to be reminded that the End had taken his voice. Nothing came out of his throat, no matter how hard he tried. No matter. Long waved his arms and jumped down from his horse, rapidly closing the distance between himself and his friend.

Plucky son-of-a-whore! The man charged him, and it was all Janks could do to get his weapons up in time. He must have been a coward in truth, too, for the stranger pulled back and dropped his arms. Janks spat in contempt and climbed up to meet him. Still, the stranger had his arms up and silently mouthed something the corporal was sure had to be magic. Fuck him! Janks rushed in, swinging both long knife and axe. The other man leapt back, a look of shock on his face. *That's right, fucker!* Janks thought. *I'm going to kill you!*

What new madness was this? Janks attacking him without pause or quarter? Was the man angry that Long had been captured? Did he somehow blame his old friend for all that had happened since? Pure lunacy. Over and over, Long entreated his long-time companion to drop his weapons, stop his assault. It made no difference. Janks came on like a man possessed. Like a thrall, Long realized.

At first, he thought to parry his friend's blows until Janks realized his error or spent himself. But it soon became clear Janks meant to kill him. Long dropped his whip and drew his sword. Maybe he could knock the man unconscious and make amends later. In came his friend, with long knife and axe. Long was afraid.

This was the first man in control of his own wits that Janks had fought since this little war started, and even this one seemed a bit demented. Even as Janks pressed the action, his foe parried, deferred and otherwise surrendered all advantage. Unless it was a ruse of some sort. Quickly, Janks swapped his weapons from left to right and vice versa and went for the man's legs. If he could take the fellow down, he should be able to gut him rather easily.

Long made a two-handed sweep across Janks' mid-section with his sword, dropping his right hand at the start and punching his friend in the face. Janks didn't go down, but he did back up a step. Long gestured to his face, hoping to penetrate the fog of war that surrounded Janks' brain. No such luck. Janks redoubled his efforts to overwhelm his friend, pinwheeling his arms in a frenzy of blows that Long found increasingly hard to counter. Not knowing what else to do, he gave ground.

He had the bastard on the run at last! A feeling of euphoria seized Janks as he continued to press the other man. Janks was the better fighter! It was only a matter of time until he—

The other man's sword punched through his mail and tore into his chest. Janks slowed up, stared down at the sword that had killed him. For some odd reason, it looked familiar.

It was an instinctive move. Long hadn't meant to connect, only drive his friend back. Now, Janks froze halfway down his sword, a look of complete bewilderment on his face. Long shared his confusion.

He thought about cursing the man, but he hadn't the breath or the will. He was done, worm's meat. He struggled to stay alert. Bollocks. He wondered if his old friend Long was still alive, somewhere…

Long watched the light go out of his friend's eyes, saw his face go slack, heard the sound of his weapons hitting the ground. Janks seemed to be struggling to form words, to say something with his final breath. And then he was gone, the words unspoken. Long let go of his own sword, fell to the earth, and pulled his friend's head into his lap. "Janks," he yelled in silence. "Janks!" Nobody heard him.

THIRTEEN

Vykers, the Queen's Army

Snow continued to fall, and the combatants continued to die—by the hundreds, by the thousands. Fire and noxious gasses bloomed in the heart of each army. Arrows flew in numbers too great to track. Great boulders crashed down on one side or the other. Gradually, inexorably, the End's host pushed its way uphill.

Looking down on the action from the Shapers' platform, the Reaper scowled. Too many good men were dying while he waited for his moment. At his side, Pellas was entirely focused on countering the End and his Shapers' efforts to decimate the Queen's bowmen. Vykers pounded the railing with his fist. He wouldn't have long to wait once the cavalry attacked.

What are you doing right now? He asked Arune.

Conserving my energy, she answered curtly.

What could he say to that? He was doing the same. To his left, two of the Three leaned, like him, over the railing. Only 17 engaged the enemy, launching arcane salvo after salvo into the advancing thralls.

He'll burn out, eventually, Arune said.

What do you mean, 'burn out?'

Exhaust himself. Utterly and completely. Die.

"Take it easy!" Vykers commanded the chimera. "I don't want you killing yourself over a few thralls at the front."

17 paused, shook his head as if emerging from a daydream. He looked Vykers' way.

"I will need you later," was all the Reaper said in response.

Number 3 spoke up. "Master, do you truly believe we can survive such odds?"

Yes, Vykers bobbed his head. "Kill the brain and the body dies."

The End, In Battle

He should have done this from the beginning, as he had everywhere else he'd been. The all-out assault was undeniably his host's strongest tactic. Yard by yard, his thralls and mercenaries advanced, drawing ever closer to the heart of the Queen's army. It was only a matter of time and patience—a lesson he'd almost forgotten over the last day or so, but which he swore to himself he'd never again ignore. To be sure, he'd had unexpected distractions, but such things only made him sharper, more powerful.

The End-of-All-Things watched the carnage from high above the meadow, where he fluttered and floated like a hummingbird. He might have been in some danger if the Queen's Shapers had been capable of seeing him. As it was, he enjoyed the best possible view of the action. Every now and then and at intentionally unpredictable intervals, he blasted a random section of the Queen's front with pestilence, fire, or lightning and then darted to a new location. He felt giddy as a child with a new-found toy, so addictive were the screams of his victims.

Something unseen smashed into him and turned reality inside-out. A fleeting hint of ozone bedeviled the sorcerer. For a split second, the End was overcome with dizziness and nausea. *Damn that Pellas!* The man was an irritating burr, stuck to the End's leggings, a nuisance that would not go away. The End sought him out, smirked in satisfaction and hurled him right off his Shapers' platform, tumbling out into darkness. It was too much to hope the man would fall to his death; the End gave him an ample dose of humility, though. Out in the snow, Pellas picked himself up with delightful difficulty and dragged himself back towards his perch. It would be some time before he attempted another attack on the End-of-All-Things.

Shifting to a new position, he sought out his sister. He did not, could not find her. But the hostile presence In the Forest had grown considerably. Once more, Anders weighed the advantages and disadvantages of fighting two enemies simultaneously. He believed it could be done, was certain he'd win, eventually. Crushing the Queen's forces as quickly as possible and then turning again to those in the woods still seemed the better choice, however, so the End opted to stay the course.

And where, General Long? The End did not want to miss the pathetic fool's demise. After all, he'd invested so much time and energy in tormenting the man, it would be a shame not to see the grand finale. Ah, yes…there, cradling the head of a fallen comrade! Wonderful, wonderful. The bathos of the moment was fantastically ridiculous. The End exulted in his ability to debase these humans in evermore imaginative and subtle ways. Truly, the sorcerer was an artist—*the* artist—of a new age. Too bad none lived who could appreciate his genius.

And now, to draw this so-called Reaper out of hiding! He thought, as he dropped towards the front and drew his sword. The hummingbird dipped down into spot after spot along the line, killing scores of men in short flurries of violence and then moving on. Let the word of his presence spread. Let it pull the Reaper into the center of his host. The End's victory was a foregone conclusion.

Looking out from the arboreal shadows, Aoife champed at the bit. "Will we never join the fray?"

"We will fight."

"Yes, but when? It appears the Queen's men are losing!"

"We shall see," Toomt'-La smiled, inscrutably.

The A'Shea huffed in impatience.

Long, In Battle

When the snowflakes began settling on Janks' face without melting, Long knew his friend was well and truly gone. He lifted his eyes to the battle swirling around him. Amongst the myriad things he could not understand was how it happened that he, himself, had not been killed in the last several minutes. No one on either side seemed willing to acknowledge his presence. He felt like the boy, Spirk Nessno, except that, unlike the boy, Long wanted to die and no one would oblige him. Fine. If that's how it had to be, the old soldier would force the issue. With a final pang of regret, he retrieved his sword, now encased in a thin sheath of Janks' frozen blood, and howled at the thralls pressing towards him. "You wanna fuckin' die? Come to me, then: I'll fuckin' *kill* you!" As he made no sound in screaming this, they ignored him.

Long had never been anything like a master swordsman, but he whirled and danced through the mindless thralls like a thing possessed. He aimed for legs more than anything else, but would gladly take arms or heads if they presented themselves. His fury powered him with an almost inexhaustible supply of energy. Soon, he had cleared a space perhaps ten yards square. The ground was covered with mewling, crippled thralls, but none presented any further threat to Long or the Queen's army. Still, Long punished the End's troops for everything that had happened to him since the death of Short Pete, made them pay for every indignity, every lost or wasted moment.

"Here, what the fuck d'you think you're doin'?" Someone yelled at him.

Long spun, lashing out blindly with his sword and caught nothing but air. Some distance away, another of the End's "generals" sat astride his horse, a look of extreme displeasure on his face.

"Gone battle mad, have you?" the general asked. "Then you'll need to be put down!" Abruptly, he spurred his horse into a gallop and charged at Long.

This was it, the chance Long had been waiting for, the chance to die. It would have been easier to drop his sword at the last moment. For some reason, he raised it instead and braced himself for the general's attack. The other man had stowed his whip and came barreling towards him, a large mace held high over his head. Long laughed and nothing came out. Just as well. He suspected he'd be frightened by the sound of his own laughter at this point. Crash! Long parried the man's first blow, a bone-jarring hit, and was grinding his way down the haft of the man's mace when the other fellow's momentum carried him out of reach. In the infinity of time between the man's departure and his wheeling back around into position, Long slashed at a few more thralls, sending each to the ground with damaged legs.

The snow was accumulating in earnest now, Long realized. Part of him wanted to ponder that, as if it were somehow important. A rumbling noise brought him back to the present, in which a horse bore down on him. Oh, yes: the other general. This time, it seemed his opponent intended to trample him and perhaps swing in the aftermath. Long was at a distinct disadvantage. He raised his sword again, uncertainly, and a crossbow bolt sprang from his assailant's shoulder, causing the other man to veer to one side at the last moment. Long followed the man's gaze as he searched out his new attacker and a second bolt punctured his skull, sending him from the saddle like a large sack of onions thrown to the earth. The man's horse skittered awkwardly off to the right several yards and began wandering. Within moments, the beast was pulled to the ground by ravenous thralls. *What in all hells*? Long wondered. And then he thought of his own horse: nowhere to be seen.

He did, however, see a huge, bloody-faced warrior in Queen's armor, holding a crossbow on him. Next to this stranger was a more-familiar face: Rem, who also held a crossbow he'd apparently just finished reloading. A ways behind these two, over at Janks' body, Long could just make out Spirk, sprawled across his old friend, sobbing like a lost toddler.

"Drop your weapon, mate," the big man ordered.

Long dropped it.

The big man muttered something to Rem and then turned back to Long. "Walk this way, and don't do anything stupid. I got no reason to let you live and plenty to kill you."

Long shuffled forwards. As he did so, Rem arced away from him and circled around to retrieve his sword. Then, the actor gasped.

"What?" the big man asked, irritably.

"I know this sword, Sergeant" Rem yelled back.

The unnamed sergeant suddenly fired his crossbow and Long heard a dull thump off to his left. A thrall fell to the ground. "Don't get any ideas. I can still kill you with this thing, loaded or not," the sergeant warned. "Keep coming." At ten feet, the man stopped him. "That's good, right there. Who are you?"

It was futile, but Long told him. Unfortunately, the sergeant didn't speak mute.

"Got no voice, eh?" the man observed. "Now, I really got no reason to let you live..."

"This is my old sergeant's sword!" Rem said, finally returning to his new sergeant's side.

The man looked down at the weapon. "That a fact? And what about this fellow?" he asked, pointing to Long. "You recognize him?"

Rem scrutinized Long's face, his attire. "No," he said, sadly. "I'd love to know how he came by Long's sword, though."

A second friend had failed—or been unwilling—to recognize him. It had to be more of that Mahnus-fucking End-of-All-Bullshit's work. Long pantomimed writing.

"He wants to tell us in writing," Rem said.

The sergeant seemed skeptical. "You can write?" he asked Long incredulously. "The fuck kinda soldier can write?"

"An officer," Rem told him. "And, er, me," he added almost shyly.

The sergeant looked at the actor as if he'd offered to bugger his commanding officer. "No wonder we're losing this damned fight!" he spat. "Okay," he sighed heavily, "Get him back behind the lines and see what the prissy poet wants to write for us."

The cavalry, led on the right and left sides by Generals Branch and Lescoray respectively, exploded around the ends of the Queen's front and stormed down the alleys between the End's forces and the woods. The End-of-All-Things, having enjoyed tremendous success to this point without a cavalry of his own, was not overly concerned at this latest development. He should have been. While the being that was the End had spent hundreds of years studying magic of every sort, the Queen had studied military strategy. Though not a soldier herself, she knew the function, value and strengths and weaknesses of every type of unit imaginable and had taken great pains to train or acquire the best. The End had faced cavalry before; he had never faced the Queen's cavalry. In front, her heavy lancers overwhelmed the sorcerer's thralls, smashing them underfoot like so many eggshells. Behind, knights in full armor with massive swords, axes and hammers obliterated each and every body they encountered.

But no battle is completely one-sided, especially when the enemy's fighters do so without fear or scruple and appear to have no end. If a knight paused for any reason, thralls attached themselves to him and his mount like leeches. When enough thralls gained purchase, the knight and his horse went down, often causing the next knight to stop or stumble and suffer a similar fate.

The noise of the cavalry's twin charges pulled the End from his games at the front and back into the sky. Naturally, he intended to intercede on his army's behalf; the question was: how to do it? If he came to the aid of those on his left, he could no longer monitor the progress of those on the opposite side, across the wide meadow, and vice-versa. Frustrated, he sent a short burst of fire into the ranks of the cavalry on his right and swept down upon the knights on his left. The End saw that brief blasts of fire had little effect on the heavily armored knights; Lightning had a much more desirable result. The enemy screamed and howled and cooked in their little steel ovens. Weirdly, Anders found he liked the odor.

An unearthly wailing commenced at the End's back, and he knew he'd guessed wrong. The real action was on the other side of the field. Up he went, again, more determined than ever to break this enemy. For all that, he was unprepared for what he saw: the forest itself descended upon his right rear flank, drawing many of his thralls off the Queen's cavalry and into an altogether different engagement. When he looked back to the left, he saw the same thing occurring on the left rear flank. His sister and her strange allies had leapt in on the Queen's side.

Everyone he hated, gathered against him.

Vykers stalked over to the old Shaper. "You're gonna have to adjust your plans, friend. I'm not sittin' out the biggest battle in ages."

Pellas, looking drained and more than a little beleaguered, continued to urge patience. "Can't you see? Our enemy is trying to draw you out, in conditions that favor him."

"Yeah? Well, they ain't gonna favor him as soon as I show. You do what you gotta do, and I'll do what I was made for." Without another word, Vykers made for the ladder and started heading down, his three chimeras in tow.

"Well," Pellas sighed to the empty platform, "I suppose we can try it your way."

Don't worry, Arune told the old man. *Whenever and wherever you appear, it'll still be a bigger surprise than the End-of-All-Things is ready for.*

I hope you're right, child, Pellas told her.

Child? Funny thing to call a ghost, old man.

Pellas wheezed in laughter, stepped off the back of the platform and floated to the ground.

The children of Nar and the Queen's cavalry made uneasy allies, but they immediately recognized each other as such and refocused their attentions on the legions of lunatic, bestial peasants the End threw at them in wave after wave. In fact, as the Queen's men discovered, the wisest choice was to ignore the fey folk altogether. Something about them was terribly beguiling, almost hypnotically dangerous. They also killed their adversaries in a far wider array of ways than most humans thought possible. These forest folk, the men thought, would not make good enemies.

On his way to the front, Vykers was intercepted by Major Bailis, who wanted to introduce him to some new recruits—volunteers. The Reaper barely glanced at them, until one face in particular caught his eye: a red-haired hill man with a broken left cheek and a broad chest. Seeing the Reaper had recognized him, the man looked down at his feet.

"Wasn't there something you wanted to say to me, friend?" Vykers prompted the man.

The redhead said nothing, looked uneasily left and right.

"Something about how Tarmun Vykers is a son-of-a-bitch and other suchlike pleasantries?"

The redhead's companions backed away from him. The man, himself, seemed to shrink in upon himself, blushing furiously all the while. "I...regret...my choice o' words when last we met..." he began.

Vykers let out a lusty laugh and clapped the man on both shoulders. "You picked a good day to die, my friend, and good company, too. Welcome, to the Queen's army!"

You never saw such a look of relief on a mortal face! The redhead smiled sheepishly and received a hearty ribbing from each and every one of his mates. Good company, indeed!

The Reaper erupted from the Queen's front, his sword flashing in great, lethal arcs and making an eerie keening sound. Behind him, the Three tore into the nearest thralls with a speed that all but defied human vision. Tarmun Vykers was home, at last.

Long, the Queen's Army

Long bent over a scrap of parchment he'd been given by Rem and was just about to put quill to paper when someone called his name.

"Long Pete?"

He looked up and his jaw dropped. D'Kem stood not fifteen feet away, a look of astonishment on his face. Long was certain it was the twin of his own expression. D'Kem looked at once taller, older and more powerful than the old sergeant had ever seen him.

"Long?" Rem questioned.

D'Kem waved a hand and Rem stumbled backwards.

"Alheria's tits! It *is* Long! What in the infinite hells happened to you?" Rem stammered.

Long tried, but still could not speak.

D'Kem crossed nearer and placed a hand on Long's shoulder,

frowned. "An enchantment disguised your face. Easy enough to dispel. I'm afraid I cannot reverse the damage done to your voice, though."

"Some wine, here!" Rem yelled.

"Wine won't help, either," the old Shaper said.

"It'll help," Rem scoffed. "It just won't help his voice."

A shadow loomed over Long's shoulder, offered a wineskin. Long grabbed it and took a tremendous swig. Then, another.

"Sergeant Long," D'Kem said, "May I introduce Sergeant Kittins."

Rem shot him a furtive glance that warned him this was deadly serious: Do. Not. Laugh.

"Sergeant Kittins," D'Kem continued. "Sergeant Long."

"So you're Long, eh?" Kittins asked, for want of anything else to say.

Long nodded.

"That explains why you were killing thralls and fighting one o' the End's mercs."

Long shook his head. But he couldn't explain. He knew he'd lose it if he tried.

"Well," Kittins said, "this little reunion is nice and all, I'm sure, but we're gearing up for the final push. It's-shit-or-get-off-the-pot time."

"Where's Spirk?" Long scribbled on the parchment.

"Back in the mess tent," Rem replied.

"Good," Long wrote. "Keep him out of this." He stood and Kittins jabbed him softly in the ribs with the hilt of his own sword. Long tossed the now empty wineskin aside and gladly accepted the weapon.

"The Reaper's just charged onto the field!" a panting soldier yelled to everyone within earshot.

For the first time in memory, Long Pete smiled. But it was a cold, eager smile.

Surrounded by her "children," Aoife stood in the middle of the conflict, cloaked in a kind of protective haze. Her brother could see her now, she knew, but would have difficulty hurting her while attempting to orchestrate the overall battle. Aoife used the time to help and heal as many of the Queen's Knights as she could reach. Most were shocked to see her, of course, but none refused the A'Shea's ministrations. In battle, a gifted A'Shea could keep a man in action almost indefinitely. Of course, Aoife's attentions were spread too thin for that; she had the whole of the cavalry and some of her children to care for. The thralls could not penetrate her protections, it was true, but neither did she possess limitless energy.

The End-of-All-Things was thoroughly engaged with raining fire, lightning, poison and disease down upon the fey folk and the Queen's cavalry, and yet he did not—could not—fail to notice Tarmun Vykers' arrival onto the battlefield. Just southwest of him, up the hill, Vykers and his thrillingly freakish chimeras wreaked havoc on the End's thralls and mercenaries. Truly, it was like watching a quartet of giants attacking a bunch of blind school children. The End took a second—just one selfish second—to marvel in envy at the Reaper's gift for destruction. Shame to kill such a man, but if the fellow wouldn't be reasonable, what choice did the End have? Besides, in order to be great, Anders had to conquer the great—wasn't that the warriors' trite standard? He made a quick assessment and judged that his troops could hold the left and right flanks until he'd defeated Vykers. It would be a challenging duel, but, he felt, shouldn't take more than a few minutes. And the death of the Reaper might very well destroy what little morale the Queen's men had left.

Her Majesty's troops came pouring from the line behind Vykers like angry wasps emerging from a threatened hive. Wherever the Reaper went, the Queen's men followed in his wake, putting the sword to anything that so much as moved one muscle. It is fair to say, though, that each of these men grabbed his chance to watch the Reaper at work.

Vykers continued to make the impossible routine. His anticipation was uncanny, his speed, inhuman. A soldier standing witness could see a hundred or more thralls incapacitated or killed before he could count to twenty. And

Mahnus forbid the same soldier stole a look at the Reaper's chimeras. The Three were surrounded by a constant mist of blood that never dissipated, so long as they moved. It was the kind of carnage an army was capable of, in mere seconds.

The Reaper had always loved combat; for him, this was better than sex. And his sword made it so much better; he almost wished he could tackle the End's host by himself. With this sword in his hand, there was no limit to the ways in which a foe could be killed. It was endlessly fascinating and invigorating. And he was making an obvious dent in the enemy forces. What had been an unbroken wall of thralls was now a more manageable, more familiar mob. So what if it stretched back a mile or more? Vykers and the Three would kill them all.

Vykers was a weapon in and of himself, and a weapon could not be killed.

The End and Vykers, In Battle

The End appeared in the air, not far from Vykers, and blasted the Reaper with a full barrage of arcane energies. They scattered every which-a-way well before reaching their intended target. That had to be the sword, the End knew.

Vykers' head snapped 'round and he stared right into the End's eyes. "Aha!" he sneered. "The sniveling bully appears at last!"

"Sniveling? Bully?" The End shook the earth at Vykers' feet, intending to send him into a chasm. Again, his spell dissipated before reaching its goal. The End touched down and drew his own sword. Instantly, both men's swords began shrieking. "It appears our weapons like one another no more than we do."

Like a great cat, Vykers circled stealthily to his right, hoping to observe his opponent's adjustments to his movement. The Three spread out.

"It seems your pets need something to occupy their attention," the End said and beckoned to his nearest thralls. As before, this group of thralls began to wriggle and writhe, struggling within their own skins. Again, they burst in showers of gore, leaving glistening crimson ghouls in their stead. Two of the Three were upon them before this change was complete; Number 17 stayed put and incinerated the closest with a flash of light so bright even Vykers winced.

"Well done! Well done!" the End crooned. "But I can do this all day. Can you?" He eyed Vykers and shifted his stance to protect himself against a sudden onslaught. His sword whined with ever-increasing urgency.

"I won't need all day," the Reaper smiled, showing eye teeth that had, mysteriously, gotten a good deal larger and sharper than normal.

The End found this somewhat unsettling. "Been mating with dogs, have you?" He barely had time to parry the Reaper's opening effort—and certainly wouldn't have, if not for his own magic sword. When the two weapons made contact, the noise was bizarre and ear-splitting.

The Reaper feinted a thrust at the sorcerer's left shoulder and instead muscled his sword around for a swipe at the End's right knee. For a second time, the man was saved by his sword. Vykers stepped back, circled to his left for a change.

The End made more of his ghouls bloom into being in order to keep the Three out of this fight and held his sword upright, in what he understood to be a guarded position. His sword did not resist, though it clearly wanted to reengage Vykers' weapon.

Vykers' ears were abuzz with the sounds of flesh rending and sinews snapping. Beyond his immediate vicinity, he heard the more usual sounds of battle—weapons clanging, bones crunching, flames burning, men screaming in pain or fury—but he kept his eyes entirely focused on the End-of-All-Things. So far, the man was fighting a defensive battle, which seemed out of character for one so ruthless. Vykers goaded him.

"You wanna die while attacking, or die while defending yourself?"

The End arched his eyebrows in mock surprise. "Oh, are you offering a choice? How kind of you, really. But this is my fight, my day, my vict..."

The Reaper came at him like some sort of demonic whirlwind. His blows came so rapidly and with such fury that even the End's sword barely blocked them all. Indeed, the sorcerer found himself cut in a dozen places, and each was singularly painful.

"That's just a taste," Vykers growled in an almost carnal manner.

The End had never been hurt. Never. It made him angry. With a colossal effort, he sent forth shock waves that blasted everything away from him for twenty-five, fifty, seventy-five yards. Except for Vykers.

The Reaper surveyed the scene. He and his foe now stood alone in the center of an enormous circle. Beyond its perimeter, the fighting continued. He hoped his chimeras were still alive. "Nice trick, that," he said to an enemy noticeably unhappy to find him still present.

Finally, the End came at him, swinging his sword with lethal intent, but nominal skill. His sword, though...his *sword* had skill. It feinted and jabbed, thrust and slashed. A normal man would have been dead a hundred times over; Vykers was a ghost it simply could not locate. On the rare occasions when the Reaper needed to parry, the End's sword hung greedily upon his own, as if attempting to mate with it. Throughout, both weapons continued their unearthly, plaintive songs.

"Stand still, damn you!" the End screamed. "Your cowardice is unbecoming!"

Vykers froze. "Cowardice?"

"You heard me. Stop dancing around like a two-penny harlot. If you would cross swords with me, cross swords. Otherwise..." The End extended his left hand, made a circling motion over his head and stepped backwards, smirking.

"Otherwise what?" Vykers said.

"I shall play games, as well."

Keeping his eyes fixed on the End's, Vykers queried Arune, *???*

I am here.

I bloody well know that. What the fuck's this bastard on about?

It's something unfamiliar...I can't quite...Alheria's mercy!

He didn't have time to ask what the problem was before everyone on both sides began shrieking in terror. Vykers risked a glance to one side and, sure enough, the End came at him the moment he looked away. This time, the Reaper didn't move;

he knew whence the blow came and batted it down before it reached the midpoint of its journey. The End tried again: same result. In the background, the panicked wailing of both armies reached a fever pitch. Vykers looked beyond his nemesis and saw something that made no immediate sense: blood—everyone's blood, anyone's blood, all the blood—was catching on fire, burning with infernal black flames, producing a ruddy, noxious smoke. Another strike came towards the Reaper's head; he slapped it away.

"You're the coward, here," Vykers snarled. "You can't touch me, so you torch everyone else? You child!" He launched himself at the sorcerer, bashing the other man's sword over and over with transcendent rage. He added several more cuts to the End's growing list of injuries and succeeded in driving the madman to his knees. Still, the furor around both combatants grew.

Out of nowhere, Pellas appeared not five feet from Vykers. "I can stop this butchery," he told the Reaper. "But it will be costly."

"Will it save the Queen's army?" Vykers asked, between blows.

"It will," Pellas said grimly.

"Then stop it!"

Pellas nodded and started—there's no other way to describe it—*expanding*, until he exploded in a cascade of shimmering white sparks that sailed in every direction. Vykers staggered back, and the End fell onto his backside. The sorcerer's spell had been snuffed out.

*Pellas...*Arune whimpered into the silence that followed.

It began to snow harder.

"Now, you die!" Vykers said, closing in on the End.

The sorcerer scrambled to his feet, his expression a mixture of anxiety and exhaustion. Resolutely, he lifted his still-whining sword.

Vykers attacked.

And the End lifted blithely into the air, just out of reach, smiling smugly. "How does it feel, Reaper, being unable to strike your foe?"

Vykers flew up after him. The surprise he felt was surpassed only by the surprise evident on the End's face.

You're welcome, Arune said.

Incredibly, the End laughed. "Tricky bastard!" He pointed his sword at Vykers' chest. "What *are* you?"

Vykers swung at the sorcerer's weapon with a little too much force and went spiraling away.

"Not used to flying, I see." The End smirked. "Good." With that, he blinked out and reappeared behind the Reaper, intending to finish him with a quick stab between his shoulder blades.

But you can't stab Tarmun Vykers in the back. It cannot be done. Anticipating the move in a way only Mahnus knew how, Vykers spun and smashed his fist into the sorcerer's face. There are many arcane protections that are highly effective against arrows, swords and spells, but few that work well against the unexpected punch in the nose. The End dropped to the snow like a rock and sprawled out, dazed, on his back. Vykers swooped to his side as quickly—if awkwardly—as possible. When the sorcerer regained his feet, he was bleeding from both his nose and mouth, though Vykers suspected the blood from his mouth came from an internal injury sustained during the fall. On top of all the blood that dripped from the countless nicks and cuts the Reaper had already given him, the End looked in bad shape. Still, he laughed.

"Bravo! Bravo. I concede you're the better fighter. And yet, I endure. I am the End-of-All..."

Both swords were now squealing and moaning uncontrollably. Frankly, both men were tired of the noise, but it was Vykers—of course!—who pressed the attack. In he came, unleashing a series of lightning fast combinations his enemy had no chance of deflecting. Except...the swords were getting... stickier and stickier, harder and harder to separate. At last, Vykers could not pull his sword apart from his rival's, and in that moment of distraction, the End struck, triumph ablaze in his eyes.

The Reaper felt the most burning, blinding agony he'd ever experienced and looked down to see the sorcerer had stabbed him more or less right through the liver with something...

invisible. Blood gushed from the wound in front and in back. Vykers felt his knees go weak and buckle from the sudden stress to his system. In the back of his mind, he heard Arune screaming. Enraged, he turned to lock eyes with his foe, who continued to smirk at him. Vykers abandoned his sword, extended his claws through the fingertips of his gloves and spoke:

"Rot in hell, you whoreson dog!" In one motion, he thrust his hand into the End's throat and tore the man's trachea right out of his neck.

The End stopped smirking, his mouth choosing to gape instead. Wider than his mouth, though, were his disbelieving eyes. This! This was something he'd never anticipated, something that could never have *been* anticipated. With shocking speed, strength and sensation fled his extremities. Still, the Reaper stared at him with evil intent. Still, the End struggled to find an escape, some means of salvation. His peripheral vision disappeared completely. He was dying. With the last of his conscious will, he glanced down at Vykers' wound, a mysterious, taunting smile on his lips.

Vykers threw the man to the ground and stomped on his spine, reveling in the sound of grating, fracturing vertebrae. The End-of-All-Things had been a self-fulfilling prophecy. He was dead.

Vykers collapsed.

And woke up in a dark, quiet tent, in terrible pain.

"We're here," a vaguely familiar voice assured him.

He tried to sit up, could not. Tried to speak, same result.

A nearby lamp was turned up, and into its soft glow floated the face of someone he…

"I'll not lie, Tarmun Vykers. This is as ghastly, as perilous a wound as I've seen," Aoife said. "But you also seem to possess… reserves…that defy understanding. You should be dead."

With tremendous effort, Vykers blurted out, "But…?"

Gently, insistently, she pushed him back down. "But…you're not."

Number 3 floated into the light, to join the A'Shea.

Vykers smiled, in spite of the pain. He raised his eyebrows, inquiringly.

"Dead," Number 3 said sadly. Vykers had never seen his companion so diminished.

"Wh...wh..." He tried.

"What injured you?" Aoife asked.

Vykers bobbed his head slightly.

"A hellish thing, an invisible dagger of some sort, a powerful relic from before the Awakening, as near as we can tell." Vykers noticed she held his left hand. For all the pain, wonderful sensations came from her touch.

"I need to make you sleep for a while. It's the only way to keep you alive, until we figure out what's happening to your wound."

Another head bob. Vykers slept.

They were thralls no longer. Upon the End's death, the peasants he'd enslaved first became inert and then gradually came back to life as their memories returned to them. Many fell to the ground, suffering from malnutrition, dehydration or worse. Others sat intentionally, taking the time to sort through their muddled thoughts. A few took their own lives. Whatever their choices, confusion was their master now and might be for some time to come. Bodies littered the front and sides of the battlefield. Many were covered in snow—white, pink and, in some cases, bright red, depending upon the state of the corpse beneath. Other bodies had somehow defeated the freeze, remaining defiantly bare despite the weather. Children, adults, the old, mercenaries, Queen's men, horses—all shared the ground with the gently falling snow.

If a man listened, he would hear weeping. Plenty o' that. Some voices called out to others who would never respond. Some voices cried out in pain. A horse whinnied. A chill breeze wafted across everything.

Toomt'-La watched from the trees, ambivalent. Mother-sister had left him for the human camp. He suspected she'd gone for good. Perhaps it was time he and his left, as well. Nar had gotten its revenge, and the old gods were satisfied.

Generals Branch and Darwent (Lescoray had fallen in battle) oversaw the organization and short-term rehabilitation of the End's former thralls, commanding various officers of lower rank to ensure the bewildered peasants were fed and, as far as possible, given some sort of shelter from the on-going snowfall. No army carries triple supplies, but the Queen's men found room in their tents for the most desperate cases. Nevertheless, it was an effort that would take days if not weeks to resolve. Yet, the Queen's men were happy to assay it; it beat the hell out of the certain annihilation they'd faced only a short while earlier, praise be to Vykers. And Pellas.

Long Pete had one heavy burden he needed to address. As he poked his head into the near-empty mess tent, he found the young man right where he'd expected: mourning at Janks' side. Long wanted to call out, to offer words of…what? Solace? But he could not speak, would never speak again. It was just as well. How in Mahnus' name could he ever explain what had happened? What he'd done? Long shuffled over, so as not to catch the boy unawares and frighten him, but it was he who was frightened when Spirk finally looked up. The "lad" appeared to have aged ten years, at least. Gone was the boyish innocence, the naïveté. For better or worse, tragedy had made Spirk a man. His expression brightened slightly when he sighted Long, but grew even sadder again, as if he was afraid to tell his old sergeant that Janks had died. Fighting back tears of his own, Long joined the young man at Janks' side, where the two men sat unmoving, until dawn of the next day.

It was almost amusing, really. Whenever Vykers came to believe he understood pain, that he'd survived the worst it could throw at him, life handed him a larger dose. In his current straits, merely breathing was about the most heroic thing he'd ever done. The cool, energizing caress returned to his forehead, and Vykers opened his eyes. There she was, the radiant A'Shea he'd met In the Forest. What was her name again…?

"Can you speak?" she asked quietly.

It was agony, but he could manage now. "Yes."

If he thought this bit of progress would bring a smile to her face, he was wrong. She was as taciturn as ever. "It's been about two and a half days since you fell," she said. "You have a hole through your body a person can see through. It's not gotten worse, but neither has it gotten any better. There's a magic involved that none of us has been able to neutralize."

"Pellas?"

The A'Shea looked mystified. "Pellas?" she repeated.

Ah. No Pellas, then. *Arune?* He called.

Tarmun? She sounded distant, preoccupied.

Still with me?

Still with you.

Good, Vykers relaxed. *Good.*

He awoke some time later, to the sound of conversation just outside his field of vision. "Yes?" he said aloud.

"He lives!" came a sardonic reply. Her Majesty had arrived.

Vykers struggled to sit up, but Aoife leapt up and urged him back down. The Queen stepped into view. Behind her, a bald Shaper lingered in the shadows. "I suppose I must thank you for saving my realm—the whole world, really."

The Reaper wanted to laugh, found he could not.

"And so," Her Majesty continued, "I find myself in an awkward position: the second greatest threat to my throne has destroyed the first greatest threat to my throne, but lies near death, presenting me with an opportunity..."

"I'd kill me, if I were you," Vykers managed through gritted teeth.

"Sound advice!" the Queen declared. "I think I'll ignore it," she added. "For now."

"Why?"

"Because, Reaper—destroyer, monster-that you are—you are now also a hero, in spite of your worst intentions. My soldiers revere you, and that is good enough for me."

"Then...what are...you...going to...do with me?" Vykers spat out.

The Queen cackled with genuine mirth. "I'm going to let you rest for another day and then I'm bringing you back to my castle, to convalesce."

Clearly, Vykers didn't get it.

"To get better, to heal," the Queen clarified. "Won't that be wonderful?" she asked, impishly. "I get to watch you in pain every day, for weeks and weeks, as long as it takes!"

But he could tell she wasn't that hard. For some reason, the old bat cared about him. Days gone by, indeed. Vykers pretended to nod off. He spoke to Arune, instead.

Looks like this is your chance, he said.

For what?

To be free of me, to get your own body. Can't be any shortage o' good candidates in the field surgeon's tent.

You don't get it, do you? Arune complained, disappointment evident in her tone.

What now?

I'm all that's keeping you alive, you big, selfish idiot!

Vykers was stunned.

I got a good taste of that dagger when it came in. It's meant to cause wounds that never heal.

Never heal, Vykers asked, *or can't be healed?*

Let me put it this way: it's not healing.

But it's not getting worse…

I'm working on that, Arune answered.

Thank you, Arune, Vykers said and passed out again.

The Reaper showing gratitude? Now, she *was* worried.

Some time during the last hour or so, Spirk had deserted him. Maybe the boy—the *man*—had finally succumbed to hunger or decided to visit the jakes. In any case, Long was alone with his old friend at last. If not for the cold, he felt sure the odor of decay would have driven him off long since. But Janks was frozen, or nearly so. He was, in point of fact, the only meat of any kind, frozen or otherwise, to be found in the mess tent any more. Janks would have laughed at that, Long knew. He would have had a good, merry laugh.

Janks' hands had been folded over his chest, over his wound. Looking more closely, Long noticed something peculiar: a small, round stone...Spirk's magic stone. A worthy gift, Long reflected. And what had he to give, but words?

There were so many things Long would have liked to say, had he only been able, beginning of course with an apology. An apology for never taking his friend seriously, an apology for running off and getting captured, an apology for killing him, an apology for leaving him in the field to go fight thralls. Too many things to apologize, for, really. And then, what good's an apology to a dead man? He'd tried that with Short and gotten nowhere—no forgiveness, no relief. Suddenly, Long pictured his two dead friends in the afterlife, sharing a pint or a keg of something marvelous and having a good laugh at their foolish, hopeless, stupid old pal, Long Pete. Strange, that no matter how he tried, he couldn't envision Janks doing anything other than laughing right now.

Ah, my old friend, I hope Mahnus and Alheria treat you better than we did down here.

"Sarge?" Rem's voice broke into the silence.

Long turned and his heart leapt. There in the doorway, right next to the expected actor, stood Mardine.

"He can't talk any more," Rem warned Mardine.

"He's talking just fine," she said, as she strode over and into Long's arms. Their embrace went on and on, until Rem found it too awkward to remain. "I'll...uh...see you both soon!" he said, and scuttled nervously out of the tent.

Long gazed up into Mardine's eyes. Oh, he loved her. Alheria's mercy, how he loved her, and who'd have thought that half a year ago?

In minutes, the couple was drenched in tears, both sad and happy. After some time, Mardine was able to speak again. "When the End-of-All-Things died, the mercenaries cut and ran. They looted whatever they could and left me chained to a wagon. Seemed like forever 'til the Queen's men found me, but I'm glad they did, Petey, I am so glad they did. I can't even tell you how glad." She paused, got a mischievous look in her eyes. "But I reckon I could *show* you..."

Another day passed. Vykers had been seen by an endless array of A'Shea and Shapers, none of whom seemed particularly helpful or hopeful. Yet, Vykers found he was able to sit up a little, with help, to take broth whenever he liked, with help, and to speak for longer periods, without help. In the evening, he heard a man singing along with a stringed instrument of some kind. The Reaper knew the song, a sentimental old piece about his deeds in younger days. But then it veered off into new lyrics, a lengthy and quite satisfying passage about his triumph over the End-of-All-Things. Huh. Even if he died from his wound, that song was a reasonable epitaph.

When Aoife came in with the Queen and her Shaper, Vykers knew he was being moved.

"I. Meant to. Ask," he said.

"Yes?" Her Majesty responded.

"The End's body?"

"We burned it. I had intended to put his head on my gates, but some thieving wretch got to it first and stole it, along with his heart. No mistaking his body, though, and that's nothing but ashes now, which I fully intend to scatter to the four winds."

"Good," Vykers grunted. "And my sword?"

"Your...companion has it. None else could touch it," the Queen replied. "I'm told it has changed since you saw it last."

"I. Need. It."

"Oh ho! Do you, now? I thought the great Tarmun Vykers had no use for magic swords and the like!"

Vykers was not amused.

The Queen sighed rather melodramatically and whispered in her Shaper's ear. He promptly left the tent. "You're awfully demanding for a near corpse."

"And savior. Of. Your realm," Vykers countered.

The Queen's dark eyes sparkled. "Er, yes."

The Shaper returned with Number 3 in tow. "Master," the chimera said, and held the sword out for inspection.

It had changed. It had, if appearances could be trusted, devoured the End's weapon, in much the same way the Five had eaten one another. Now, the sword was larger, longer, uglier. It clearly featured elements of both swords in its shape and design, and it radiated chaos.

"Let me. Touch."

Aoife objected. "I don't think that's wise."

Her Majesty sniggered. "Wise? Tarmun Vykers? Ha!"

The A'Shea looked gobsmacked.

"Let him touch the damned thing," the Queen ordered.

Ever so gently, Number 3 set it down near Vyker's left hand. Cautiously, he laid two fingers upon its hilt. He grimaced as if in pain. Aoife was about to try to remove the accursed sword, Queen's orders or no, when Vykers at once relaxed. The shadow of pleasure crossed his face. "We will," he said, apropos of nothing, and returned to sleep.

By week's end, entire divisions had headed back south, often accompanied by large numbers of bemused peasants, looking for direction, purpose, a new start. The battlefield, which some joker had christened "the End of the End" (and the name stuck), had been largely cleared of bodies. That had been an arduous process, involving the separation and identification of remains, whenever possible, and, ultimately, their mass cremation. Fortunately, the snow had melted, which made the job somewhat easier, if a bit more foul-smelling.

The few larger tents remaining in the Queen's army were mostly occupied by soldiers and officers in the final throes of celebration. It had truthfully seemed the world was about to end, but it had not. Hence, the prolonged festivities. There was only so much feasting, drinking and public farting a man could tolerate, however, before the mind wandered to more productive pursuits. Such was the case for everyone seated at Long's table.

Joining the old sergeant, whose expression was now more or less permanently bittersweet, were Mardine, Spirk, Rem, the twins and even Sergeant Kittins. All were delightfully, visibly pickled, with the exceptions of Long Pete and his bride-to-be.

"Once more to ole Bash!" Kittins shouted out, raising his flagon high and sloshing himself and Spirk with a goodly amount of ale.

"To Bash!" everyone yelled and drank.

"To Pellas the Great!" Rem sang out.

"To Pellas!" everyone cheered.

"To Corporal Janks!" Spirk blurted out.

"To Janks!" everyone agreed and drank.

Long, alone, seemed to voice a silent prayer on top of the toast.

"To Long Pete!" a voice called from the doorway.

For the first time since setting eyes on Mardine after the victory, Long broke into a wide, genuinely happy smile. Yendor Plotz stood in the tent's open doorway, looking like hell and grinning like the village idiot. Long jumped to his feet and ran over to embrace his old comrade in arms and intoxication.

"How ya been?" Yendor asked.

Long demonstrated his inability to talk.

"'S just as well," Yendor said. "We're men of action, anyways, ain't we?"

Long's shoulders shook in silent laughter.

Yendor came further into the tent and extended his hand to each person at the table. "Yendor Plotz, former general and gen'rally good guy!" he announced, by way of introduction. Without waiting for an invite, he squeezed himself onto the bench, between Spirk and Kittins.

Kittins was already amused. Yendor had that effect on people. "Former general, is it? You fought for the End?"

"Fought for? Nah, I drank his booze, shit in his latrines and spent a lot of time passed out drunk. What the hell else was I gonna do? Kill innocent people?"

Kittins roared with laughter and slapped his new friend on the back.

Rem asked the obvious question: "How did you survive the battle and where have you been this past week?"

Yendor actually giggled. "Wunna you bastards put my horse down, so I just huddled beside it, drinking the last o' my Skent 'til I took a snoozer. Horse kept me warm for a day or so, b'lieve it or not, and then I just joined these roving bands o' the lost until some officer put me in line for a good meal and a blanket. Finally, I sobered up enough to start thinkin'—always a dangerous thing, by the by—and asking around for Long Pete and this Janks fella he was always goin' on about."

At the mention of Janks, the table grew quiet, Yendor

noticed. "Oh, it's that way." He looked over at Long. "I am truly and sincerely sorry for your loss, my friend."

Me, too, Long mouthed. *Thank you.*

Yendor grabbed the pitcher from which the table's various mugs and flagons had been filled and lifted it. "To them's have gone on and to those as are coming!" He nodded to Mardine with a wink and a twinkle in his eyes that set the table on a roar. Long blushed, and everyone laughed all the more.

EPILOGUE

It was the single most comfortable bed chamber Tarmun Vykers had ever experienced, with the best bed, too.

Man could get used to this, he thought. *Except the gaping-hole-in-the-gut part.*

Reunited with his sword, Vykers had improved steadily, and yet the wound refused to close. The existence of that damned dagger had been the End's one real surprise, and Vykers almost admired how well the egomaniacal fiend had kept it a secret until he absolutely needed it. It just happened that Vykers' many secrets outweighed the Ends'.

An A'Shea came in to change the dressings on Vykers' wound and assess its status. This was another of those very rare male A'Shea. Hard to admit it, even to himself, but Vykers missed Aoife. But, as she didn't seem to miss him, there wasn't much point in dwelling on it. He'd saved the world; surely, there were plenty o' women willing to share their...*gratitude*...with him.

Ugh, Arune groaned in disgust.

Still there, then? Been so long since I've heard from you, I thought you'd gone away.

Keeping your sorry carcass alive's a full-time job.

And that had been the biggest riddle in the aftermath of the battle: why had the Shaper chosen to stay with Vykers and keep him alive when she could finally have had her freedom and a body of her own once again? He suspected he knew the answer, but dared not express it, even to himself.

The A'Shea said nothing as he left.

Vykers' appetite had improved, so he picked at a chicken carcass sitting on a nearby side-table. And then the door opened again and Aoife stepped through. Vykers was genuinely happy to see her.

Uh-oh, he thought.

A lone figure struggled and fought its way up the icy mountainside, carrying dual burdens. In his left arm, shielded against his chest, a small child peered out into the snow with eyes devoid of emotion; in the figure's right hand was a roundish bundle, dark with dried blood.

"Soon," General Omeyo said, more to himself than the child, "we'll find shelter soon."

Appendix A

Cast of Characters

Tarmun Vykers, A.K.A, "the Reaper"—a legendary warrior
Arune—A spectral Burner who shares Vykers' body
Anders Cestroenyn—the self-proclaimed "End-of-All-Things
General Schere—One of the End's men
General Wims Deda—Another of his men
General Omeya—Another of his men
Three—A chimera and friend of Vykers
Aoife Cestroenyn—An A'Shea or "Mender," sister of Anders
Too-Mai-Ten-La, A.K.A. "Toomt'-La"—a satyr, born of Aoife
The Historian, A.K.A, "the Ahklatian"—An ancient sage and Shaper
Long, A.K.A, Long Pete
Esmun Janks—A friend to Long
D'Kem—a washed up Burner
Mardine—A giantess
Yendor Plotz—A drunk and friend to Long
Spirk Nessno—An idiot and friend to Long
Remuel Wratch, A.K.A. "Rem,"—a famous actor
Major Bailis—An officer in Her Majesty's Army and Kittins' Commanding Officer
Sergeant Kittins—An officer in Her Majesty's Army
Bash—A halfbreed soldier
Her Majesty, the Virgin Queen—Ruler of the Central or Midlands Kingdoms
The Five—Chimeras who serve Vykers
Mahnus—God of Creation and War
Alheria—Goddess of Earth, Nature and life

Appendix B

A Guide to Character Name Pronunciation

Author's note:

If you've read this far, these are your characters as much as mine. You may imagine their names however you'd like. This list is really for the sticklers amongst us.

Tarmun Vykers = Tahr-muhn Vahy-kurz
Aoife = Ee-fuh
Arune = Uh-roon
D'Kem = Di-kem
Bailis = Bey-liss
Mardine = Mahr-deen
Deda = Dey-duh
Omeyo = Oh-mey-oh
Toomt'-La = Toomt'-La
Mahnus = Mahn-us
Alheria = Uh-lair-ee-uh
Ahklat = Uh-klaht
Ahklatian = Uh-kley-shuhn

ABOUT THE AUTHOR

Allan Batchelder is a professional actor, educator and former stand up comedian. He has written several plays and screenplays, dialogue for computer games, and online articles about theatre and/or education. *Steel, Blood & Fire* is his first novel, the opening act in a planned series. Allan lives in Washington State with his wife, son, and two cats. And his computer.

Dear Reader:

Thank you for reading *Steel, Blood & Fire*. If you enjoyed it, please consider writing a review on Amazon, Goodreads, or anywhere else books are reviewed. Vykers is one tough bastard, but he can't survive without your support!

For updates and news about sequels, go to:

www.immortaltreachery.com

https://www.facebook.com/SteelBloodFire

And on Twitter at: @TarmunVykers

Immortal Treachery is:

Steel, Blood & Fire

As Flies to Wanton Boys

Corpse Cold

The Abject God

And, coming in 2018, *The End of All Things*

And now, turn the page for a preview of *As Flies to Wanton Boys*...

CROSSROAD
PRESS